ALSO BY PIPER CJ

The Night and Its Moon
The Sun and Its Shade

The Gloom Between Stars

PIPER CJ

To the bisexuals:
Remember, September is bi visibility month.
Commit your crimes by midnight on August 31st, lest they
perceive you.
Resume escapades October 1st.

Published by Bloom Books, an imprint of Sourcebooks
P.O. Box 4410, Naperville, Illinois 60567-410
(630) 961-3900
sourcebooks.com

Cataloging-in-publication information is on file with the Library of Congress.

Printed and bound in the United States of America.
LSC 10 9 8 7 6 5 4 3 2

Continent of Gyrradin

Sulgrave
Mountains

the unclaimed wilds

the Frozen
Straits

Raascot

Gwydir

the
Etal Isles

the university

Uaimh
Reev

Stone

Raasay
Forest

enemies at the university

Farleigh

Yelagin

the regency's road

campfire

Farehold

Priory

the Temple
of the All-Mother

Aubade

Henares

coliseum in ruins

the Selkie, defunct

allies in Henares

Tarkhany
Desert

listen along with

The Gloom Between Stars

 the beginning

hide and seek	*klergy, mindy jones*
witch	*karliene*
trøllabundin	*eivør*
twisted games	*fjøra*
ymir	*danheim, gealdyr*

 the middle

vendetta	*unsecret, krigarè*
throne	*saint mesa*
tarot	*small million*
soldier, poet, king	*cullen vance*
goldie's goldie	*the sidh, colin goldie*

 the end

tomorrow we fight	*tommee profit, svrcina*
hard to kill	*beth crowley*
mares of the night	*glen gabriel*
the sword of destiny	*jillian aversa, erutan*
avalanche	*cellar darling*

Pronunciation Guide

Characters

Amaris: ah-MAR-iss
Ceres: SERE-iss
Gadriel: GA-dree-ell
Malik: MAL-ik
Moirai: moy-RAI

Tanith: TAN-ith
Yazlyn: YAZ-lyn
Samael: sam-eye-ELL
Zaccai: za-KAI

Places

Aubade: obeyed
Farleigh: far-LAY
Gyrradin: GEER-a-din
Gwydir: gwih-DEER
Henares: hen-AIR-ess

Raasay: ra-SAY
Raascot: RA-scott
Yelagin: YELL-a-ghin
Uaimh Reev: OOM reev

Monsters

Ag'drurath: AG-drath
Ag'imni: ag-IM-nee
Beseul: beh-ZOOL

Nakki: NAH-kee
Sustron: SUS-trun
Vakliche: VAK-leesh

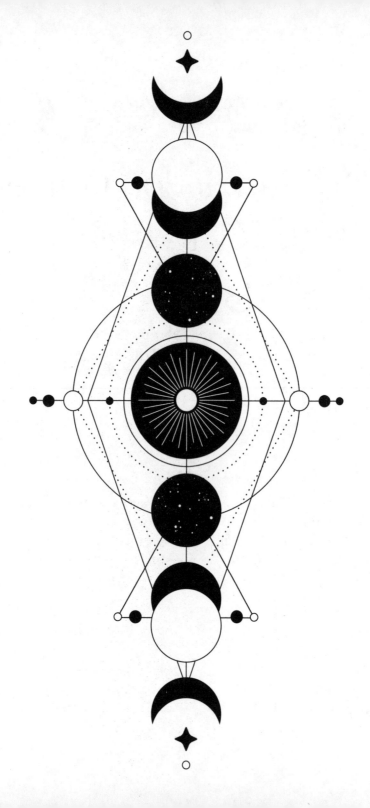

PART ONE:

The King of Fire & Mud

Chapter One

OBSESSION IS A BEAST WITH TWO MASKS.
Sometimes it's a thing of beauty, gilded with poetry and devotion. It's called many names, though in its cleverness, it often passes for love. Turn it over, however, and discover obsession's prickly, poisonous edges. It consumes wholly, whether worn affection or pain. Few perceive the subtle lines between the monster of compulsion and infatuation as love and hate blur, for they are not opposites. Toothless, benign indifference is obsession's true counterpart.

Nox knew of loathing. She was no stranger to hate. She craved indifference. She was desperate to remove the obsession's shroud and burn in it the snaps and pops of their campfire.

She'd felt only rage while she and the entangled group of reevers and fae picked through Raascot's jagged mountains. They'd left the castle grounds earlier that morning. Every step that took her farther from Gwydir carried her closer to the sharpness of her disgust with everyone around her. She hated Gadriel—this fae man with his fallen-angel wings and deceitful intentions responsible for dragging Amaris across the border. She hated Moirai for cursing the border, she hated her mother's husband for beating the woman to death before they could ever meet, and she hated Matron Agnes for hiding the truth of her parentage for her for so very, very long. She despised King Ceres—the man who was supposed to be the only father she might ever have the chance to know but who had devolved into madness. She hated Yazlyn most of all. The fae sergeant sat across the campfire now in the rapidly darkening mossy meadow with her stupid auburn curls, her blackened feathered wings, and the apologetic smile that she would cast any time Nox looked at her. She hated the thinly disguised glances of infatuation Yazlyn shot in her direction. The fae bitch had thrown the world into chaos when she'd sent her single, treacherous raven to their lunatic king.

Nox had demanded to know why Yazlyn couldn't be hung by a tree and left for dead, and Gadriel had made some half-hearted attempt at a joke about how hanging wasn't terribly effective for execution when your target had wings.

Her scowl let him know she hadn't found the joke amusing.

She noticed how the winged fae members of the military walked on eggshells around her. After learning she was the only living person to have a claim to the northern throne, they'd undoubtedly realized what a terrible mistake they'd made. She hoped to make it clear to the Raascot fae that they wouldn't be appeasing her anytime soon, but Gadriel did his best to remain solution-oriented. She wanted to be annoyed, but the general's patient diplomacy made it difficult. He refocused energies and efforts time and time again to keep the party on the task at hand. They'd continue to push forward until they intercepted King Ceres and his war party—Amaris in tow—before anyone crossed into Farehold.

She glanced around the fire, counting herself in the sorry band of five.

Malik and Ash were the two highly trained reevers she felt had become her family, though as she looked to where they sat across the orange flickering, she began to wonder if they'd grown to mean even more. Gadriel and Yazlyn represented Raascot's military dissent, and while she didn't like them, she also saw this wisdom in their allyship. The fifth and final member, Nox felt like more of an obstruction than an asset. She had almost no battle training, unless she counted her love for her axe or the number of times Malik had made her practice swinging her dagger.

The group might have been bigger, had the oldest reevers left their station in Raascot's capital to join the rescue mission. Elil and Grem were to stay in Gwydir. When they learned the mounts they'd ridden from Henares had been seized in the raid, Grem—whose horse had been safely stabled while the others had been left tethered susceptibly outside—had handed over his horse to the traveling mob as an amicable gesture. Now that the throne had been left unattended for Ceres's mission of vengeance, Raascot was on the precipice of falling to whatever forces had been invading from the mountains. Elil had argued that whether or not Ceres and Moirai were stopped from destroying each other was irrelevant if there was no home to which they might return.

Nox had looked between Elil and Ash while the redhead fae male spoke. One might have thought them the same age, but she knew enough of posturing and relationships to understand there was something long unhealed between the men. Ash had set his jaw but said nothing as Elil spoke of the creatures from below the soil that continued showing up in greater numbers than they had in centuries. He'd insisted that their reevers' oath prevented them from abandoning the kingdom to the throes of magic altogether.

She didn't care for diatribes on demons. She'd seen fae in their ag'imni form. She'd lodged an axe in a spider's sternum. But the true devils were beautiful, smiling faces, masquerading as friends, folding wings, and leading kingdoms.

The night would have been a rather pleasant one under different circumstances. The weather was mild for the time of year, and very few clouds dotted the blue-black sky. Stars seemed sharper and cleaner somehow among the northern pines.

"Hey, can I talk to you?"

The sound startled her from the depths of her miserable thoughts. Nox dragged her eyes away from Yazlyn, the object of her wrath, to touch the garden-green eyes she'd come to know and love.

"What?" Nox hadn't meant for the word to come out in a bite, but she hadn't been feeling particularly well. Aside from her dark spirits, her body had also been threatening the early signs of some strange flu. Her muscles ached, her eyes felt dry, and Nox had been unable to shake a chill that had plagued her all day.

Malik offered his hand. "I think this would best be discussed in private."

She frowned a bit as she slid her fingers over the rough calluses of his palm. Malik helped her to her feet and offered the bend of his elbow like a proper escort. She accepted it, wrapping her hands around the firm muscle of his upper arm. Nox felt Yazlyn's eyes on the back of her neck as the sergeant marked their departure from the camp.

"What's this about?" she asked. Nox succeeded in softening her words as she studied his profile in the moonlight. The barest glint of stubble reflected in the pale, silver light. Malik's answering breath was soothing, somehow. He'd grown a knack for understanding her moods.

He didn't answer right away. Instead, he led her gently by the arm down a trail that took them from their mossy campsite. They meandered through a collection of towering boulders, many of which had been split in half by their descent from the rocky grounds overhead. The evergreen trees were a bit sparser given their altitude, but enormous igneous and sedimentary rocks provided impenetrable walls of privacy at every turn. She wondered as to the secrecy of whatever it was he needed to tell her, given how far he was taking them away from the camp.

Nox was too exhausted from fighting battles of the mind and body to bother making conversation, so she chose to remain quiet. When she wasn't stealing curious glances at Malik, her eyes were focused on choosing the safest steps between the rocks and tenacious little plants that jutted out of the stones. The sounds of their feet scraping on the ground joined the occasional hooting of owls. After a time, the burbling sound of a distant creek greeted them. The gentle river noises seemed to signal whatever distance Malik had needed before breaking his silence.

"How are you holding up?" His voice held more tenderness than she deserved.

Nox choked out a humorless laugh. It was a sharp, angry staccato sound.

He made a face as he continued guiding her through the forest toward the river. "Yeah, I thought as much. Is there anyone you don't hate right now?"

"I don't hate you. Or Ash, I guess."

She felt the warmth of Malik's smile at that. "I never thought you hated me. I'm delightful."

She leaned her head briefly against his shoulder. "Indeed, you are."

"At least you're here," he said.

Her brows puckered. "What do you mean? Of course I'm here."

She nearly stubbed her toe on a rock. Malik seemed to consider his phrasing. "Sometimes you're here, even when you're not. Or maybe it's the other way around. I've just noticed that sometimes even when you're present, you...go away."

He was speaking of the void. He knew about the darkness.

And because she trusted him, she opted for honesty.

"It used to be the only way I could escape. Now I try to stay present...though it may be killing me."

"I can tell you've been feeling...unwell. I don't think you're joking when you say it might be killing you."

Nox looked up at him from hooded eyelashes. She didn't

5

know how much she could admit to without giving herself away. He was right. She had been feeling exceedingly unwell. She didn't have a mirror, but looking down at her arms alone told her that her skin had lost its vibrance. What she could see of her hair was lackluster. Her eyes felt dry and bloodshot.

This was her curse.

Love, sex, and the cocktail of emotions that sustained her had been complicated and had taken a variety of shapes over the course of her life. An upbringing full of mutual, selfless devotion between her and Amaris had sustained her for years. She'd had the affection and adoration of suitors at the Selkie even behind the bar. Once she'd taken the first patron into her rooms, her true feasting began.

In the absence of love, she had no way to feed. She hadn't consumed a soul in its entirety since she had taken the Captain of the Guard. Even that dwindling bit of life had been given to Malik when he'd fallen to the spider's clutches. The reever's steadfast infatuation had certainly been helping, but it wasn't enough, even though it may very well have been the only thing keeping her hanging on to whatever threads of life she loosely clutched.

The pair reached the banks of the shallow, happily gurgling stream. It was silver with the light of the moon as it snaked past stones and over protruding roots, carving its way out of Raascot and onward into what would eventually become Farehold. Nox was quite certain it was no deeper than her shins even in its middle. It was the flat type of river that seemed scarcely large enough for a single fish, though there was doubtlessly some form of aquatic life under its chilled, reflective waters.

Nox took a seat on a large, flat stone next to the river and removed her leather shoe to dangle her toes into the stream. The cold felt wonderful against her aching feet. Malik slid into the space beside her, nestling his arm around her. His large hand cupped her hip. She had to admit the sensation was incredibly nice. His body heat was a welcome relief from the chill. He kissed her gently against the temple through the silk of her hair.

A small sigh warmed her. She wanted to be kissed by him. She leaned into the press of his mouth, releasing another slow breath. There was a sadness to her sound. "Malik, about what we discussed—"

His murmur against her hair stopped her from continuing. "You love Amaris. That doesn't bother me at all. She deserves all of your love."

The land around them even smelled a bit like Amaris. The moonlit girl had always shimmered with juniper and the fresh scent of snowfall. It was hard not to think of her with each inhalation of the northern forest. Nox had been desperate to be close to her for so many years, and as soon as she got what she'd wanted, it had been dragged from her arms. She closed her eyes against the memory of Amaris, unwilling to acknowledge the other complicated thoughts that had plagued her for weeks.

Nox's eyes roamed over the golden man who sat beside her. He hadn't released his hold on her, nor did she want him to. He had such strong features. The masculine shape of his jaw, the tendons of his neck, the ripple of his muscles all made him so much lovelier when he smiled.

"I care for you, Malik. You know I enjoy whatever this is between us." She closed her eyes once more. She didn't want to see his face as she danced around admitting to the monster she was. "But you don't know what I am, or you wouldn't even want this from me. I did mean it literally when I said you wouldn't survive a night with me."

He nodded contemplatively. "I've been thinking about that. I've turned it over in my mind quite a few times, actually. You said the duke was turned by whatever abilities you have because he, like many men, was a taker. I'm pretty sure I know exactly who and what you are, and that's precisely why I'm not asking anything of you: I'm offering." He shrugged, but a smile tugged up the corner of his mouth. He squeezed the palm that had been resting against her hip gently and ran a finger from his free hand down her arm. "I'm a giver."

Nox's heartbeat hiccupped ever so slightly as he traced lines along her arm.

Her breath hitched as she trained her gaze on his every movement, caught between want and fear. His finger ran over her shoulder, then grazed her collarbone. Nervous adrenaline pricked her. A curling sensation twisted in her darkest parts. Still, the warm trails left by his hand felt so nice. She missed being touched. She missed the hunger, the excitement, the oxytocin that she'd engorged herself on when she'd lived at The Selkie. She craved the thrill of gulping deeply from another's life and watching their eyes twinkle out beneath her. She'd grown wild and reckless, drunk on the feeling time and time again before she'd learned to control it.

Nox bit her lip as she looked at Malik.

"Do you want me to stop?" he asked, continuing the idle movements of his hand.

He had never been bold with her, which had been something she'd always liked about him. He had been endearingly bashful for their first several weeks together. Malik was genuinely good. He was caring, he was respectful, he was often shy as his honor guided him. He had tried to apologize for his feelings all those nights ago in Henares, but Nox had cut him off. She wouldn't deny that she preferred women, but she didn't want whatever chemistry they'd discovered to end. Perhaps even this little bit of tension, this electricity, would be morsels able to keep her minimally nourished. Unless she was ready to resume the body count that had added more than a few tombstones to the cemeteries of Priory, she wasn't sure if she'd ever be able to truly feed again.

Her hair tickled her shoulders as Nox shook her head.

No. She didn't want him to stop.

She chewed her lip as she continued to eye him. He'd never explored her like this, but it was wonderful. She savored every sensation. His featherlight fingertips continued tracing painfully slow patterns around her body, moving from her arms, then to her stomach, then growing closer to more sensitive places. Her breath hitched when his thumb grazed her breast. She felt that familiar, primal hunger thump in her blood.

Nox could barely breathe out a protest. "We can't. It's not safe for you."

His breath warmed the bare skin of her throat as he gave his low, husky response. "We can't, or you don't want to? Because if you don't want to, say the word and we'll forget this ever happened. I'll walk you back to the campsite right now, and you know me well enough to believe me when I promise that nothing will be strained between us. We'll just be Nox and Malik."

Her hips had begun moving on instinct, rocking against the desire that warmed her. Her intake of air was accompanied by a small, involuntary sound that told them both exactly what it was she wanted.

She rested her fingers over his still-moving hand. The motion was not intended to stop him but to partake in his movements. Despite her better judgment, she guided his hands to places she desired most. These were the touches of a lover. Her mouth felt dry, as if she hadn't had a glass of water in a week. But this was no thirst of the tongue. She was so, so hungry.

When Nox spoke, it came out in a quiet, pained whisper. "I do want you. But I don't want to hurt you."

He nodded wordlessly once more as his hand continued moving lower. He slid it slowly up her thigh, bringing his mouth to her shoulder in the same motion. The moan she couldn't prevent from escaping encouraged him as he traced kisses from the cloth of her shoulder over the bare skin of her neck.

"I've been thinking about that," he said into her throat, "and I don't really see it being a problem for us."

Goose bumps flashed over her as the deep vibrations of his voice coursed through her. Nox's vision glazed as she felt the chemicals fill her. She battled through the fog, trying her best to look at him.

His green eyes twinkled. "I told you: I don't take. I give."

Malik's hands drew closer and closer to her inner thighs until it happened. With the lightest brush, he moved against the place she wanted so badly to be touched. Another sound escaped her, and she leaned her head against his chest, bending into him while he worked over her. She didn't just want this—she needed it. After her years at The Selkie, she had come to know what it was like to be truly full. She understood what it meant to radiate effervescence and hum with power. Swinging from one extreme to her current state of starvation would be the death of her. She hadn't told him precisely what she was, but he was a reever. She'd suspected that both men had guessed what type of demon they'd adopted into their sorry band long ago. He knew, and still, he was here.

Whatever this was, she wanted it.

Malik's fingers found the edge of her pants and she stifled a moan. She lifted herself off the rock, allowing him to tug her clothes over her hips. Despite her thirst, she was still watching him cautiously, ready to protect him at the risk of her own health, yet Malik made no gesture to remove a single article of his own clothing.

And as she watched, she understood. She melted into blissful comprehension. The anticipation had been beautiful. Every touch, every squeeze, every tug had been a build to this moment. By the time she was naked from the waist down, she was fully drenched. Malik pushed her shirt upward to expose her breasts and lowered himself to his knees on the ground beside the rock while Nox lay fully on her back, basking in the moonlight like one of the old gods about to be worshipped. He kissed her navel, then her lower stomach, then moved his mouth to her leg. Each sound of pleasure she made emboldened his advancements. One hand held her leg as he used his mouth, tongue, and teeth to drag kisses and touches from her knee closer and closer along her inner thigh to her most sensitive place.

He pressed his mouth to the center of her with terrible gentleness. His lips and tongue were as soft as a butterfly landing on a flower. Her hips arched off the rock as she breathed in deeply through her mouth, her eyes completely closed. Endorphins filled her from the crown of her head to the tips of her toes. The stream beside them covered their small noises, though she was too lost to sensation to care who might hear. He continued to kiss her, his tongue relaxed and moving in slow, patient, gentle circles. Her hips rocked rhythmically, wanting more. He growled a sound of approval, and the vibration from his throat felt so good against her.

One of his hands wandered upward, cupping her breast and pinching her, rolling her nipple between his thumb and index. It was just firm enough, just a small pain to elicit another gasp. His mouth began to move more quickly then. His tongue transitioned from relaxed to a force of pressure as he moved against her soaked, tender area. Nox continued to ride the pulse of pleasure, each thrum, each stroke, each lick matching her heart, her blood, reverberating through her very marrow. Her hips rolled as she leaned into him, her lower back curving up off the rock. Her legs began to quiver, and the calloused hand that held her thigh tightened to pin her against him.

Her toes curled in reaction to his intensity, loving the worship, the strength, the domination, and service as he gripped her, keeping her still to give her everything.

Her entire body began to tighten. She was one single, flexed muscle from her shoulders and back to her ass and thighs. She clenched in rhythm with the impending climax. She was frozen as she tensed against the final moments before she was pushed over the edge. She hovered for a beautiful, terrible, perfect moment. Her heart stopped, silence ringing in the space between beats as he continued to devour her.

The tight cord snapped. Nox bucked, her entire body

jerking with the intense and sudden release. Malik did not stop. His mouth continued to move upon her as her stomach, her thighs, her chest, her every muscle tightened and released time and time again in aftershock. His pace slowed, his mouth, his kisses, his affection becoming more and more gentle as her body twitched and melted. She trembled until his lips were the butterfly once more.

There it was.

The world was vibrant. The moon was ablaze. Joy and energy and life filled her with a wide, satisfied smile. She hummed with the delicious flavor of oxytocin. This had been the feeling she'd quite literally killed for.

But there he was. A human man. Alive.

He pulled himself up onto the rock and rested an arm over her, kissing her on the neck. She opened her mouth as if to say something, but she was too drunk on her own pleasure to spit comprehensible words. She attempted to thank him but could feel his smile through his words as he said, "Like I said, I'm a giver."

It took some time, but eventually, she found herself lucid once more. Nox pulled her pants up over her hips and curled up into him, one of her knees bent over the lower half of his body while her head rested on his chest. He held her tightly, and she could practically hear the grin of his self-satisfied victory. Somewhere against her calf she could feel how hard the exchange had left him, which was its own compliment and reward.

Even through her heavy eyelids, she caught a glimpse of her wrist, her fingertips, her shoulder, and smiled at the glow that had returned to her skin. Perhaps it wouldn't be the otherworldly shimmer and power of the true consumption of life, but this exchange had been a glass of water in the desert. Quenched, she was tugged into the depths of sleep while his strong, loving arms held her.

Chapter Two

NOX KNEW THE MOMENT SHE OPENED HER EYES THAT they'd slept for several hours.

After several groggy blinks in the first hours of twilight, Malik stirred.

She should have felt stiff and miserable after a night on a flat rock, but she awoke feeling warm, buzzing, and refreshed. Distant sounds told them their camp was packing up to get moving. She didn't know why, but she felt almost shy when Malik opened his eyes and smiled at her. He gave her a squeeze, hugging her to him before they stumbled their way from pleasurable rest onto their feet.

She dusted herself off and did her best not to overthink their night as he offered his arm and led them back to camp. She released him just as they rejoined the others.

Ash shot a disapproving look Malik's way, but the blond reever acted as if he either didn't notice or couldn't be bothered. Nox caught the exchange but knew why Ash felt the need to protest. Not only were they playing a dangerous game with Malik's physical safety, but as a friend and brother, Ash was also trying to protect the hearts involved. He'd inserted himself before, chiding Malik for his infatuation and all but demanding that Malik apologize. She remembered the night with a small upturn from one corner of her mouth. The apology hadn't ended the way any of them had anticipated.

Nox wasn't given the luxury of rumination.

Gadriel looked like he hadn't slept. His voice was low but authoritative when he spoke. "Ceres's party is moving forward on foot since his force contains so many humans and half fae. I think Yaz and I should fly in to try to close the gap while you three continue on foot."

Ash narrowed his eyes. "Are you joking?"

Gadriel twisted his mouth to the side.

The coppery reever had enough anger to go around. "None of this would have happened if you hadn't dragged Amaris into Raascot under your false pretenses of asking after the king, Gadriel. And you." He gestured angrily to Yazlyn. "If we live a thousand years, don't expect any of us to forgive you for what you did."

Yazlyn's eyes were downcast. "The fact still remains, I can fly. We'll cover ground so much more quickly—"

"No." Ash was firm. "Gadriel, fly me with you. The reevers have a much stronger claim to this rescue mission than you do. Malik, if you take the horse, you can cover nearly enough ground to keep up with us. Nox, that leaves you with—"

"Absolutely not. She's not touching me. I'll take the horse."

Yazlyn's voice was apologetic but had a sharp edge around her words. "Malik and Ash are too heavy for me to carry." She fidgeted as she dared to continue. "I know you don't like me right now. I know you aren't ready to forgive me, though I desperately wish you would. My reasons are useless, so I won't try to excuse what I've done, but I love my country. You're the heir and blood of Raascot, Nox. Until we get to a better place with one another, surely we can be civil at the very least."

Nox looked her squarely in the face. Her coal-black eyes burned into Yazlyn's sad, hazel gaze. The winged girl kept her hand outstretched in an olive branch, willing Nox to step closer to her. The power that had returned filled her with formidable energy as she glared at the sergeant. "Then I'll walk."

Gadriel and Yazlyn exchanged looks. Gad raised a gentle hand as if placating a wounded animal. "Nox, you have to understand. We can't just leave you alone."

"Why the hell not?" She crossed her arms tightly. "You didn't know I existed two days ago. Go back to pretending the king has a son."

He dismissed her request entirely. "Two days ago, we were watching Raascot be driven into the dirt. Now we know you're the only surviving heir to the throne. As much as you hate us, we would die before we let anything happen to you. I speak for both Yazlyn and myself when I tell you that our swords are yours, Nox."

Nox scowled. "I'll ride with Malik."

Malik shrugged unhelpfully. "That could work…"

Gadriel's voice remained controlled, but he didn't budge. "That'll slow the horse down significantly. You'll already be trailing behind us just because you and your mount are bound to the ground. Additionally, any of our supplies will have to ride with you on the horse if Yaz and I take anyone by air."

Yazlyn took another step toward Nox while lifting a hand as if to beckon her forward. Nox spun on her, snapping, "Don't touch me."

Yaz looked like she had been slapped. It had taken exactly the same amount of time for them to learn that Nox was their monarch as it had taken Nox to despise them. She knew enough of lovelorn glances to know that Yazlyn looked at her with hopes for more than friendship. It was something of a relief to watch Yazlyn's crush ebb from desire to impatience. Nox neither wanted nor needed her attention.

While their squabbles unfolded, Ash's cut in impatiently. "None of us are happy about this, Nox. No one liked walking through the rain, but we had to anyway. No one liked losing their homes or weapons, but that's life on the road. No one likes backstabbing demons abducting Amaris and handing her over to their mad king, but here we are."

Ash shot his glowering eyes to the winged fae at his last statement.

Malik agreed. "Right now, we just need to make forward progress. Let's close as much ground as we can between ourselves and Ceres. His war party will be moving slowly from sheer size alone, so we have the advantage. If we don't get moving, they'll be at the border within the next two days before we can stop them."

Gadriel took off toward the southern border with Ash moments later. Malik urged the horse forward to follow. Nox grimaced but allowed the sergeant to touch her. Yazlyn flinched under the daggers being drilled into her through Nox's unforgiving gaze as she scooped her up and took to the sky.

✦

"What are we supposed to do?" Amaris yanked against her chains. The cold cuff bit into her wrist. She would have hated the sensation had the sharp metal not been a reminder that she was alive. Her heart throbbed. Every time she closed her eyes, she saw Odrin bow his head. Being still with her thoughts meant hearing his final words. She shoved and fought and battled to put the nightmare in her airtight box. She needed her faculties. She needed to be able to think, to breathe, to move forward. She couldn't do that if she thought of the man she'd considered a father. She couldn't do it if she thought of Gadriel and his betrayal. She couldn't be strong or fight or move forward if she remembered the pain and panic on Nox's face as Amaris broke her heart once again.

Numbness needed a counterbalance. Amaris yanked on her cuff again, frowning down at it. Her eyes followed the chain wrapped around the pole in the center of the tent. It was too thick for her to break. Perhaps if she'd been wholly fae, or been able to access her goddess-damned powers, but no. For now, the pink and purple bruising that evidenced her each and every tug was a reminder that she had survived. She had to continue surviving, if only for Nox.

She'd left Nox behind in Farleigh. She'd been dragged away in Aubade. She couldn't leave her now. Not again. Not like this.

Amaris didn't know the geography of the northern kingdom well enough to pinpoint exactly where they might be, but she knew she was manacled to a post in a tent somewhere in the flatlands of the Raasay Forest. Their shelter was made from a thick, off-white canvas material that concealed the pines and boulders beyond them. The foliage had grown denser and the trees taller as they'd descended in elevation. Zaccai had volunteered to stand guard over King Ceres's unwilling champion and had been more or less keeping her company as they marched south. She wanted to be angry with him, but she wasn't. Amaris couldn't conjure resentment for any of them. Her glass heart had been shattered into such fine shards that it was little more than powder beneath her fingers. Where fury should have burned, there was only void.

The ag'imni—the true ag'imni—had told her this would happen. Gadriel had pushed himself against her as he'd hidden her in the hollow of a tree while the demon had hissed about how the general knew what she was and the role she was meant to play in his game. Ag'imni lied, she had told herself, but its words had been as much a warning as they had been a nightmare. It had told her that her name had been on the wind for eighteen years. The demons used their gifts of speech for fear and deceit, she'd told herself. She'd failed to consider that the best lies were born of truths.

Amaris had been torn from Nox's bed with the scent of plums and the tingle of her tongue still on her lips. She had given everything she had to Gadriel only to be handed over to his ruler the moment they'd entered Gwydir. King Ceres had slain the only man she'd ever known as a father solely to gain her broken compliance. She was in the care of a wounded sovereign who was so consumed with mourning over his lost love that his grief had stolen his sanity. The Raascot troops marching south were not alive with the thrill of battle. There was no sparkle, no joy in the eerily quiet war camp. This was a kingdom of sorrow.

She looked at the reddish-purple mark left on her wrist from the chain, then up at the only person she might count as a friend in the camp.

Zaccai was sitting on the ground near her with his arms propped on his knees. He rested his head in his palms, wings limp behind him. His posture looked every bit as defeated as Amaris felt. He shook his head without attempting to meet her eyes.

He had no more clue what to do than she did.

Amaris was not being treated unkindly, but there was no question as to her status in this camp. She was no equal. She was in shackles, serving an agenda of vengeance upon the threat of slaughtering what remained of her loved ones. A sick part of her wondered if the king was allowing Zaccai to stay close to her knowing that she had grown familiar with the fae commander. Perhaps even this Raascot fae's life would serve as a threat to punish her in a pinch, should she fail to comply.

She was quiet when she asked, "Cai, do you know what Gadriel was saying about the king's heir? In the throne room?"

Zaccai exhaled into the hands that cupped his face. "I've been thinking about that ceaselessly." He moved his hands to rake them through his hair, further betraying the stress that gripped him. "I understand why the king would want to dismiss Gadriel's announcement as convenient timing, but Gad has never lied to Ceres, no matter how much easier the lies would have made our lives. Gadriel didn't say anything to you?"

"No, nothing. We had spent nearly every day together for an entire summer, and he's never mentioned a thing... though to be fair, even if he hasn't lied to Ceres, he was lying

18

to me." Amaris stared at Zaccai's face to see if he'd react, but he continued to face ahead. His eyes remained unfocused while she spoke. "He'd told me of the king's search for his son. He hadn't told me that Ceres had already learned his lover and son were dead, nor had the bastard informed me he was hunting for the fantasy of some white-haired, goddess-given answer to avenge their deaths."

He met her eyes long enough to reiterate a truth she didn't want to admit.

It wasn't a fantasy.

Their absurd mission, the nonsensical message, the impossibility...she fit.

Zaccai shifted the weight of his head into only one hand. He'd closed his eyes tightly against the night, lost to his memory of the exchange in Gwydir. "But Gadriel only lied through omission. He would have no reason to have changed from believing the king had a son to saying that Daphne bore him a daughter. He would have no reason to deceive with regards to any gender of the heir. That doesn't make sense."

"So, you're saying you believe Gadriel's telling the truth?"

"I'm saying that I'm ready to believe he might be."

Amaris leaned her head against the pole. She looked up to where the canvas ceiling vaulted and stared at the pool of shadows above her. "The only thing that changed was the arrival of my friends at the town house. It's possible that the other reevers had come with information and I was too preoccupied to learn anything from them."

Zaccai considered this. He lifted his head from where he'd been pressing it into his hand. "Who arrived?"

"My brothers, Ash and Malik, and my childhood friend Nox."

He chewed on this information, the gears in his mind turning. "I met Nox once as well, right after they escaped the castle. Uriah and I had been posted to await Gadriel's return, which by now we all know never came. The three of them were camping in the forests just outside of Aubade. Your friend could understand us, even in the south."

Amaris cocked her head at this. The only person south of the Raascot border who'd been able to understand them had been Master Fehu, who, despite seeing the demon she was meant to perceive, presumed her northern blood allowed her a tether to them. "Nox could understand you in your ag'imni form?"

Cai's brows pulled together in thought as he stared into his memory. "She does look very northern, doesn't she?"

While thoughtful lines formed on Cai's forehead, Amaris felt her pulse quicken. Her eyes sharpened as she whipped her head to him. "Are you implying what I think you are?"

"She's the only variable, Amaris."

Amaris tried to run her fingers anxiously through her hair, but they snagged on the tangles. She shook her head in denial, watching the small snarls dance in front of her vision in her rejection. "No, we grew up together as orphans. She has no family. Neither of us has a family."

"Isn't that why you're here?" His voice was quiet. "Aren't you in Raascot because you aren't who—or what—you thought you were?"

Anger flared through her. "You've said it yourself: Ceres is mad. Nothing he has said to me or about me made any sense. The man is incoherent. He's not rational."

He frowned. "Ceres didn't invent this information. The priestess who's been with us in Gwydir told us of your birth. She was the one who told of Daphne's death and her prayer. The priestess you saw in that throne room was present at your birth. It's how she had your description. It's how we knew to look for you. And then when you could see us..."

Amaris's voice grew louder. Anger knotted in her throat. "You can't trust anything said from a prisoner, Cai! Someone being tortured will say anything to have their suffering end!"

He stood from where he'd been sitting near her and began pacing the small area within their tent. His brows furrowed, muscles tensed. "That's the thing—the priestess was never harmed. Even if she had been, people invent simple answers to questions when under duress. They can create fictional locations when asked where something is hidden, they might supply fabricated names when pressed for sources, but they don't craft entire stories about prayers and curses and goddesses and babies with no prompt. She had no reason to invent such a tale. And then look at you, Amaris. No one can be mistaken for your features. You have hair and eyes and skin that were created to be found. It's as if you were meant to stand out for just this reason."

Amaris scrunched her eyes tightly. Her voice was quiet as she said, "I should have just killed you in that glen."

She heard Zaccai crouch before her but didn't look at him as he rested a hand on her arm. It was a gesture that was meant to make her feel better. She turned her face away from his, eyes still closed, but he continued the comforting rest of his hand. "You don't mean that."

She absently wondered how much of their conversation could be heard beyond the flaps of their tent. They were not in the company of the rambunctious war march of blood-thirsty men. Quiet pressed itself upon the encampment like a damp quilt. The men and women, both human and fae, were moving and talking in subdued tones somewhere beyond their tent. Horses shuffled and whinnied occasionally. Fires were popping, but even the flames seemed melancholy.

"Do you believe Gadriel?" she finally asked.

"I do," he said, no hesitation in his answer.

"Then do you believe in your king's mission for self-destruction? If he takes you and your men into Farehold..."

"It's a death sentence," Zaccai agreed.

Amaris echoed her question. "So what do we do?"

Chapter Three

YAZLYN'S FEET HAD BARELY TOUCHED THE GROUND BEFORE Nox pushed out of her arms. The sergeant wasn't very good at hiding her emotions, and Nox was perfectly aware that everyone saw the conflict for what it was. Nox marked the successful blows as each new insult chipped away at Yazlyn until her emotions transitioned from wounded flinches of rejection to a tangible anger.

Good. Let her be angry. The fury would never match Nox's own.

Perhaps Yazlyn had only sent her raven in an attempt to end further suffering in Raascot. Maybe it was true and Yazlyn hadn't wanted to cause pain for anyone. Nox had heard the arguments as many times as Yazlyn could spit them out: she didn't want any more Raascot men to have to die.

But Nox didn't give a damn how well intentioned the bitch may have been.

Yazlyn's eyes narrowed slightly as Nox walked away. From behind her, she heard the sergeant's sarcasm.

"'Thank you for flying me, Yazlyn,'" the fae said, attempting her best impersonation. "'I'm sure it was very hard for you to carry me through the sky.' Oh you're welcome, Nox.

How kind of you to think of me. Yes, it was taxing, but I was happy to help."

Nox rolled her eyes and retreated to where the others stood. Ash and Gadriel had landed a long time before the women had landed. Yazlyn was smaller, and the weight of a passenger had taxed her greatly. Malik and his horse were the last to arrive.

They were up to speed in a matter of minutes.

Gadriel had shot upward and had managed to spot the war camp less than an hour's walk away. As Ceres had many winged men among the southbound troops, Gadriel recommended they stick to the ground as they covered the remaining distance.

Ceres had utilized the tried-and-true tactic of camping his men in a depression, Gadriel informed her. His camp of choice prevented their fires from being seen by prying eyes. The Raascot soldiers were in a basin near a low, flat river that seemed to flood in the spring and dissipate by late summer. This time of year, its waters were exceedingly shallow and the typically soggy grassy expanse in the valley had dried out.

Nox wasn't thrilled to hear that they were headed to a river, but she supposed she had little say in the matter. She followed at a glowering distance as they began winding their way up an outcropping of jagged rocks and tall, thin pines. They needed a way to peer down into Ceres's camp without being detected. The five had yet to come up with a plan to extract Amaris and convince Ceres of his living heir. It was pointless to concoct anything too specific before understanding the makeup of the camp, so they focused on putting one foot in front of the other. They'd need to assess the manpower, appraise the layout, and gauge points of entry and exit before they had a hope of crafting a strategy.

"Shouldn't you know the manpower?" Nox's question came out as a disapproving accusation.

Gadriel nodded. "I should. But Ceres is no longer recognizing his general. Who knows what else he's changed."

She didn't bother asking him to elaborate.

They walked in single file for the majority of the trail, save for when the path was wide enough to allow pairs to stand side by side.

Ash had been acting decidedly bitter toward all parties, Nox and Malik included. He had stormed ahead of the rest to lead the group, perhaps so he wouldn't have to look at any of them. She wondered how much he knew about a romantic development between herself and his brother-in-arms. She thought back to Ash's push to end Malik's expressions of affection in Henares and wondered if it had been out of honor and altruism or if Ash had simply been wary of his human brother's susceptibility to Nox's deadly charm. She had, after all, once tried to snare Ash in her trap.

Up ahead, Malik led Grem's horse, a mount called Seven. She'd wanted to ask why the mare had such a strange name but hadn't possessed the energy when the gruff, older reever handed over the reins. Malik had hurried the mare to catch up with Ash so the reevers could quietly argue about something or other. Nox trailed toward the tail-end of the crew. She was particularly irritated at how often the Raascot fae turned around to check on her. Nox had more than two decades looking out not only for herself but also for those around her. Being treated as though she were made of porcelain simply due to a piece of information regarding her heritage that had never affected her life was fiercely agitating.

Gadriel slowed to meet her pace.

Nox bristled as the rhythm of his steps matched her own. She tightened the arms folded across her chest.

"I'm Gadriel," he said.

She wasn't interested in his attempt at friendliness. She kept her eyes trained ahead after the others as she said, "I don't know if you realize this, but we've been traveling together for several days. I'm starting to question your capacity to serve as general if you don't remember who you've met."

He smirked. "I'm hoping you might allow me to

introduce myself for a fresh start. If this were the first time we were meeting, I'd attempt to make a better first impression."

Avoiding his gaze, she looked past the thorny boughs of touching pines to the pink shades of afternoon that peeked through. Her peripherals informed her that he'd kept his comfortable, easy pace, the patient expression still on his face. When she finally turned to meet his eyes, she meant to scowl at him, but a disconcerted frown made her brows furrow instead. They hadn't been afforded a lot of opportunities for one-on-one time, both because of the urgency of their travel and her desire to put as much space between herself and everyone else as possible. Now that she looked at Gadriel, she couldn't help but see something eerily familiar in the lines of his features.

She sighed, self-soothing as she tightened her grip on her arms. "I don't know that we can have a fresh start."

His mouth went a bit crooked, and he shrugged. "Ceres is my cousin. If you're his daughter, that not only makes you our princess, it makes you my family."

She regarded him again, this time with a bit more intentionality. His features were far more angular and masculine. His skin was a richer depth of bronze than hers, but both denoted their Raascot lineage. There was something more than that, though. There was a feature in the bridge of his nose and in the curve of his chin that she had recognized, however faintly, in her own mirror. She faced the trail again, uncomfortable with the unfamiliar feeling that tugged at her. She had never had family beyond Amaris. She wasn't sure if some general's arbitrary proclamation could make her feel any differently.

"You shouldn't forgive us," Gadriel said.

That gained her attention. She arched a brow.

He continued. "Daphne left you as close to the border as she could so that we could find you. Your mother did everything in her power to bring you to our doorstep. Not only did we fail to locate you, but because of our mission,

25

the person you care most about in this world is now marching south."

She sucked her teeth in response, returning her irritated gaze to the trail ahead.

"I care about her too." He said it with such tenderness that she almost believed him.

Anger pricked through Nox. Her lips pressed into a line before saying, "If you care about her, why would you bring her to Gwydir?"

Gadriel's face slackened a bit as they continued their winding through the trails, ascending the hills that would bring them to overlook Ceres's men. "Hope?" he offered. "When I met Amaris, I was in shock that Ceres's information had been real. None of us thought there was anything to it—another fruitless chase in a long line of empty missions. Then I got to know her. She's strong. She's capable. Not only could she hold her own, but surely, Ceres would see everything in her that I did. I thought that maybe she'd work with Ceres—with Raascot—as a team. Reevers want peace, right? This could bring it. I don't know what deluded me into thinking Ceres could see that."

"Love," Nox offered.

Gadriel stiffened.

She clarified, "You love your cousin. You wanted to believe the best in him, I'm sure."

Nox wasn't sure what Gadriel knew of her affections for Amaris or their complicated path. She also couldn't pinpoint the nature of his relationship to Amaris, save for the way he'd put himself between her and his men when they'd taken her from the town house. She'd seen the look on his face, the defensive posturing in his shoulders, heard the tone in his voice as he'd barked orders on her behalf. She knew enough of men to identify affection when she saw it.

Defeat touched his words as he said, "I guess I thought if anyone could talk sense into him, it would be his most recent object of obsession. If this answer to prayer turned out to be real, surely he'd at least listen to her and they'd be able to work together. After we got into Gwydir, though, I didn't have enough faith in him to bring her to the castle. I wanted a chance to prepare her, to tell Amaris everything before she met him. She deserved to know what she was getting into."

"Until your goddess-damned sergeant betrayed you." She could practically taste the acid of her words on her tongue.

She wasn't shocked that Gadriel did his best to defend her. "It wasn't betrayal, Nox. If anything, I was betraying Ceres by hiding Amaris so close to his home. I know you hate Yazlyn, and I don't expect that to change. But Yaz is good—almost to a fault. She believes in her country and in her people. She has no ill will toward any of us, even after we've made it very clear that she fucked up. She's my friend and a damn good sergeant. Besides, I'm pretty sure she likes you, and for what it's worth, I know she made a spectacular partner to her last lover. Though she also makes something of a formidable enemy, so you might want to ease up on antagonizing her."

Nox watched the dark, chestnut-haired curls of the fae in front of her as they swayed with each step, dangling just to the space in the middle of her dark, glossy wings. There were more foul adjectives that colored her thoughts when she looked at the otherwise beautiful fae girl. Stupid, stupid, stupid.

"I don't care."

"I don't expect you to. That's okay. But it doesn't change who she is, nor does it change what she would do to protect you now that we know who and what you are."

Nox scoffed and was glad when he made no attempt to redirect her emotion. She had been abandoned as an infant, raised with neither love nor family, and sold for her body. The idea that she was suddenly valued simply because of a title was utterly disgusting. She had been as worthy of protection for the past two-odd decades. Her personhood had not been any less important when she was orphaned, or when she worked at a pleasure house, or when she was a nobody traveling with two reevers. Gadriel may as well have possessed the ability to infiltrate minds for how well he read the message in her single dismissive sound.

"It would be yours, you know. You could lead Raascot however you wanted, Nox. If you don't want to be a princess, that would be your call to make. If you wanted an egalitarian society that didn't recognize titles or monarchs, you could create that reality."

This hurt her heart in a way she hadn't expected. Gadriel seemed to sense the shift in energy and didn't press her any further. They walked side by side in silence for a stretch of time until he gave her a brief, light touch on the arm before departing to rejoin Yazlyn. She was sure he and the fae woman had plenty to discuss regarding how they were expected to exchange a lunatic king for a hateful, bitter princess. She breathed in deeply through her nose and could smell only cold, mountain air along with the heart-piercing scent of juniper.

Gadriel's assertion hadn't been the only thing that had tugged at her heart. It wasn't merely what her ascension to a title and throne could mean for the lost and abandoned children like her and those with her at Farleigh. The scent was pulling at a deeper thread that had wrung her heart ever since her dream. Watching Amaris's birth had not been the encouraging vision that Yggdrasil had perhaps intended. Seeing the snow-white babe born to a surrogate priestess may as well have filled her with vinegar. She had retreated within herself, not speaking for the two-week ride from Henares to the Raascot border after that dream. Still, all the silence in the world hadn't allowed her to truly process what she felt or what it meant.

Nox parted her lips and opted to breathe through her mouth. She didn't have the emotional capacity to filter every juniper-laden breath through her painful memories. She adjusted her arms, holding herself tightly, though not from the chill. The last lights of evening weren't as cold as they

28

had been the nights prior. She wasn't sure if the temperature had truly changed or if the fuel Malik had offered warmed her from within. She looked up to the space between pine needle branches at the few neon wisps of orange and red that illuminated whatever shreds of clouds that remained.

They'd be cast into the black parts of night in an hour or so, and moonlight would do them no good if they stayed under the canopy. She craned her neck to see what appeared to be a break between trunks ahead. Just beyond Seven's steady plodding, the forest fell away to an open horizon. The silhouettes of those in front of her were still clearly distinguishable against the fading light. If they were approaching a cliff, then they had to be on top of Ceres's camp.

Agitation and uncertainty were replaced with nerves. She buzzed with anxious anticipation. Amaris had to be close.

Nox couldn't see any sign of Ceres's camp from her spot in the line, but Malik had begun to tether Seven to a tree. If he was stopping, then surely they'd reached the outlook. She scanned for the other reever, and the flash of red was the only confirmation she needed. Ash was already crouching his way to the edge of their vantage point.

Nox dipped her head, though she wasn't entirely sure what she was hiding from. She was adept in espionage, but her skillset had been honed in silks and heels, not on cliffs and in camps. She picked her footing carefully to join Ash and Malik, kneeling beside them as they peered over the lip into the valley below.

This was what she'd wanted. She'd fought at every turn to be reunited with Amaris. Now looking down at the winking campfires and dotted glow of canvas tents in the last purples of dusk, she felt only acute, controlled terror.

She may not have liked the Raascot fae, but she was grateful to be sandwiched between trained military and elite assassins. The general whispered something to the reevers about waiting until after sundown, but the men seemed to throw up irritated hackles at the suggestion that they would barge in, swords upheld, before night had even fallen. She could have acted as translator if she'd felt like brokering peace. She understood that Gadriel was used to being a general and all the orders and assumptions that accompanied it. The reevers were familiar with equality in the sword-end of a society intended to uphold peace. They were not the most intuitively collaborative campmates. Still, this was war. No one was rash enough to let petty differences botch what needed to be done.

✦

Gadriel felt a pang of sympathy at the memory of Amaris and her surly attitude as he watched Ash and Malik bristle at his every word. He wondered how off-putting he truly was to anyone who had been raised outside of the militant hierarchy of his lifestyle. The men and women beneath him had been kept alive because of the order and structure he commanded. His troops thrived under his leadership. He felt like a fish out of water in this band of competent, loyally neutral assassins who had no need of his orders. He knew his systematic tackling of things and ability to dominate logistic scenarios were assets nine times out of ten, but he would have to refrain from too much self-reflection for now. Their mission was united regardless of their backgrounds or training. They needed to extract Amaris and intercept Ceres before the people of Farehold perceived hell's army to be descending upon them.

It was Nox who spoke next. "If you were the mad king, where would you have stashed Amaris?"

Gadriel continued scanning the tents for any tell-tale signs. "I'd want to keep her as close to me as I could, since she's his primary asset. I assume her tent is as centrally located as possible."

Ash spoke. "What conditions would he be keeping her in?"

Gadriel shook his head. "I honestly don't know. I had hoped they'd be able to work collaboratively. I obviously

30

misjudged him. I've never known Ceres to be cruel, but grief makes people do terrible things."

He knew this told them little, save for offering the barest of hopes that Amaris was not in any sort of immediate danger.

"What have his war camps been like in the past?"

Gadriel frowned. "It's been a long time since we've had open war. I've been to battles and skirmishes with Ceres, but it's been decades, if not a century, since the last time we truly met blades with an enemy the way he intends now. He was a different man then. His people loved him. They were going to war for love."

Nox's voice was quiet. "He's still going to war for love."

Gadriel felt such a profound loss when he regarded Nox, he couldn't explain the emotion. He felt a helpless urge to comfort her. He wished he could make her years of pain and abandonment disappear. Maybe the emotion came from compassion, or perhaps they were sourced from guilt at his own failure. He had spent decades knowing just how fiercely loved and sought after she had been, while she had grown up feeling rejected and unwanted. His parents were still happy and healthy well beyond Raascot's borders, where they'd retired in Sulgrave. He couldn't imagine what it would have been like to have become a man without their guidance or leadership. He couldn't fathom what it might feel like to overlook the camp of a father you'd never met—one you knew to be irreparably broken.

"I want to talk to him," Gadriel said.

Everyone vehemently disagreed, some verbally, others through huffs and balled fists. Even Yazlyn, who had done her best to remain quiet through the majority of the night, couldn't bring herself to see any wisdom in his statement.

"Last time you tried to speak with the king, he had you seized and thrown into a rune-guarded cell."

"This time we have Nox."

Malik and Yazlyn looked equally horrified. "You mean to bring Nox down there?"

Gadriel raised a calming hand as if he were soothing a startled horse. "I wouldn't unless I knew it was safe. I think if he could meet his daughter—"

"I'm sorry, but no. You can't do that." Yazlyn had snapped back at him as a friend in the past, but he'd never dared to make such a directly defiant statement to him as her general before. "I love Ceres and will serve him until he takes his final breath, but our responsibility extends to his daughter now. We can't guarantee her safety in that camp. Not with him in this mental state."

Even if he hadn't seen the irritation flash through Nox, the audible grind of her teeth would have warned them that she was not ready to make peace with Yazlyn. She snapped, "I don't need anyone guaranteeing my safety. You have no idea what I'm capable of." Nox pushed up from the ledge and took a few steps to stand by Seven.

Nox may not have had any combat training, but it was a relief to believe her to be wise. Even in her agitated state, he could leave her be and focus on their plan of attack without worrying she'd take off into the forest, forcing them to spend another twenty-one years hunting her down.

Gadriel and the reevers returned to discussing strategy in hushed tones when a peculiar sound emerged from the valley below. It wasn't quite a scream. There was something wet and strangled about the noise that bubbled from the depression that hid the camp.

His brows gathered in confusion. He knew camp chatter, the clatter of scrimmages as troops practiced their footwork and swordplay, forest sounds, river noises, even the sounds of ag'imni, beseul, and the demons that lurked in the dark. This was a new sound. He and Yazlyn exchanged looks to confirm that they'd heard the same odd disturbance.

At his side, the reevers leaned as far as they dared over the outlook to scan for the source of the unfamiliar sound. The camp below seemed to grow even quieter following the noise. The war camp was listening just as intently as those overhead.

A second clipped noise, one of pain and shock and water, emerged from a slightly different part of the gully. There were no signs of light, of struggle, or of movement. Yazlyn was the first to point.

"There, by the water. Do you see something?"

It took a moment to follow her extended finger. Dusk had ended, and night was upon them. Only the orange flickers from the bonfires glinted and reflected off an unusual shape. Something that may have been a snake lifted a glistening tendril from the shallow water of the river below. As it rose, it became clear that they were not looking at the neck of a snake but at the arcing tail of a bipedal creature. The monster rose from the waters, pulling itself from the mud on two legs that were as long and spindly as its nearly circular tail. Gadriel heard a frustrated grumble at his side and knew without tearing his eyes from the monster that the sound came from Malik. The reever was left at the greatest disadvantage, as he was the only member in the overlook with purely human blood. Gadriel and Yazlyn, however, were able to discern something even more troubling with their eyesight.

He'd never seen anything like it.

The creature was nearly a bird, though its skin had an amphibian wetness. The mouth had a sharp, beaklike protrusion. They couldn't fully ascertain whether or not it had eyes from where they lay flat on their bellies on the overlook. As the monster crept quietly toward the camp, they were able to see its target.

At the camp's edge stood a man, pants tugged downward, cock in hand as he pissed into the river in peaceable ignorance. Gadriel wasn't even allotted the time to have a conflict of conscience over whether or not he should alert the monster's unsuspecting victim or maintain their cover. The creature was upon the man in a second.

When the monster attacked, it was not with its mouth. The tail that had seemed to arc in such an unusual sphere struck as if it belonged to a scorpion. The tip of the tail had conjoined with two blade-line pincers, severing the head of the man before he'd had time to tuck away his pecker or scream. Gadriel understood the wet sound with horrifying clarity as the man's head rolled, separated from its body, and the monster began to feast. It perched one of its large, taloned feet on the fallen man's body while the beak of its mouth tore at the victim's flesh.

Gadriel looked to the men beside him for answers. If anyone in the kingdom knew what they were facing, it would be a reever. His chest tightened as he soaked in the bloodless faces of true shock at his side.

"They're supposed to be in the desert oases of Tarkhany. No one has seen a vakliche in five hundred years," Ash whispered, his voice strained.

Malik mustered a semblance of bravery. "Beseuls detest sunlight. Vageth blood will cause wounds to go septic. Ag'drurath knit and heal more quickly than anything in our tomes. What do we know of vakliche?"

Ash ran a hand down his face, failing to hide a frustrated, desperate frown. "I thought they were extinct."

Gadriel turned to Yazlyn. She was still trained on the reevers. She set her jaw, tone stoic as she asked, "These are water demons?"

Ash was breathless. "They're mud demons. They shouldn't be here. They shouldn't be *anywhere*. It doesn't make any sense. It's just as bizarre as the spider—"

Another movement sliced his sentence short, catching their collective eyes. The vakliche was not alone.

"Okay," Malik said, keeping his voice steady. "The problem isn't how to kill them. Almost anything can be dismembered. It's getting close to them with that tail."

"The problem *isn't* how to kill them?" Yazlyn hissed. "Demons can't be killed. It looks to me like this one can't even be slowed down if we can't get close to it!"

Gadriel swallowed as conversation buzzed around him.

He kept his gaze on the river, watching for disturbances between the silver moonlight and fireside glow that caught on the gentle rapids.

There. Another vakliche was pulling itself up from the water on the far side of camp while the first one they'd spotted finished its bloody meal. The tail Malik referred to was twice as long as the monstrosity's legs, making it nearly impossible to reach the torso of the beast without being caught in the horrific, snapping razor of its pincers.

Yazlyn's voice was fast and weak. "Demons have been pouring in for years now. I haven't seen mud demons, but the forests—"

Malik cut her off. "We have to focus on the here and now. Why are the vakliche targeting the camp? What's drawing them now? Why would these creatures infiltrate this camp out of nowhere?"

"We know demons are attracted to fire," Yazlyn said quietly. She didn't need to tell two reevers what drew monsters from the dark, but they were all doing whatever they could to work through the problem. "Raasay Gully is always dark and empty. There are never bonfires. Could that…"

Ash spoke over her, offering, "Could this be some breeding ground? Maybe a nest they didn't know about?"

Gadriel countered that this gully had been their primary mode of travel for years whenever they wished to avoid the road between the kingdoms. He stopped at Nox's urgent, shushing gesture.

"Do you see that?"

"What, do you see another demon?" Yazlyn hissed.

Nox waved as if flicking water from a damp hand. Her gesture was sharp and dismissive as she gained the attention of the others. "Do you see that hill?"

"The vakliche would be by the water—" Yazlyn was cut off again. Gadriel was glad the princess's weapon was by the horse, as Nox looked like she might throw her axe at his sergeant if she didn't shut up.

Nox gestured to a small outcropping on the far side of the valley.

A sound rose in the encampment below as the men began to find the bodies of the fallen. A vakliche launched itself into camp more brazenly, tearing its way toward men who had been sitting near a fire. The reevers were drawn to the carnage below, but Gadriel followed her intense, outstretched finger. His voice was hushed as he responded to Nox. "Blue?"

"Do you see it too?"

"There's something blue," he confirmed. "Excellent catch, Nox." And he hoped she knew he meant it. Whatever it was, it didn't belong. He looked at Ash and Malik. "You're going to hate me for this, but let's deal with that fallout later. I'm a general, and we might not get another distraction. Ash, Malik, you have to investigate the far side of the gully."

Ash's eyes flashed in protest, but Malik was quick to interject. "He's right," Malik said. He turned to Nox as he went on. "If this blue anomaly just happens to coincide with a historical attack of demons—"

"Then that's one hell of a coincidence," Nox finished for him.

"Listen." Gadriel cut the argument off before it began. "Yazlyn and I are winged. We can bolt from the pincers and are a hell of a lot more useful in a Raascot camp than either of you. We'll go in, find Ceres, and free Amaris."

Malik nudged Ash, and it seemed to free him from his indignation. He was ready to do whatever had to be done. "We've got this," Ash said in agreement. The reevers began to unsheathe their swords, and the dark fae readied themselves while below them pandemonium erupted.

Gadriel turned to the only one in their party without a mission. "And Nox—"

"Don't be a hero?" she finished for him.

"Just stay alive. We've gone through too much to lose you now."

36

Chapter Four

"DID YOU HEAR THAT?" AMARIS FROWNED AS SHE LISTENED. It could have been anything. Maybe it was nothing. It was just something odd, something that didn't feel quite right. But the hairs on the back of her neck pricked as she leaned toward the noise.

Zaccai tilted his pointed ears toward the opening of the tent. The following yelp told her it was most certainly not nothing. Her breath quickened. It didn't take long for the pounding of feet, and soon the sounds erupted into hollers. Amaris's emotions flashed from alert to trained to panic. She couldn't be a reever if she was chained to a pole like a mistreated dog. She tugged against her chains as she jumped to her feet.

"Wait here!" He darted from the tent, shooting skyward.

"Cai!" Amaris tensed as she stared into the dark flap of the tent where he'd disappeared. The commotion around her swelled with calls for action, running, the powerful flapping of wings, and the metallic ring of weapons pulled free from their sheaths.

She'd kept her eyes peeled throughout her time as Raascot's prisoner, always looking for an out, a weapon, or anything else that might prove useful. She scanned the tent for something she could use in defense, praying she'd missed something. She'd had years of training in both offense and defense, but her fists might not do much for her while she was constrained. There was a lantern on the tent's second-most pole. It didn't make much in terms of a weapon, but any metal object was a blunt force when used in conjunction with surprise. She lurched toward it but cried out in pain as the chain jolted her shoulder socket, jerking her backward. She stretched her arms outward but couldn't make contact. There was nothing. She had nothing. She couldn't use persuasion. She couldn't use true sight.

Shock wave. She had a shock wave.

She didn't know how to summon it, but she'd used it before. If she could topple the lantern or crack the tent pole, she might have a chance. She closed her eyes and focused, calling to her magic. It seemed as fruitless as a human attempting the All Mother's holy manifestation. She felt like she was reaching into an empty room. Her hand grasped at nothing. The space inside of her was that of an empty, shallow, powerless box.

"Come on, *come on.*"

She tried to feel the panic she'd felt that day in the woods when Gadriel had helped her access her power. At first, she was doing her best to imitate the sensation, but as the sounds grew louder, she felt a true helplessness begin to rise in her. The sounds outside were of pain and falling warriors. The screams of men and women mingled with an unfamiliar animal crack and snarl. She heard the inhuman sounds of crunch and bone and the sopping noise of something unnaturally wet. The panic began to grow in earnest, building in her like the stoking of a fire. She reached for her magic again, clawing at the empty walls within herself. The shock wave was somewhere. She had used it before. She needed to focus. She needed to find wherever it hid within her.

A sound tore through the air like that of a bird underwater.

It was the terrible, drowning cry of a beast. The shrill, piercing sounds of a dying scream were far too close. Whatever it was, it was drawing nearer to her tent. The thunder of something just outside the canvas nearly stopped her heart. Amaris jumped out of her skin as Zaccai landed in front of the flaps to the tent. He sprinted to her, clawing at her shackles.

"What is it?" Her question came out strangled.

"We have to get you out."

"Cai, what is—"

His eyes were hard, face tense, expressions bobbing between panic and control. "I have no idea. But we have to go. We have to go now."

Her eyes widened as she absorbed the sheer terror he failed to conceal. Zaccai was a spymaster. He was military. She'd seen him friendly. She'd seen him strong. She'd seen him sad. But this...

His jaw flexed as he gritted his teeth. "We don't have time. I'm picking up this whole fucking tent. Cover your head and neck."

The fear behind his eyes answered any questions she may have had. Amaris dropped to the ground and sheltered the back of her head and neck as if the building were about to collapse around her. Zaccai yanked at the tent and its poles until it collapsed. Under the white canvas, she could see nothing. She heard the pole snap. Zaccai had to be as blinded as she was, but he kept working. He maneuvered one end of the cuff from the splintered end of the pole.

"Can you move?"

Amaris gave her hand a shake. The remaining cuff was cold, tight, and chafing, but she was free. "I'm free," she confirmed. She shoved against the fallen canvas, attempting to tunnel her way toward an edge.

He shouted to her from elsewhere in the collapsed tense. "We have to go."

Another animal noise stopped her in her tracks. She felt the pressure as something stepped onto their collapsed tent. Amaris froze as the fabric pulled taut around her. She would have remained immobilized, but Zaccai reached her at long last and crashed into her, shoving her to the ground. He covered her with his body, enormous wings sheltering them both. She stayed quiet as the canvas stretched tight. The enemy had to be nearly on top of them.

She opened her mouth to ask what it was, but Zaccai's hand clamped down over her mouth. Every one of his actions heightened her fear. Her heart thundered. If she only knew what it was, she could come up with a plan. They couldn't just cower silently. She felt his muscles tighten, coiling as the fallen canvas tightened even further with yet another step from the unknown creature.

The sound of broken glass and death stole the breath from her lungs.

The curdling cry of whatever sodden monsters were in their camp was directly over them. Zaccai's final tightening hold was an apology, and she knew it. She was an unwilling, wingless fae in a camp of winged Raascot men. She shouldn't have to suffer the fate of her exposed spine and flesh because of their failures. He might lose his wings to the creature, but if she was exposed, she'd be done.

She was going to die, and she wouldn't even have the luxury of knowing what killed her. She tucked her head against Zaccai's chest. He was her friend. In that moment, all she knew was that she didn't want to die alone.

A new sound cut through her final, silent prayers to the All Mother. A man's yelp—a cry for aid—was a sword slicing through the tension. It took three bounds. One to close the space; one crushing, sharp step directly on them; and a third to clear the tent and set them free. Zaccai stifled a pained grunt as he bore its weight before the monster was gone.

"Go!" he urged, releasing the shield of his wings as he pushed her forward. Amaris didn't need to be told twice. She scrambled as quickly as she could to fight free of the canvas.

Zaccai grabbed her arm in the final moment, yanking them both forward as they burst into the night.

They emerged to face the fires and beasts of hell itself.

Amaris couldn't believe what she was seeing. Two-legged demons seemed to be pouring in from the river, dripping in mud, covered with glistening, amphibious skin. The creatures possessed the horrible, wiry legs of the great desert birds she'd only seen referenced in Tarkhany, except these were the slick legs of reptiles with blackened talons and sharp, charcoal beaks to match their birdlike legs. The body they possessed was nearly the beginning of the half circle that gave way into a tail with sharpened, scorpionlike pincers.

Vakliche.

The nightmares were everywhere.

Amaris's lips fell open. She'd never seen so many monsters. She'd never heard of a reever taking more than three of any creature at once. No training could prepare her for a conquering army of vakliche. This was not a battle she could win. The demons were innumerable. This was a slaughter.

A small voice in her mind told her that she needed to be useful. A piece of logic called to her training, it summoned her muscles to readiness, but she was frozen. Arms at her side, she turned to Zaccai. He mirrored her disbelief. He hadn't released her arm. His fingers still pinched around her tender flesh, poised to tear her forward.

All around them, tents were ablaze as collapsed canvas toppled into campfires. A foot-soldier screamed as she sprinted from the camp—the impossible form of a woman wholly engulfed in flames sending Amaris deeper into shock. The nightmares of bodies on fire would surely haunt her for the rest of her days, should she survive the night. The soldier had been set to an orange, white, and crimson glow as fire engulfed every hair and fiber of her torso. Her screams had boiled within her throat as she ran fruitlessly to escape the inferno. The melting soldier's noise drew the attention of the demon as it took off after her. The monster seemed forged

41

with the leftover, disposed corpses and parts of whatever drowned creatures hell had rejected.

Amaris spotted it then, and her breath caught as she swallowed against the dry pit of fire and despair that clogged her throat. She looked up at Zaccai.

"Cai," she choked.

He hadn't moved, and she knew why. His men were dying. Troops were falling. Everything was crashing in as hell ate his people alive.

"Cai, listen," she insisted. She dug her fingernails into the flesh of his forearm to get him to listen. He blinked, turning toward her. "Cai, hear me! The demon—it has no eyes."

His eyelashes fluttered as the information drilled into him. It brought him back to awareness. She'd gotten through. They had an important piece of information. The horrific shape of the aquatic scorpion thundered past them, and Zaccai raised his wings in a knee-jerk reaction to shield them, but she noted the moment he understood. The vakliche was chasing after the gargled form of the flaming woman, but it couldn't see. It wasn't following the fire or the shape of the soldier. The frothing beast was sprinting toward her screams.

Zaccai looked at Amaris, and she knew what he was asking. "Save your people," she said.

The sky above the camp filled with smoke as trampled tents caught ablaze. Winged fae shot into the air, darting to the ground to scoop up their earthbound brothers and sisters in arms. A fae woman launched into the air just as her leg was caught in the clawed tail of the beast and she was dragged back to the blazing campground.

"The king!" Zaccai shouted. All semblance of shock had left him. He was armed with information and bound to king and country. He didn't even look over his shoulder as he shot toward the royal tent, leaving Amaris unattended.

Amaris was no helpless maiden, and he'd known it. She summoned everything within her to survive. She had to move, and she had to do it quietly. The metallic shackle cutting into her tender flesh was already absorbing the heat around her. She winced, gathering her chains into her hands. She clutched the hot metal tightly, mobilizing while she minimized her noise. Tents, men, and cries in every direction told her she was in the middle of camp. Anywhere was better than here. She picked a direction.

The sounds of fire, screaming, and the drenched noise of chomping beaks against fallen, bloodied bodies filled the air. A high-pitched ringing filled her ears, drowning the godless noises of the dying. She couldn't allow herself to observe any of it. She couldn't pause to mourn. She couldn't allow herself to gape in horror at the blood, the gore, or the unholy consumption of humans and fae alike.

It may as well have been the bright light of high noon. Despite the midnight hour, the camp was glowing in crimsons and yellows as canvas shelters lit all around her. Amaris's head jerked from side to side between the rows of war tents, but she wasn't sure which way to escape. If she made it to the river, she could leave camp only to encounter more of the demons. Her body was hot from the fire of the tent she'd barely escaped. She refused to look back at the fate she'd scarcely avoided.

She froze.

Another thundered past her as a creature took off in the direction of a screaming soldier. Her mouth dropped open in a mixture of disgust and horror as the immense shape of the creature was illuminated by all-encompassing firelight. The monster was wrapped in the black, salamanderlike skin of semi-aquatic beasts that should never have been found above the water's surface. The description in the tomes could never have prepared her for the horror of seeing the vakliche in person.

Amaris forced herself to focus. "One." She clocked the first beast in front of her and slightly to the right. "Two, three." She counted two more fully on her right, in what would have been an eastward direction. She spun slowly, holding her chains to her. "Four, five, six." Three more creatures were in the western part of the camp. Another sound came from the south, alerting her to at least one more. Her best bet for survival would be to the north, back toward Gwydir.

The monsters were even more terrible in the golden flicker of the inferno illuminating them. They could have been mud-caked cousins to the ag'drurath as their horrible, twisted bodies tore into the camp.

The warriors on all sides had their weapons drawn. Men hacked and cried out as they sprinted, swords outstretched, but she knew their fate long before they reached the creature. The archers were landing shots, and arrows were no killing blows for demons.

"Ten," she grunted as she ran past a crowd of armed men. They barely noticed her. Amaris rounded the corner and sucked in a breath, silencing herself.

Eleven. Twelve.

She didn't have time to appreciate the soldiers around her who knocked their bows and launched their arrows at the demons. They may not kill the monsters, but the agitation and confusion bought troops much-needed time. A few winged fae had taken to the air, their great, feathered wingspans thundering as they held a steady position, as if treading water above the camp. The aloft fae brought their bows to aim and knocked arrows before releasing them onto the demons. The twangs of bows and clinging, metallic sounds of metal began to join the sunken sounds of flesh as tar-like blood dripped to the ground.

North. Go north.

An armed woman made eye contact with her. From her widened eyes, it was clear she recognized Amaris. For the barest of seconds, she thought the woman might lunge to contain her. The woman shook her head once, and the message was clear.

Go.

Amaris was about to run past the woman when she stopped

short. The woman jolted in surprise. Amaris wrapped her fingers around the warrior's arm and with hushed urgency whispered, "The demons can't see. Don't make a sound."

Their eyes met for a charged moment before Amaris nodded and took off into the night.

She needed to make it back up the mountain pass beyond the camp. She rounded another tent and skidded to a halt, frozen in her tracks. She'd nearly slammed into a demon, hidden as it bent and devoured a winged man. The slain man looked up at her with lifeless, unblinking eyes, body moving only as the demon jostled its meal. Amaris took a careful step backward. The monster ceased pecking through the man's chest cavity, red blood and the gore of organs dripping from its great beak as it lifted its face and turned in her direction.

She stopped breathing.

Amaris didn't move a muscle as she scanned the monstrosity, searching for a weak point, a soft spot, something she might use against it if it lunged for her. Two enormous slits lined the side of its head as if to function like the gills of a salamander, but its face contained only its enormous, blade-sharp beak. Its slits flared as it listened. The flames behind her licked at her back. She knew if she held her place for any longer, her shirt may catch on fire. Heat punished the skin of her arms, the back of her legs, her shoulders, but she refused to move. The metallic chains and cuff soaked in the cooking temperatures around her, eating into her wrist. Sweat trickled down her brow, both from the heat and from her suppressed urge to cry out in pain.

The fire popped, blistering her, but she held her ground. Her years of training, of powering through pain, of adversity and self-denial culminated to this moment. If she moved, it would all be for nothing. Blood mingled with the drool dripping from its beak as it leaned in toward her, gills flaring as it tested the air. Her eyes burned as she refused to blink. And then she saw it.

Salvation came in the form of a flash of wings.

Someone shot overhead, calling out to the troops below. The monster turned its attention upward as it followed the sounds overhead. She recognized the cry as a figure darted past again.

Zaccai. He was drawing the beast away from her.

As soon as the monster took a few steps toward the noise, Amaris gulped for air, choking on smoke as she leapt from the burning tent. She glanced down at her arm just long enough to see the sloshing liquid of blisters dotting her skin. Her head swam against the pain. Relief was only temporary as she ran. The heat lived on in her skin.

Amaris tried to make as much space between herself and the fires around her as she could, but everything was ablaze. Crackles of fallen logs, screeches of running demons, and the collapsing sounds of toppled canvases greeted her at every step. Nowhere was safe.

She looked to the north and fought the urge to cry out with helplessness. The fallen tents had formed a blazing barricade. She'd never be able to escape back up the gully.

In the distance, the small, dark comfort of the murky river waters broke through the flaming light of the tents. *Relief.* The only true cooling agent would be the rapid river through which the demons seemed to be mercilessly spawning. Her mind felt the swirling, toppling sensation as if she'd been pushed over a cliff with no chance at equilibrium. Her head spun again against the sensory overload as waves of sound and heat hit her time and time again. The only clear path was to the stream.

Rallying her breath, Amaris tried to move as quietly as possible. She clutched the blistering hot metal of her chains to her body as she advanced toward the source of the danger.

Chapter Five

THE SHARP INTAKE OF AIR AT HER SIDE TOLD YAZLYN THAT he'd found her. Yazlyn followed Gadriel's line of sight. *Amaris.* The reever was a speck of white against the crimsons, oranges, and embers.

"I've got to get to Ceres," he said urgently.

He didn't have to elaborate for Yazlyn to understand what Gadriel was saying. "I've got her."

Gadriel dove from the cliff, wings tucked until he'd nearly reached the river below. His great wingspan opened up, carrying him toward the king's tent while Yazlyn took off toward Amaris. Somewhere on the ground, she knew Ash and Malik were picking their way toward the distant, bluish glow that didn't belong in such an unholy setting. With any luck, their new princess would avert her eyes, stay by the horse, and avoid being any more traumatized by her time in Raascot than she already was.

But Yazlyn couldn't think of the others now. She closed in over the speck of white between the blaze of toppled tents. She swooped in and closed her wings, thundering to the earth, wings flaring once more to steady her. She'd been so focused on Amaris, she'd failed to secure the ground before landing. She sucked in a quick breath of horror as a monster immediately turned for her.

Yazlyn locked eyes with the reever for a fraction of a second. It was all she could spare before the demon sprinted for her. She shot into the air, hovering a few paces above the earth, and became acutely aware of the extent of the monster's reach as it stabbed upward. Its tail nearly grazed the leather of her shoe as she jerked away from the mud demon.

Amaris used the distraction to take off in the opposite direction. She didn't have the luxury of wings, and with the demon's long legs, it would overtake her on foot in seconds if it found her.

The sergeant watched the reever's white hair like a beacon as it disappeared around one of the few still-standing tents. She continued to bait the demon, ensuring Amaris had the time she needed. With Amaris no longer in her line of sight, Yazlyn gave the monster her full attention and shuddered in terror. Its scorpion pincers continued to threaten her from where it stood, beaklike mouth dripping with anticipation of its kill.

There. That should be enough.

It took her nearly three upward beats of her wings before she was beyond the shredding clutches of its tail. It looked up after her and roared its sunken, guttural noises. But no... it wasn't looking at her, was it? She strained to look down at the abomination and saw its face fully for the first time.

She went four beats higher into the smoky night air before she started screaming to the camp of Raascot soldiers.

"Everyone!" Yazlyn summoned the most authority her voice could muster. No one could hear her. There was too much commotion, too much terror. She bit her lip as she looked between the distant space where Amaris had disappeared.

She'd made a promise to Gadriel, yes, but Amaris was a reever. Not only that, but she'd been perfectly silent when Yazlyn had landed. *She knew.*

Amaris would have to survive on her own for a moment longer. Her people needed her. Yazlyn darted across the sky, shouting, "Be quiet! They can't see you! They hunt by sound!"

She repeated the same information as her eyes watched the frenzied scurries of her countrymen. Some responded instantaneously, skidding to a stop and silencing themselves. Some seemed to hear her, but the panic of the dying was resistant to logic. No matter how much she called to the men who scattered beneath her, they couldn't control the fear that tore from their throats.

The camp had descended into hysteria.

Yazlyn flew over where Ash and Malik had been picking their way to the opposite hill and shouted her information. She wasn't directly above them, so her noise only drew the creatures to a slightly off-center position as their tails shot up after her. The change in the reevers' postures and speed of their advancement told her that they had understood her warning. If anyone would survive this night, it would be them.

She'd done all she could. Now, she had to retrieve Amaris. She dove and turned with the agility of a bird of prey. Her eyes burned from the smoke as she searched the camp, but the lost, pale girl was merely another blistering spot of blindness in an already scorching basin.

She'll be fine, Yazlyn told herself again and again. *She's a reever.*

She heard another scream and shot into the sky after an earthbound troop. Gadriel wouldn't be happy with her, but it seemed she lived to let him down. There was too much to be done. She couldn't ignore her countrymen in favor of a tool for Ceres's vengeance who didn't wish to be found.

Yazlyn darted about the turmoil of the troops and started helping. She dove for the Raascot humans who lacked the power of flight, grabbing anyone she could hold. They clung to her as if she were the only rope in the midst of the ocean. The men weighed her down significantly, and there was no calm or gratitude in the face of the dying. Their thrashing nearly dragged her under into the flames with them, but this was not how she died. She refused. She grunted, summoning all the will and fortitude she possessed as she forced enough strength into her wings to carry others to the opposite bank of the river.

"You!" Yazlyn commanded one of the enlisted troops in a firm whisper. "On the king's honor, it's your job to keep *everyone* silent." He nodded, tears from pain and shock carving lines down his soot-stained face. "And you." She turned to another. "Get the others up this cliff. They have to move slowly. If a single stone dislodges and you draw their attention uphill, you may survive the demons, but you will not survive me. Do you understand?"

"Yes, sergeant." The troop swallowed, throat bobbing as he kept his voice low.

The other winged fae who'd accompanied the south-bound march followed suit, scooping up the flightless and dropping them on the riverbank. The frenzy had already consumed so many soldiers. Anyone who wasn't eaten by a demon would cook within the camp's inferno.

✦

Nox couldn't stay on the outlook.

Restlessness and adrenaline forced her from the ledge. Pebbles bit into her palms and knees as she shoved herself onto her feet. She'd watched in horror for too long.

She didn't give a damn if she was an orphan, an escort, a succubus, or the damned queen of the kingdoms; she couldn't stand idly by while death consumed the world around her. Her conscience would haunt her for decades to come if she remained on her stomach while demons devoured the entrails of those below. Her friends were out there. Malik was maneuvering through the tents and across the grassy plane. Amaris was somewhere in the camp, possibly lost and scared.

Everyone had told her to stay put. Even as the command had left their lips, it had a split chance of her obeying or rejecting their advice. She'd watched the reevers scale down the mountain and head toward the distant, anomalous glow. She'd waited as Gadriel shot like a hawk toward the king's tent. She kept her eyes trained on Yazlyn as the sergeant went looking for Amaris, and she saw the flash of white against the chaos as the sergeant slammed to the ground. A moment later, Yazlyn shot into the air, abandoning Amaris as a demon advanced. The sight stole the breath from her lungs.

That spineless bitch.

She couldn't trust anyone. She couldn't live with herself if she did nothing, and right now, Amaris needed her.

Adrenaline precluded wisdom as Nox scaled down the mountain. Rocks shifted and tumbled from her uneasy footing. She caught Yazlyn's voice as the sergeant called to others above the din. Her flutter of wings kept her safe from monstrous pincers as she tried to tell everyone that the demons lacked eyes—commanding them to be quiet, shouting for those on the ground to move silently.

Another stone slipped, and Nox yelped as she braced herself against the cliff. It did her no favors as the tumble of rock had already begun to draw attention, but she picked her way sideways, sidling on the opposite bank like a crab while the monster that had sensed her remained fixed on the spot where she'd scrambled from her outlook. It kept whatever it called a face focused on the cliffside she'd abandoned. She may not have been trained for agility, but what she lacked in practice, she made up for in cunning.

That's right. I'm over there, you watery motherfucker.

The demon opened the prongs of its maw, and Nox realized that she had mistaken a beak for multiple connections of four forward-facing teeth. Strands of slime connected the roof of its mouth to wherever its tongue rested as it growled after the noise she had left in her ripple. She tore her eyes from the monster to look toward the camp.

Nox saw only flame and carnage. Bodies had fallen in wet, vermillion puddles around the campsite. She heard

51

cries, the crunching of bone, the wet sounds of the river and its monsters. The bipedal stampede of demons continued to thunder through the camp as each new sound drew their attention. The pops and snaps of canvas and fire filled the silences between breaths. Smoke and wings filled the sky. Warriors were slowly collecting and scaling the mountain farther down the cliff—too far for them to spot her place in the shadows. No matter how hard she searched, she saw no trace of Amaris.

Even if the goddess allowed her to see Amaris, Nox wouldn't be able to call to her. Sound was their enemy. She choked down every sensation that begged her to cry out.

She drew closer to the river, and her skin pimpled in gooseflesh. Every survival instinct in her body told her to run as far from the water as possible. She hesitated along its banks.

Water was fine in a chilled glass. It was lovely in a bubble bath. Those were the only two conditions under which she approved of any body of water. She'd nearly driven a wedge between herself and the reevers in the rain. She had once given away her position to the enemy in a shallow, harmless creek when a turtle brushed against her calf. But these were not turtles. She was surrounded by otherworldly demons birthed from the river muck.

Come on, you coward, she chastised herself. *You've been through the worst things imaginable, and you've come out stronger. There's only one thing you couldn't survive, and it's the knowledge you let something happen to Amaris because you were too scared to help. Get it together.*

She sucked in a breath and held it as she dipped her foot into the water. Her lungs burned against her refusal to breathe, but something about remaining tense made her feel safer. She plunged her entire foot into the water and winced, closing her eyes as she did so. Nox knew she needed to be on high alert, but it was all she could do to keep from turning and running in the other direction as terror gripped her.

She had no reason to hate the water as she did. Men,

sure. They'd given her a glorious abundance of reasons to hate them. Women in power, the church, most of humanity, really, had let her down. Kings, queens, and princesses had failed her. But those failures had made her indifferent, cold, and strong. It was something else entirely, something primal that drove her to fear the blackened bottoms of riverbeds.

She plunged her second foot into the water. Then her shins. Then her knees. She was met with an onslaught of icy desperation to jerk her limbs up from the watery grave. The cold kept her focused on the task at hand, allowing the camp, the beasts, the world around her to vignette as she put one foot quite literally in front of the other. She'd been right to fear the river, especially now that she knew there were *faceless scorpion demons* in its depths. And yet, Amaris needed her.

As she shifted her weight into one hip, a single foot searching for the river bottom, her sole did not find hard sand, nor did her feet slide over slippery rocks. Instead, as she eased her weight off the shore and into the water, she began to sink into the silt of the river's squelching, bottomless mud. Everything within her begged her to cry out for help. Nox felt a desperate panic as the entirety of one foot, then her ankle, then the lower half of her leg disappeared beneath the shallow river bottom. She drew blood from her tongue from the force of biting into it, begging herself to maintain silence. Silence was a matter of life or death.

Nox twisted aggressively from the river. Her torso turned to clutch the rocky banks and the small grasses and shrubs at its ledges. There was no way she'd be able to walk across the river muck. She'd be lucky to escape even the single step she'd taken into its infinite, loamy bed.

An unnatural bubble surfaced from the gurgle of the stream, drawing her eyes.

Three arm's lengths from her, a serpentine coil rose from the murky water.

Nox froze.

The creature continued to rise, its elongated tail the first to break the surface. The body that emerged was not the rough, crocodilian body of a truly scaled reptile but the soft, froglike body of the demons of nightmares. Mud and water slid from its surface. The gill-like slits at its side flared, and it opened its mouth, tasting the air.

Her mouth parted in a noiseless, horrified scream.

She did not move. She did not breathe as her leg was sucked deeper and deeper into the muddy waters of the river. Her worst nightmares hit her from above and below as she continued to slowly sink. She swallowed scream after scream as she stared at the demon. The river had no care for her urgency. It continued to gobble her leg, slurping her into its depths while demanding her silence.

While the slippery creature had no eyes, the attention of the mud demon seemed to be staring directly at her. It tasted the air around, parting its sharpened, forward-facing teeth and revealing the black hole of its gullet. The water swallowed her thighs, then her hips. Gentle rapids licked her navel as she silently begged the monster to leave. If she didn't get out of the river soon, she'd drown.

She could feel death. It was as inevitable as time was to gray hair and wrinkles. Nox knew that, whether in three seconds or three minutes, she would scream and claw her way onto the shore. If the mud consumed any more of her leg, she wouldn't be able to free herself even if there were no monsters. It would take two able-bodied men and a large rope to pull her from the ravenous river bottom. As it was, hell's most heinous creature clicked its pincers as it tested the sound, listening to the river burbling around her.

Then the cry of a wounded foot soldier drew its attention.

She whipped her head at the same moment the creature spun in the water.

She saw the man collapse to his knees on the opposite shore. Her eyes widened in both horror and gratitude as one man's impending doom signaled her lone chance at survival. The soldier had been too consumed with his pain and grief to see the beast approaching. Nox took full advantage of the monster's lunge toward the mortally wounded man, using the ripe sounds of his violent death to her advantage as she sucked her leg from where the river had gripped her and pulled herself onto the bank. She blocked the cathartic scream that begged to free itself from her throat as she squirmed wholly onto the shore.

Nox shuddered on the riverbank once, then twice. Dark, dense mud gripped her from the knee down. The danger hadn't passed. Nothing had changed. Demons filled the camp. Her friends needed her. Amaris needed her. She only allowed herself a moment of panting before getting to her feet. She'd found strength against impossible odds before, and she could do it again now.

Then, like a phantom, there she was. The spectral figure Nox had been rushing to save, the one she'd been hoping against all hopes to see, stood on the far shore. Amaris had yet to spot her, and Nox understood Amaris's plan at once. She was lowering herself to the ground, readying herself to cross the river.

Nox silently waved her hands above her head, jumping once until Amaris saw her. She gestured forcefully for Amaris to stop, lifting both palms in a flat, wild gesture. She hoped Amaris could see the intensity of the whites of her eyes. Nox pointed at the river and then made the gesture of a throat being slit several times to indicate death.

No, she mouthed again and again.

Amaris stared at her from the flickering hell of the sweltering camp on the opposite side. It had only been a matter of days since they'd held each other in the bed, but it seemed as if years had separated them once again. Nox was on the cool, dark side of one bank while Amaris burned in the fires on its far shore.

She knew Amaris was a reever now. She'd fought an ag'drurath. She'd survived unspeakable odds. She was powerful enough that Raascot's king had forced her to march south as his champion. Yet as Nox stared at the pale features obscured by night and shadow, she saw only her snowflake.

Please, no, she pleaded.

Nox didn't know what Amaris was able to ascertain from her frantic, unintelligible attempt at body language, but after several long moments, Amaris turned from the river and angled her body south, toward the front of the camp.

Nox's fists flexed in frustration. She couldn't wait helplessly on the far edge of the battle. She would rather die in the fires or in the jaws of the monsters than be the girl who'd stood and watched as her friends, her presumed father, and what remained of her love wandered amidst the beasts and flames. She had to find another way across.

One leg thick with the blacked mud of the bottom it had barely been freed from, she began to walk forward, then backward, scanning the shores of the river until she saw what she was looking for. A low-lying dam of water-logged tree trunks and sharp, jutting sticks had begun to pile up on one edge of the river. Biting back her breath, Nox set out toward the makeshift bridge.

Chapter Six

MALIK LOOKED OVER AT ASH FOR THE NOD IN CONFIRMA-tion as the two closed in on the far side of the gully. The sound of their advance was muted by the wetland grasses of the marshy stretch. Their bodies were mirrors of crouched tension, each moving with silent intent. Whatever the winged fae had to do in the Raascot camp tonight, their focus had to remain on the magical anomaly.

It pained Malik to know people were suffering so close by, but he understood that something bigger was at stake. If this truly was related to the attack, they'd save more lives by staying focused than they would by plowing forward, sword in hand, at creatures that would cut them down before they reached the soft parts of their torso. He summoned his training to grow utterly numb to the world around him, blocking out the sounds of fire, terror, and death. He couldn't allow himself to smell the burning canvas, flesh, and hair. Only that which posed immediate danger was able to perforate their bubble of awareness. He pressed forward toward the bluish spot on the hill, not sure of what it was nor why they sought it.

But it couldn't be a coincidence, could it?

He tensed as something caught his attention. With Ash's faeling reflexes, he was spinning to face the new, unseen enemy a split second before Malik absorbed what was happening. His vision darkened as the glow of fire was blotted out by an enormous, black expanse. A gust of wind mussed his hair as feathers rustled over them. A winged fae landed behind them on the balls of his feet, touching down as quietly as possible. His breath caught as he drew his weapon on the newcomer. Ash brandished his blade, ready to fight.

The tall, muscled fae raised his hands to show he meant no harm. The look on his face, youthful, clean-shaven, told Malik that this fae expected something of them. What, he couldn't tell.

The fae whispered, "It's me, Zaccai! I'm Gadriel's second-in-command. I—"

Ash nodded beside him. "Yes, I remember the introduction."

Malik frowned but relaxed slightly. He recognized the name from their time with the ag'imni in Farehold. Neither Malik nor Ash had room for surprise, nor could they bother to ask what he was doing here or how they had found him. Time and questions were not luxuries afforded to them. Reunions would be allotted to some other day.

"The beasts can't see," Ash hissed. "Be quiet."

Zaccai nodded, communicating he both knew and was ready to act in accordance with the information. Zaccai crept on his feet closer to Malik, keeping his voice as low as possible. "Imagine my surprise when I spotted two reevers crossing the back of the battlefield. Where are you going if it isn't toward the demons?"

"So, curiosity drew you over?" Ash said.

"If it has your attention, it must be bad. The world is already on fire. We don't need any more bad news tonight. I thought you might need help."

Malik's voice was so low, his words were barely discernible

above the chaos of the camp. He lifted one finger, pointing to the hilltop. "There."

He watched the man's face. Zaccai found the ominous blue swell on the cliffside and swallowed. A distant wail snaked through the camp. He turned away, looking over his shoulder at the truly incomprehensible magnitude of damage.

"It can't be a coincidence," Malik said.

"Shit," Zaccai muttered under his breath. He patted two hands down his torso until he landed on the circular weapon that had been pinned to his hip. He procured a whip made of thin chain, saying something about its runes. Zaccai extended the whip to Malik. "I have to go help the men in my camp. If the problem is magical, you'll need backup. Here."

Malik accepted the whip and saw the hundreds, if not thousands, of runes that had been carefully etched into the interlinked, delicate chain. He had never used a whip, but he gave Zaccai an appreciative nod.

Zaccai was off in a silent dash, his crow's wings flashing into the night as he soared toward the surviving northmen. Malik was the first to turn his back on the flames. The reevers couldn't spare time to watch him.

The far edge of the gully had a bit of a lip. The bluish lure drawing the reevers forward had been perched on an overhang in the middle of the hill where a small, sheltered cave had appeared to jut from the rocks around it. The men pressed up against the hill underneath the object of their pursuit.

"Do you hear that?" Ash mouthed.

Malik nodded. Quiet, unintelligible muttering trickled down from the cave above. It was feather-soft and would have been impossible to hear if they hadn't been carefully listening.

Someone was speaking.

If the magical glow signified man or fae, Malik had no idea how the two of them had gone undetected as they'd crept forward, especially as even Zaccai had spotted them from across his battlefield. Still, the gentle words showed no signs of disturbance, no indication that they had identified anyone approaching.

Malik scrunched his face. They were far enough from the disaster that the firelight did little to help him find footing on the cliffs. Moonlight was his primary aid as he searched for an area to summit. Despite the gentle slopes of the gully around them, the rock elected by their glowing anomaly was perfectly sheer.

Ash was both limber and quick on his feet, but Malik was the one who had proven to possess the grip strength and upper body power necessary to pull himself up and off obstacles time and time again. He'd have to be the one who used his chest and shoulders to pull himself over the lip.

With a nod, Ash linked his fingers together to offer Malik the first step. Ensuring his weapons wouldn't sound against the stone, Malik took off his sword in favor of his knives and the rune-engraved whip. He stepped a single foot into Ash's interlocked hands and made his body as light as he could as he reached up with his right leg and left hand, finding the smallest of divots and pockets in the rock face onto which he could latch. He knew Ash could do nothing except stand helplessly by and spot his friend from the grass below. Ash would have to focus on keeping them safe from any threats on the ground. Whatever Malik found in the cave, he'd have to face alone.

✦

Gadriel landed as quietly as he could outside of Ceres's tent. A single hand braced against the warming grass, leveling the feet that absorbed the impact of his landing. He closed his eyes tightly and forced a rallying breath. The last time he'd seen his cousin, he'd been sent to the dungeons.

The threat of death superseded whatever tension lingered between them.

Gadriel pushed his way into one of the few remaining canvas tents where he knew he'd find his king. He wasn't sure what he expected, but it certainly wasn't a man slouched on his chair, half-empty bottle of wine resting on the arm of the makeshift throne. Gadriel gaped at the unfazed form of his cousin. It took him no time at all to realize Ceres had been left alone. None of the men sworn to guard Raascot's king had remained at their post. They had doubtlessly sprinted into action to protect the war camp.

"Ceres, your men!"

"Why are you here?" the king asked in a normal, tired voice, not bothering to open his eyes. He was rubbing his temples as if utterly unaware that his men were screaming and tents were ablaze all around him. Whatever migraine that had dug its maddening ice picks into Ceres's temples must have been so crippling that he couldn't differentiate between the screams from beyond his tent and the wails of his men beyond.

Horror gripped Gadriel. Ceres had been unreasonable for years, but Gadriel had never fathomed his cousin could sit idly by while the world burned. Ceres had sent men on missions for two decades, not caring if they died, but Gadriel had always assumed it was because his cousin was too far removed from the problem to understand the weight of his royal decrees. And yet, here he was, face-to-face with disaster, and the man showed no emotion.

Gadriel took another step into the tent.

An ominous caution pressed over him. He lowered his voice with unease as his eyes darted to the shadows and flames that revealed themselves on the canvas of the king's tent. "Ceres, have you seen what's attacking?"

"What do you want?" Ceres asked, still not looking up from where his headache plagued him.

Gadriel lowered his voice further, almost as if trying to soothe an animal. "I'm here to help you, Ceres. Let's get out of here."

"Why do you use my name like I'm a child?" Ceres's fingers stilled as Gadriel looked at him, their eyes meeting at last.

Gadriel had spent so much of his time over the past twenty

years south of the border that he hadn't seen the slow progression of gauntness and misery that had etched themselves into his cousin's face. The fae were invulnerable to time but not impervious to the effects of starvation, neglect, and illness of the mind. Even when Gadriel had stormed into the throne room, he had done so fueled with an agenda that prevented him from truly seeing the face of the man who had spent hundreds of years on Raascot's throne.

At one time, Ceres had been a good king. Perhaps Gadriel had been both unable and unwilling to see the visible evidence of the madness that had claimed him. He was neither king nor cousin. The man's eyes seemed disconnected from his body. They were so red, so bloodshot, it appeared as though Ceres had not slept in years. Gadriel's gaze traced from the sunken cheeks to the odd angles at which Ceres's shirt loosely hung.

"Come on. Let me get you out of here," Gadriel tried again, this time intentionally avoiding his cousin's name. He stretched out a palm.

"I would rather die here than return to my throne a failure," Ceres said.

Gadriel's jaw hardened as he looked at the man he'd loved and served, hardly recognizing the wan, hunched figure who now sat upon the throne.

Ceres loosed a short, barking laugh. His fingers dug more deeply into the flesh of his temple. The purple bruises beneath his eyes were rimmed only by the dark line of his eyelashes as the king dropped his gaze once more.

The urge to fix everything surged through Gadriel. He wanted to reassure his cousin, to save him, to end his suffering. He shook his head, reaching within himself for reassurance, for comfort, offering stability. He left his hand extended as he said, "You're not a failure. You've made something—someone—incredible. I've met your daughter, Ceres, and I'd like for you to live long enough to meet her too. She's smart. She's resourceful. She's strong and clever and everything that would have made you proud."

Ceres laughed again. The sound was a dark, cruel thing like glass across skin. "You're callous, cousin, but I've never taken you for evil."

Gadriel advanced another step. "You have a daughter. Daphne had no son. She bore you a daughter. I've met her. She's here. I don't mean in Raascot—she's here just beyond the camp."

Ceres stood. "Do you know where I was the day I heard Daphne birthed a son? I was in my war room, planning how I might extract her from Aubade. Her vile bitch of a mother had already married her off to a monster, thinking a marriage could do anything to dissuade me. It didn't, and they both knew it. Moirai knew I would come. It took a curse on the entire border to truly keep Daphne and me apart. Isn't that something? Doesn't that speak of our love? Only a curse dividing the very continent could separate us."

Gadriel dared another step forward. "Daphne's husband beat her, didn't he?"

Ceres continued to look off into where a sane man might have seen the fire and screams of dying men beyond the flaps of his tent. His eyes seemed to hold only memories. "Moirai would rather see her daughter with a devil who looked like a typical citizen of Farehold than with a good man who she thought looked like a demon on the outside. So, she made everyone see what she saw."

Gadriel took another step forward, using the advantage granted by Ceres's reverie. He advanced again, doing his best to close the space between them. "I know why you believe you had a son. It's what we were all led to believe. It's what I continued to believe until a few days ago. Daphne bore no male heir, Ceres. She had a daughter. A daughter who looks like you—"

Ceres's eyes sharpened. "Don't try to tell me—"

"A daughter who looks so much like you that Daphne had to switch the babe at birth. The princess took your daughter to an orphanage close to the northern border and exchanged

63

her for a male babe who might pass as her husband's coloring, a golden-haired boy to live in the palace under a false name and false title. The girl was raised a two-day ride from the Raascot border, in a place run by the church. Your child's name is Nox. Daphne named her for the kingdom of night in hopes that you might find her."

The king's presence faded in and out as he lost himself to the distance of his thoughts. His brows had connected into something of a furrow.

"No, she had a son. Word spread—"

Gadriel took another step. He sucked in a calming breath, but the tent had become an oven. The hot, dry heat burned his lungs. It was all he could do to keep from coughing and disrupting Ceres's thoughts. "Word spread of the son Daphne wanted everyone to believe she had. Daphne was smart. She needed the world to believe she'd given birth to a boy so that no one would go looking for your daughter."

A tuft of hair tumbled loose from the ringlet atop the king's head as he shook off the information. "The priestess said—"

Another step. "The priestess said that Princess Daphne had been beaten nearly to death and brought both herself and the lifeless body of a boy. Her husband had discovered it was not his son—but nor was it hers. Her child was a changeling, Ceres. Daphne's prayer was that the goddess would find a solution. She prayed to the All Mother to heal the land and protect your natural-born child."

"That can't be true," the king said, getting to his feet. His silhouette was the only darkness in the orange glow around him.

"She never told you in the dreams you shared? Could you not speak to—"

"Do you think I didn't try!" Ceres barked. Gadriel had only meant to keep Ceres talking as he approached but realized his mistake immediately. Of course, if Ceres could have visited Daphne through his abilities, Raascot wouldn't

64

have spent twenty years in calamity. The general redirected his efforts.

"Daphne's prayer was to protect your child."

Ceres's mouth twisted. "The vengeance—"

Gadriel edged ever closer. He was almost within reach to be able to disarm his cousin, if he could keep the king focused on their conversation. Sweat trickled down Gadriel's face. If he looked anything like Ceres, black, damp curls would be plastered to his forehead and back of his neck. His sweat-soaked shirt clung to him.

Gadriel opened his mouth in an answer. "Amaris is not vengeance. Your child of moonlight was the answer to the princess's prayer for healing and reunion. Daphne begged for an answer to reunite you with your child. The goddess heard her prayer. Amaris grew up beside your daughter. The All Mother ensured that Nox wouldn't be alone. The goddess sent this miracle to see through enchantments and heal the kingdoms so that you could find your heir. Amaris isn't vengeance. She isn't a weapon. She's hope."

He was so close. Gadriel kept his eyes on the king's face but stayed wholly aware of Ceres's proximity to his weapons. His hand was loose on the hilt of his sword. "No, my son—"

Repetition was his friend. He wanted Ceres to realize the truth, but he was satisfied with distraction as the man remained lost in his thoughts if that's what it would take to subdue him and get him out of the camp. "Daphne was too clever to let Moirai know about her child, *your* child. You know of her cunning. You loved her—don't doubt her now. She knew that if she spread the word that she had birthed a son, it would be the cover she needed to shield your child." Gadriel opened his hands as if presenting his final piece of information. "She's here, Ceres. Your daughter is here. Her name is Nox."

Ceres swallowed the name as if truly hearing it for the first time. It seemed to speak some deeply resonant piece within him that even Gadriel could not understand. Ceres found a stillness in the chaos he'd been ignoring. The king finally repeated the name, eyes fluttering shut. "Nox."

His eyes remained tightly shut, but a single tear leaked from the lashes that had pressed together. "Night?"

"Yes," Gadriel breathed. Relief washed through him, and he did nothing to hide it. The general was one arm's length from his cousin. "Her name means 'night.' Her very name and her black-jeweled crown were the only clues that Daphne had left her so that the two of you might find one another."

It was too much, and he knew it in an instant. He saw the flicker of his progress flash to distrust before he could blink. He'd pushed too far. Ceres shot to attention. The king realized how close Gadriel had gotten, and before he took the last step necessary to close the space between them, Ceres drew his weapon, extending it toward his cousin.

Gadriel unsheathed his sword.

For a terrible moment, there was nothing but betrayal on the orange glow of Ceres's face.

Gadriel lunged to disarm his opponent, hoping he could fling the sword from Ceres's hand. The king must have taken the advance as confirmation of deceit. An angry growl tore from him as he flung himself toward his cousin. Rage, fury, and animosity were as clear as the high, sharp sounds of crossing blades.

Gadriel parried, evading a blow as he ducked and found firm footing once more. This would be no easy battle. They had grown up together. They'd learned the same tricks and steps and maneuvers in the training camps of their youth. They fell into familiar patterns they'd executed far too many times as brethren in the ring. The primary difference was the bloodlust on the king's face. All Gadriel wanted was for Ceres to lose his weapon and stand down.

Swords crossed again and again. The scraping sounds of sheer metal joined their grunts, the shuffling of feet, and the distant battle cries of men beyond the tent who still fought for their lives. Ceres threw his weight into a downward motion that Gadriel blocked, holding his sword with both hands as he pushed his king back. The metal hilt of his sword burned within his hand.

"Stop!" Gadriel commanded, trying again and again to disarm his king.

"Don't you think I know?" Ceres's voice broke. The emotion shocked Gadriel, but Ceres would not relent. He swung again. "Don't you think I know how mad you say I've gone? The whole kingdom says I've lost my mind. No one tries to hide it!"

Ceres pivoted. He took three steps in retreat before holding it on guard once more. Every move the general had learned, Ceres had learned in tandem. Every step Gadriel took, Ceres took to counteract. But the king and his blade were not the only threats in the tent. The heat nearly took physical form as it rippled around them, their tent glowing red with the fires just beyond the canvas.

Gadriel grunted as he advanced, each thrust and strike aimed to disarm. He pleaded with the man he'd loved as both a brother and a king. "Prove them wrong, Ceres!" He swung his body as he met another sharp blow to deflect the man's blade. "See reason!"

Ceres laughed as he spun with his sword in an arc.

Surprise was nearly Gadriel's undoing. He'd grown so familiar with the king's far-off gazes that he'd underestimated how astute Ceres's swordplay had remained. The metal of his blade continued to punish Gadriel's hands as it absorbed the temperature around it. His fae ability to procure heat from within was a separate beast entirely from the inferno that pressed down on them externally.

Ceres swung again. There was no mistaking his intent. He was swinging to kill.

Gadriel used every drop of training to deflect and defend. The battle would be over if he went on the offensive. He could hack or slash in an instant. All he wanted to do—all he was willing to do—was loosen the blade from Ceres's grasp. Gadriel attempted to flap his wings to knock the king backward, but the space in the tent threatened that such an action would bring the entire tent down upon them.

"How convenient," Ceres cried between grunts from the thrusts of his sword, sweat beading down his forehead. "That you would discover such information as soon as the girl you're sleeping with turns out to be the tool I've been searching for."

Gadriel dropped to a knee to dodge a blow and countered, pushing Ceres back. He didn't know how his cousin knew of his relationship to Amaris, but it hardly mattered. Ceres had spat the information to rattle him, and he couldn't let it work. He continued to face Ceres while retreating toward the tent's only entrance. If he could draw Ceres out into the open, they might have a chance at surviving the night.

"I didn't know!" Gadriel gasped, swords clanging as Ceres took the retreat as opening. He could barely grip the metal hilt through the slick sweat of his palms. "No one knew until Nox found her way to Gwydir! She has proof, Ceres!"

"What proof?" The king let out an angry sound as he forced his sword down again, shoving both backward. His face was wild in the red light of the fires beyond the canvas. "What proof could you possibly have?"

Gadriel refused to relent. "The Gray Matron at their orphanage met Daphne that night!" He blocked again, baring his teeth as he forced logic and reason, hoping it cut as sharp as any weapon. "Daphne left her daughter with her crown of black gems."

Ceres was unmoved. He broke the advance with a dodge and countered with a swing. "Anyone can forge black gems."

Gadriel swung again, each sentence punctured with a clang, a parry, a duck, a lunge. "Nox ate the fruit from the Tree of Life! She saw Daphne die! She understood the curse long before she knew Daphne was her mother. All she knew of her father was that he was from Raascot. Nox didn't know it was you. She didn't know she had royal lineage. No one knew it was you, Ceres. There was no reason to create a crown known for Raascot's royal family."

Ceres panted, the heat shoving itself down his throat. Gadriel knew the broiling temperatures roasted his cousin's blood and flesh every bit as much as his own. This time when Ceres struck, Gadriel tucked to the side, rolling onto the ground and sprinting from the tent.

They were out of the frying pan and into the flame, no longer in an oven but now susceptible to the very demons raining hell down on the camp. The open air amplified every strike. Ceres swung twice, each of his thrusts bringing him closer and closer to where Gadriel drew him out. His cousin's eyes sparkled with an unknowable grief, rage, and distance.

"The monsters have no eyes," Gadriel hissed as the mad king continued to swing. He blocked the sword from overhead and pushed down upon his king to whisper into his ear. "Kill me if you must, but do it quietly."

In a desperate attempt to save both of their lives from the tell-tale sounds of the metallic clangs of swords no longer muffled by the tent, Gadriel dropped his sword to the ground upon his final backward leap. It was a risk. Ceres could cut him down where he stood, should he not accept the bid for hand-to-hand combat. He raised his fists and cocked his head, ready to fight.

Ceres raised his sword, paying no mind to the mud demons and their razor-sharp scorpion tails as they littered the camp with their destruction and gore. Gadriel saw Ceres's eyes flicker ever so slightly to a monster only five tents away as it struck a man down with its razor-sharp tail. He knew the king was weighing the dangers between forgoing his weapon in favor of silence and risking the loud cut and crunch of blade and bone that might bring the creatures to them.

Gadriel had not flinched from his stance. Ceres eyed him for a long moment before slowly lowering his sword to the space on the singed grass beside him. Embers flew between them like fireflies, deathly sparks illuminating their profiles and outlining their silhouettes with the dramatic flames of night.

Then, the king raised his fists.

Chapter Seven

MALIK LIKED TO BELIEVE HE WASN'T AFRAID OF ANYTHING, but he knew that wasn't entirely true. Snakes and centipedes and things that went bump in the night had never deterred him. Kings and laws and reputation had never seemed important. It was not what he was afraid of; it was who he was afraid for.

He'd felt sick with fear for his mother when she'd been caught out in a storm alone. He'd been overcome with dread as he'd watched helplessly from behind the iron bars of Aubade as his brother in arms was dragged into the queen's coliseum. He'd been afraid for Nox when she'd fallen into a silent, distant escape. And now, he was afraid for the continent and its people as he finished his ascent toward whatever might command the very demons from the muck.

He didn't dare breathe as he raised his upper body over the lip of the stone, ready to face magical weapons, armed forces, terrifying witches. Instead, it took a moment for his eyes to adjust in the dark to what stood before him.

The blue that Nox had spotted from across the ravine belonged to a small fae girl. His eyes widened as he took in the silhouette that stood just at the edge of the stone's lip. He brought one knee up as quietly as possible, leaning forward onto the plateau. He understood why she hadn't spotted them, why the Zaccai's fluttering wings hadn't caught her eye, and why the rustling of rocks and battle had done nothing to startle her. The dark-haired fae appeared to be in something of a trance, engrossed in her meditative state as she channeled her magic while a blue glow burned her hands as they stretched and morphed power between her palms.

With aching slowness, Malik used all the power and control he possessed to secure himself on the cliff. He eased himself onto the balls of his feet, moving with excruciating stealth to keep from waking her from whatever hypnotic state possessed her. She was a few short steps away. One wrong move, one kick of a stone, and he'd forsake his cover. He controlled his breath as he slipped noiselessly into the space behind her.

An ominous warning slithered down his back.

While Malik wanted to spring into action, he understood the stillness of this moment to be the separating force between life and death. He was overcome by the combination of the hazy night sky, the distant orange flame of the gore in the valley below, and the incongruous blue threat before him. She was nearly half his size in both height and width. He couldn't see her face, but from where she twisted in her dance, he could see the tell-tale sign in the moonlight of her ears poking through the cropped angle of her black hair. She didn't look like the countrymen of Farehold or Raascot.

He felt at first that if he could just get close enough to her, he could take her from behind. But to what end? He was fully human, facing a threat who appeared fully fae. If this being was powerful enough to summon an army of monsters, could he really contain her with his human arms, regardless of her size? He willed himself into a state of quiet invisibility while he searched his options.

The fae remained in her trance. Between her concentration and the chaos, Malik was certain she was orchestrating the creatures below. The lives of the humans and fae that had fallen, consumed by the beaks of the demons, was blood that stained her hands. With monastic stillness, Malik pulled the whip from his side. He wasn't sure what the rune-etched weapon would accomplish but understood enough of magic to know that the whip would serve him a hell of a lot better than mortal weapons he wielded. He raised the chain-link rope with one hand and, though not particularly religious, said a silent prayer to the goddess that he would make his mark.

Malik brought his upper arm behind him and lashed the whip forward as it coiled itself around the young woman. In the blink of an eye, the blue glow from her hands winked out. The screams of the monsters rose from the valley as they were freed from her hold, shrieking as they retreated to the swampy waters from which they came.

The young woman unleashed a feral cry as the metal bit into her. Malik moved quickly to contain her, certain he had little time. She squirmed as he pinned her to the ground, straddling the space above his captive. She cried out again as she fought back with physical strength rather than magic. He yanked the chain once, forcing her arms between his tree-trunk thighs so that she could create no space in the trap as he pulled the rope tighter and tighter until she had no room to maneuver. Countless lives hung in the balance of his ability to keep her within the tightly wrapped tendrils of the whip.

He gaped down at the fanged teeth bared in anger, the sheen of sweat reflecting in the glow of moonlight and flame, the dark eyes of surprise and anger as he stared into the delicate, beautiful face of a murderer.

Chapter Eight

THE INHUMAN WAILS OF THE MONSTERS WOVE TOGETHER with the sound of Ceres's fist against Gadriel's cheek. Gadriel had been caught off guard by the blood-curdling sounds of venom and water that had erupted through the full bellies of the demons as something seemed to change, like a snapping tension. The mud demons pounded the earth as they sprinted toward the river. It had been a mistake to look away. The momentary distraction cost him greatly.

Rather than fight the impact, he leaned with the blow, pivoting backward from his cousin in the direction of the man's punch.

Once more, Gadriel realized he'd spent decades taking Ceres for granted. The man had been so consumed with his loss that everyone had begun to see him as weak. Even Gadriel, despite training with him for centuries, had assumed his cousin had forsaken most strengths one might want in their king. If the swordplay hadn't been convincing enough, the shock against his jaw rocked him backward completely.

Ceres stumbled forward. With the mud demons gone, Gadriel had all the time in the world. He could talk sense into his family member. He could disarm him. He could make him see reason. He made a motion to kick Ceres's legs out from underneath him, but his cousin avoided the movement. Ceres used his lofted vantage point to come down hard on Gadriel's face—a crush to the cheekbone with cracking strength. Once again, Gadriel was caught by the disadvantage of an unwillingness to harm his king.

He winced against the pain. In the time it took him to stumble backward, a metallic glint from the corner of his eye told him that Ceres had picked up his sword once again.

"I've been a fool to think you'd stand beside me, cousin." Ceres adjusted his hold on his weapon. He made his first thrash with the blade. The sharpened points of his teeth reflected in the firelight, reminding Gadriel that it didn't matter what happened if he didn't stop Ceres—hell was here and now.

He rolled out of the line of contact and scrambled for his own weapon, but he'd abandoned it too far from where he now lay prone. He paused his outstretched hand as a monstrous creature sprinted toward them. The demon shuddered liquid from its hide as it barreled between the two, its talons shaking up embers and red coals, paying them no mind as it blew past them.

Gadriel's desperation cracked through as he pleaded, "Your daughter is here, Ceres!"

"Stop lying!" Ceres swung downward. Each of his lunges and blows was meant to silence the general permanently. Time after time, he was one thrust away from murdering the fae—whether or not he was his last remaining family on the continent. Gadriel now had the open room to use his wings to his advantage, beating backward enough to create the space he needed to find his sword. Ceres, though a winged fae, had not attempted to flex the appendages at his back. His eyes glowed red with the fire around him.

"What would it take to convince you?" He lunged for his blade. Gadriel raised his sword. He'd scarcely held it aloft for a moment before he needed to grip it with both hands in defensive block of yet another descending blow.

Between the monsters, the fire, the heat, and the wildness of the king, Gadriel knew in his heart that he'd have to murder Ceres if he hoped to escape. He also knew his love for king and country would never allow it. He'd sooner die than commit treason.

"Ceres, let's go! Come back to Gwydir with me. We'll sort this out."

The king looked like a dog shaking water from his hide as he rejected the offer.

Gadriel ground his teeth in helpless frustration. If he took to the sky, would Ceres follow? He'd said he'd sooner die in this camp than return to the throne a failure. Did that mean his cousin would remain on the ground as flames closed in on them? He wouldn't leave Ceres behind. Gadriel hadn't put much thought into how he would die, but he'd certainly never suspected it would be this.

After a parry and a duck, Gad tripped backward on the crumbling coals of what had once been a tent pole. He was so consumed with trying to keep his king alive that he hadn't been paying attention to his surroundings. He was nearly flat on his back when the arc of the sword cut through the hot, spark-flecked night air.

Ceres swung again, but Gadriel would do nothing more than defend. Maybe if he was lucky, Ceres would tire first. But as he faced what might almost be his death, he didn't see the fallen bodies of the military, soft innards bleeding into the earth. He didn't waste his time on crumbling camps or the hate in his cousin's face. He thought of his years serving at his cousin's side as friends, as family. He thought of how they'd trained, they'd sparred, they'd joked. Memories of their shared pints, their hunts for women to bed, their adventures flashed before him. He thought of toasting whiskey with his friends, crossing blades with his troops, the spirit and smile on the starlit face of Amaris. He gritted his teeth against the killing blow that never came.

✦

Nox had nearly crossed the dam, feet wet with a mixture of the silt from the river and her own blood. She had lost both of her shoes to the mud and had shredded her feet on the sharp edges of beaver-gnawed wooden spears as she'd scaled her way across the dam. The destructive firelight of the quickly falling campsite had illuminated her path.

With an exasperated grunt of frustration, she leapt from the dam.

She sucked in the sound, terrified she'd drawn the beasts' attention when the creatures made some unbridled relinquishing cry. The scraping noise wrapped its way down each of her vertebrae as she cringed in startled revulsion. It was a strange, strangled contrast to the gory screams that had belted from their throats for the hour prior. She stared out at the camp as the creatures buckled and shuddered as if each of them was hearing a shrill too high-pitched for their sensitive, gill-like ears to absorb. The sightless creatures writhed in pain for the barest of moments as Nox stared on in horror. Their vibrating movements stopped, each demon righting itself as it turned from the camp and ran for the water.

Nox clutched herself against the dam. She closed her eyes tightly, shutting out her fear as demons plunged into the river. Water hit her chest, her arms, her face as they splashed below its surface. She didn't move a muscle as she clung to the split logs while the slurping noises of mud, water, and chaos settled to little more than a ripple.

When she opened her eyes, there was scarcely more than the circular evidence of bubbles popping far beneath the surface.

A profound, vindicating shudder raked her body, as she had always known that every body of water was filled with unspeakable horrors. All that remained now was the shallow, harmless waters of a terrorless night. If it weren't for the river running red with the blood of slain men, the picked-over carrion, the entrails that littered the ground, and the inferno of the tents that had been mere tinder to their destruction, one may have thought the whole thing just a gruesome nightmare.

Nox released the blade-sharp logs and made the final jump onto land. She picked pained, shredded footsteps toward the last place she had seen Amaris. An eternity had passed from the moment they'd locked eyes on opposite shores, but she had no other plan to help. Her bare feet stepped over the fallen splinters of tents and white-hot embers of the inferno that raged on all sides. The firelight illuminated every corner, every passage, and every hiding place. All she could do was search. Her eyes moved rapidly amidst the fallen rows of tents, the ghost town of an encampment as if the land before her was little more than lines of text. She studied each sentence, each phrase, each question for signs of her moonlit half.

Amaris had disappeared. Nox winced against another sharp bite to her feet as she stepped on a terribly hot coal. She swallowed a curse, refusing to let the pain deter her. For all she knew, Amaris had fallen to smoke poisoning or was trapped under the charred remnants of a tent pole. Maybe she'd been wounded by a demon, violet eyes plucked from her very skull, clutching her face, bloody and blinded.

Stop it. Focus. Focus, Nox told herself, shoving down the gory, hopeless parts of her imagination. She swallowed down the urge to vomit as her fears were justified only seconds later. She stopped short at the shredded body of a man and flinched as she stepped carefully over his corpse. There was no one to be found. Everyone had either fled beyond the reach of flames and demons or been slain.

The front of the encampment had to be near. The line of crackling fires had almost reached the dark, clear air where the river bent and the tents ended. If Amaris had escaped to the front…

Nox's eyes widened, breath catching as she nearly walked into a fight. She skidded backward at the sudden movement as two men stumbled into view, swords raised.

Gadriel. The man on his back was the general. Her lips

parted in surprise as she absorbed the sight of him clutching his sword with both hands, grunting against the power of the opposing blade pressing down upon him. He was sweat-soaked, teeth bared, wings pinned beneath his own weight as he used two hands to keep the blade aloft, arms shaking as he pushed through what had to be the final remnants of his strength.

Paralysis gripped her as she stared at Gadriel and the second winged fae Raascot warrior. Sweat dripped off his brow, drenching his hair. The light caught the small, silver ringlet that rested on his crown. It had surely been only three seconds that felt like an hour as she looked in horror between the general and the man who may have been his brother. There was something upsettingly familiar about the attacker. It wasn't just what she saw in his face but the same dark hopelessness in his eyes that she'd seen so many times in the mirror in her first days at the Selkie.

She'd seen other citizens of Raascot. She'd spent days with Yazlyn. She'd looked at the vacant expressions on the fallen warriors as she'd picked her way across the battlefield. Gadriel had possessed black hair and bronze skin, and she hadn't recognized him to be family. The other fae of Raascot that had sprinted past her in the burning encampment all had vaguely similar features as harbingers of their region. Other than broad strokes of the familiar heritage separating her from the colorless faces of Farehold, she saw no similarities in jawlines, eyes, or noses. Nothing had tugged at her intrinsically as the view before her did now. Maybe it was because Gadriel had said he was going to search for the king, perhaps it was because she knew Ceres was Gadriel's family, or maybe it was just a connection that couldn't be explained beyond the ties of fate. When she beheld King Ceres leaning his entire weight over Gadriel with the intent to murder, she knew precisely whom she saw.

"Father?"

Nox wasn't sure why she said it. She wasn't even certain

it was a word she'd spoken before. The title had bubbled from her throat almost as if she'd had no control over its release.

She had seen Princess Daphne in her dream. She had been told by Matron Agnes that Daphne was her mother. It wasn't until the screaming and chaos at the town house following Amaris's capture where reevers and fae shouted for attention that they'd aligned their pieces enough to discern that Daphne and Ceres had been lovers. She had known her father would be someone of northern heritage, but seeing him now in his half-wild crouch over Gadriel shoved her soul from her body entirely.

As if in a dream, she felt herself connect to a small possibility that might have occurred in some alternate reality. Absent from the charred world around her, she pictured Princess Daphne hugging her, placing the small tiara of blackened gems upon her head. She heard her father call to them both and thought of how she'd run into his arms. She saw her parents hold hands at the dinner table, her mother resting her head on her father's arms. In a disembodied dream, she'd had a family. She'd been loved. She'd been safe.

Another sharp spark of fire burned into her skin, drawing her back to reality. She sucked in a sharp breath of scalding air, blinking rapidly at the men.

Ceres looked up to meet her eyes. For a moment there was no recognition, only the feral intent he'd held over his cousin. It wasn't in the first heartbeat, nor was it in the second. After several moments had passed, she saw something flicker behind Ceres's eyes. He still pressed his weight down on the waning strength of his general, but something had changed.

As he observed Nox, he seemed to share in whatever soul-bare experience had pulled Nox from the flame-riddled pain of their present into the same sickening, unachievable alternate reality. In the space it took for Ceres to relax his weight, Gadriel rolled out of his disadvantageous position to his feet. He took a defensive stance near Ceres. The general's mouth parted as if to speak to his cousin but closed when he could see against the reddish firelight that Ceres's face had completely slackened.

"Nox!" Gadriel exclaimed, breath and body utterly spent. He took a few staggering steps away from his cousin, putting himself nearly between his king and her.

Ceres did not release his sword, but it dragged beside him as he stepped toward the pair. Gadriel lifted his weapon again. Nox recognized the stance with a start. He'd said for days that she was their heir, and they would treat her as such, but seeing it in action did something inexplicable to her.

Ceres seemed to understand the general's defensive position as if it were the most familiar thing in the world. She saw the recognition in his face as his expression softened: his general was protecting a princess. It was as if it all made so much sense, and no sense at all.

"Nox?" Ceres repeated the name.

It wounded her to look at him through the rippling, shimmering heat in the air, the smoke of the night, and the unchecked bonfires that banished all shadows. His fae face was ageless. Even still, there was a sorrow that betrayed his centuries. He didn't look like a father may have in their story-books. He wasn't a graying gentleman with a gut full of ale or the friendly, wrinkled face she'd see in cobblers and butchers and farmers bringing their wares to market.

He was the king.

She nodded numbly. She had no weapons. No words. Nothing to say or argue or add. She wished she'd prepared anything for this meeting, but all she could do was dip her chin to acknowledge her name. It had been the one thing her mother had given her.

"You..." He shook his head at the sight of her, disbelief clear on his face from his raised brows to the drop of his chin.

Her lips parted slightly, hoping she might say something impactful, something that mattered, but nothing came out. All she could do was stare.

"You look like her," Ceres said, taking a step forward.

81

A supporting beam from a tent somewhere behind him crashed to the ground, sending copper flares into the sky and backlighting Ceres dramatically as he advanced. His steps were lurching like the undead of legend.

Nox took a half step back in reaction, and Ceres and Gadriel both appeared to recognize her fear. The king stopped in his tracks. The general took another half step, positioning himself closer to Nox. Ceres's face slackened. He looked like he might cry. "You're afraid of me. Of course you are. Of course..." His face pinched, hands flying to his head as if struck with a sudden, piercing headache. It took him a few painfully long heartbeats before he dropped his hands and looked at her once more. "Are you truly my daughter?"

Nox swallowed. She had forgotten how to speak. When she opened her mouth to find her voice, heat pressed down her throat. She was acutely aware that she was in the middle of a sweltering fire. Truth be told, she didn't know if she was Ceres's daughter, despite what anyone said. She had only one fact to share, and she did her best to summon her courage as her lips parted before the King of Raascot. "Daphne is my mother. I bore too much of a resemblance to my father to stay with her in Aubade. She hid me so that I might live."

His posture softened further at this. The air sizzled around them, popping and hissing flames revealing every minute feature on his face.

Nox pressed on. "Come with me. We'll talk about it across the river."

Conversation was a dance. Body language was an art. The moment the suggestion left her lips, she knew she'd made a grave error. The wounded look on Ceres's face suggested that she'd gravely insulted him or that he'd insulted himself. Yes, perhaps she'd spoken to him as if he didn't see the bloodied, charred corpses of his men or the crimson and coral colors of the tents as they danced around him. She, along with everyone in Farehold, had known the northern king to be mad.

But as he stared back at her, it wasn't with insanity. It was with a broken heart.

Ceres didn't move.

"Daphne truly was your mother, wasn't she?"

It wasn't a question. He peered into Nox's face, and then his eyes drifted to her other features the way one might look with disconnected curiosity at a painting. Beyond the Raascot skin and glossy hair she'd inherited from the north, perhaps he was looking to see if she had the curve of Daphne's nose, the lines of Daphne's chin, even a build he might recognize. He searched her not as a person but as a phantom, looking for a familiarity he wouldn't have seen in more than two decades. There was a lucidity in his gaze, a clarity in his eyes as he sharpened while examining her.

A knot formed in Nox's throat as she choked on nerves. For a moment, the man she knew as Ceres was so perfectly sane. Perhaps she'd been the key that had locked him behind his lunacy for decades. Maybe now she twisted the handle, opening the door at long last as he was reunited with his daughter. Maybe their pain had been separate but equal, sharing in their suffering across the continent, never knowing the salve for their wounds had a name, a face, a life.

Nox's brows knit together. She stretched a hand forward.

"All I've ever wanted was to give you the world," he said. He took a step closer to them. Gadriel tensed beside her. The subtle flex wasn't lost on Ceres as his eyes drifted slowly from his cousin back to her.

Nox left her hand outstretched to Ceres.

"Nox," he said, smiling to himself. "It's such a clever, beautiful name. Your mother was the most intelligent, perfect person I'd ever known." He was talking to himself as his eyes drifted over the fallen war camp. The site of the burning tents, the corpses, the sparks, and gore flickered in his dark eyes. He spoke to her, to them, to no one at all as he went on. "I've dedicated every moment for so many years to the pursuit of my child. Every troop I've had, every man I could spare, went to finding you—except I didn't know it was you I was looking for." There had been no warmth behind his injured smile, but it saddened further as he watched her.

The smile was telling, as he was both appreciative of Daphne's cleverness and wistful about his wasted years. His voice was so very distant when he spoke again, as if the king were speaking to an audience of only himself. "When word spread through the kingdom that she'd had a son, of course I never looked into the faces of the daughters scattering Farehold. How cunning she was to have switched you for a boy. No one would look for you. No one could harm you." Ceres's eyes became clearer as he took another step closer. One more step and Nox would be able to take his hand. She didn't know what she'd do once their hands clasped, but she knew they didn't have much longer if they hoped to escape the flames.

"Let's go," Nox urged. Sweat from the blistering flames pooled and trickled down every part of her body. Any bit of exposed skin heated, scorching like a sunburn as the fires towered. She was certain that Gadriel had tried everything in his arsenal to assuage the king. It was up to her now to soothe the man. If they could get him over the river, away from the fires, they might still have a chance.

Ceres was speaking to her, and yet he wasn't. Nox had the vague feeling that even though his words were addressed to her, Ceres was speaking to Daphne. "I wanted to give you your childhood. I wanted to give you a life. I wanted to give you everything… And I took it all from you. I gave you waste and ruins. I gave you fire and ashes and madness."

She extended her fingers, almost able to grab the king and lead him away from the horrors raging around them.

"But I can still give you the kingdom." He met her eyes. Ceres closed the gap then, but it wasn't the space between himself and Nox.

Her scream was a sharp, dizzying intake of air.

His final step was toward his general. Ceres gripped the end of Gadriel's sword where the general had remained tensed to defend Nox from the mad king. Ceres pulled himself inward, sinking the sword as he guided it into the space between his ribs. It made no sound as it punctured his leathers and sunk into his flesh. The sharpened blade disappeared noiselessly as half of it buried itself in the king before either she or the general realized what was happening.

Nox's hands flew to cover her mouth, jaw on its hinges in a noiseless cry. Gadriel's eyes were wide, frozen in shock as he hadn't been allowed the time to react.

Ceres's eyes saw the terrible plea in Nox's eyes. His hands tightened around the sword, preventing Gadriel from yanking the blade free. Blood painted his lips. Slow, sanguine droplets dribbled over his chin as he stared at her, releasing his final words as his body crumpled over the remaining steel. He held her gaze with the small smile the King of Raascot was able to summon. The ashes of his army fractured around them in the reflection of his eyes as he met her dark, horrified look.

Nox's body roiled between the need to vomit and cry. At her side Gadriel released the blade. He braced her against the swaying motion threatening to drag her to the ground. Nox heard a sound. It was loud, angry, scared, and horrifying. If it weren't for the ache in her throat, she wouldn't have realized that she was the one screaming. Her cries against the goddess clouded her eyes with tears as she looked into the dying light in her father's eyes.

Ceres still had a smile on his face as a trickle of blood dribbled from the corner of his mouth. It was clear that seeing his child was the final joy he'd needed in this life. His journey had come to an end. As he held the blade against his body, he maintained his hold on her dark eyes as he coughed up four final words.

"You deserve the world."

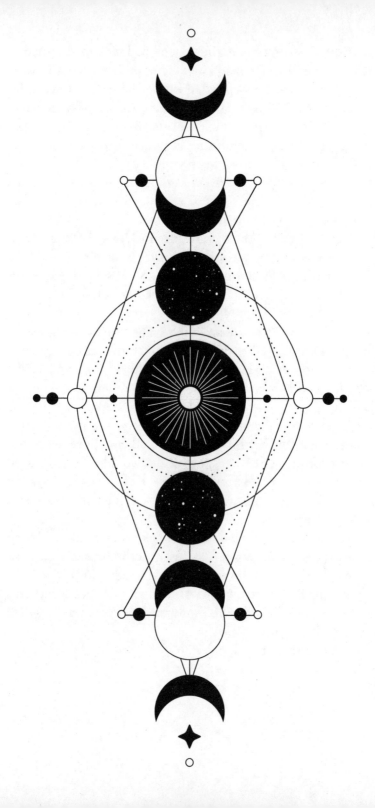

PART TWO:

The Daughter of Madness and Ruin

Chapter Nine

KINGDOMS HAVE COLLAPSED FROM THE THIRST OF TREASON as poisoned wine touched the lips of their debaucherous kings. Empires have gone to war over land, titles, vengeance, and glory. The old gods and All Mother alike have fueled zealots, destroying peoples and cultures for centuries.

King Ceres, who had reigned fairly and benevolently for two hundred years, had fallen to the grips of a love that had consumed him wholly. Something meant for beauty had become utterly toxic. When his beloved passed over to be with the goddess, he had allowed his kingdom, his people, and his sanity to fall along with her. Years later, the story-books would refer to the night that claimed his life as the Raasay Valley Massacre.

In his final moments, the best he could do for his people and his daughter was to see that history remembered him for the things he would do for love.

At least, Nox knew that was his intent. Good intentions were worthless contrasted against their consequences.

It had been Yazlyn who'd found them in the gully. She'd checked in with her general, kneeling amidst the coals in the pool of blood beside their late king. Yazlyn hadn't broken the miserable silence that Gadriel and Nox had established throughout the remainder of the twilight hours, and for that, she supposed she was grateful. Instead, Yazlyn left Gadriel with the king as she pried Nox's numb shell from Ceres's bloodied body. She'd held Nox close and remained quiet as she relocated them from the gully to the very tree at which Nox still sat.

It was one tragedy too many.

Nox leaned her head against a pine tree, too exhausted to stand. She wanted to say it was the worst night of her life, but a detached part of her wondered how many worst nights she could experience before the word lost all meaning.

More than one thousand had marched south. She'd heard the numbers. She'd seen the clean, canvas rows before the world had fallen to pieces. Only a few hundred Raascot troops—injured and charred human and fae, some badly wounded or burned—limped their way northward to Gwydir before the sun came up over the ashen remains of their encampment. She'd been too tired to hear or care about much, save for the information buzzing around her as military and reevers shouted reports, whispered sad truths, and updated those around them to the best of their abilities.

Zaccai, whose name she recognized from their camp beyond Castle Aubade, did his part to help them before returning to his men, intent on assisting their return to the capital city. She wouldn't have known the name of the winged fae at all, had Ash and Malik not been using it as they spoke a few paces away.

Her vision was fuzzy, the dark vignettes of shock and sleeplessness creeping in at the edges as she slouched into the tree. Still, she'd been sharply aware that their small party had grown by a very unwelcome fae member. Nox had listened from her place on the ground in muted, disconnected horror as Ash explained the source of the nightmarish blue glow to Zaccai. The reevers had subdued and retrieved their prisoner and carried her as far as they could.

Zaccai had kicked up a tiny cloud of dust as he'd landed with a small, unconscious fae woman in his arms. Their party of five was now seven. Eight, if they counted the prisoner, which Nox didn't. The captive responsible for summoning the mud demons was a tiny ball of hate wrapped in the bindings of the metallic rope of the rune-etched weapon. Nox looked at the fae long enough to know what she *wasn't*.

Nox had known humans and fae from Farehold, Raascot, and Tarkhany. She'd never met anyone from the Etal Isles. And as far as she knew, no one living had met anyone from Sulgrave. Wherever the girl was from, she wasn't welcome here. Nox's disgust toward the stranger was energy she couldn't spare, particularly as Amaris arrived.

Nox would have been horrified to see Yazlyn land with a blistered, wounded Amaris in her arms, but the emotion was useless. Yazlyn had set her down with such consideration that Nox forgot her hatred for the sergeant long enough to extend the barest flicker of a grateful smile.

Seeing Amaris—skin stark in horrible shades of pinks, reds, and purples—in the sergeant's arms hadn't been nearly as irritating as she'd expected. Yazlyn had moved noiselessly to Nox's side and lowered Amaris gently until her head rested in Nox's lap. Smoke had muddied her silvery features into a flat, muted gray.

Nox didn't even have the energy to brush the flecks of ash from Amaris's hair. Instead, she waited, and she listened. Somewhere in the distance, the sounds of a grave being dug let her know that Gadriel was seeing his cousin's final rites before he joined them on the cliff. She dipped in and out of sleep as the able-bodied built the funeral pyres to respectably cremate the remains of the troops who had fallen to demons and flame.

While Nox couldn't commit to being asleep or awake, Amaris remained fully comatose. They'd scavenged enough healing tonics from the encampment for everyone to take what was needed. Nox drank one, then used no fewer than four as she rubbed them into Amaris's blisters, burns, and dribbled as much as she could down her throat.

Skin and wounds knit together beautifully as the face in her lap became moonlit once more. Knowing Amaris was safe and cared for, Nox could let her mind wander. She attempted to absorb the brief life and death of her father.

He'd be marked for his sacrifice. The Raascot fae had said as much.

Loose promises were made that a monument would be erected where he'd fallen so that the late king might be visited and remembered. Words were exchanged. Labor was spent. And through all of it, Amaris remained dead to the world, and Nox forced herself to cling to consciousness. No one, save for Amaris, had truly slept in more than twenty-four hours. The solemn party agreed to take turns guarding their prisoner while the others rested.

Malik took the first watch, nodding in silent reassurance as Nox felt she could truly let go. Amaris's sleepy mumbles vibrated in her lap, letting her know Amaris was, at the very least, alive. It wasn't relaxing, but she was comforted. It was a far cry from ideal, but she and Amaris were alive, and they were together.

For now, that would have to be enough.

✦

The night came to an end.

Evidence of the tragedy permeated the very air around them, banishing all hopes that the unspeakable events had been a nightmare. Cold morning light stirred Amaris and those around her. Whether or not they were ready to face the shape of the world in the wake of Ceres's death paid no mind to the hour or their exhaustion.

Amaris opened her eyes, seeing the gray first light from one eye, the crinkled fabric from a warm lap in the other, and a miserably stiff neck between both. She moved gingerly, pulling herself into a half-sitting position. She didn't have to crane her neck to know who owned the soft lap, the steady breath, or the cinnamon scent that supported her. Despite the wooden tightness of running, of chill, of battle, she relaxed into Nox as much as possible.

She recognized Ash and Malik. They were already up, though they hadn't yet spotted that she was awake. She felt the flutter of a raven's wings belonging not just to Gadriel, but as she tilted her head ever so slightly, she caught a cascade of smooth, auburn curls.

Dissonant whispers rushed over the ashes as the fae and reevers spoke. Nox chimed in a time or two, the vibrations of her voice feeling awfully nice against Amaris's cheek. It was almost enough to lull her back into a deep and healing sleep.

But they were not the only ones at camp.

Amaris's eyes settled on a dark-haired prisoner, tightly wrapped in a silvery chain binding. The red she wore was in stark contrast to the grays, greens, blues, and blacks of the clothes and forest around her. The prisoner tilted her chin up once as Malik knelt to question her, revealing a foxlike, angular face, then dipped her head once more without saying a word.

Amaris didn't attempt to speak. Physically, she felt tense but fine. Her throat tingled, but it probably wouldn't have impacted her speech. The exhaustion was deeper than muscle tissue or sleeplessness. It was heavier than smoke inhalation. It was the bloodied memories of men, their dying cries, the pounding thunder of birdlike feet, the abominable terrors that lived in the mud, and the knowledge that she was in the mixed company of those who had come to save her and those who were responsible for her betrayal.

Still, she listened.

There was a short-lived debate amidst the crew about whether or not they should return to Gwydir or proceed south to Aubade. As tempting as it was to press onward and march gallantly toward a curse that needed shattering, they were at least two weeks and change from the royal kingdom at the south, with no plan and very little in terms of forces. And that was before they accounted for the evil bundle still tightly wrapped in the rune-engraved chains.

Amaris watched her reever brother try more than once to get the prisoner to drink water, but she kept her lips shut firmly, forcing the water to dribble over her chin. Amaris's lashes fluttered closed as she both admired and was tired by Malik's goodness. If the young fae was a prisoner—particularly given the horrors of the night—perhaps she didn't deserve water.

Gadriel announced that he would begin transporting the others through the air to Gwydir, where they had an abundance of both supplies and time. Once he made it to the castle, he said, he'd send Zaccai back to make another trip. Whoever remained on the ground could urge Seven forward with their limited supplies and the prisoner draped over her saddle.

The pillow of Nox's chest reverberated pleasantly against Amaris's cheek as she spoke. "What, Yazlyn? No offer to fly me this time?"

Even with her eyes closed, Amaris recognized the quick retort as Yazlyn said, "Apologies, *Your Highness.* I have more pressing things to do than pander to the spiteful."

"Please," Gadriel said, as drained and defeated as Amaris had ever heard of him. "Save your fighting for the castle. Right now, the most important thing is that we get everyone away from the gully and back to Gwydir. The time to assimilate will…"

His sentence drifted at Nox's visible discomfort. Perhaps he saw the wisdom in giving Raascot's new monarch the chance to let her shock abate before forcing talks of her new life in the north. The conversation between them halted, mountain sounds of mourning doves, the crunching of foraging animals over dried pine needles, the rustling of leaves filling the quiet.

Amaris grunted in sleepy disappointment when Nox was taken first, her pillow, her comfort, her safety net disappearing

94

as Gadriel scooped her into his arms and took to the sky. Sometime later, Zaccai joined what remained of the band on their overlook from where he'd been tending to the wounded to fetch and carry Amaris.

"I'm sorry," Zaccai said quietly.

Amaris tried her voice for the first time in an eternity as she asked, "Did you do this?"

The steady thud of wings pushed against air as they punched through clouds and cool, mountain breezes. Zaccai said nothing.

Amaris tried again. "Did you call the demons, or send your people to their slaughter, or kill the only father I've ever known?"

"Amaris, I—"

She rested her head against his chest, closing her eyes to resist the light rather than to accept sleep as she said, "I'm not angry with you, Zaccai. You aren't responsible for any of what happened."

And she believed every word of it. Victims took more shape than one.

If she'd asked, she would have undoubtedly been given answers. She could have inquired about how her brothers had made their way back to the castle. She could have checked on the horse, the journey by foot, the methods and means of the Raascot fae who'd been at her camp that morning.

But she didn't.

She'd been handed off to attendants and remained too tired to fight. She was in Raascot, where she'd been betrayed. She was in Gwydir, where Gadriel, the one she'd cared for, she'd been vulnerable with, she'd trusted, had deceived her. Everyone here had undoubtedly known him for decades, if not centuries. She didn't want pitiful exchanges or well wishes if she didn't believe the kingdom-loyal mouths that eschewed uncomfortable truths. Lines seemed blurred here, somehow.

She was bathed, and fed, and put to bed between silken sheets. She accepted a healing tonic and an accompanying vial for pain she knew wouldn't help, as the wounds that afflicted her were not of the body. The attendants spoke in hushed voices as if she weren't there. Between drawing her bath, setting out her food, and tucking her into bed, she'd learned all she needed to about the rumors of Nox's ascension. They'd muttered this and that about reevers in their kingdom, perhaps not knowing it was a reever they scrubbed and bathed. When one breathed a hushed speculation of Nox's time at a brothel, Amaris had jerked her arm away from the brush that chafed her, still naked in the bath. She'd glared up at the women, and the attendants stared back in horror as if they'd forgotten they shared a common tongue.

She thought of a glossy, black carriage. She thought of a life debt that had hung over her head in Farleigh like an axe. She thought of the peacocking woman and a distant pit of suffering in Priory that some had called the Selkie. Amaris slipped open the lip of the box within herself and shoved in the implication. Amaris had escaped the fate intended for her, after all. And Nox was here, the heir lost on the winds, the fairy tales and decades of turmoil brought to fruition. Amaris had spent years avoiding the gut-sick guilt whenever she thought of her naïve command to ask Nox to wait for her. Persuasion had forced her to stay behind at Farleigh and remain with the matrons. She'd pictured Nox in linens, scrubbing floors, going about her chores, stuck in servitude of the church. But when Amaris saw her in the dungeons as a free woman, it was with relief that she became certain that Nox had escaped any terrible fate.

Amaris relaxed as they dressed her and put her in bed. That's all their ill-informed mutterings had been, after all. Rumors.

"Excuse me?" Amaris asked, startling an attendant exiting the bedroom.

The woman turned with wide eyes. It was the first time Amaris had opened her mouth in quite a while.

"The reevers? One gold of hair, one faeling with red hair. Have they arrived safely?"

96

The woman swallowed. "They have, my lady."

"I'm not a lady," Amaris said, unfolding herself from the sheets. Her feet dangled over the tall bed. "What do you know of the prisoner? The fae who returned with us in chains?"

"Only that she's under lock and key in the dungeons by order of our general, my lady."

Amaris forced herself not to glare at the strict use of the incorrect title. "And my friend—the woman you've all been talking about? Nox? Where might I find her room?"

"I'm not so sure I—"

Amaris's feet hit the plush carpet. They'd done her a kindness by putting her in clean trousers and a tunic rather than a nightgown, but she still hardly recognized herself. All uncertainty left her as she leveled her gaze. "Nox and I have known each other since infancy. We grew up together. She came for me. Don't withhold this information from me."

The servant shot a nervous look over her shoulder as if there might be someone sager to give her an answer. Perhaps she was another in a long line of Raascot citizens who didn't wholly adhere to protocol, or maybe Raascot was a kingdom without the stringent formalities of Farehold. The attendant steadied herself, smoothing her apron as she gave directions to Nox's room.

Amaris thanked the woman and abandoned her bedchambers for the long, tall corridors of Castle Gwydir. The blue-black labradorite that had seemed so ominous only days before as Amaris had cried in Ceres's throne room now felt strangely beautiful. Each time a lantern or candle refracted the iridescent glow of the stone, she was reminded of the night sky and the sacred lights of mythos that danced only in northernmost dreams.

A frown tugged at the corner of her mouth as she made her way through the halls. She'd ascribed Nox's presence in the dungeons of Aubade to fate and the All Mother, as much as her own. They'd been thrust together by destiny, after all.

But what if they hadn't? What if Nox had been on

the southeastern coast for another reason entirely? What if the servants...

She desperately hoped they were mistaken. A memory of Nox kneeling before her cell in a black silk dress bloomed behind her eyes. Nox had always been beautiful. It hadn't crossed her mind to question the paper-thin gown on someone so stunning before now. Though she tried to push them down, thoughts of a bejeweled madame and a far-off brothel gnawed at her.

She shook thoughts of the jewel-toned madame from her mind as she eyed the door before her. The attendant's instructions were apt. She found the room with little trouble, even if the strange twisting in her chest and sudden tremble in her hand suggested otherwise. She pushed down the baseless feeling and wrapped her hand around the elaborate iron handle. She didn't bother to knock on Nox's room, pushing open the heavy wooden door and letting herself in.

A season had passed since they'd sparked the ember in the dungeons of Aubade that had spread through her like a wildfire, greater and hotter than the tents in the gully, more powerful and overwhelming than the destruction that had consumed the world as she'd finally admitted to herself how badly she wanted every part of Nox, as friend, as family, as lover, as life. Their precious moments in the town house had consumed her, shoving themselves down her throat and filling her belly with a fortitude that she did not truly feel.

Because when she thought of Nox, she felt love, yes. She felt want, she felt comfort and familiarity, but she also felt fear. They'd become young women side by side. They'd grown into adults apart. Their kisses, their stolen moments, their tenderness had been shredded. And in the season that had followed the ag'drurath, and in the march following their time in the town house, her mind had whirred. Amaris had thought of survival, she'd thought of food, she'd thought of Ceres and the fight and the demons, but between every breath, she'd thought of Nox.

Uncertainty fractured each second, creating a sluggish push and pull as she entered the room. Afraid though she was, her heart was as ready as her body was willing. Maybe things had changed—but hadn't they already? They'd been society's discards for years before their paths had torn them asunder. The sword arm of the church from Uaimh Reev, and a young woman left behind at an orphanage to become...a princess? Yes, the world around them had crashed to a standstill as they'd learned that Nox was of royal heritage, but it made no more or less sense than anything else that had happened to them. Time and history had been a string of fables, woven together with lived experience that had seemed so impossible.

Amaris gulped her last breath of air before walking farther into the room. For the time being, at least, Nox was in accommodations very similar to her own. Perhaps once Ceres's possessions were put into a kingly tomb and the royal chambers were made suitable for their new monarch, Nox would find herself in different rooms. For now, they were simply down the hall from each other. The arrangement was perfect.

Amaris's anxiety melted like caramel over hot cinnamon buns the instant their eyes met—sticky, sweet, and unspeakably wonderful. Her flickering smile was hesitant and hopeful as she searched the face that met hers.

Nox smiled faintly from where she had been reading on her bed, legs still under her covers. The heavy, dark-blue blankets seemed to shimmer with the same meteorological light that reflected in the stone. "I'm glad to see you're up and about."

It wasn't quite the warm, tearful reception she'd hoped. She hedged as she said, "The servants are treating me as if I'm back from the dead. I've felt fine for at least two days. Did they scrub you as hard in the bath as they did me? I think my wounds from their brushes are harsher than any wounds from the fire."

Nox laughed at that, but her laugh was disconnected. She

pushed aside her text—what appeared to be some old tome of Raascot lineage. Amaris attempted to imagine what Nox was going through, but she couldn't shoulder any such royal burden. Maybe she didn't understand, but she hoped Nox would teach her.

Amaris bit her lip as she shifted her weight from one foot to the other, waiting for an invitation farther into the room. Suddenly, their quiet moments on the cliff didn't feel so comforting. Nox hadn't been exceedingly talkative as they'd rested after their time on the battlefield, which Amaris had found terribly logical. But the time for silence had come and gone. She didn't want space or small talk. She didn't care to discuss the weather or the tomes or the politics of the kingdom. Yet the energy was not primed for the things she wanted.

She twisted her mouth and attempted stilted conversation. "What are you reading?"

Nox shrugged as she looked at the leather-bound book she'd discarded. "My family, I guess. The paternal half, anyway."

"What's it like to discover you have a family?" Amaris wasn't totally sure that she was joking. She meant it to be lighthearted but wasn't confident her delivery had landed. From the look on Nox's face, it seemed it hadn't been received with levity.

The gaping void of the room wouldn't serve them. Cowardice had no place in the ring, no room when facing demons, and certainly no right to interfere between her and Nox now. Amaris left the place she'd been indecisively occupying near the door and approached the overly large bed. All of the mattresses in Raascot and their four elaborately carved posts seemed crafted to fit the large wingspans of their fae. They made Amaris feel terribly small. She thought of her oath, of her runs up the mountain, of her duals with man and beast as she closed the gap between them.

"Amaris—"

If this was a dance, she'd take the lead. She shook her

head in a plea for silence, crawling onto the bed and folding herself into the space next to Nox. In years past, Nox would have lifted her arm and allowed Amaris to cuddle in underneath, but today Nox maintained her distance.

It was okay. So much had happened. The world as they knew it had shifted. Amaris was sure that no matter how much empathy she conjured, she couldn't truly comprehend the nuances and complexities of Nox's roiling emotions, no matter how much she wanted to. Learning not only of one's parents but of such a terrible, tragic lineage all in one fell swoop was a devastation she couldn't fathom. Amaris fidgeted slightly, unsure how to best comfort her. Nox had been there for her for her entire life. She had to chip away at the mountain of repayment that was due by being there for her now.

When Nox didn't raise her arm, Amaris lifted it for her. Sometimes one needed a nudge to return to familiarity. Only a few nights prior, they'd been tucked in the safety of the town house on the edge of Raascot's capital, the luxurious scent of dark spices and plums, the feelings of warmth and safety, the sensations of want curling through her. She inhaled the same plums now as she nestled into the young woman who was whispered to be queen of the northern kingdom.

The silent apology of folding herself into Nox was all she could do. She chastised herself for the years they'd wasted and the moments they'd squandered. Amaris had learned that the All Mother laughed when moments were delayed, and she wouldn't make that mistake again. If there was one thing Ceres and his agenda had taught her, it was that tomorrow held no guarantee.

Be strong.

Unspeakably terrible memories attached to the words. Her chest tightened. Her breath caught. She couldn't be a coward. She couldn't squander the life she'd been spared, whether or not she deserved it. She had to be brave, now and always.

"Nox," she said slowly, "when we were in bed together,

do you remember what I said? I know so much has happened between now and then, but then again, hasn't that been our lives? I need to tell you all I was going to say there. All I felt. All I feel still."

Amaris thought of touching a snail, watching the once-happy, loose creature recoil until it disappeared completely beneath its protective shell as Nox's energy withdrew. Amaris cursed herself. She was certain Nox's reluctance had come with years of hesitation from the walls she had unknowingly put up between the two of them. There was a darkness to her spirit that felt somehow heavier in the deep blues and blacks of the dark stone room. She wanted to tear down those walls and make her intentions abundantly clear.

She'd try again, and when she did, she'd be the one whose underbelly remained exposed. It was only fair.

With another swallow against her cotton-dry mouth, Amaris leaned boldly forward and grazed her lips in a kiss against the sharpest edge of Nox's jaw.

Nox turned away from the kiss, closing her eyes. In angry, kicking hindsight, Amaris realized she'd misread the signal entirely. She'd shifted her body weight closer, seeing the motion as an opportunity to trace a second kiss on Nox's now-exposed neck. She'd lowered her pink, soft lips onto Nox's throat.

Nox murmured Amaris's name, and Amaris had smiled at long last. Fear still thundered in her ear, but she continued to call on bravery.

"Amaris" came the hesitant voice once more.

"It's okay," Amaris reassured.

Amaris lifted her body from where she had tucked herself underneath Nox's arm and swung herself into a far more intimate posture. She put one pale leg over Nox's deeply tan thighs, positioning herself in Nox's lap, holding her face in her hands as she straddled her.

She looked down into the beautiful, radiant face she loved, and her brows drew together like pulled curtains. Nox's lips were pursed in a gentle, disapproving frown.

This wasn't the face she was hoping to receive, but it was all so new. She'd never been in this position before. She'd never initiated anything so bold or acted in any such way with the soon-to-be queen. The way her nerves rattled her now felt wrong. This wasn't the unsure anxiety she'd felt in the town house. This wasn't the tension she'd felt in her dreams as Nox had tugged at her chin. Something was different. The only new variable was what Nox had learned about herself. Amaris needed to be sympathetic while showing that her emotions didn't scare her. She could handle whatever Nox was feeling.

"I understand," Amaris said, leaning into her. Nox opened herself up slightly as Amaris relaxed into her, planting kisses on her forehead, her temple, her mouth. For a beautiful moment, Nox returned the kiss, her hands finding Amaris's hips. The fire sparked once more, igniting through her just as it had in their intimate moments in the town house on the edge of Gwydir. This was what she wanted. This was why she'd come. Amaris moved gently, pressing herself into Nox with one hand weaving its way into the hair above Nox's temple. One of Nox's hand's tightened against Amaris's hip. It was the encouragement Amaris needed. She opened her mouth more, deepening her kiss.

Nox turned her face, breaking the connection.

"What is it?" Amaris murmured, pulling away ever so slightly.

Nox shook her head, berry-dark lips turned downward.

Amaris swallowed again, her mouth unnaturally dry. She wanted a glass of water more than anything. She didn't know why her nerves wouldn't relax. She did her best to catch Nox's eyes, but a lattice of thick lashes barred them from one another. Amaris battled through it, saying, "I want this, Nox. I want us. It took me so long to understand what's between us, but I know now."

Still, Nox refused to meet her gaze. Amaris followed her line of sight to see little beyond the starlight trapped within the dark blue-black stones. Amaris sat backward, shifting her weight off Nox, as her eyes widened in slow realization.

She took in Nox's pallor and her sleeping clothes. She looked across the room to the tray of untouched food. A fire was warming her hearth, but the room held all the signs of someone who hadn't left her bed all day. Amaris began to shake her head as she created even more distance, scooting herself to the edge of the bed. "Oh, goddess. I'm so sorry. I'm so goddess damned stupid. After all you've just been through with your father, your parents, the battle, the death...of course right now is the most inappropriate time. I'm such an idiot. I'm so sorry, Nox. Please forgive me; this was such inconsiderate timing. Take all the time you need."

"It's not that," Nox murmured.

Amaris frowned, trying once more in a fruitless bid to catch Nox's dark eyes, but the barricade Nox built was unrelenting. Uncomfortable lengths of time stretched between them as she waited for Nox to expand.

"This has nothing to do with my father, or his death, or anything in Raascot."

Amaris slid until her back rested against one of the ornate bedposts.

Nox sucked on her lip and straightened her posture. The agony on her face was worth a thousand words, yet Amaris was quite certain she wouldn't be gifted with nearly so many. She studied the lines in Nox's face, the way she twisted the sheet between her fingers, the crestfallen energy that dripped through her words as she asked, "Amaris, what do you know of your birth?"

"What?"

Nox sighed. "What do you know of your parents?"

Amaris shook her head. "I've never known a thing about my parents, and you know that. The king raved about me being born by some prayer. It means nothing. The man was insane." Anger knitted her muscles into tension as she wrapped her arm around the bedpost for comfort. Amaris truly understood nothing of Nox's posture, her tone, nor the direction of her conversation. Only moments ago, she'd been trying to kiss her. Now, nothing made sense.

Amaris grimaced. She was fucking up but couldn't stop herself. She tried rewinding time, saying, "I'm sorry. I shouldn't have called him that. He's your father—"

"He had gone mad. There's nothing wrong with stating the truth."

Nox untucked her legs from the bed and pushed herself into a standing position on the plush rug. She crossed to a writing desk and located a dirty, black velvet bag. Amaris watched her as she pulled a handkerchief from it and unwrapped what remained of an apple. It appeared fresh and firm, though it looked as if two large bites had been taken from it.

She extended the fruit in her hand.

Amaris didn't touch it. "What is this?"

Nox sighed. "This is the fruit from the Tree of Life at the Temple of the All Mother. The temple was sacked—though if you want to hear that story, you're going to have to ask Ash or Malik, as I'm afraid I don't have the capacity to relive any more fires. It was hell, Amaris. When I walked into the temple, its priestess directed me to the apple. It was her dying wish that I take it. A few days later, I ate the fruit. The tree showed me its memories."

Words. Garbled nonsense. Gibberish tumbled together like gravel in her mind as she looked at the very ordinary apple. Amaris peeked between the stoicism on Nox's face and the outstretched offering. She accepted the fruit, blinking at it with puzzlement.

There were a number of things that came to mind, but she chose to bite her tongue on most of them. Instead, she asked, "What do you mean? Are you implying the tree had memories?"

Nox only shook her head, looking every bit as deflated as Amaris felt. "I have no more use for the fruit. Perhaps if you eat it, it'll show you the same thing and then you'll carry the same burdens I carry now. All it did was bring me dreams of things it had seen. It showed me my mother and how she died in the temple. It showed me her final prayer. It also showed me you—the answer to her prayer."

Amaris looked up from where she'd been eyeing the apple and met Nox's face. "The answer to...why would it show you that?"

Nox brought her fingers to her temples and closed her eyes. She swallowed audibly, physical and existential exhaustion painting itself through each movement and noise. It sounded as if she were having some trouble breathing. "I don't fully understand it. I also don't know if there's a right or wrong way to tell you what I'm about to tell you, so please offer me some grace here, Amaris. But, if the tree's memories are to be believed, then you have no human or fae parentage. You're not..."

"Not human?"

"Not either." Nox's face scrunched as she dug for the words she needed. "You were born of the goddess out of an answer to a prayer—my mother's prayer. Daphne's dying breath was a petition to the All Mother that a curse-breaker would be sent to save the land and protect her daughter. In the next dream I saw what that meant: the priestess bore you."

Amaris frowned. "You're saying the temple priestess is my mother?"

Nox's sound was a mixture between a sigh and a frustrated grumble. Amaris could read body language well enough to understand that Nox wanted to go to sleep, that she wanted Amaris to leave, that she wanted to bury her head in a pillow. Unfortunately, Amaris wouldn't be granting her any such favors.

"No, the priestess is from Tarkhany. You are paler than snow, from your eyelashes to your lilac irises. There's no way you share her blood. If the dream is to be believed, the priestess was a surrogate for the prayer as she was there when my mother died."

Agitation roiled into something else entirely. First, Nox had become a princess. Great. Then, she'd rebuffed Amaris's romantic advances. Fine. *Then*, she'd implied that Amaris had no parents whatsoever. Nox had been a lot of things, but she'd never been cruel. Amaris's lip quivered in thinly controlled anger. "What are you saying?"

Nox buried her head in her hands completely, hiding behind the curtain of fingers and hair. Her voice was tired and sad, a kaleidoscope of other emotions that Amaris couldn't begin to piece together as she replied, "I'm saying, I don't know anything anymore. I'm saying, I don't know what I saw and that it has destroyed me to deal with this information. I'm saying I've loved you from the moment I saw you. I was there when you were brought to Farleigh, and I was the first child there who laid eyes on you. My first memory is of you, Amaris. My first memory is of that night when you were placed on the manor's doorstep. I knew then, even as an infant, that you were the most special thing I'd ever seen. We were family, we were friends; I've loved you so deeply and so intensely for so long in so many different and complicated ways. I've always wanted to be with you. And now that I've learned this… I don't know if what I feel is real."

Amaris had been slapped. Nox might as well have marched across the room and struck her with her own palm. Lips parted in breathless horror, she held the apple away from her as if it were a spider. She repeated Nox's final words numbly, feeling like an echo chamber. "If what we feel is real?"

Nox tightened the grip she had on her shoulders as she hugged herself. "Listen: I don't know if I love you because I love you or if what's between us is some tether from some *prayer* so that we'd find each other. This tether, this connection, it might feel too good to be true because that's exactly what it is: too good to be true. What if the things we feel were merely meant to keep us together so that some dead woman's wishes could be fulfilled? Princess Daphne asked the goddess for someone to save the land, and here you are, a girl who can see through the curse. She asked for someone to protect her child, and here you are, the only one I've ever loved. I want to look at the tree's memories and everything it showed me and find it beautiful, but it's just so, so upsetting. It's disconcerting to my truest and deepest core. It feels like it cheapens everything I've felt for you. I don't know how I can have any certainty if these feelings and pulls I've carried for you are real or merely the product of some magic beyond our control. I don't know what to tell you, except that I'm so confused, it makes me sick."

Amaris dropped the apple onto her lap, her hands balling into fists. Her fingers bit painfully into the meat of her hand, tendons flexing in disgust. "You feel confused? You, who has been such a constant in my entire life, even when I've had crushes on boys or liked men and spent years questioning what this relationship meant to me, only to finally accept that you are my exception. I love you, Nox. You're the only woman I'll ever want. Meanwhile, if the kingdom's rumors are to be believed, you've been off fucking anyone and everything—"

Nox's back stiffened. Her dark eyes flashed as she raised a single, hostile finger. All confusion left her as she seemed to find firm footing. "Back off. I know you're angry, but you are acting so unkind right now. Don't say something you can't take back."

Amaris found her feet as well, the bed now perched between them. "You've spent your whole life knowing the goddess made your heart for women, haven't you? That wasn't me, Nox. Do you know how confusing it's been for me? I grew up liking boys! I like men. I do. I like fighting with them, I like training with them, I like wrestling and flirting and spending time with them. I've tried and failed on more than one occasion to create something with a man. And here you've been, destroying my feelings and twisting my head for years. You've had years to experience the world, you've let goddess knows who into your bed—but you were it for me. I thought that made this special, Nox. Finally, after all this time, I want the same thing you've always wanted. But the *instant* it was my choice in return, you turn me away. Do you know how fucked up that is?"

Shades of crimson blotched across Nox's chest and neck as she attempted to calm herself. Her inhalation shook with emotion. "Fuck you."

"Are you serious?"

Nox's eyes narrowed. "Your cruelty and childishness are astounding right now. You can't force me to be ready to deal with this information. You know I've loved you. I am telling you that I'm struggling to understand what the tree showed me. Things are complicated. All I've asked is for *time*. Give me a goddess-damned moment to adjust."

Amaris answered with a shout, not caring who in the castle might hear her anger. "We've had our whole lives to adjust! We've had two decades of time! Meanwhile, I still can't get rid of my goddess damned maidenhood while you—"

"While I what?" came the question, dripping in acid. Nox met her intensity, her voice burning with an anger she had never in all of her years directed at Amaris. Every sentence she spoke got louder and louder. "While I took your place in the whore house? While I was shipped off with Millicent to sell my body for the deposit she made on you so that you could get away and run off to live your best life? Is that what you're accusing me of? Giving you a shot at freedom? Because if you are, you're more of a goddess damned ungrateful bitch than I ever could have believed. You escaped and left me behind. I didn't hold it against you. I continued to fight for you—for us *both*. I've spent the last few years as an escort. You stand before me, judging me for the things I've done to rescue you from a life that was meant to be yours?"

"Nox..." The room suddenly seemed too small. The velvet, the wood, the crackling fire shrank as the walls pressed in on her. The nutmeg and plum Amaris had always treasured filled the room with a threatening intensity.

"Get the fuck out of here."

Amaris went limp. "Nox, that's not what I meant—"

"I don't care what you meant. It's what you said. And you know what? Maybe I will go sleep with goddess knows whoever I want. Because you don't know the half of who I am or what I can do. And frankly, it stopped being your business the minute you left me in Farleigh. I could throw a stone down this hall right now and whoever it hit would gladly warm my bed."

The spring within Amaris snapped. The pressure from regret, from sorrow, from repentance released. "Then do it." Amaris seethed, grabbing the door.

"Get out," Nox snarled.

"Oh, trust me, I'm gone."

"Don't speak to me again until you realize what a royal bitch you've been!" Nox shouted, chucking the remnants of the fruit through the doorway and into the empty space Amaris left behind her.

✦

Nox heard the fruit hit something and churned with fighting rage. She burst from her room, chasing after the fruit that was surely pulp against the corridor wall. Her anger didn't ebb as she emerged to find Yazlyn, wide-eyed, clutching the apple in her hands.

"Did you seriously just throw an apple at me?" She blinked her too-large hazel eyes, incredulity bleeding into something irate. She glared at Nox, wings flaring slightly behind her as she glowered as if to say her patience had reached its final straw. She looked as if she might throw it back in Nox's face.

Rage. Pure, beautiful, succulent fury pulsed between them.

Nox made no attempt to conceal her loathing as she assessed Yazlyn, eyes passing over her in an up-down as she absorbed the winged fae and the fruit in her hands. Her teeth were bared in a growl as she saw Yazlyn's agitation.

Yazlyn's cherry-brown curls were smooth and freshly brushed. The fighting clothes she'd worn for the last several days had been exchanged for leather pants and a long-sleeve tunic that must have had slots for the wings. She should have smelled of soap and oils, but instead, she radiated walnuts and blackberries. She was beautiful, which only made Nox hate her more. She closed the gap between them in three quick steps, savoring the flash in Yazlyn's face as she lifted her forearm to the fae's throat.

It was the look of someone struggling to decide whether she should use her military training to murder the new queen of Raascot.

Nox shoved her forearm harder, pinning the fae against the stones of the far wall. One hand moved with lightning quickness to intercept Nox's arm. The fingers on Yazlyn's other hand closed around the apple as she stared wide-eyed into Nox's eyes. She savored the look as the sergeant's fight or flight switched to battle mode as her new queen descended on her.

When Nox spoke, her tone was angry and low. "Do you still want to fuck me?"

Yazlyn's lips parted in wordless bewilderment.

Nox savored it, salt and honey on her tongue all at once. It had been a moment since she'd had the chance to appreciate the shock of a new conquest, watching the lights in their eyes as they understood what was about to happen. After several heartbeats, rapidly blinking hazel eyes and a half-hearted attempt at a pathetic shrug, she nodded once.

"Good. Get in."

Chapter Ten

Yazlyn was Nox's equal in nearly every capacity, which was a satisfying change of pace from demur sweethearts who'd shared her bed, or the obnoxious and unworthy, whom she'd quickly ended. With Yazlyn, they were two fierce, powerful sides of the same coin. Two women of northern blood, only a few inches difference in height, relatively similar build, an equal affinity for women, and most importantly, identical, white-hot tempers.

The rage that had spent many moons boiling between them could have been worked out in one of two ways. The women could have fought their differences in the combat ring, where Yazlyn would have had training, tenacity, and leverage. But if Nox took the lead and dragged the war to her advantage, they could take their sparring to the bed.

Nox had been gentle with many lovers. But Yazlyn was not a lover.

Any other woman may have been intimidated by the aggression Nox brought to the sheets, but for the sergeant responsible for betrayal, the fae who sent the raven, the doe-eyed enemy who'd punctured her world with a hot knife, it was clean, vicious passion.

Between the enthusiastic bite and tear of lips, tongues, hands in hair, nails on skin, Yazlyn barely managed to gasp, "What are you—"

"Shut the hell up," Nox ordered.

Their clothes didn't have time to make it all the way off in their haste, shirts bunched over breasts and hands shoved down the fronts of pants as they clawed every scrap off one another, tearing and shredding the fabrics that had contained them. Nox tasted the sweat on Yazlyn's throat, mouth moving rapidly to the tender push of Yazlyn's breasts, and tasted only the hot, burning liquor of rage. She knew the sensation well. It was one that scalded your throat, warmed your muscles, made your head light, and guaranteed regrets in the morning as one pounded strong drink after drink. They drank the bar dry, gulping dark spirits as they pressed themselves into one another.

Their intensity hadn't left much room to get from the hall to the bed.

Whether passion or violence, Nox couldn't decide which surface to slam her prey against—though some of it was from the sadistic joy of the tasty yelps each time she rammed the fae into something hard.

Nox's shirt was easy enough to get off. She didn't bother figuring out the panels on Yazlyn's tunic that allowed for wings. She bit into Yazlyn's lower lip hard enough to draw blood as she ripped the fabric down the front. Yazlyn's cry was a mix of pain and protest as her top was torn to shreds.

Much to Nox's delight, Yazlyn was a fighter.

She wasn't sure if she'd ever been grabbed and kissed in return with as much passion as she dished out, but the sergeant had no shortage of hostility, which tasted awfully similar to the delightful flavor of lust.

Their frenzied undressing at the door knocked a candle from the wall. She was more or less sure it didn't catch the castle on fire, but she didn't pay particular mind as they roughly shoved one another against the desk. Glass bottles of ink shattered on the floor as neatly stacked papers fluttered around them like obscenely academic snow.

The bruises, the pains, the shoves felt good against the breaking waves of their anger. Anger for the sergeant, sure. Anger toward Raascot, yes. Fury toward Amaris, absolutely. And most of all, the unadulterated rage at the culmination of events that led to the building steam of this moment and its volcanic release.

She inhaled sharply as Yazlyn scooped her onto the writing desk. The blackberry scent intensified as she tuned in to her senses, feeling the tug of cloth, the softness of a mouth coupled with the sharp drag of fanged teeth, the crackle of the fire, and the glorious sounds of mingled, heavy breathing. She lifted her hips in consent as her pants were slipped over them and discarded on the floor.

Naked on the writing desk table, Nox pulled Yazlyn's body against her, and the fae woman dragged her teeth down Nox's throat. Nox grabbed a handful of hair and yanked the winged woman back, asserting the dominance she needed so badly to exercise. She missed this. Life had been out of control for long enough. She was itching to exert a little authority.

"Get on the bed and lie on your stomach."

Nox watched the flicker in the battle of wills as a dozen emotions played out behind the fae's too-large eyes, each green, brown, and yellow stitch of her irises throbbing with conflict. Their eyes locked in a standoff, but Nox knew the moment she won. Yazlyn's large, hazel eyes flitted between her and the mattress that called to them. Nox's cocky smile spread as she recognized the hunger. Yazlyn wanted whatever was coming next more than she wanted to be right, to be dominant, to be victorious over her new queen.

She obeyed.

Triumph had a luxurious, cashmere flavor as she crawled onto the bed over her conquest, brushing over flesh and feathers as she slid over Yazlyn's back. She pressed her bare breasts into the shoulder blade space between the sergeant's raven wings.

"This doesn't mean I—" came Yazlyn's first, half-hearted sign of mutiny. The roles had been established. There would be no switches tonight.

With a quick, authoritative sweep, Nox wrapped her left hand around the fae's throat and then stuck two of the fingers of her right hand into Yazlyn's mouth. It was effectively silencing. A wet tongue and pursed lips sucked on them until they were satisfactorily wet, before Nox used the fae's own saliva as she traced lines down smooth, soft skin, tucking her hand between hips and sheets and sliding two fingers inside of her.

Yazlyn's gasp was as satisfying as rich, red wind. Nox sipped the moment, drinking in the blackberry scent that flooded the room as it wetted her hand. The movements started slowly as she absorbed satisfaction from each tense muscle, each moan low. Her fingers curled in a "come hither" motion inside the fae before grazing her teeth over Yazlyn's naked shoulder. Nox's mouth connected with the tender muscle where the neck and shoulder met, drawing a small yelp of pain. As before, each cry was immediately followed with a total-body release, a rush of water, an encouraging moan—the perfect, masochistic counterpart.

Nox's speed and intensity increased gradually at the soaking appreciation of each motion. Yazlyn made her pleasure no secret, which was wonderful. Nox took pleasure of a different kind. She continued her pumping, clamping her left hand down on the fae's mouth as the fae grew louder and louder. Now that she knew how to make the sergeant scream, she was relentless. She channeled her rage, her resentment, her betrayal into every stroke. Her fury over the treacherous raven sent to the king, the violence she felt in response to the downfall of the town house, the heat and ferocity of every passing moment spent hating each other channeled into stroke after stroke after stroke. She had all the time in the world and proved as much with glorious consistency until the satisfying cry of her finishing gave way to several deep, wet, full-body spasms.

Nox's entire body hummed, throbbing with each delicious gulp as the glorious wet, loud evidence of pleasure soaked the bed.

As it turned out, they had more anger than could be resolved in a single tussle.

By the time the sun came up, the sheets were damp with puddles, there was a broken vase, a lantern had clattered from the wall by a stray wing, and each girl had climaxed no fewer than three times. It had been furious, erotic, and raw, and a splendid release. There were no good-night kisses or attempts to pretend they were friendly.

Nox arched something of a surprised eyebrow when the morning light woke them and she saw Yazlyn had fallen asleep in her bed, though the sheer physical taxation would have taken a toll on them both. She supposed she'd allow the overnight stay on such grounds. There was no shame or semblance of regret between them. Nox had a feeling Yazlyn had needed the night every bit as much as she herself had.

A sweep of sheets, a fluster of fabric, and Yazlyn was out of the bed. She turned to Nox. "How's my hair?"

Nox reclined in bed, pillows propped behind her back. "It looks like you've just spent the night getting fucked, if that's what you're wondering."

"Perfect." Yazlyn closed the door behind her on the way out.

Nox smirked at the barrier between herself and the sergeant, enjoying the satisfying exchange of using something for precisely what it was. Love, lust, and coin all had their place in the bedroom. Then again, sometimes one just needed the septic feelings souring one's soul pounded out of them.

Nox found a fresh pair of clothes but didn't bother bathing. She enjoyed the buzz of clinging to an orgasm long after the sex had finished. She reflected on her lovers and their flavors, from the clients she'd hated and fed on to the strange women she'd brought home from the bar, to the sweet, naïve Emily, the gentle, generous Malik, and now Yazlyn's mess. Chaos was truly delicious in the wake of how tiresome it had been to spend years tenderly loving Amaris, only to have that love thrown back in her face the moment she asked for time and understanding.

Nox settled into the stool in front of the mirror, brushing out the sweat and sex that tangled her hair while she readied herself for the day. She was taxed in every sense of the word. Betrayal still twisted her stomach at how selfish Amaris had been. Nox was angry at herself for how the night had gone, rebuffing the advances of the lone person she'd loved for so many years. Maybe if she'd been able to sort through her thoughts and feelings more quickly, last night could have been the culmination of years of waiting. They might have fully been together, unlike their final hours at the town house where pain and want and confusion had led to fretful, stolen kisses, words left unsaid, and the last restful sleep before their worlds unraveled. The night could have faded into soft kisses, with lovemaking; instead, it had been sharp teeth and nails and hate-fucking. But, if Nox wasn't going to get a fairy-tale ending, she should at least get some drama-free oxytocin.

She hadn't been in the castle long enough to know her way by heart, but she followed the scent of cooked ham that mingled with foggy memories of navigating the halls. She joked to herself that she should have used her pocket watch to ask for the location of the dining room but stumbled into it after two turns down the corridor.

Surprise circumvented her hunger when she saw Malik at the table. It was far too late for someone of his disciplined sensibilities to be eating breakfast. From their travels across the continent and their time in Henares, she knew he was normally awake with the sunrise and off training before she'd picked her head up from her pillow.

His entire face lit when he saw her. "How'd you sleep?"

She took a few steps into the dining room, appreciating it in the mid-morning light. The spread of breakfast meats,

117

fruits, pastries, jams, pots of tea, and pads of butter left nothing to be desired. The table was large enough for a military, but the neat stack of plates and cutlery made it clear that everyone was to come and go as they pleased. She piled her plate high and offered him a half smile, not sure why guilt tugged at her. Part of her wondered if he could smell sex on her. "It ended up being a pretty good night."

"I'm glad to hear it. I've been worried about you."

She looked down to keep him from seeing her flinch.

This was why she felt guilty. She didn't want to look into the sparkling green eyes and gentle smile that contained everything that she was not. Malik was a good person who genuinely cared for her. Not only that, but without her ever having to explicitly explain that she was a succubus, he'd discerned enough to keep her fed. That was long before considering that the man had been an excellent, gentle, selfless lover. They hadn't discussed how she couldn't offer him anything in return if he hoped to keep his soul safely encased in his body. She chewed her lip, wondering if she was under an obligation to have a discussion with him about the sort of things that had taken place in her bed the night before. She decided that yes, she would talk to him about it out of decency, but it would not be while she ate her fruit and eggs.

Malik propped his weight onto his elbows. He leaned forward as he said, "Gadriel needs to speak to you. He thought you might be more comfortable if I came as well."

She frowned into her breakfast while chewing. "Why you?"

He smiled. "I'm pretty sure he felt the most handsome reever would be best suited for the task, but it may also be because Amaris hates him right now and Ash has been bitter toward everyone for days."

Nox took another bite as she mused, "Amaris is losing friends in the castle quickly, isn't she?" Her sourness broke into a half smile as she added, "Ash probably just needs to get laid."

Food and conversation only did so much to ease the

gnawing discomfort at what lay ahead. After breakfast, Gadriel appeared to fetch Nox and Malik. He led them down Gwydir's fortified corridors, far from the bright, happy daylight and into parts of the castle that couldn't be breached. He pushed his hand against the door, waiting for a clinking sound to greet them before tugging open what she could only assume was the door to the war room. A large, oval table with a map of the continent sat in its center. Despite its lack of windows, the combination of fae lights and lanterns created a friendly-enough ambiance.

Part of her had braced for a familiar fear as he led them to a place deep in a stone-walled castle with no escape, but the fear did not come. She didn't like Gadriel, but he was not a bad man. Besides, she was quite confident Malik would sooner die than let anyone look at her sideways.

"Zaccai and Yazlyn should be joining us any moment," Gadriel said as he pulled up a seat and gestured for the others to do the same.

"Yazlyn is coming?" Nox fidgeted in her seat. She'd both enjoyed and benefitted from their night together, but she wasn't sure how she felt about their passion between the sheets rolling into a war room council. Perhaps she'd be clearer and sharper at the meeting thanks to her fresh dose of oxytocin, but she didn't know if that meant she could tolerate its supplier outside of the bedroom.

Gadriel had opened his mouth to respond, but his answer was unnecessary. The door opened and Yazlyn, hair neatly braided and clean clothes on her back, entered. She was free from any evidence of the previous night's entanglement. Her face was utterly impassive, which reassured Nox that the sergeant's military training would enable her to maintain whatever separation might be needed between pleasure and profession.

The muscles between Nox's shoulder blades relaxed, if only slightly.

She ignored Yazlyn long enough to appraise the

fresh-faced fae who entered the room behind her. There was a youthfulness to his appearance, though she supposed things like age could never quite be determined when it came to matters of the fae. She'd been too miserable to take stock of the newest member of their party after the massacre. As she regarded him now, her eyes flitted to a small, black silken bow tied around his wrist. He'd kept the scrap of fabric she'd torn from her dress to differentiate ag'imni so long ago.

He lifted the decorated hand in a polite wave.

"Zaccai," she said with a smile, the memory of their exchange outside of Aubade flooding back with the simple, silken token.

The others exchanged a mixture of puckered lips and brows, but she paid them no mind.

"You look…warmer," Zaccai offered with a crooked smile.

Nox didn't have to force the smile that lit her. She didn't know why the man hadn't bothered to remove the small silk bracelet, but she felt a surge of platonic affection for the second in command. Perhaps she had more friends in the castle than she realized.

Malik translated the nature of their acquaintance for the general. "Zaccai met us outside of the castle the night you and Amaris flew off with the ag'drurath. Nox was attempting to escape through the woods in…what…silk underwear?"

"It was a dress" came her clipped response, "and it was perfectly appropriate for events that didn't evolve escaping through the trees."

Zaccai rubbed at the back of his neck a bit shyly.

The newcomers took their seats around the war table and eyed Gadriel expectantly to start the meeting. And start it, he did.

"King Ceres is dead," he said, wasting no time on easing them into their first council, "and Nox, you're his only surviving child. I wish we were welcoming you to the kingdom with more fanfare, but we were all there for the slaughter of his troops. Those who survived are home with their families on reprieve. Word of Ceres's death has spread like wildfire, and we need to smother the flames with good news rather than panic. Our next move is to disseminate information that his heir has been successfully located. I'm the only other family member who might have challenged your claim to the throne, and I can promise you: I don't want the title. I vote that we post a decree along with a very brief heritage—your mother as Princess Daphne and you as the one we've sought for twenty years—so that the people of Raascot can begin familiarizing themselves with your name. Then we'll need you to pass a sentence on the prisoner. What do you think?"

Nox tried to suppress her laugh at first, but the harder she tried to push down the burble of amusement, the more ridiculous the thought became. "You want to know what I think? I think prostitute turned princess is a pretty outlandish rags-to-riches story. I think this whole thing is absurd and that if I keep slapping myself, eventually I'll wake up. I think the best I can offer you is to step into the position as a placeholder until you find someone better suited to serve as monarch."

Malik's frown was not unkind. The Raascot fae, on the other hand, sat on pins and needles while they watched their general for a response.

Gadriel eyed her carefully. "I know this isn't a life that you wanted or asked for, but even though this is new for you, we've spent twenty-one years looking for you."

Yazlyn spoke for the first time. "I think your age will put a lot of people at ease."

Nox folded her arms over her chest. "Oh, they'll be thrilled to have a monarch who's scarcely out of her teenage years?"

Yazlyn shook her cherry-dark waves, her face both calm and serious. "No, you're in a peak magical year. Farehold may have a human-to-fae majority, but Raascot still honors the old magics. Seven and three are both enchanted numbers, and your age is their multiplication. I think the people will see it as a sign that you remained hidden until your twenty-first year and were discovered only at the fullness of time."

The others, Malik included, nodded as if this made perfectly logical sense. Nox did her best not to roll her eyes. "I'm a bastard," she said matter-of-factly. "Even if both of my parents were of royal lineage, they weren't married. I'm not a sanctioned birth."

Gadriel waved her comment away. "That hardly matters outside of Farehold. Which brings me to my next point: unless we find out what happened during the massacre, there may not be much of a northern kingdom left. What should be done about the prisoner?"

Nox frowned at Gadriel. "What are her official charges?"

"She's charged with war crimes and murder in the first degree."

She chewed her lip. "I'd love to just kill her and be done with it, but first we need to know if this was an isolated incident or if she's part of a large-scale attack."

Gadriel rubbed his chin. "Yazlyn spent some time with the prisoner this morning. What have you learned?"

The sergeant's face settled into serious lines. "I was able to get her to eat and drink a little, but she still isn't speaking. She seems very sick, Gad. She's looked unwell since we arrived. On the one hand, I can't imagine I'd look well if I were in prison. But something seems terribly wrong. As for what I've learned...I've never met anyone from Sulgrave, but she seems to fit the physical description. If her display of power is any indication, I think it's essential that she stay in engraved chains. We'll need all the help we can get in dampening whatever skills she possesses."

"Did you get any indication of what the most effective way might be of making her talk?"

The military fae briefly discussed interrogation techniques, then surprised Nox when they turned to her as the deciding factor. She understood that they were on some sort of mission to think of her as their leader, but she had no experience, no skill set, and no know-how when it came to any facet of rulership.

"Me?" was all she could say.

Gadriel nodded solemnly.

She made some vague, shrugging agreement to do whatever they thought was best, and that was that. After a few more parting words and muttered commands, Gadriel dismissed the group. Nox got up to leave but was stopped.

"Nox, is it okay if I have a word with you?" the general asked.

Malik shot her a parting look to ensure she felt safe, which she assuaged with a single nod. Once the others were out of the room, Gadriel leaned onto the table, propping his weight with both hands as he looked at her.

"Are you a succubus?"

Her jaw dropped. She blinked, taking a defensive step backward. Suddenly the large, stone room felt too small and too cold all at once. Her hands flexed at her sides. Her mouth tasted of copper as she sputtered, "Excuse me?"

He waved it away with a hand. "I can see what you're feeling, and trust me, this is not an accusation. Succubi and incubi are powers in fae that manifest in the north from time to time. Before the battle, you and Malik disappeared from the camp together. You came back hours later looking ten years younger and like you'd just returned from the brink of illness. It seemed so obvious to me then. It's more than just a useful gift, but it's important for those in your inner circle to know how to help you."

Nox shook her head so hard that she set her vision off kilter. "I don't know what you're talking about."

She knew enough of body language to tell Gadriel was doing his best to make himself look as reassuring as possible. He said, "I want to make something very clear about whatever you may think about the term ascribed to this gift, or any beliefs you might have about your ability. There is nothing dark, nothing bad, about who you are or the way you were made. In the north, we were raised under a creed that I need you to internalize: a power is only as good or as evil as the one wielding it. Now you're in Castle Gwydir, and your survival is vital to the kingdom. If you become sick or are close to death, a healer would need to know what fuels and revives you. A good general should have knowledge about how best to protect his queen. I left Ceres on his own for years. I left him alone with his struggles when I should have been safeguarding him. I won't make that mistake again."

Her lungs felt too heavy. Her eyes were too dry.

The only person who had ever ascribed this word to her was Millicent. The reevers seemed to have gleaned what she was, but they left it unuttered. If the evidence with the Duke of Henares hadn't been enough for the men, Malik's intervention on the eve of battle certainly had been.

She opened her mouth to speak, but the very word made her ill.

Solemnity slackened from Gadriel's face as he became less of a general and more of a person. His posture softened. "Can I ask you something?"

She nodded numbly.

"When you returned with Malik, he was still intact. How have you learned to master it?"

Nox felt terribly uncomfortable. "I don't…"

He raised a hand at his side, swearing some invisible oath. "Consider this something like doctor-patient confidentiality. I'm asking as your general and as your fae advisor."

Death. She wanted to die. She wanted the floor to open up and swallow her whole. She was the game master. She was the coordinator of moves, of actions, of words. She decided who lived and died. She'd been so powerful. And now…

She twisted her mouth against the truth, but the time for denial had come and gone. One thing she had yet to try was telling the full truth. She closed her eyes and took a slow, steading breath as she said, "It's the oxytocin—the love chemical. It's almost like drinking a tonic. I can feed fully when I take it from someone. The act of taking is how I'm able to gain control, which either ends in their death or relinquishing whatever remained of their sanity. But strictly in terms of self-sustaining, I'm able to meet my...nutritional needs...when someone gives as well. It's not quite the same as taking, but I've had a lot of success with it."

He nodded. "So, your partners—"

"I'm not entirely comfortable..."

A hand covered his face as he rubbed at his eyes. "I mean this with all the respect you're due as my queen, but I don't give a damn about your sex life. I do, however, have to know how to best advise you."

"Fine," she said somewhat tersely. "My partners are women—Malik being an unusual exception—and being a succubus doesn't seem to affect my female partners. They give me the chemical I need for sustenance without me draining them in return. It's victimless. My true *feedings* have been male patrons at my former place of employment: the Selkie. I'm sure you've slain many in battle, General, but I'm not without a death toll. Many died before I learned how to control it, more still before I was able to use it to my advantage. The Selkie's Madame was so thrilled to have me under her roof that she was entirely too happy to clean up evidence of what I was—what I am. I did eventually learn how to leave them with enough of a consciousness that they survived while I retained control. I have a few men running around Priory whom I can still call on in a time of need. To date, my most powerful asset is the Duke of Henares."

"That's very useful to know. He would back us in war?"

"He would back us in anything. He has no say in the matter. And truth be told, he's quite happy about it."

She studied Gadriel carefully, watching for any subtle tightening of the eyes, any flex of the shoulders, any twist of the mouth. None came. He remained staring thoughtfully into the nothingness at the center of the table, absorbing everything she said as no more than an advisor.

A second wave of relaxation moved through her, unclenching fight-or-flight muscles that she hadn't realized she'd been flexing.

"Forgive me," he said, breaking the silence, "but most of the fae succubi I've met—though rare—have been able to feed from the familial love of their parents and affections of families through childhood. At least, that's how we've determined so many of them go undetected until they come of age. But, without a family, being what you are...how did you make it out of the orphanage?"

She had sensed something like this might be coming. Millicent had asked the same, though she hadn't understood it at the time. The answer hurt her, particularly in the wake of their fight. She and Amaris had been many things, but they'd never been at war.

Still, it didn't change the truth of her answer. Her voice dropped a register, quieting as she said, "The same way any succubus would, I guess. Love. I didn't have parents, but I was never without love."

She was enough of a student of the male face to see the subtle flash of emotion, though he concealed it well. She didn't know why, but her answer had hit some sort of nerve with him. Given how hard he'd worked to establish a nonjudgmental environment, she had to fight down the reaction that stirred within her as she struggled to understand what had triggered him. A memory from her fight with Amaris itched her behind her ear, recalling how she'd shouted that she preferred men. Had the general been one of them?

"That makes a lot of sense" was all he said.

Nox had rallied enough confidence to ask the question that had been irritating her from the moment Ceres had marched south, leaving their motley crew to fight outside of the castle. She leveled her gaze. "How can Raascot entertain this? This conversation we're having right now...how can you even consider allowing a queen like me to ascend? My body count is just as long in bedded partners as it is in the deaths I've caused. I understand where I thrive and the power I hold. I was running a kingdom of my own in Priory. I understood how I might succeed in this world. Everything you're suggesting here…it's absurd, Gadriel."

His eyes softened, brows tilting up in the middle. "I want to be empathetic. You have to understand that you feel this way about yourself because of where you were raised. This wouldn't be a question on your mind if you'd grown up in Raascot. There is no shame in being either succubus, incubus, or any of the manifestations of ability that Farehold has spent hundreds of years calling 'dark power' in the north."

She pushed out a breath of air. "Gadriel?"

He perked. "Yes?"

"Can we be done with this for today? It's been…a lot."

He was distinctly sad as he said that yes, of course their meeting was hers to adjourn. He said this or that about maps to pore over, but she felt his eyes on the back of her head as she exited the room. She barely had time to relish in her escape before a bright spot of gold moved.

Malik had waited for her. He shoved off from where he'd been leaning against the wall just beyond the war room's heavy doors. He fell into step easily with her, asking, "So, boss, what's our next move?"

She laughed. "Who are you calling boss?"

He flashed a winsome smile. "Who are we fooling? You've led the charges long before they gave you a crown. Any idea when or where we're going now?"

She followed the distant glow of daylight. "You mean, right now in the castle? Or is this more of an existential question? Because right now, I'm just trying to escape the tomb."

They continued down the hall until their paths were meant to diverge to separate wings of the castle. They kept up pleasant, idle chitchat for the majority of their walk, but before they parted ways, Nox felt a tug in her lower stomach. It was a guilt similar to whatever had struck her at breakfast.

After discussing things so frankly with Gadriel, she felt like now was as good a time as any to talk to Malik.

"I'll see you at dinner?" he asked, eyes hopeful.

Nox attempted to plant her feet, but for the second time in an hour, she wished the ground would gulp her down. "Malik? About what we did in the forest…"

His green eyes reflected nothing of worry. They were merely quizzical as he regarded her. "Is this an invitation for round two, or is this a conversation about how it can never happen again?"

Her gaze dropped to her feet. She gnawed on her lip but felt like sharing this information would be a bit like ripping wax from oneself: do it quickly and lessen the pain. "Neither. I feel like it's only decent of me to tell you that I took Yazlyn to my bed last night. Just given how unconventional my relationship to you has been, I felt like I needed—"

The sound he made may have been a light laugh. It drew her eyes back to him, only to find him smiling. His expression was gentle, which was no surprise. Everything about him was infinitely kind. "I have no claim of ownership over you, Nox. No one should. I care for you, and I believe you still enjoy my presence. You can call on me whenever you like, whether it's to enjoy each other in the bedroom, to discuss politics, or to practice throwing your axe. Where is Chandra, by the way?"

Her gasp faded into a grin over how expertly he'd side-stepped discomfort and changed the subject. She truly detected no jealousy or hurt on his features. He had known that she preferred women. He had known that she was a succubus. He had known that she'd spent years pining after Amaris. She began to wonder why she thought he'd react any differently now. Nox reached out and squeezed his hand in response.

He planted a kiss on her forehead. "I'll meet you on the archery range later this afternoon, okay? You can't go too long without practicing."

Sunbeams cut inwardly, warming Nox's very center as she returned to her rooms. Somehow, despite how tumultuous and miserable the past few days had been between the massacre, the demons, her fight with Amaris, and the sight of her father perishing, her life had also never been better. Maybe that said less about her current state and was more of a commentary on how terrible her life leading up to this moment had been, but she'd take her happiness wherever she found it.

Chapter Eleven

H I, ASH." AMARIS LIFTED HER HEAD FROM WHERE IT HAD been buried in her arms at her sitting desk. She hadn't been crying, or moving, or breathing. She'd merely pressed her forehead into the creases of her forearms and lost herself to the pain of memories. Her room had provided a perfectly beautiful cage for her wounds. When she hadn't answered the knocks at her door, he'd let himself in, presumably to see if she was still alive.

"Hey, Ayla." He offered an unconvincing smile. Ash closed the door behind himself, then leaned against the desk.

The sting of tears threatened her over the nickname. It had been so long since she'd been with her reevers. For years, she'd trained with them, lived with them, truly become one of them. Being ripped from their side had been the worst moment of her life…but terrible things had a way of being topped. The brittle shell where her heart had once been now contained little more than desperate wishes that Odrin was alive, that Nox was still her friend, that she could go back in time and change everything.

Nothing had been right in her life from the moment their feet had crossed the cursed threshold of Castle Aubade. The queen turned the reevers into enemies of Farehold. She had thrown herself at Gadriel, someone she believed she'd trusted, only to learn that she had given herself to a traitor. She had set fire to whatever she and Nox had shared.

And then there was whatever hell Nox had said about apples and priestesses and prayers. She hadn't asked to hear of her supposed heritage. She didn't want to know about her past or about any prophetic purpose the goddess intended for her.

All she wanted was to be Ayla, the reever.

Her minor success for the day had been sitting at the desk to mourn rather than spending the day under the covers of her bed as she wanted. She wasn't sure how she'd summoned the strength to get up from the mattress, but she couldn't imagine doing much more than that.

"Penny for your thoughts?" he asked.

She wiped at a treacherous tear. She attempted a half-hearted smile. "Oh, you know. Just my entire life falling apart. It's no big deal."

The corners of his mouth turned down. "Is burying your head on your desk offering any solutions?"

She squinted her eyes a bit, raising two fingers of each hand to emphasize the point around her words. "I'm not really in the 'solution stage' of grieving, I'm afraid."

He accepted this. "Would it make you feel any better to punch it out?"

She chewed on her lip. "Are you offering?"

"It's been a while since you've kicked my ass. I need someone to keep me humble."

✦

The castle's training ring was beautiful, though she hadn't expected any less. Despite the traumatic connection she had to her first encounter with the northern lights that had been captured in the rock that composed the castle, it never ceased to take her breath away. Maybe if she stopped hating the Raascot fae long enough to hold a conversation, she'd ask someone what feat of manufacturing had accomplished a castle made of blue-black crystal.

They had gotten lost in their initial attempts to find the ring, but a servant pointed them in the right direction to the enormous, open-air gymnasium toward the castle's center. Gwydir made the training center at Uaimh Reev look like a child's playpen for all of its equipment, space, obstacles, and weaponry. The courtyard wasn't just perfunctory, its night-colored stones were also covered with beautiful flowering vines. The plants thrived in the final pushes of summer heat, each giving off a strong, plum-like scent. Soon autumn would be upon them, and then she'd be able to train with the flowers wilting and drifting to the ground, leaving her in peace.

Amaris wasn't ready to think of plums. She breathed through her mouth, denying the scent its chance to make her cry.

"Damn," Ash said appreciatively.

She planted her hands on her hips. "Given their limit-less training supplies, I'd almost expect the Raascot fae to be better than us."

"Nobody's better than us," Ash said, plucking a thick roll of protective gauze from the wall. He wrapped his knuckles carefully, readying for their hand-to-hand sparring. Compared to the daily arduous training at the keep, their time on dispatch had left them borderline rusty. Since they were both a bit out of practice, they took their time bouncing around on their feet and getting their muscles warm, stretching and moving before either of them was ready to throw the first punch.

He beckoned her forward, and Amaris obliged. She punched hard, wincing at the sharp impact in her forearm as he blocked her. True to his offer of being her punching bag, Ash took it upon himself to block her. This was her chance to labor through her pain.

"Do you want to tell me what happened while we were apart?" he asked. Sweat had already beaded on his brow. He panted as he absorbed a kick, taking the blow. He grimaced as she advanced, but his footing remained firm. He'd lost none of his readiness, nor she her agility.

"Where do I even start?" She grunted as she threw two successive punches; one blocked, the other dodged. This particular ring within the training court was not the sand of the coliseum, nor the polished stone of Uaimh Reev, but a soft, stretched lofted surface that allowed them to fall and bounce without fear of truly injuring themselves. It came with its own set of positives and negatives, as the ring's bounce was both more forgiving to their falls and also offered less leeway should they step, roll, or dodge beyond the hard outlines of the sparring ring and tumble from the platform onto stone.

"Well." He jumped backward to create more space. "Last item I saw you, you and an ag'imni were flying off on the back of a dragon. I think I preferred Gadriel when he was a demon. I don't know that there's room for more than one pretty boy on this team."

She raised her eyebrows and went for a sidekick. She understood her mistake. He'd been distracting her while he created space once more, and it had worked. "We made it to the university. We located the curse's orb. He tried to strangle me to death—"

He grabbed her foot rather than simply blocking her kick at that, his temper flaring. "Gadriel did what?"

She spun free, landing on the balls of her feet and finger-tips of her right hand, left arm in the air behind her for balance. Amusement tickled her at his reaction. "Oh yes. Apparently, their training tactics are quite barbaric. They make our morning runs look like picnics. I want to hate him for it, but I'd asked for it. What's more, it worked. Did you know I can create a shock wave? Because neither did I."

Ash was still bouncing on his feet to stay lithe as he leaned backward, dodging her advances. "Are you saying you discovered a power?"

She gasped for air as she nodded, bobbing and lunging.

133

"So far, I have three, to my knowledge. Though I don't really understand how the last one works. You should ask the general what he can do sometime, but be prepared for him to make you break his neck."

"True sight," Ash confirmed as he threw an elbow. "Persuasion," he said as he misjudged his distance, throwing too much body weight into his thrust and stumbling past her dodge. "And shock waves? Are you a witch?"

She aimed her kick for his jaw to shut him up.

Her redheaded friend put everything into the next few steps, giving Amaris an opportunity to tuck and roll on the floor of the ring. Dirt clung to her shirt and pants as she found her way off the ground.

"Did you say 'break his neck'? Do I even want to ask what you mean by that?"

Amaris flashed a breathless, heated smile. "Come on, faeling. Your dad is full fae, right? Do you know if you have any other powers?"

His kick glanced past her face. "Other than good health" (a grunt), "devastatingly good looks" (a punch), "and resistance to certain fae charms, no, I haven't really explored it."

She couldn't spare the energy to nod as she spun backward, throwing an elbow into his sternum. He groaned as the blow cut through him. She panted as she said, "Be prepared to get thrown off a cliff, then. They take it to some extremes to help you unlock whatever you've got. If you have any."

He swung, stepping into his punch. "If Nox does and she's only half-fae, I don't see why I wouldn't."

Amaris was distracted enough that his punch made contact. He breathed in a sharp inhalation in apology, but she shook it off. "What power does Nox have?"

Sweat dripped down the side of his face. He lifted his shirt, exposing his abdominals as he wiped it clean. There was genuine confusion when he asked, "You don't know?"

Their fight wasn't over, and Ash would live to rue whatever tactic this was. He was still mopping sweat with his tunic when she advanced. Acid colored her retort. "She doesn't have powers."

He had to jump back twice and leap to the side to avoid her lunge. Rather than let up on his cruel, untoward distraction technique, he doubled down. "She's a succubus, Amaris. And a pretty dangerous one at that."

"No." Amaris shook her head sharply and spun for another kick.

Anger threw her off her balance. Her foot glanced past him, but she couldn't stop herself in time. Ash clamped one arm around her thigh, immobilizing her.

"Trust me, I'm not thrilled about it either. Malik's in way over his head."

She pulled him in close, bringing her elbow down into the back of his neck with bruising strength. Reevers didn't pussyfoot when they trained, but they rarely went for cruel blows. Ash had crossed a line, and she would too. "You don't know what you're talking about. Nox doesn't even like men."

She was losing her advantage. Emotion clouded her judgment as Ash gained ground.

"She doesn't have to like them to use them. Don't get me wrong: I think she's swell, and not too hard on the eyes if I have to choose a traveling companion. But at the end of the day, perhaps because I'm fae, I'm not under her spell the way Malik is." Each word was punctuated with winces, exertion, the scraping of feet on stretched platform, and rage.

Amaris's anger shook her from her footing once more. "You're wrong."

This time when Ash grabbed her, he didn't release his hold. His honey-gold eyes burned into hers with a bit more intensity. "I think you two need to talk. Clear this up with her, Ayla."

"Stop!"

"You'll always be an oak tree." His mouth gave way to a crooked smile. "Don't fight it."

He'd won the fight, and she loathed herself for it.

"Do you concede?"

"I hate you."

Amaris shoved off of him and began to walk away. She felt disgusted, and not just with her inability to knock Ash to his ass. She rejected everything being said to her. She didn't know how or why he'd come to believe these things about Nox, but he was profoundly mistaken. Her fighting spirit had died, but her energy was far from satiated.

"Run with me?" she asked. She took off before he could respond, but he was on her heels in moments.

They jogged laps around the perimeter of the training court, ivy leaves blowing gently as arms and powerful legs brushed past the vines. The pair made an entire lap before the conversation picked up again.

"Okay." Ash pumped his arms to keep up with her. "Enough about Nox. Why is your life falling apart?"

Amaris was pushing herself too hard. She knew her stamina would burn out long before it should, but she couldn't bring her legs to a reasonable pace. She felt as if she were outrunning her problems, as if reality were wolves currently at her heels. Her lungs burned. The rocks and flowering vines and weapons were blurs as she pushed herself harder and harder in her laps. "What do you know of the dream Nox had? About...about what King Ceres said about me?"

She heard the suction of hesitation at her heels. They'd spent years running up and down a mountain. Holding a conversation on level terrain shouldn't have been so demanding. "I know that whatever she saw really messed her up. She didn't talk for two weeks after her dream." Then, "Slow down. You're going to burn us both out."

"Good," Amaris said through gritted teeth.

"I've heard what they've said about you. I don't know what to make of it."

"Are there any other legends or myths about the goddess doing anything like this? Because it all sounds like impossible bullshit to me." Her voice was barely a gasp between the thundering of her running steps.

"I don't know." He dragged air through his lungs. "I think it would be pretty cool to learn I was a demi-god."

She hit a mental and physical wall all at once. Her run slowed at that until she was at a complete stop. She pulled as much oxygen as possible into burning lungs. Her muscles ached. Arrows pierced her sides. She hadn't been this out of shape since she'd first arrived at the reev. The high walls of the gymnasium blocked any wind from blowing, refusing her any relief.

Her hands dug into her knees as she bent in half against the stitch forming in her side. "Is that what they're implying? That I'm a demi-goddess?"

She and Ash righted themselves from where they'd been doubled over and walked across the ring to a wooden barrel of fresh water. The pair had no cups, so they opened the spigot directly into their mouths, drinking deeply as the tiny waterfall quenched their thirst. Amaris let the small stream run over her face and into her hair, savoring the cool shock of water.

Ash swallowed before nodding. "What else would you be?"

Her breath found its equilibrium, heart rate slowing once more, but her mind had found no relief. "A goddess damned orphan with no home and no plan."

"You have a home, Ayla."

He motioned for them to abandon the training grounds, and they did.

They exchanged plans to meet for daily training but had been too taxed and absorbed in conversation to pay careful attention to where their feet had carried them. Every turn, every corridor looked the same. By the time they came upon a circular staircase, she knew they were in the wrong area, but curiosity and a lack of anything better to do got the better of her. "What do you think? Up or down?"

He shrugged, the pink of his exercise slowly leaving his features as they walked. Their sweat had almost completely cooled by now. "Princesses are usually in towers, treasures are typically in vaults."

"Well, I have no use for a princess. Down it is."

The stairs curved in a spiral of identical stone stacked atop one another, each as gemlike as the ones around it. They followed their curiosity down several flights of stairs and through a narrow hallway. They seemed to realize where they were at roughly the same time as the underground room opened and iron bars lined the sides. The atmosphere changed, heavy with secrets. Amaris could practically taste the flavor of something forbidden the moment her feet hit the landing.

They had found their way into the dungeon.

The room flickered with firelight, which told her that someone must be regularly keeping up with these cells, despite how empty the castle had appeared. Fae lights could be left unattended. Torches had to be replaced.

"There's nothing for us down here," Ash said quietly.

Amaris nudged him in response, gesturing to the corner cell. While many bars were the dull, matte black of iron enclosing empty chambers, the cell in the corner shimmered faintly in the dim flames. Ash trailed slightly behind her as she approached the cage. She thought of the university and its hordes of well-kept treasures as she eyed the rune-etched bars that sparkled with whatever magic had activated them.

The need for runes was immediately apparent.

Amaris looked right into the eyes of the foxlike fae who could conjure monsters.

Seated on the ground with her back to the far wall, the prisoner tilted her chin upward as if in quiet, defiant strength as Amaris approached. The once-red tunic she wore was now brown with the grime and filth from her time in captivity. Amaris sized up the enemy, from her arched ears and her angular, beautiful face to her tiny stature. There was a gild about her skin, somehow both similar to and entirely separate from that of the fae of Raascot. She looked back at Amaris with dark, almond eyes.

Amaris had heard some in the castle whisper about how the prisoner might be from the Sulgrave Mountains and tried to picture a life beyond the Frozen Straits.

Ash and Amaris exchanged uncertain glances. She supposed a rational person would have left, but Amaris hadn't been feeling particularly rational as of late. The girl's sentencing would have been the king's problem, but Raascot was without a king. Perhaps a reever would suffice.

"Who are you?" Amaris asked.

The prisoner narrowed her eyes slightly. "I'll tell you who I am if you tell me what you are."

Amaris blinked with no attempt to conceal her surprise and felt the small, semi-startled step at her side as Ash did the same. As far as they knew, the prisoner hadn't spoken to anyone before this moment. Amaris's ears itched at the unfamiliar curve to the woman's consonants and vowels. There was a musical lilt to the way she spoke, though it was the common tongue.

Amaris opened her mouth as if to reply, but the prisoner stopped her. "But not with the mongrel present."

Amaris looked between the three of them. She followed the prisoner's glare toward the other reever. "Who, Ash?"

"For fuck's sake" came Ash's low disgusted reply.

In a silent exchange, Amaris made a vague, apologetic gesture in an attempt to communicate that no matter how bizarre her interaction, it was useful to get the prisoner speaking. The skin by Ash's eyes went taut. With controlled anger, he made a parting comment about waiting for her in his rooms, leaving Amaris alone with the most dangerous fae on the continent.

Chapter Twelve

W HILE AMARIS NEITHER APPRECIATED NOR UNDERSTOOD the prisoner's insult, she didn't exactly expect manners from someone who'd summoned mud demons to slaughter an entire encampment.

The scrape of shoes against floor and the rhythmic noise of steps grew fainter and fainter until they were alone.

"You have your wish. I'm Amaris. What's your name?"

The prisoner was shackled by both her wrists and her ankles. The engraved manacles shimmered just like the rune-etched iron bars between them as she gestured toward her chest.

"Tanith."

"Hi, Tanith." Amaris knelt so she might face the prisoner at eye level.

The prisoner spoke again, her voice jarringly light and sweet in contrast with how dark and terrible her power had been. "I've held up my end of the bargain: who I am, in exchange for what you are. You are neither human nor fae."

It was not worded as a question. Tanith arched a brow expectantly.

Amaris chewed on her words for a moment before opting

for honesty. "Would you believe me if I told you that I don't truly know? There are theories as to what I am that have only recently been disclosed to me, but they're too bizarre to hold truth."

The sweat from her run had fully cooled, leaving her clothes damp and chilly in the dark, underground dungeon. Gooseflesh pimpled her skin and she frowned. If she was already cold, she couldn't imagine how the small fae had been here for days with neither cloak nor blanket. She opened her mouth to ask Tanith about it, but the fae spoke again.

"Go on."

She sucked in a breath as she considered her options.

The first thought was that it was unwise to speak to a deadly stranger and that she should end the conversation now. The second was that Nox was the only person she had wanted to speak to, yet not only had Nox hidden her own identity, she had thrown her out of her room and rejected her only one night prior. The final thought was that it was so often easier to speak to strangers who held no bias than it was to talk to those who truly knew you.

"I've been told I'm a prayer brought to life," Amaris said.

Tanith's brows pinched. There was impatience in her voice as she corrected Amaris. "Any woman can pray for a child when she is infertile, and you would be a prayer brought to life. This is not what you are. Fulfill your end of the bargain and tell me."

Amaris saw an opportunity and took it. "Would you expand upon our bargain?"

Tanith seemed unamused by the negotiation. She pursed her lips. Her eyes scanned the empty rocks and stones of her cell before she answered. "You have the advantage, as I don't have much else to entertain me. Let me hear what you're offering."

Amaris agreed. "I'll tell you everything I know about myself, and you tell me not only who you are but why you're here and what you were doing with the vakliche."

"The vakliche?" Tanith repeated. "Is that your word for the mud demons?"

Amaris nodded.

The distant ghost of a smile flickered behind Tanith's eyes. "You'll tell me everything?"

Amaris dipped her chin. "I'm afraid you won't get anything from me regarding the continent, but I don't see the harm in telling you about myself, if you promise to do the same."

"I swear it."

Amaris settled fully onto the floor as she readied herself for a long tale—one she was not used to telling. She described being raised in an orphanage, the food, the matrons, the children. She told the tale of escaping a purchasing claim and running off to train with the reevers. Tanith inclined her head with particular interest when Amaris reached the part of her tale where the mad king told her that she was some tool for the goddess's vengeance. She explained how she'd written the statement off as lunacy until Nox spoke to her of the dream. As Amaris talked, the choking, weighted noose around her neck began to loosen, freeing her from a heaviness she hadn't realized she'd been carrying.

"A demi-goddess?" Tanith smiled. "I am honored to be in your presence."

"Why?"

Tanith tilted her head, her dark, shoulder-length hair cascading to the side. "What purer magic exists?"

Amaris looked away. "It's your turn."

With the wooden confidence that came from familiar repetition, Tanith said, "I am an agent of purity in the same way that you are an arm of the goddess. I honor magic and its sanctity in a way that Raascot and Farehold have not for nearly one thousand years."

Amaris frowned. "You murdered all of those people in the name of...magical purity?"

Tanith's head had already been cocked to one side. Like

a curious cat, she deepened her tilt. It was as if she were not interested in the question itself so much as why a demi-goddess might be asking it. "Any pure fae would have easily been able to fly from the gully."

Amaris's lips tugged downward.

Tanith's chains sparkled, magical charge coursing through them as she waved a hand. "The All Mother's problem is the scourge that has divided the continent. The pure fae of Sulgrave have been alienated—preserved—against the chaos and dilution of the southern kingdoms."

Stiffly, Amaris said, "Your problem is with humans."

With a tired sigh, Tanith said, "Humans have no business fighting with or under a fae king, nor should they be inter-mingling and breeding with fae lovers. I have no quarrel with humans if they remain amongst their own. Though other purists might prefer that the scourge be eradicated altogether."

"The scourge being humanity?"

"Why do you ask such questions, demi-goddess?"

She grimaced. "Don't call me that. I don't identify with the All Mother or her supposed role in my life. I'm just asking what kind of hate would drive you to slaughter."

"Hate?" Tanith asked.

Amaris's stomach twisted. "You murdered countless men and women."

The fae frowned. She looked at Amaris with gentle curios-ity. Amaris watched her chew the thought before responding. "Does a doctor hate influenza? Does a physician hate weak hearts or the fever spots that spread in close quarters? Or do the healers and medicine men identify a natural disaster and take steps to eradicate and prevent the virus from spreading?"

Amaris struggled through the analogy. "Humans are a virus?"

Tanith seemed to smile this time, a real smile. "Magic is blood, demi-goddess. Humans are antibodies, diluting the magic that the goddess has granted our world as they fight against it each time they breed. They are a vaccination, creating insusceptibility to magic every time they reproduce with the fae. Don't you see it? It's divided the continent. Weakened it. Worsened it. How can you want to live in a world like this?"

Amaris's heart skipped at the revelation. She had gained more motive, background, and information from the prisoner than Gadriel, his fae second in command, or her reever brothers had since they'd taken Tanith captive.

Whether or not she believed in her birth as it had been revealed, it had opened the invaluable doors that led to her speaking to the bloodthirsty zealot in their dungeons. Amaris had trained to fight monsters but had developed an idea as to what villains looked like. Tanith was small, and pretty, and spoke with the gentle calm of a lady, yet she'd bound river demons to her and commanded them to annihilate men and women of Raascot she'd deemed tainted. Her insult to Ash made sudden sense. Tanith considered his mixed, faeling blood to be an abomination.

"Why are you telling me all of this?" Amaris asked.

Tanith's brows puckered as if once again confused by Amaris's question. "Why would I hide the good message? Why would the All Mother want me to conceal her vision for unity?"

"You're wrong," Amaris said coolly, getting to her feet.

"You may visit me again, demi-goddess. You will see things my way," the prisoner called out after her in her sweet, musical voice.

✦

Amaris didn't look over her shoulder as she ascended the stairs and walked numbly down the hall. It took her a few twists and turns before the midnight-hued passages became familiar. The dark-blue halls were palatial with their high ceilings, the windows large as they showcased the mountainous views of Raascot beyond their glass. Gwydir was the loveliest place she'd ever seen, but she was numb to its beauty. She passed her rooms and navigated her way beyond the throne room to the windowless war room at the castle's heart. It was a gamble, but she had a hunch about who she might find there. She opened the door without knocking.

Gadriel looked up, surprise scrawled across his face. His weight rested on his hands as he stood, leaning over the map that overtook the table's center.

She had refused to speak to him or even look at him in the moments following the massacre. She hadn't missed his concerned glances, but he'd been wise to keep his mouth shut. The last time they'd exchanged words, he'd barely looked in her direction as he'd been begging Ceres to hear of his heir. The time before that, she'd been naked in his bed, draped in his arms. So much had changed. Maybe he knew her well enough to understand she wouldn't have listened if he'd made any attempts to explain himself.

Good.

"Amaris." He blinked through her name. Pain was as evident in his expression as was the unexpectedness of her arrival. She believed in the validity of his unseen wounds, and she didn't care. She'd erected a palace of stone and ice with walls as thick as those of Gwydir around what had been her feelings and affections for the general.

"I spoke with your prisoner."

Several moments passed between them. His voice was low when he responded. "And?"

She answered as if giving a report at Uaimh Reev to Samael. "Her name is Tanith. She's a magical purist. I believe she belongs to a religious organization from Sulgrave from the way she spoke of the All Mother. She made it sound like she isn't alone in the desire to eradicate not only humans but those who intermarry and reproduce. Sullying magic, or something like that. Honestly, even the sympathizers, such as any man who lived or fought beside the impure, appear to be in her war path. Tanith said that any true Raascot fae would have been able to fly away from the massacre, but I don't think this is a problem specific to Raascot. That's all I've learned."

Amaris turned to walk away without waiting for his reaction. She had relayed the information to the general and had completed any obligation required of her.

"Wait." His command was swift. She disregarded it, her back to him as she left the doorway and strode into the hall.

He had already navigated around the table and was closing the space between them with the speed and agility famous to the fae. He reached as if to pull her back into the war room. She kept her face unreadable as he eyed her. "Amaris, talk to me."

"I did."

His hand tightened around her arm, and his words were decidedly un-general-like. For a moment, he was simply a man pleading with a girl, though he stretched his tone to remain as strong and emotionless as he could feign. His coal-dark eyes and too-large irises bore down into her. "Please, speak to me. I never meant to hurt you. I've done everything I can since the moment you were taken—"

She swung her arm to shake him off, but his grip became a shackle. Anger heated her. She bared her teeth.

His military training may have been what kept his tone even and calm, but she didn't miss the faint edges of his words colored with a feeling that may have resembled desperation. "Please talk to me. You built a wall once before when we were at the university, and we found our way back to each other. Talk to me, and we can fix this."

Amaris made another jerking motion, but when he didn't release her, she met his dark, pleading expression with fury as she said a single, icy word.

"Snowbird."

Gadriel's grip slackened and he released her, freezing where he stood, as she turned her back and walked away.

Chapter Thirteen

Amaris was so lost to her fury that she collided into Yazlyn as the winged sergeant attempted—and failed—to slip out of Nox's room undetected. With a flutter of dark feathers, they untangled themselves, each taking a stumbling, backward step. A pained silence clouded them as Amaris wrinkled her nose at the sergeant. She forced herself to make a terse gesture of acknowledgment, but neither could bring themselves to speak.

Yazlyn muttered something that may have been excuses or apologies as she stepped around Amaris, leaving the door to Nox's room ajar. Coming off her unsettling exchange with the prisoner and freshly unnerved from her encounter with Gadriel, she gritted her teeth and stepped into Nox's room. The run-in with the sergeant had been one insult too many.

Her eyes widened. She shook her head, half apology, half confusion upon finding Nox's nude shape draped lazily on her bed.

"Goddess damn it, Nox, should I come back later?"

Nox's shrug was one of casual disinterest. She relaxed into the headboard, making no movements to tug at the sheets. Amaris's face heated. It wasn't that she'd never thought of

Nox unclothed. Her thoughts had wandered into shadowed corners of curiosity and want on more than one occasion, particularly after the kiss they'd shared in the town house, though it had ended fully clothed, with little more than deep, unsatiated wants. She'd missed Nox in more ways than she could articulate, from the comfort her presence to the soft touch of her skin. This was not how she'd hoped to see Nox naked. She forced her eyes from bare skin to the bed, sheets draped over one leg, hardly concealing the space between her legs.

"Why are you here?" Nox asked, question dry with disinterest.

In nearly two decades on this earth, Amaris had never known Nox to be cruel. There was a challenge in her eyes that dared Amaris to instigate a fight like she had the night before. The ascending queen was making a statement, and the message was loud and clear.

One's life was said to flash before their eyes before they passed. Maybe it was true at the death of an era too. She pictured Nox's worried face as she examined Amaris for scraped hands or knees. She saw the pretty rocks they'd gathered by the pond and the stolen laughs they'd shared when whispering about the Matrons. They'd held each other through thunderstorms and seasons of sickness and fears over the future.

Nox had always been beautiful, that was a given. It was her wisdom, her patience, her fortitude that had anchored them. She's been an unwavering constant for Amaris. Their moments in the dungeons of Aubade, their night together in the town house, had illuminated the barest outline of their years apart. Nox had crossed continents to find her, ensnared guards to rescue her, and trekked north of their kingdom to be reunited. Whatever had happened between her apple-laced dream and their fight had broken a tether that Amaris hadn't recognized until it snapped.

"Would you at least make an attempt to cover up?"

Nox sighed with dramatic disappointment and left the bed, stepping into a dressing gown. "I didn't take you for such a priss. Then again, what would I know? After all, I've been whoring my way through Farehold."

Amaris made a small, anguished noise as she finally dared to look into Nox's eyes. Her glare held no glimmer of forgiveness.

"Nox, I know I said some things last night—"

Nox scoffed.

"I really need some understanding right now."

Unwavering, Nox said, "You need some understanding? You spent your entire life knowing you were cherished, loved, and set apart. I protected you, Amaris. Who looked out for me? Who watched my back? That bitch of a Gray Matron did more to guard me than you ever have."

Amaris pressed her fingertips into the soft skin of her temple, forcing down the bubble of confusion and hurt. She fought the urge to snap over the freshly sexed Yazlyn, who'd collided into her in the hall. It should have been *her* stumbling, mussed hair, flushed cheeks, from Nox's room. Amaris chewed her lip until she felt like she could control her tone. Fists flexed at her side, her nails offered a grounding sting as they bit into her palm.

"Nox, you discovered you were a princess—sorry, a *queen* if I'm not mistaken. Forgive me, but I'm having trouble empathizing with how hard it is to learn that you're the sole heir to not one but two kingdoms."

Without missing a beat, Nox said, "Coming from the divine prayer herself."

Amaris was aghast. "My revelation left me with nothing! I have never had a family. I've had one person my entire life—*one*—who I've always loved, who I've always counted on, who used the heritage that I knew nothing about against me. You've taken this knowledge, even though it changed nothing about who I am and what I feel, and wielded it as a weapon."

Unruffled, Nox said, "Did you come here to fight? Because honestly, I woke up in a pretty good mood and would prefer that you take your energy elsewhere."

Amaris couldn't help herself. "You're having a good day because you just fucked someone? That's great, Nox. I suppose it would make someone like *you* feel better. Do you want to hear what I learned from Ash? Apparently, the person I've known for my entire life is a succubus. Not just any succubus: a powerful, dangerous one at that. Do you want to explain how you kept this from me?"

Nox examined her cuticles. She remained impassive as she said, "If you're just here to yell, I'd prefer that you save it for another time. I'm not in the mood."

Amaris's shoulders slackened. It was like being in the ring all over again, except she had no idea how to handle her opponent. All she wanted was the safety and love she had known mere days before.

Amaris had done nothing, yet the world around her had changed. She didn't want this. She squeezed her eyes shut to halt any emotion, fighting against the wound that threatened to rally her temper. She just wanted things to go back to the way they were.

"I'm sorry," Amaris whispered. "I'm not here to fight. Will you talk to me?"

Nox deflated ever so slightly. She returned to her bed, crossing her arms as she reclined against her pillows. Cracks shone through her hardened exterior as she fixed her sights onto the rumpled comforter that remained in a discarded bundle at the foot of the bed.

Amaris approached the corner of the four-poster bed but didn't dare sit. An alarm bell rang in the distant corners of her mind, warning her that the chains that contained her boxed emotions would break at any moment. She couldn't swallow down the beast and its horrid tentacles for much longer.

"I just don't understand how things have changed," Amaris said through choked emotions. "Even if I am some product of prayer, it would have always been the case, right? It would have been true when we were five, and ten, and fifteen. Why should a new piece of information color a lifetime?"

Nox was quiet. Distant sadness seeped into her bitterness as she said, "I was struggling with the revelation even when I met you at the reevers' town house at the edge of Gwydir. I tried to tell you what had been plaguing me that night. Seeing you again, holding you, it was overwhelming in the best way. But…"

Amaris motioned to interject, but Nox spoke over her before she had the chance.

"Then you made it perfectly clear what you thought of me."

Her feet planted firmly in a warrior's stance, fight filled her once more as Amaris corrected, "I tried to bridge the gap so we could be together."

"Is that all?" Nox laughed.

"Nox…"

Her glossy hair danced around her shoulders as she shook her head. "I've been clinging to a fantasy. I wrapped my fingers around a vision of how things could have been between us and held it so tightly that I didn't stop to consider if it was you and us that I loved and missed or if I've spent the last few years mourning an invention of my own imagination."

"That's not fair," Amaris said shakily. She couldn't wholly comprehend Nox's anger. Her journey to understanding her own heart had been slower than Nox's. Her path to understanding was being punished, and she didn't know why.

"I agree," Nox said. "It isn't fair that I took the fall for you and went to Priory. And it sure as hell isn't fair that you would use that against me."

Tremors claimed Amaris's hands, causing her words to wobble as she spoke through the threat of tears. "I didn't know, Nox. I couldn't have known what would happen when I ran."

"And I never held my fate against you," Nox said quietly. She bit her lip as she looked out her window. Amaris cast a glance to the glass, to the dark river that surrounded the castle, to the stone city sparkling in the distance, but she knew Nox looked at nothing in particular. She was looking away, not toward.

"I love you."

Amaris rested her forehead against the post. Rejection loomed like an impending storm, but she had to speak her truth, regardless of what it cost her. She opened her eyes just long enough to see Nox pull a pillow to herself, soothing whatever need for a hug she might be feeling. If this had been any other time in their life, Nox would have raised her arm and Amaris would have tucked herself into the gap, a puzzle seeking its missing piece.

"I wish I could believe you," Nox said. "I just can't see how any of it is real anymore. I've tried to accept whatever brought you into this world, but I can't move past it. If it's true—if you really were born to break some curse directly tied to me—I don't see how I can ever know if what we feel is real or if it's just a tie that fate needed us to feel. That I was meant to take your place at the Selkie all along. Especially now that I know what I..." She looked at her hands, rolling a pinch of the bedding fabric between her fingers. Amaris understood what Nox wouldn't say, and it pained her. She opened her mouth for rebuttal before Nox said, "Was it love that tethered us, or were we pawns of destiny?"

Oncoming tears strangled Amaris with barbed wire. "Why didn't you tell me what you are? It seems I might be the only person in this castle who didn't know. Why did you hide that from me?"

Nox focused intently on a distant point beyond the glass pane, deep within the city of Gwydir. "I didn't know until I was in Priory. And as it stands, I don't see that it's any of your business."

Amaris hadn't even realized her fingers had begun anxiously twisting the fabric of her shirt. She couldn't look at Nox. She couldn't look around the room, at the desk, at the rug, at the northern lights caught in the blue-black walls or the crackling fireplace. She fixated on the small twists and turns of her thumb and forefinger as they pressed into her shirt, pulling its threads between her fingers. She examined the hurt and pain that stretched between them and could see only one spark of light at the end of the tunnel, glowing as the lone solution.

Amaris slowly released her shirt and breathed out a slow, steadying breath. She leveled her purple gaze to Nox's dark eyes. "I guess the only way for us to know if it's really love will be after I break the curse."

✦

The declaration sent the resolution from Nox's lungs.

She opened her mouth to say something, anything, but a flash of pearly white glimmered on whatever remained of the light as Amaris disappeared from the room, closing the door behind her.

Everything she'd bottled uncorked. She buried her face in her pillow, wetting the fabric as she rocked into it with tears of outrage and fragmented dreams. All she had ever wanted was for Amaris to return the love she'd freely given. Now the very thing she'd prayed for so many years was within arm's reach, and she couldn't accept it.

What if Amaris broke the curse? Would the tether be released?

She knew better than to ask fruitless rhetoricals and cursed herself for wasting another moment on what-ifs. This wasn't something that would break and be set free. This was something she wanted to carve out of her chest, plopping the wet, parasitic hope on the table and being free of it at last.

She'd lose her mind if she stayed in her room.

Barefoot and in little more than her robe, Nox stumbled from her bed and down the hallway toward the kitchen. If there was ever a time for a stiff drink, it was now.

Nox would have had no trouble barging into the kitchen

at the Selkie at all hours of the night or day. She'd never been one to be intimidated. But she was in an entirely new environment, and given the royal blood pumping through her, she felt pressure to make a good impression on the Raascot citizens working around the castle.

She'd do her best to mitigate the damage. But first, alcohol.

She hadn't had the opportunity to get to know any attendants or staff at Gwydir Castle, and the feeling of stepping in on people who didn't know her raked her with further guilt. She did her best to introduce herself to the startled cook, but when Nox asked for a bottle of wine, the middle-aged human woman seemed to sense the edges of pain that dictated the request. Nox did her best to introduce herself as the woman fetched two bottles of their finest red. Nox waved away the effort to give her glasses to accompany the green bottles. She had no need for them. All she needed was a corkscrew.

She tucked one bottle under her arm, walking and twisting as she navigated the way back to her room on little more than muscle memory. She abandoned the cork on the rug and took her first several gulps of the spiced, robust wine. Pain pulled her forward like a leash, guiding her to her bedroom door as tears blurred her vision. She kissed the bottle again and again before she made it to the safety of her room.

A loud gasp known only to the drowning escaped her as she came up for air, then polished off the rest of the bottle as she crawled beneath the sheets.

"Come on, come on!" she grunted at the second bottle as she struggled with the cork. It crumbled under the pressure of her urgency, breaking before she'd accessed the second store of delicious, numbing medicine. "Fuck!"

She threw the bottle onto the bed a little too forcefully. It rolled to the corner, stopping on the bedpost just before smashing onto the floor.

She'd been an orphan, a whore, a no one. At least in Farleigh, she knew friend from foe. At least at the Selkie, she was valued for what she was. At least before she'd bitten into that goddess damned apple, she'd always had Amaris.

She wasn't an orphan any longer. She wasn't in a brothel. She didn't have Amaris.

Malik had claimed to love and care for her regardless of what she was or what she offered, but how could she believe anything he said when his human blood whisked him under whatever spell she cast? The fae among her were predisposed to treat her with reverence now that they knew who her father was. For the first time in her life, she was wholly and inconsolably alone.

Chapter Fourteen

Nox cracked open a single, unwilling eye. Despite the groggy dredges of sleep that clung to her, she knew she had survived until morning. There was just enough ambient gloom to discern the rectangle separating her from whoever was rapping on the door. She opened her mouth to speak, smacking her lips against the way her tongue stuck to the roof of her mouth. She winced at the ice-pick headache piercing her right temple.

"Go away."

Malik's voice called through the door. "Hey, you alive in there?"

"I'm asleep." She buried her face in the pillow, glad her curtains were shut against the sun that lit the kingdom. She didn't want light, or company, or—

"I've brought tea and muffins."

She perked slightly, tilting her face toward the door.

"I'm coming in," he said. He didn't wait for an answer.

She jammed her face back in the pillow, seeking reprieve like a rabbit scurrying back into its hole.

Malik left the door open. She listened to the clang of dishes and cutlery on the desk and the scuffle of feet as he crossed the room to open her curtains. She groaned as the warmth of daylight hit her back.

"Everyone in the castle knows what I am," she said, words muffled as she spoke into the pillow. "So it seems like a good time to inform you: succubi are allergic to daylight."

He placed a warm, heavy hand on her shoulder and shook her gently. "Get up before your tea gets cold."

She shook her head.

"Fine," he said in a sing-song voice as he shoved away from the bed "Then I guess I'll have to drink the tea myself."

Nox pushed herself up slowly. She rubbed her eyes. "Leave the tea and no one gets hurt."

He smiled patiently and scooped up the cup. "Do you want to talk?"

She accepted the warm mug and took a sip. It wet her mouth, warmed her throat, and hugged her from the inside out. She wished she could relax, but all she wanted was to go back to bed. She looked mutely into the middle distance as she sipped her tea.

After a prolonged silence, Malik asked, "Do you want me to get Amaris?"

"Absolutely not."

He shuffled his weight from one foot to the other. "Is there anything I could do? Anything at all?"

Nox stiffened as she weighed his words. She wondered if she was reading more into them than he meant to imply. She finished the rest of her tea in one gulp and held the cup out to Malik. "Can you ask Ash if he would speak with me? And, when he comes, if he could bring more tea?"

Malik's brows lifted in surprise. He didn't look hurt, per se, and she understood why he might be confused. He eyed her for a moment before obliging. Leaving the empty teacup and muffins, he disappeared into the hall. Seconds became minutes became the better part of an hour. It was long enough for Nox to settle back into the bed and let the warmth of sleep wrap itself around her, lulling her into escape once more. She

157

was dipping her toes into the delicious sensation of waking up too early and falling asleep once again when a voice broke through her heavily weighted eyelids.

Ash knocked lightly on the open door, pausing at her threshold before entering.

"Nox?"

She regretted allowing herself the comfort of falling back to sleep, as she felt eminently worse off than she had before. The near-sleep amplified her hangover and made it nearly impossible to sit up in bed. She stacked the pillows behind her back, leaving her hair askew, not caring about the crease marks of sleep as she greeted him. She extended her hands for the teacup and saw that he held one for her and one for himself. She lost herself in her cup of tea, vaguely aware of how he fetched the muffins from the desk and perched gingerly on the edge of the bed.

"What time is it?" she asked between swallows of over-steeped tea. This pot was far too bitter. She wrinkled her nose but continued to sip at it out of sheer habit.

"Just past the one o'clock bell," he answered, voice heavy with skepticism. He passed her the muffin, and she accepted it. "I'm going to be honest, Nox. I don't fully understand why I'm here."

She was grateful for the pastry as she set down her tea. It gave her something to do with her nervous energy. It was filled with apples and crumbles, and the stickiness of its fruits and honey was uncomfortable against the tips of her fingers.

"You're here because I think you might be the only person in this castle I can trust."

She looked up at him long enough to see how he slumped against the farthest post of her bed, his face arranged in puzzlement.

She echoed the expression on his face with a small, humorless laugh as if she could read his thoughts. "I under-stand your confusion. I know how it must sound. Would you sit with me for a minute? I promise: I have no intentions of seducing you. In fact, that's part of why I think you're the only one I can talk to."

Ash nodded, though his lips remained twisted in a frown.

"I know you don't approve of the relationship between Malik and me, and I don't blame you. I don't think I can be trusted around any human male, which is part of why I can't speak to him about this. When it comes to Zaccai, Yazlyn, and Gadriel, they're duty-bound to listen to me by whatever unintelligible ties to royalty they feel legally bound. Amaris—"

She stumbled over the name and paused to pick at her muffin, bringing one crumb at a time to her mouth. She chewed on a small chunk of the baked apple while swallowing the pain that came to her by speaking the girl's name. "Amaris and her origin are an entirely separate issue I'm trying to work through. But it's why I don't know if anything she tells me or feels for me can be trusted."

Ash reiterated, "So you're talking to me because I have no loyalty to you. I'm not fully human, and I was born of no prayer to help you. You think I'm the only person who isn't obligated to like you."

Nox nodded slowly. She selected another crumb, nibbling at the food despite the cramping of protest in her gut. "You've spent enough time with me to know me, while remaining a true neutral."

Ash sank into the bed post more fully, relaxing as he asked, "What did you want to talk about?"

Her laugh mingled with a sigh. "I'm not sure. I wish it were so clear that I could just ask you a question and trust your affirmative or negative, but things are muddier than that. I have these Raascot fae who've brought me to their castle just because I'm supposed to be the bastard child of their king who didn't know I existed until moments before he died. I've loved Amaris from the moment I met her, but I don't feel like she's even attempting to be empathetic about why this is difficult for me."

He pushed back. "Why being a princess is difficult for you? Wait, I'm sorry, are you queen now? I've lost track."

She was exasperated for a moment before reeling her feelings inward. "Ash, do you know how deeply I've loved her? I attempted to single-handedly amass an army to march north and rescue her. I'd believed..." She laughed as she looked at him, remembering what she'd once thought of the league of assassins. Millicent had so cleverly woven truth with lie. Nox shook it off, deciding against going into the grit of her hatred for reevers. She went on. "I learned Amaris was not only in the castle in Aubade but traveling with reevers of her own volition. My life, my choices, my paths have all revolved around my feelings for her. Do you understand how jarring that is? How disorienting it might be to realize that the person who'd shaped your life isn't a human, or a fae, but some tool for a destiny to which you didn't agree? I feel as though all my life's choices were predetermined. I feel like it's just another in a long line of things attempting to rob me of agency."

He chewed on this. "Couldn't that be comforting?"

She balked. "Excuse me?"

He made a dismissive gesture. "I can only speak for myself, but the idea of someone being constructed for me as I was molded for them is unspeakably beautiful. It seems like the kind of blessing no one in the history of the continent has had the chance to experience. You might be the luckiest woman on the goddess's earth."

The air was knocked from her lungs, leaving her lips parted in a gape.

He amended, "I'm just saying how I would feel in your shoes. I'm sure what you're feeling is valid. You're wondering if anyone loves you for who you are, or if they only feel the way you do because of your power. With the fae, it's a power of monarchy. With Malik, it's the succubi power. With Amaris, well, who knows exactly what's going on there."

Her handful of crumbles fell into her lap, shoulders slumping as she frowned at him.

Ash laughed to himself before saying, "I appreciate you

talking to me, if only so I could have the chance to tell you to your face that you're pretty damn great. You're capable, you're clever, you're loyal, and you're unarguably cool. You took a hatchet to a spider demon without any training. You saved Malik's life. And that's coming from me, who has no interest in serving under you or sleeping with you." He chuckled before waving away some preempted insult. "You're beautiful. I just value my own life too much to get tangled up in whatever you have going on in there. That being said, I do think you could use more practice time in the ring and that you're acting more than a little ungrateful."

She was so taken aback that she wasn't sure what to latch onto first. She echoed his final word. "Ungrateful?"

He seemed bigger—more commanding, somehow—as he folded his arms over his broad chest. He relaxed into the bedpost and arched a brow. "You have the opportunity to steer nations. If you've ever had any ideals as to how the continent should be run, this is the time to seize that opportunity. You could change people's lives for the better. I know you didn't ask for any of this, but it's on your shoulders now."

She reeled from his scolding as he got to his feet. He'd nearly made it to the door before she asked, "What of Malik?"

The faeling's lips turned down. "Do you care about him?"

She chewed her lip. "I don't have any intentions of hurting him."

His frown deepened as he abandoned his movement for the door. "Sometimes intentions aren't good enough. Do you feel like he truly understands what he's getting himself into?"

She swallowed down the urge to react defensively. She'd asked him here for this reason. The least she could do was trust his council. "I do. He knows what I am, who I love, and our limitations. I've made no advances on him."

Ash's brows puckered thoughtfully as he leaned against the doorframe. "Perhaps I underestimated the two of you. I'm invested in keeping Malik alive. But at the end of the day, it's none of my business."

She watched the empty doorway for a while after he departed. Ash's presence hadn't totally soothed her, nor did his absence wound her.

The way she saw it, she had precisely two options. The first was to ignore his advice and paint all of his words in the color of her own self-doubt, dismissing whatever assurances he'd offered. The other was to trust that he was telling her the truth, that she was worthy of whatever affections and relationships she'd received. Ultimately, she was the only one who could shape her reality into belief or disbelief.

She'd already wasted half the day and managed to turn her bed into a patisserie floor by scattering crumbs throughout the sheets. At the Selkie, the girls who worked behind the bar were responsible for changing the bed and tidying the house. In Farleigh, the children were assigned chores. She was sure that someone would come along and fix the bed, but she began tugging the sheets loose to leave them in a half-helpful pile atop the mattress just in case.

She'd nearly finished when a kindly fae woman poked her head in the door. Her hair had been piled in securely woven braids atop her head. If she hadn't possessed the loveliness of the fae and the features of the north, her attire, hair, and demeanor might have reminded Nox of Matron Mable.

"Your Highness," she said, eyes wide, "you needn't do that."

Nox smiled apologetically. "I'm not really sure what to do with myself," she said honestly. "I was just going to draw a bath…"

"Please," said the fae, eyes wide, "for the love of the goddess, let me do that for you." She disappeared through the suite into the bathing room.

Nox trailed behind her. "I'm Nox," she said.

The fae looked over her shoulder, hands busy with her task. "I know who you are, Your Majesty," she said with a bow.

Nox fidgeted. She'd hoped the attendant would provide her name as well, but she didn't want to force anything unnatural.

The servant didn't look up this time as she said, "Several of us will attend to you, and you're 'Your Highness.' We're not as formal as the southern courts up here, but you'll still be hard-pressed to get any of the attendants to refer to you as Nox."

"Oh," Nox hedged, "I'm not...I wasn't a part of the courts."

"No matter." The attendant gestured for the bath. "You're in your kingdom now. I'll get you some fresh bedding and lay something out for you on the bed." She startled Nox when she squeezed her shoulder as she passed. She held her eyes for a moment, sucking in a rallying breath before saying, "And for what it's worth, we're all very glad to have you."

She was relieved the attendant closed the door behind her so she could be by herself. She'd need some time to make sense of the million ways in which her life had changed.

By that evening Nox had bathed, dressed, and done her best to amend her attitude. Whatever had happened in the past was not to alter whatever happened moving forward. She would regard Amaris with neither the love nor the bitterness she'd cultivated and instead receive her, along with the fae and the reevers, with a new openness.

The collection of reevers and fae shared raised eyebrows and looks of surprise when she turned up at dinner.

She was equally surprised to find that everyone else, regardless of their disdain for one another, had made it to the dinner table at roughly the same time. Gadriel and Amaris appeared to be sitting as far from one another as possible. Yazlyn made room for her at the table, but Nox ignored the others to sit closest to Ash and Zaccai. Ash smiled into his potatoes as if they were the lone recipient of their private joke as the attendants dished up their plates. The cook had recognized Nox and had an additional bottle of wine sent out for her, accompanied by a wink and an encouraging thumb as the doors between the dining room and the kitchen swung shut. Nox forced the budding smile into a flat line and poured a very generous helping of wine for herself.

"So," Nox said over the polite if a bit tense conversation that was being attempted amidst the dinner table, "what do we do next? Gadriel, take it away."

The general's mouth parted. Nox lifted her wine glass and waited expectantly. Perhaps it was neither the time nor the place, but she'd been informed multiple times in the past twenty-four hours that she was queen. She may as well act like it.

Gadriel cleared his throat. "Amaris was able to speak to the prisoner this afternoon."

The clatter of forks and knives stilled as everyone looked up at him. No one so much as chewed as they waited for the general to continue.

He straightened his shoulders. "Our captive is a Sulgrave fae on some purity mission, and from the sounds of it, she isn't alone. I don't think the monsters in the north are an isolated incident. If this intelligence is correct, Farehold is no safer."

Nox considered the information. "Maybe so. But we can't very well protect Farehold while they still perceive Raascot fae as ag'imni, or while Moirai's on the throne."

Yazlyn propped an elbow onto the back of her chair. She reclined as she said, "It's been a thousand years since the last time a fae reigned in Aubade. Farehold and Raascot had intended to unite under one banner. I think we're long overdue for a reunion party. What do you say, Nox? Can your ass fit onto two thrones?"

Caught between agitation at Yazlyn's nonchalance and appreciation at her ability to act like nothing had changed between them, Nox made a face and lifted a shoulder with as much nonchalance as she could manage. "Honestly, at this point, ask me to juggle fire and speak to cattle. If this is what's in front of us, then this is what we'll tackle."

Gadriel appeared to be doing his best to fight down a grin. She wasn't sure if he was amused, or if his heart was genuinely warmed, though she hoped for the latter. After all, the man who'd fathered her had been mad. His shoes may not be too difficult to fill.

"I have a question," Zaccai said, chewing his food. "Why did the prisoner speak to you?"

Amaris swallowed her mouthful of food. "Well, her name is Tanith, and apparently I'm the most magical being among all of you as I'm a direct descendant of the goddess. I'll be accepting your prayers and gifts of offering whenever is most convenient."

The taut cord of lingering tension snapped with her joke.

"Okay." Nox quieted the room. "So, she wants magical purity. Where does that leave us for her sentencing?"

A muscle in Gadriel's jaw feathered, his eyes darkening as everyone's thoughts returned to Tanith's sentence. "That depends on your desired outcome. How do you think justice would best be served?"

Nox considered this. "What I want is unrealistic."

"Give it a shot," Malik suggested. "You can be very persuasive."

She leaned back in her chair and thrummed her fingers against the table for a few long moments. "I don't want to insult the deceased by leaving the war criminal unpunished, but more importantly, I don't want to be the queen who lets it happen again. I don't know that justice would be served if we eliminate her until we truly understand whether we're protected against Sulgrave. How do we know that Gwydir is safe at home in their beds with people like her on the loose? This *Tanith* may be our only resource."

Zaccai looked at the room seriously. "As spymaster, I can confirm that knowledge often comes at a terrible price. I'm an advocate for intelligence. But to what end? Do you want to get it out of her and then carry out an execution?"

The room watched Nox carefully. She appeared to be studying her food with unblinking intensity. After a long time, she said, "I want to turn her."

Several sets of brows perked.

"You do aim for the stars," Malik mused.

"If a Sulgrave threat is on the continent, we aren't equipped to stand against others with her power. But she is. What's the saying about fighting fire with fire?"

"Not to?" Yazlyn mumbled into her drink.

"I want to try," Nox said firmly.

"Then we'll try," Gadriel said in agreement.

Amaris raised a cup. "And we'll replace her religion with the Church of Amaris."

"Here, here!" The reevers returned the toast while the rest of the room laughed and groaned in equal proportion.

Dinner played out with mouthfuls of food, smatterings of conversation, and laughter. They found a relaxation that had evaded them for a long, long time. While no one knew how long it would last, for at least the meal before them, the fae, the reevers, Nox and Amaris exchanged pleasantries, told excited recountings of their role in ending the massacre, swapped road-weary tales, and took turns laughing about the woes of training.

Zaccai blessed the table with an anecdote from when they were newly enlisted about how Gadriel had learned of his ability to make his skin burn and didn't learn how to turn it off for nearly three months, leaving everyone in a panic over a scalding fae-in-training. Yazlyn shared that she had been yanked from her bed in the middle of the night in her underthings and tossed into the snow to discover her manipulation of ice. The snowbank that had been meant to drive her to her breaking point was reshaped as a batter-ing ram to bury her then-commanders in a wave of cold, wet regret. Amaris grumbled something about how she'd joined an elite club of masochists. Off-handed comments were made about how Ash might be the next to be tossed to the wolves, and Nox caught the demi-fae grinning into his vegetables at the image.

Despite the heightened emotions, the uncertain future, and the amalgamation of problems on the horizon, she was able to dip her toes into a glimpse of how "normal" could one day look.

✦

Amaris would probably go back to feeling disillusioned when the wine stopped flowing, but for now, each sip tasted an awful lot like an evening well spent. Between her brothers and the military fae, the dinner at Castle Gwydir reminded her so much of the easy camaraderie at the reev. Nox seemed to be enjoying herself, which took a weight off Amaris's shoulders that she hadn't realized she was carrying. She even slipped up long enough to laugh at Gadriel's jokes a time or two. He caught her eye for the barest of moments while the others erupted into spirited debate over his remark and returned the smirk.

The meal came to a close, and everyone filtered out of the dining room at staggered intervals. Nox swiped the bottle of wine. She and Yazlyn seemed to finish their dinners at precisely the same time, which everyone at the table politely pretended not to notice. Ash and Malik made a few ribbing comments as one claimed he would hit the bullseye with his arrow and Zaccai insisted that even if they did hit the center of their mark, any arrow of his could split the reevers' arrows between the fletching. Whether it was the booze or the air of geniality, the boys decided to settle their bets immediately and took off for the training ring before it became too dark to shoot.

Amaris wasn't sure what made her stay in her seat, but she was acutely aware of the building curiosity over the unknown as the general lingered. He was waiting for her, and she knew it.

Once the table emptied, Gadriel moved from his end of the table to join Amaris. She covered her expression by lifting the wine goblet to her lips.

"And then there were two," she murmured.

He offered a crooked smile. "I would like to be the first

to place my prayers and offerings. Would you prefer goat sacrifices or naked dances under the moonlight?"

"I'm still mad at you," she said, setting down her cup, but her voice lacked cold conviction. An evening of laughter would do that to a person.

He dipped his chin. "You're entitled to your anger, and I'm more than happy to weather it. Now, back to your ceremony."

Appreciation for his spirit mingled with amusement as she said, "I've never been one for goat meat. Tell me more about these naked dances."

"Well," he began, taking a drink of whatever was in his goblet, "normally I'd wait for a full moon, but I think we're in waxing gibbous tonight. I'd have to defer judgment to the goddess over whether or not that's acceptable."

She made a daring amount of eye contact, thrumming her fingers against the table as she leveled her response. "Hmm, the goddess is a bit more interested in the nudity you mentioned than she is in the phase of the moon."

"I think you should attempt to add a little more structure to your religion. But if you don't care about the phase of the moon, then I suppose I'd have to show you what remained of the ceremony."

She lifted the glass again but merely held it to her lips. She didn't drink as she eyed him over the crimson liquid. "And during this ceremony…would you call me goddess?"

His eyes flashed, teeth glinting wickedly. "We both know that's not the dynamic you like me for, witchling."

The general winked.

She choked on her sip. Amaris wasn't about to tell him that he was right.

"To be clear," he said, "I'm just happy you're talking to me again. Whether or not our clothes are on or off."

She cocked a brow. She didn't realize she'd been biting her lower lip until she caught his eyes on her mouth. "Maybe when I sober up, I'll stop speaking to you again."

He leaned in closer, invading her space ever so slightly. "Perhaps I'd believe that if you were drunk."

She pushed the boundaries between the high-wire of anger and arousal that they'd grown so accustomed to walking. "Maybe the worshippers shouldn't be the only ones with their clothes off."

Gadriel's eyes narrowed almost imperceptibly, evaluating her. "I don't think that's what you want."

Her gaze didn't budge, though it found a bit of its edge as she stood her ground. "And why is it that everyone else is telling me what I do or don't want? I'm quite sure that I know myself well enough to stand by my question."

"And your question is about what happens under the moonlight?"

She didn't breathe as she waited to see where he would take her challenge.

His lips twitched in a smile as he leaned forward onto the table. He propped himself onto his elbows and eyed her. "Any proper ceremony should take place at night. I'll pour the wine, but then I think the goddess would like to take a night off from thinking."

"And," Amaris swallowed, cheeks heating, "how would she do that?" She closed her eyes briefly, inhaling through her nose as her memory reflected on exactly how his voice had sounded when she'd gotten to her knees. Her toes curled within her shoes. She didn't move, nor did she speak while she waited for him to continue. Her heart skipped once as she looked into what could only be described as a distinctly predatory gaze.

"By leaving the decisions up to the one in charge of the ceremony. Let him tell her what to do so she can truly relax. I'd think that the best way to ensure she was free from any worries about what to do would be through my humble offering of ropes and ties. I'm fairly confident that even a goddess couldn't break through the knots I could wrap around her wrists and ankles. Though I'd welcome any struggle, should she want to test the binds."

Heat spread through her neck and chest. She drank a bit too deeply from the red wine just as an excuse to look away. Their dynamic was her favorite dangerous game. Warmth filled her belly as she dared to prompt, "And then?"

He'd leaned even closer, lowering his voice. "I'd expect an all-night affair. I don't think any deity could be properly honored until she was so exhausted that she could no longer move, think, or talk back to her general."

Obstinance spiked through her. Her eyes widened. "Hey, you're not my—"

He took the wine glass from her hand in a swift movement and exchanged it for a cool, clear glass. "Be a good girl and drink your water."

Gadriel made a sound with his mouth almost like a click of his tongue as he winked. He stood and left the table, leaving Amaris to burn with her thoughts and whatever feelings had passed between them. She set down the water he'd given her and returned to her wineglass, knowing that once again, she'd be left alone for the night with her bathtub, her hand, and her imagination.

Chapter Fifteen

Y AZLYN DID HER BEST TO KEEP HER SHOULDERS BACK AND her chin high as she trailed behind Amaris. She clasped her hands behind her back like she used to when being lectured by her drill sergeant, only to keep from nervously fidgeting. Combat, she could handle. The emotional discomfort between herself and the reever was a different beast entirely.

The two had spent very little time together, which Yazlyn expected. She knew everyone in the castle blamed her for the horrors that had occurred in the wake of her well-intentioned letter to the king. With Amaris at the epicenter, Yazlyn wouldn't blame the young woman for hating her most of all. And that was prior to considering the complicated dalliances that resulted in her waking up in Nox's room.

Even if Amaris hadn't had reason to hate her before...

She's been too shocked to sputter out more than an unintelligible greeting when she'd opened her bedroom door to find Amaris holding a tray of food and a pitcher of water. Her face creased in confusion as she looked between the modest meal and the one holding it, but the reever hadn't sought her out for a showdown or for a picnic. Instead, the two found themselves in a tense alliance as they went down to the cells to talk to the prisoner. As spymaster, Zaccai knew a thing or two about reconnaissance. He'd decided that a pure-blooded fae and a demi-goddess would be their best bet at getting Tanith to talk. While either he or Gadriel could have gone, he suggested Yazlyn be sent in their stead in case a male presence might negatively affect Tanith's willingness to share. Being the ones to deliver the prisoner's meal couldn't hurt their case either.

Yazlyn had been born and raised in Gwydir but had never had occasion to spend time in the castle before now. She had her own apartment in the city, though nothing called her home. Her plants were long dead. Her cupboards were as empty as her bed. And given that she'd gotten the royal family into this mess, she was determined to stick around while she made it right.

This meant, however, that she was even less familiar with the layout of the castle than Amaris appeared to be. The reevers had taken to snooping—exploring the territory for weak points and exits, they claimed—which meant Amaris knew how to get from their rooms to the dungeons. The corridor ended in a spiral staircase. Before the oranges and reds of torchlight cut through the dark stairwell, she felt the hum of magic.

Yazlyn identified its source a moment later. In the far corner, manufactured bars glistened with containment spells.

She hadn't seen the fae since their moments on the cliff following the massacre, but she could have picked out Tanith's angular face in a crowd of ten thousand. The captive had been absently staring into the middle distance as they arrived. Nothing about her posture changed, but her eyes sharpened, focusing on them as they approached.

"Amaris," Tanith said in quiet acknowledgment.

Amaris paused before the shimmering bars. "This is Yazlyn. She's a Raascot fae. I was hoping the three of us could talk."

Tanith said nothing.

Amaris settled onto the ground, crisscrossing her legs so they sat at eye level. "Are you comfortable enough in here?"

Tanith cocked her head slightly. "I'm your prisoner. Does my comfort concern you?"

Amaris twisted her lips. She shot Yazlyn an uncertain look. Rather than responding, she slid the tray into the cell using the small metallic opening at the bottom and carefully placed the pitcher on the ground.

Interrogation was not an area of Yazlyn's expertise. Then again, she supposed reevers weren't known for taking prisoners either. Perhaps they were equally out of their depth.

"Are you cold?" Amaris asked.

Tanith's tone remained impassive as she said, "I wouldn't refuse a blanket."

"I'll have one sent down as soon as we're finished speaking," Amaris said. Yazlyn joined Amaris on the floor, using the action to cover whatever expression might betray how impressed she was by the reever's ease with authority. She spoke as if she ran the dungeons, which she may as well have, for all intents and purposes. Tanith had no way of knowing any differently.

Tanith pressed, "I could also use a book."

"How about we'll see how much you're willing to share in this meeting, and then I'll decide whether or not we have a book sent down with that blanket."

While Tanith and Amaris talked, Yazlyn took the opportunity to examine her more closely. The Sulgrave fae was beautiful, as were all fae. Beauty was a weapon that nature had honed in flowers, birds, snakes, and insects throughout time both to lure in prey and warn the cautious. Her loveliness told the tale of far-off lands.

Farehold fae had been fewer and further between, as they'd intermarried for so many generations that very few presented with telltale features. Hell, she'd dated the first and only Farehold fae she'd ever met and didn't expect to encounter more anytime soon. Southern lineage had given way in Farehold to humans who now presented with the small magics as a distant connection to their fae ancestry. It was even more unusual to see a full fae from Farehold than it was to see one from Tarkhany, despite geographical improbability.

Yazlyn's mind wandered beyond her kingdom to the fabled, empty nothingness that separated the world from the Sulgrave Mountains. The vast, arctic wasteland known as the Frozen Straits—as expansive as the sea—separated the continent from the mountain range beyond. Cartographers estimated that it took one month to cross the Straits, but there was no food, water, shelter, or provisions for the entirety of your journey. Raascot boarded the northwestern sea, and she knew from the human sailors that one might manage a month on the water with the abundance of fish and sunshine, but the sub-zero temperatures of the Straits would freeze any living tissue that remained exposed. She had no desire to spend time on a ship as it was, let alone one made for the ice. Most of her knowledge of the Straits came from campfire lore and empty threats from one's superior. If you didn't fall in line, you'd be sent to join the graveyard of ghost ships and their frozen men, icicles of flesh and bone.

Yazlyn recalled Gadriel mentioning that his parents had moved from Raascot to Sulgrave nearly two hundred years prior, which was a fate achievable only by fae who possessed gifts of heat or fire, which he'd inherited from his father. She hadn't asked him anything further, as she knew there'd be no answer. Even if they had survived the trek to Sulgrave, they'd never dare to journey back again.

"What do you know of Sulgrave?" Tanith asked.

Yazlyn snapped back to attention. They were both looking at her.

Yazlyn shook her head. "No one knows anything. The Frozen Straits make it impossible to access."

Tanith tilted her head. "Impossible?"

Amaris propped her elbows on her knees and rested her chin in her hands. She seemed entirely too relaxed around the violent murderer, in Yazlyn's opinion. "There's a bedtime story—a ghost story, really—about Ophir, the last fae princess of Farehold, who died on the Straits."

A flicker of a smile tugged on Tanith's otherwise expressionless features. "I'd like to hear your ghost story."

"There isn't much to tell, I guess. She was fae and had the ability to call to flame. If anyone should have been able to survive the conditions and make it across the wasteland, it would have been her. She was on an ambassador mission or something of the like. I guess I don't know the details. But the story tells us that she heard something on the ice, and though her crewmates tried to keep her on the skiff, she walked out into the dark. They saw her fire in the distance, and she was never seen again. Without her flame to warm them, most of her men died when they tried to return to Farehold. The few who survived were half-mad. Her death meant the end of the fae dynasty in the south. Whatever dangers live on the ice, whether arctic temperatures or monsters, if even a well-guarded princess of fire stocked with enough provisions for royalty can't survive them, then no one can."

"Yet, here I am."

Amaris made a thoughtful noise. "Yet here you are."

Yazlyn opened her mouth to make a comment, then closed it before saying something that might make her sound stupid. The legends that emerged from Sulgrave were a mixture of fact and fiction. While some claimed that the fae beyond the Straits were the size of giants and had the powers of gods, others had insisted they were more beautiful than angels and had the wings of the seraphim. Some said that Sulgrave was the Kingdom of the All Mother, where no illness or enemy dare penetrate their barriers. While some were relatively easy to discern as fairy tales, others... Yazlyn wasn't so sure.

This Sulgrave fae had, after all, displayed unheard-of power.

Yazlyn was little more than an unnecessary fixture in the dungeon as Amaris carried the conversation. The reever asked, "How old are you?"

"One hundred and seventy. And you?"

"I'm eighteen, and Yazlyn is sixty-three."

"You are a child," Tanith stated as fact.

Amaris bristled, which Yazlyn took as her cue to ask a question. She kept as much authority in her voice as she could muster. "How did you cross the Straits?"

Tanith smiled. Echoing Amaris's ghost story, she said, "With the gift of fire."

Yazlyn spoke again. "Did you come alone?"

"No."

Amaris pitched a negotiation. "Tell me of your mission to the continent, and for every satisfactory bit of information, we'll add a book to your cell. Do we have a deal?"

"What kind of book?"

"I have a few in mind," Yazlyn said. She'd be offering her nothing of beasts, politics, or religion. Certainly, there would be enough fictional tales to satisfy Tanith's want for entertainment without giving her any further ideas about how to attack.

Tanith made a small, satisfied noise to indicate her agreement.

"Whenever you're ready," Yazlyn said, back straight, tone level.

Tanith smiled coolly, showing no teeth. "Five of us crossed on a ship that has carried many before and will carry many after."

"Who sent you?" came Amaris's question.

"I was not sent. I was called."

Where Yazlyn succeeded, the reever failed. Amaris was not as good at concealing impatience. "Then who called you?"

Yazlyn didn't recognize the emotions in Tanith's eyes. She seemed neither cruel nor insane. She had the long-suffering, quiet energy of a parent speaking to a toddler. The Sulgrave fae answered Amaris's question with a question. "What do you believe in, demi-goddess?"

"I'm sorry?"

"You are a child of the All Mother. Do you visit the goddess in Her temples? How do you worship?"

Amaris shook her head. "I'm not particularly religious."

Tanith chewed on the inside of her cheek while she considered the response. "How very interesting. I suppose you would not be the first child to scorn their parent."

Yazlyn's brows met in the middle. "Are you implying this massacre was a religious issue?"

Tanith tsked her tongue once in calm disapproval. "I've honored the All Mother for my entire life. We are fortunate to live among the goddess made flesh in Sulgrave, and Amaris, you would be most welcome in our lands. The most tangible way to express reverence is to unify the people with magical perfection. I honor the unadulterated magic of the goddess. This is how I worship the All Mother."

Yazlyn turned to Amaris as if they weren't sitting directly in front of the prisoner. "So we're dealing with a religious zealot. Any ideas?"

Amaris held up a finger toward Yazlyn. She held Tanith's gaze. "Can you clarify what you mean by that? The goddess made flesh?"

Tanith eyed her with great interest. "The Speaker, of course."

"What can you tell me about the Speaker?"

"She is the All Mother."

Yazlyn studied Amaris's reaction every bit as carefully as Tanith's. The reever's white brows collected in the middle, betraying her frustration. "What is your endgame?"

"My heart echoes the heart of the All Mother. I desire unity."

Yazlyn interjected, "And how, exactly, is unity achieved?"

Tanith lifted her shoulders lightly, then relaxed against the stone wall as if losing interest in the conversation. It was with some boredom that she said, "Occasionally, viruses are killed with quarantines. Some bacteria are expunged only through thorough cleansing. There are many ways to deal with a blight, and each doctor is only responsible for the tasks within their power."

Amaris stood, rubbing her temples. Yazlyn couldn't be sure as to what Amaris was thinking, but if it was anything like what was going on in her own head, perhaps the reever wasn't sure if she could confidently risk speaking to Tanith without revealing disgust over her genocidal ideologies.

"I think I'm done for today," Amaris said.

"Go ahead and grab her a book," Yazlyn said. "I'd like to stay for a minute longer."

✦

Amaris left the fae to chat, but before she was fully up the stairs, she could have sworn she heard Yazlyn laugh. Perhaps leaving them alone hadn't been the wisest choice.

It took a bit of rummaging, but she managed to procure what she was looking for. Amaris caught Zaccai in the hall and sent him with three tattered books and a wool blanket to the dungeons. She'd selected three fictional love stories, thinking perhaps the lunatic could use a change in tone from whatever had been clouding her mind for one hundred and seventy-some years.

As Amaris was leaving her room for dinner, Yazlyn stopped her in the hall.

"Can I talk to you?"

Amaris was taxed on all fronts. The emotional toll of being around her betrayer—the pretty, stupid, irreverent fae warming Nox's bed—had worn heavily on her.

"I spoke to Tanith for a while longer, and she genuinely doesn't act hostile. She seems so perfunctory; she has the conviction of a healer helping the continent."

Amaris unleashed a tired sigh. "Yes, she's used that metaphor a time or two."

"I don't think this is a full-on assault by Sulgrave. She seems like a fanatic who's never known any better. What worries me right now is her claim that five of them came over on her skiff. Even if she is a radical, it only takes the actions of a few extremists to bring a kingdom to its knees. Look at the destruction she achieved by herself in the gully."

Amaris focused on the task at hand. She chewed on her lip, shoving her feelings aside as she remembered the flames, the gore, and the vakliche. "Did you get a sense for her powers? She was able to bind demons to her will."

Yazlyn nodded. "Yes, she told me almost everything. It's like we'd speculated: Tanith doesn't seem to be concealing anything. It's almost as if she feels like we'll see her point of view and join her cause."

"Are you defending her?"

The whites of her eyes outlined her defiant surprise. "Of course not. Tanith is a fanatical murderer, and we're right to keep her in chains. I just don't think she's evil. She just seems…"

Amaris folded her arms over her chest, drumming her fingers on her bicep. "Like she's never been outside of her echo chamber?"

Yazlyn was quick to agree. "I'm finding it hard to be angry with her. She did more to us in a night than Ceres did in twenty years. But…I don't know. Talking to her, it seems like she did these things as if acting out her part in a play. She doesn't feel violent, she feels…pitiful. I don't know anything of her religion, but it seems like she's had no exposure to humans or faelings. Maybe the rest of Sulgrave isn't like this. When it comes to Tanith…we don't have any reason to believe she's had any exposure to the world outside of her cult."

Amaris made a face. "I don't remember the All Mother ever calling for murder."

Yazlyn exhaled slowly. "Fuck, don't ask me. I'm not religious. But I know a thing or two about military culture. This is what people do in the absence of a call to action, isn't it? They create a message? We have an asset on our side, though."

Amaris's fingers stilled. She lifted both brows. "Care to share?"

"If anyone has a hope of getting across to her, it's a demi-goddess."

She narrowed her eyes. "I wish people would stop calling me that."

Yazlyn smirked. "You don't seem to like anything anyone calls you."

"You could always call me Amaris."

This elicited a true grin. Yazlyn's smile faded after a moment, and Amaris debated leaving. She didn't want to spend more time around the sergeant than necessary, but she could tell the fae had something else on the tip of her tongue.

"Can I say something, Amaris?"

"Can I stop you?"

The sergeant shifted her weight from one foot to another. Amaris frowned as she watched the fae's features twist in a battle of emotion. Her expressive brows pinched. If she bit her lip any harder, she'd draw blood.

Yazlyn said, "You don't have to accept my apology. You don't have to forgive me or even be my friend. I don't want to defend my actions. I thought I was doing what was right for my kingdom and for my friends and family and troops, and I was wrong. I'm a fuckup in more ways than I can begin to describe. I will spend the rest of my time shouldering my mistakes. I'll pay for them whenever I look into any of your faces, and I'll pay for it whenever I train with the remnants of the Raascot military, or whenever anyone mentions our late king. I just wanted you to know that not only am I sorry, but no one will hate me as much as I hate me."

Amaris sucked in a breath but was too shocked to speak. If she wasn't mistaken, she might have thought she caught the glassy sheen of tears before Yazlyn turned her head. She stepped around Amaris, and as she left, choked out, "Thank you for listening to me."

She'd been hungry before bumping into Yazlyn, but

her appetite vanished along with the whoosh of reddish-brown hair.

She skipped dinner in favor of a long, quiet soak in the bath. An attendant knocked and set a tray of food on her writing desk while she was still in the soapy waters, though it had mostly cooled and the bubbles had popped, leaving her in a cold, milky tub alone with her thoughts. By the time her fingers and toes resembled the shriveled, sugary prunes that sometimes adorned their desserts, she submerged herself one final time. She was in enough pain already. She didn't need empathy for the one who'd put her in this mess on top of it.

Despite her towels and robes and blankets and fire, nothing seemed to warm her that night or in the nights that followed.

Amaris joined the war council over the next several days until it slowly grew to include everyone in the newly formed inner circle. Three reevers, three northern fae, and Nox as heir to Farehold and Raascot met to discuss, plot, and strategize against what seemed like an ever-growing number of issues. Taking over as ruler of Raascot would have been enough of a task, but between the curse at the border, Moirai declaring enemies of the north and the reevers alike, and Sulgrave who had the power to tether monsters unleashing threats, there were no simple solutions.

Amaris wasn't particularly shocked that Nox had attempted on more than one occasion to hand the crown and title in its entirety over to Gadriel—the only member of the inner circle with the age, know-how, familial claim, and skillset to actually run a kingdom—who had to patiently rebuke her time after time. He was happy to be her general and advisor, he said, but everyone was invested in Nox's success, even if she had no faith in herself. He assured the room that he'd rather set himself on fire than be king.

"Because being a monarch is a fate worse than burning to death?" Nox had asked.

Gadriel had said something about trying to be reassuring,

and everyone told him that he should stick to strategy and leave psychology for the others.

The sun rose, and the sun set, and the days wore on. They learned a little more from Tanith each day. Amaris ate, trained, and slept.

But she did not feel whole.

Chapter Sixteen

I DIDN'T THINK ANYONE WOULD BE IN HERE," YAZLYN SAID apologetically.

Nox looked back at her through the dappled shadows that filtered in from the moonlight. "Stress makes it harder to sleep. And I don't know if you've been in the same war room meetings that I have over the last few weeks, but..."

"You needed a drink?" she ventured.

"I needed a drink."

Nox was leaning against the window in the dining room late after the midnight hour. The full moon caught on the leaves as they flickered in the night breeze, showcasing its bathing, metallic disc whenever the branches moved. She turned her head to look at the intruder, wine goblet in hand. Silver outlined her inky hair, the slope of her nose, her elegant neck, the silhouette of her body in its nightdress as she continued looking out the window.

"The castle grounds are lovely," Nox said quietly. "I thought moats were for storybooks, but this river...it looks like silk in the moonlight."

Yazlyn hedged near the door. She'd spent plenty of time with Nox, but they'd kept it strictly carnal. She'd made the mistake of falling asleep in Nox's bed a time or two after a particularly spirited session but had quickly learned she was better off slipping into her pants and making her way to her own chambers before she slept, which left no time for the mistake of pillow talk. In the war room, they stuck to strategy. These poetic, late-night thoughts felt different. They were intimate, almost.

"I needed a drink," she repeated, face silhouetted against the window. "You can get whatever you need and go."

Yazlyn's face fell from disappointment to irritation in a second. She'd been an idiot for thinking Nox was capable of tenderness. "You don't own the castle."

"I do, actually."

"Have you always been this arrogant, or does the monarchy just look cold on you?" Yazlyn asked, grabbing a goblet from the cabinet. She could have excused herself to the kitchen or made herself scarce, but the agitation lit a fire within her. She picked her way around the table in the shadows. "Are you sharing that wine?"

Nox had been holding the slender neck of a green glass bottle in one hand, goblet in the other. She began to refill it slowly. The soft, loose shrug she wore around her arms against the castle's chill slipped off a shoulder as she moved. "Your general, your demi-goddess, your queen..." She let her words tangle with the breeze as the wind hummed against the window. Its whistling noises were their only companion in the silence. "Is there no one you speak to respectfully? Get your own."

"So selfish." Yazlyn extended her glass and waited.

Nox went still, which sent Yazlyn's heart into a threatening stutter. She couldn't discern the emotion behind the eyes in the darkness. Rather than filling Yazlyn's cup, she set the bottle down on the window's ledge. She brought the cup to her lips and drank deeply before taking a step toward the fae's outstretched hand.

"You know exactly how generous I can be."

Well, perhaps they didn't know how to be friends, or

even drinking buddies. But there was one thing they did particularly well.

Yazlyn set the cup down on the surface behind her, leaning both hands on the dining room table to support her weight. She tilted her head to the side ever so slightly. Nox returned the look, her face going from irritation to puzzlement to something else.

"Here?" Nox sounded genuinely surprised.

"I thought you owned the castle." Yazlyn lifted her weight slightly, sliding backward onto the table. There was no one around. No one had been awake for hours. It was just the queen, the fae, and the moon. She waited expectantly.

One curious moment. Two long breaths. Three slow, uncertain blinks.

Nox took the bait. In two steps she was in the space Yazlyn had created by widening her legs, hand in hair, anger fresh. "Where do you get your audacity."

Heat pulsed between them, energy changing in a flash.

"The same place you get your rage." Her fingers dug into Nox's back, pulling her in to close the gap as she tore the warming shawl from Nox's arms and tossed it to the side. She wouldn't give the queen a chance to respond.

She was no stranger to rage either.

Yazlyn sucked Nox's lower lip into her mouth, biting down on it as they crashed into one another. Her back arched in pleasure, demand, and longing. Her blood heated as she clawed at the soft skin on the back of Nox's neck—a fire that spread from her mouth to her stomach to her most intimate places.

Their mouths were not ones that knew kindness. Their tongues tasted of hate, cinnamon, cruelty, blackberries, passion, walnuts, and urgency. The goblet Yazlyn had fetched from the cabinet toppled over, a loud, empty gong clanging against the table as Nox attempted to shove her backward onto the surface. Yazlyn's wings flared around them as she lifted her shirt up over her head. She reached for Nox's nightdress, but the queen grabbed her hand, putting it between her legs instead.

Fuck.

Yazlyn's eyes rolled into the back of her head as her fingers slid against the thin, soaked cloth that separated them. Her thoughts blurred as Nox's mouth moved along her throat. She'd never had a shot at the upper hand. She melted to Nox's will every time they tasted each other. The hot, wet evidence of how badly she was wanted in return unraveled her resolve.

Their loveless affair was a volcanic release of pent-up fury.

Every time she was on the verge of boiling over, they found exactly how to release steam. Nox made no attempts to be with her, but by now Nox had learned exactly what her body could handle. Yazlyn wasn't an idiot. She knew Nox pushed her to certain limits for her own sadistic pleasure, but there were no scratches that tonics couldn't heal. There were no bruises or slaps or curses too hard. Even though Yazlyn's canines were sharper, Nox inflicted more damage, biting to hurt.

Yazlyn knew she'd never been quiet, whether she was being a smartass in meetings or letting the entire castle know that she had several fingers inside of her on the dining room table. She couldn't help it. Sex was her drug of choice.

"Shut the fuck up." Nox slammed her hand down over Yazlyn's mouth, crawling up on the table to keep her pinned and quiet.

Yazlyn fought back. She was just as likely to be the aggressor as the submissive, and for once, she had the tactical advantage. Nox may be queen, but she couldn't disarm a mouse, let alone someone in Raascot's military. It had barely taken Yazlyn the effort of a single hooking motion with her leg, grabbing Nox's arm as she flipped her. Nox gasped in both pain and surprise as the back of her head hit the table too loud, too hard, and it was exactly what they needed.

Make it hurt.

Yazlyn's hand stayed between Nox's legs, working her from her advantageous position. Every vindicating moment of aggression only stoked their fire and strengthened their resolve. Nox fisted her fingers in Yazlyn's hair, cinching her in as the fae moved on top of her, each touch, each swirl, each penetration, circulation, each pump a new and terrible step closer to the edge.

The silver light wasn't strong enough to show their sins to the world as it filtered in through the window but cast enough of an outline for them to see each other as the tangle of two deliciously shadowed creatures of the night.

"You know," Nox gasped, "I'm not sure if I love or loathe walnuts and blackberries."

"Good," Yazlyn replied. "I hope you can never taste blackberry jam without getting wet."

Two hands landed on the top of her head in response, shoving her downward. Yazlyn's knees hit the stone floor. Nox arched off the table as she wrapped her thighs around Yazlyn's head, pulling her closer. Her mouth moved against the plum flavors while her nails drew gashes along Nox's hips and outer thighs.

The queen was holding out on her. But Yazlyn knew she could make her scream.

There was the briefest pause in pleasure as Yazlyn waited for Nox to look up. When she did, it was just long enough to make eye contact as Yazlyn put her index, middle, and little finger in her mouth. Nox's eyes widened, gasping again as Yazlyn's mouth wasn't the only thing in her and on her. Nox buckled in response at every point of pleasure, hips rocking against the table as she drew closer and closer. She clasped her hand down over her mouth, muffling the sounds of the building climax.

Perhaps a more selfless person would have been wanting to make their bedmate come for the sake of their own pleasure. Not Yazlyn. She needed the victorious win that would only come from Nox's cry. And it was no small task. If she knew Nox at all, she was certain she'd sooner choke on her own scream than let the Yazlyn think she'd won.

All's fair in sex and war.

Nox's unwillingness to release more than the involuntary

moans didn't stop her body from responding as climax hit like a strike of lightning, shocking her as it jolted through her. She kept her hand over her mouth at the first strong wave and again at the second. Yazlyn's free hand tore upward, feeling Nox's stomach as it clenched, her back arched, her legs tightened to freeze Yazlyn where she knelt.

Then she heard it. Ten thousand angels. First kisses. Piercing rays of dawn. Tea in the morning. Promotions in rank. Taking flight. It was the deep, satisfying, shattering cry of a woman's orgasm.

She worked her way through the reverberating shutters, slowing her movements.

After a final tremble, Nox propped herself up on her elbows as Yazlyn wiped the glistening remnants from her chin. Nox twisted her mouth to the side, eyeing her. She sat up straight and outstretched her hand in a surprisingly gentle gesture, stroking Yazlyn's curls once. It was just enough to surprise her, to soften her walls as she looked up at Nox, appreciating the connection that bonded lovers.

The moment her guard was fully down, she saw her mistake. Nox popped off the table and grabbed her shawl in a lithe movement. She wrapped it around her shoulders and headed for the door.

"Hey!" Yazlyn's eyes widened the moment she realized Nox was leaving with no intent of letting her finish.

Nox paused. She looked over her shoulder. "I'm selfish, remember?"

The air punched from her lungs. "Oh, you stone-cold bitch."

"That's Queen Bitch to you." She pressed a kiss to her middle and index finger, letting it float to the ground as she wandered out of the dining room. A cruel smile tugged at the corner of her lips, concealed only by the cover of shadows.

Soaked and alone on her knees on the stone floor of the dining room, Yazlyn was left even emptier than she'd been before.

Chapter Seventeen

G REEN SUMMER LEAVES RELINQUISHED THEIR COLORS INTO oranges, then reds, then browns. The days grew shorter, and the nights fell colder.

Ash and Amaris ran and trained daily, with Zaccai and Malik joining intermittently. Nox would make appearances to throw Chandra. Yazlyn joined once or twice to toss icicles into the air to knock the boys' arrows from their skyward ascent, occasionally hitting Nox with a wayward shard of ice. They enjoyed watching her take water from the pitchers and manipulating it into whatever shape or form she required.

Gadriel spent most of his time in the war room, though he could be heard exercising and practicing in the early morning hours before the others had taken their breakfast. The general and his second in command took turns meeting and training with their troops. The shreds of what remained of the military were left out of their plans for the immediate future. Raascot's forces had suffered greatly under Ceres, and any effective plan would need to remain covert.

Their Sulgrave captive continued to be a passive, model prisoner.

Tanith made no effort to struggle, and her behavior had

stretched into further and further privileges. Not only was she collecting a small hoard of books and the comforts of blankets and pillows in her cell, but Tanith was occasionally allowed out to move her legs through the courtyard under the careful supervision of either Gadriel or Zaccai, while she spent her time on careful stretches under the late autumn sun.

While spies in the Farehold confirmed the stirs of public dissent against Raascot, the southern crown voiced no intentions of openly marching on the north.

Nox learned so much about the stronghold presence in Farehold—including the humans who had allied with the north and had been helping Raascot for hundreds of years. She suspected the sweet family she'd encountered on the shores of Yelagin's lake had existed within the spy network for decades prior to any perception curse. Presumably, they were no safer in the north than Farehold. She wondered how many of Raascot's unassuming citizens served as plants for Moirai.

It was unwise to head south of the border without any true plan of action, especially with their shredded forces. From their reports, it seemed the southern queen knew nothing of the massacre in the gully, nor how it had decimated Raascot's military. They used her ignorance to their advantage to continue planning, training, recruiting, and growing whatever strength they could. Nox did her best to take every meeting seriously, particularly as Ash continued to remind her of her ungratefulness. She truly had an opportunity to change the world for the better, and she'd be wicked not to seize such a rare chance.

In the weeks that stretched into late autumnal months, Tanith had been deemed nonthreatening enough to be kept as a ward in secluded castle rooms. Though she'd moved beyond the dungeons, her manufactured door was both warded and locked from the outside. While her religious zeal was unmoving, Tanith had been consistently willing to relinquish knowledge and data, as long as no one of mixed, magical heritage was in her presence.

A blacksmith with a gift for runes had been a deciding factor in Tanith's relocation. The manufacturer had been handsomely compensated for the two seamless silver cuffs that stretched from the base of Tanith's elbow to the onset of her wrists. Tanith's powers were as nullified as those of any human on the continent. If she hadn't been lovely and had the sharpened ears and canines of the fae, no one would have known her to contain any semblance of the terrible abilities that had leveled their forces. She was no true friend of the castle, but she was an asset, and some captor-bonding appeared to have forged a tentative alliance between her and several members of the inner circle.

Yazlyn had been encouraged from her military allies and reevers alike to continue visiting Tanith whenever she was able, as their friendship—whether real or forged from necessity—could only benefit the inner circle.

Time had not soothed the wounds that had festered between Nox and Amaris as the seasons changed, though they did their best to remain civil. Amaris had directed the majority of her attention toward the general for distraction, but he seemed pleasantly delighted to taunt her with possibility, smirking at her ever-growing frustration.

Life did what it always did: it went on.

✦

Amaris recognized the voice instantly.

She decided it was good that Yazlyn wasn't a member of Zaccai's reconnaissance team. The sergeant's face betrayed her emotion at every given turn. Between the morning walks of shame and Yazlyn's propensity for volume, the sergeant's nightly dalliances had been broadcast throughout the castle.

Amaris had felt the icy chips of her heart breaking into disagreeable pieces until she caught herself eavesdropping outside of Tanith's room one afternoon late into fall. She couldn't stop herself from pausing as two voices drifted beyond the door and into the hall.

She'd had honorable reasons for wandering the halls. At least, at first.

The chilly hours prompted her to see if the kitchen would make her a cup of hot chocolate after dark. She'd scarcely made it beyond the collection of rooms when Tanith's accented lilt was met by a sharp, disagreeable laugh.

Yazlyn had been encouraged to foster a friendship with the Sulgrave girl, but no one really knew what their rapport entailed. Amaris sucked in a breath as she listened.

"I can't say I pity you." The voice belonged to Tanith.

"I'm not looking for pity," Yazlyn replied. "I just don't know who to talk to about this. Maybe it's comforting knowing you have some unresolved issues that predispose you to side with me over her simply because I'm fae."

"You're lucky I still talk to you, considering how you sully yourself with a halfling."

Amaris pressed herself into the stones near the door. She knew this conversation had no bearings on matters of security, nor did she have any business listening. This was the intimate conversation. And yet...

"It's misguided, you know. Truly sometimes it feels like I'm talking to a child. It's hard to be mad at you." Yazlyn's voice again.

"Pursuing magical purity—"

"Yes, I've heard your speech. Her human half has nothing to do with why I hate her."

To Tanith's credit, she didn't jump at the opportunity to push her own agenda. Amaris rested her fingertips and temple against the door as she listened.

"Then why do you hate her?"

Yazlyn's volume ebbed and flowed with varied emotion. "I don't hate her. I just don't want to wake up in her room anymore. I wish I could want anybody else. She's not good for me. And don't say it's because she's not fae."

An invisible fist punched through Amaris's gut. It ripped her heart through the gaps in her ribs as she listened to the murderer responsible for the Raasay Valley Massacre and the sergeant who'd orchestrated Amaris's demise as they discussed Nox. She hadn't grown up with girlfriends, apart from Nox, but she knew enough of whispered secrets to know when information was privileged. She battled between the urge to spare herself from pain and the need to know everything. Before she made a decision, the gentle sound of the Sulgrave accent lilted through the wooden door.

Tanith's voice held no cruelty, only a question as she asked, "Then why do you continue going to her room?"

Yazlyn's laugh was short and humorless. Amaris held perfectly still, worried at the long stretch of nothing that spread between the chuckle and Yazlyn's next words before she said, "Because as much as I want to hate her, I don't. As much as I want to want someone else, I don't. I wait for her to call for me every night, and on the nights she doesn't, I seek her out. I sit at my mirror fixing my hair or painting charcoal over my eyes until I know it's time to see her. It's terrible. She's always been exactly clear about who and what we are, so I can't even bring myself to blame her. I just know she doesn't care about me. I'm a warm body for a succubus."

Amaris sucked in a breath. She knew she should leave. This was wrong.

"Do you get nothing out of it?" Tanith asked.

Amaris frowned at the question as she pressed her ear to the door.

The Sulgrave fae could have easily doubled down on demonizing the succubi powers or lambasting cruelties about the orphan queen, but instead, she seemed to be offering Yazlyn a genuine listening ear. Amaris wondered if there was truly no one else Yazlyn could speak to, that she'd needed to turn to the captive. Amaris had heard her speak once of a partner who had left her for a life on the road and knew that the rest of her days had been spent in the service of the Raascot military. Now with their forces scattered to the wind, perhaps she truly had no friends.

Yazlyn said, "I get plenty. This has nothing to do with how she is in bed—"

"Just how she makes you feel when you're not in the bedroom."

"Precisely."

Amaris's muscles were tense as if for battle, anxious over the treachery of discovery. And yet, she listened on.

"Can I offer some advice?" came Tanith's response.

Yazlyn laughed. "I should say no. You're under lock and key specifically because we don't trust your judgment."

Tanith wasted no time before saying, "Well, you're here, aren't you?"

"I guess I am."

Amaris's feet had turned away from the door. Her body language was poised to depart, but she remained glued to the wall, beholden to their conversation.

Tanith's musical voice was surprisingly gentle and understanding when she spoke. "It's okay if you aren't ready to kick your vice. Some people turn to drink, others to poppy dens, and then there are those in need of comfort and release in the arms of others. Sometimes it takes them a few nights, sometimes a few years, and sometimes it takes a lifetime. I will spare you my religious convictions for this belief: when you're ready, you will leave her bed for good, and you will not return."

A shuffle in the room sent Amaris skittering down the hall. Her heart caught in her throat, choking her as it continued its pounding. She was nearly around the corner by the time the door to Tanith's room opened and the girls exchanged their goodnights. Amaris's arms and legs were stiff as she speed-walked, hoping she could turn the final corner before she was spotted.

"Amaris?"

Shit.

Amaris stopped in her tracks and did her best to still her breaths. "Oh, hi, Yazlyn."

Yazlyn looked up and down the corridor. "It's late, isn't it?"

Amaris tried to swallow, but her most vital organ remained lodged in her throat. "I was just heading for some hot chocolate in case the cooks are feeling benevolent. Do you want to join?"

Shit. Fuck. Goddess damn.

She wasn't sure what guilt-stricken compulsion had forced her to invite the fae, but Yazlyn's eyes widened into tea saucers. She nodded hesitantly.

Amaris continued failed attempts to still her heart from the shame-filled thumps. She shouldn't have been listening. She should have left the moment she knew they were discussing something personal, especially after learning that Nox was the subject of their conversation. Amaris had built a wall, brick by brick, to prevent herself from thinking or feeling anything about the relationship that Yazlyn and Nox had shared. She didn't allow herself to visit it, ever. After she'd bumped into a mussy-haired Yazlyn exiting a naked Nox's chambers that first time, she knew it would bring her only pain to revisit.

No matter how hard she tried to bury her emotions, she felt only distinct, echoing sadness. She was sad for Yazlyn, not just because of how the fae had found herself in a loveless physical relationship but because she had no friends. She was sad that the fae felt so much crippling guilt, that she bore the weight of her toppled kingdom and the death of her king on her own shoulders. Amaris had grown up an orphan in a child mill, but she'd always been loved and accepted, if only by Nox. After that, she'd found herself a family and a purpose with the reevers. She felt distinctly pained imagining a life feeling truly and utterly alone.

She'd lost herself to her thoughts when Yazlyn made a quiet attempt at conversation. "What keeps you up so late?"

Amaris gestured vaguely toward the dark windows beyond the halls. "The wind is very loud this far north. I

195

didn't expect there to already be ice and snow this early in the season."

Yazlyn made a sympathetic noise as they began hesitant steps toward the kitchen. "Farleigh is pretty far north, from what I understand. You're no spring chicken. These winters are hard on everybody."

"Spring chicken?" Amaris echoed the phrase as they continued their path toward the kitchen.

"Oh, um, a southerner who couldn't handle the temperature. I meant nothing by it."

Amaris felt the loneliness in Yazlyn's correction. Even at the smallest turns of phrases, the sergeant was afraid that everything she said would garner a new wave of rejection. Amaris hadn't thought she'd been overly cruel, but nor had she made efforts toward forgiveness. Not only had she blamed Yazlyn for Ceres's capture, for Odrin's death, and for the blood of Raascot's military, but also for being the distraction that stood between Nox and the forgiveness needed for them to work through their issues.

Still, a tug of empathy demanded her to put herself in the winged fae's shoes.

There was still a lone attendant in the kitchen tending the fire by the time they arrived. She hid her surprise at the late-night interruption well, then prepared a cup of milk and melted chocolate for each of them before shooing them out of the room. Yazlyn made an awkward gesture as if to return to her bedchambers, but Amaris redirected them to a sitting alcove to listen to the wind. The castle was full of little inlets with velvet loveseats and fainting settees, crammed with book nooks and tall, arched windows and delightful spaces to hide. The stars were particularly bright tonight, as it was a night with no clouds and no moon. The beauty of it was made all the more wonderful with a warm drink in hand, a soft, overstuffed chair, and a fire kept glowing by the ever-attentive staff of the castle.

Yazlyn kept adjusting her grip on her mug and fidgeting in her chair, making no secret of her profound discomfort.

"Yazlyn?"

The sergeant stilled.

Amaris took a long breath. She'd been reciting this speech to herself over and over in her head and was finally ready to deliver it. "I haven't been particularly nice to you, and I wanted to say that I'm sorry. I won't ever be okay with what happened. I have wounds that won't heal. Not now, and maybe not ever. But...I understand why you did what you thought was right. And...I don't hate you."

The windowpanes groaned as northern winds pressed in on them. The howls of impending winter filled the speechless silence.

Yazlyn was statuesque with her tension, her mouth parted as if opened for some wordless argument. Between the moonlight beyond and the torchlights filling the hall, Amaris realized her months of avoidance had prevented her from looking into Yazlyn's eyes long enough to know their true color. They were almost golden like Ash's but with greenish flecks throughout. Obstinance precluded observation. She wondered what else it had kept her from seeing.

"One more thing?"

Yazlyn wasn't breathing. "Yes?"

Amaris's fingers tightened around her warm mug of hot chocolate. She gnawed her lip before asking, "Did they really throw you out into the snow in your underthings?"

The wind stole what might have been a laugh and the stories that followed.

Perhaps Yazlyn wouldn't become her best friend that night. They didn't discuss their childhoods or their backgrounds or their pains or Tanith or politics or unrequited loves or anything deep worth exploring. After the night ended, however, Amaris was quite sure they each had one less enemy in the castle.

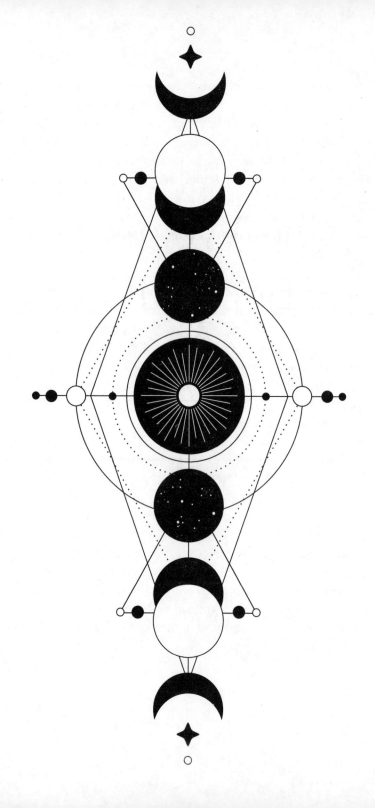

PART THREE:

The Weight of Becoming

Chapter Eighteen

W E'RE NOT READY."
    "When will we be ready?" Ash countered.
"When will we have regained the manpower, when will we have a firm hold on the nation, when will we understand Sulgrave enough to be ready?"

Nox did her best to stay present amidst the back and forth, but she'd heard this argument before. As a reever, Ash had a lot of trouble working collaboratively on the curse-breaking mission. As a general, Gadriel didn't give a fuck about the reevers' propensity for autonomous action. Her eyes glazed over, lost to the flashes of silver that caught in the enormous crystal bricks when the light danced.

She wished the war room had a window. It would be easier to waste her life away if she could at least watch the last of the leaves break free from the branches on the castle grounds, bobbing on singing winds toward the city. She pressed the heels of her hands into her eyes and left them there while the men argued.

Gadriel and Ash were going head-to-head in the war room, their weight on their arms as they leaned into the table separating them from the other's throat while other members of the inner circle watched in various states of distress. Zaccai remained near the door, leaning against the cool blue stones of the wall. Yazlyn stayed blissfully quiet at these things, though Nox supposed the fae's stillness had to do with the sergeant's rank.

Nox looked up from where she'd buried her face. "Gadriel, what exactly is it that you think would qualify our readiness?"

The general gripped his chin in one hand as he exhaled. "We need intelligence. We need reinforcements. We need a plan more articulate than 'go in and get 'em.'"

Ash was incensed. "We only need manpower if you're planning on meeting Moirai's forces in open war! I'm talking about covert infiltration. We could have focused efforts for assassination and extraction."

Amaris raised a finger. "When we kill Moirai, her crown prince will also disappear. The kingdom will go from having two sovereigns to none overnight. They have no knowledge of an heir, even a bastard claim to the throne—no offense, Nox."

"None taken."

Amaris continued, "Why do you think the void will be well received? Farehold will descend into anarchy."

From the far side of the room, Malik piped, "There have been usurpers throughout history."

Gadriel stayed firm. "Even usurpers had support and manpower. People backed and acknowledged their claim to the throne. We'd be going in like phantoms in the night and announcing that they have a new queen under the guise of 'Trust us, she's Daphne's daughter.'"

Yazlyn broke her silence. "If you're suggesting that we disseminate information of Nox's existence before killing Moirai, that would take the kind of time and presence in Farehold that we just don't have. None of us can speak or be understood south of the border. Besides, Moirai has been on a very successful smear campaign for quite some time. As far as the city of Aubade is concerned, the reevers are demon sympathizers, and all of Farehold may or may not believe that Raascot sacked the Temple of the All Mother. Putting Nox on the throne would be sending her to her death. Sorry, Nox."

"No apology necessary."

Ash was restless. "I'm hearing problem after problem, but I haven't heard a lot of solutions from any of you."

Gadriel looked like he might overturn the table. "Because these are not matters solved in weeks! The overthrow of Farehold is not something you get to sneak off in the night and accomplish just because you're well trained for combat. My military is in shambles, not only in numbers but in spirit. Even if we do go alone, as you're suggesting, we're not just worrying about how to get in and out of the castle with Moirai's head on a spike, we also need to worry about the loyalties of an entire continent. We can't hold a throne without the support of the people."

Ash began to pace. "If we have it your way, we won't leave Gwydir for another ten years."

Gadriel's eyes flashed. "Sometimes these things take years, reever. I don't mean to state the obvious, but I am a general with ten times your years in experience. Your short-sightedness—"

Malik raised his hand. "Well, speaking for the humans in the room, some of us don't have centuries to think through our plans."

This elicited many a raised brow.

Nox spoke up. "I'm only half-fae. I can't exactly wait for the humans in Farehold to die. I'd be one hundred before making any claim for the throne."

Yazlyn shrugged. "Many faelings live to be well over two hundred."

Nox puffed a strand of hair out her face, keeping her chin propped on her hand. "And I'm sure I'll be a grand two-hundred-year-old queen, but I do think the issue is a little more pressing. Besides, it would only draw attention if we were amassing forces during what everyone believes to be times of peace. Leave your men out of this, give them time to be with their families, and let's keep this within our inner circle. Moirai is stirring the south now. Sulgrave is descending now. That timing may not be convenient, but I have to side with Ash on this one."

Everyone apart from Nox flinched as if certain this would be the thing that sent Gadriel over the edge. She watched the general, monitoring his controlled way of coming back from the brink of temper. His anger was almost a visible fire that stoked and cooled to a blue glow before them in the matter of moments.

Gadriel looked to Nox. "With the information in front of you, what would you have us do?"

"Nice try, but having Ceres as a father doesn't qualify me to make that kind of call."

A tendon in his neck flexed. He took a calming breath as he relaxed his fists against the war table. He scanned the faces of the others before saying, "Can Nox and I have the room?"

She felt the weight of everyone else's discomfort, but it did little more than chase her back behind her curtain of hair, resting her forehead on her palms. She listened to the shuffling of feet and muttering amongst the others but couldn't bring herself to care. If Gadriel was going to order everyone around, he may as well step into the crown.

His voice was low and firm as he asked, "Nox, can I tell you why I believe you can do this?"

She looked up. The room felt too big now that they were alone. She didn't bother shaking her head. He'd speak his piece whether she acknowledged him or not.

She was right.

"You have met every challenge in your life with strategy and success. I know more than you think I do about what you navigated in your orphanage. I know that you were willing to take sacrificial falls to protect those you cared for, including going to Priory in Amaris's stead. I know you managed to master your fae powers with no guidance and even create critical allies of those who had intended you to be their foe or—worse—those who had underestimated you. I know that Amaris and I are alive because of your quick thinking and resourcefulness in the coliseum. You don't just have the blood of our king, Nox. You have the mind and spirit of a ruler. And it would serve everyone in Raascot if you started seeing yourself for who you really are."

She slowly unraveled her hands from her hair and straightened her posture, eyeing him carefully. She kept her face in her palms, but no longer allowed the dark, glossy locks to obscure her.

"Are you speaking as my general, my subject, or my newly discovered family member?"

Gadriel sat for the first time in the duration of the meeting. "I'm speaking as someone who has been at Ceres's side and watched him rise and assisted in his victories and then did nothing as he fell, even though I saw him struggling. I'm speaking as an advisor who refuses to leave another monarch alone like I did with my cousin. I am not going to set you up for failure. You're my cousin's heir, yes, but you are also cunning. You are quick-thinking. You are capable. But none of that matters if you don't start seeing yourself as the leader you are."

"What would you have me do?"

He pressed his lips into a firm line. "I'd have you stop asking me what you're supposed to do and start living up to your potential. You already know what to do. Of course, a good queen will take the council of her advisors and will listen to her general, but the Queen of Raascot should not be a puppet to her military's leader. I'd have you grow a spine and stop deferring to me when you know exactly what needs to be done."

The insult was daring but effective.

Nox stiffened, lowering her hands to the table before her. "You believe me to be spineless?"

He closed and opened his eyes slowly. "I believe there's

no reason for you to present yourself as such, especially when I saw you decide our path forward days ago. Say it."

Nox leveled an unwavering gaze. The several heartbeats that passed between them were a challenge. He didn't move a muscle as his silence forced her to respond.

At last, she said, "Your hope to get the support of Farehold is worthless while the curse at the border exists. We can't spread any campaign of Raascot's good intent or of Daphne having an heir while everyone who crosses the border is seen as ag'imni. Killing Moirai is the only reasonable priority, and Ash is right on that. You're also correct in that we lack key intelligence needed for effective tactical infiltration. Your spies should be gathering information on Moirai's routine within Aubade, her security, and also whatever spelled objects and wards she might possess, particularly as she seems to have something magic preventing Amaris from flexing persuasion.

"On top of that, open war is foolish with or without the threat of Sulgrave. If we expose ourselves like Ceres's men did in the gully, they're merely sitting ducks for Sulgrave's zealots to strike. Sneaking in is our best bet at eliminating Moirai and keeping ourselves safe. We have every reason to believe her curse will die with her. Ceres may have been mad, but he was right to bring Amaris south. She should lead the assassination effort. It is why she was born. Once the curse is broken, we can move forward with humanitarian efforts for Farehold."

Gadriel's eyes flickered with pride as the corner of his mouth quirked up in a smile. "And now you're a queen."

Chapter Nineteen

A MARIS? WE NEED TO TALK."
Nox used her newfound momentum to seek Amaris out the moment her meeting with Gadriel concluded. She'd stopped by her own room first and fetched a small, handkerchief-wrapped package. One long corridor and a left turn later, she was in Amaris's doorway. "I know things have been strained between us, but this is about the mission. Even as a reever, I know you want to honor your dispatch for the south."

Amaris had been sitting on her bed, fully clothed, flipping through an illustrated bestiary. She always seemed to be able to sniff out texts on monster lore wherever she went, and the castle had been no exception. Nox noted the personal library piled on Amaris's desk and bedside table.

"Did you know about these?" Amaris turned the book toward Nox, ignoring her question completely.

Nox looked at the drawing and made a disapproving sound. "What an unfortunate creature. Why would the goddess make something so ugly?"

The drawing and accompanying text appeared to be something with a body of an owl with a distinctly humanoid face. "They're called harpies. A lot of lies, fear, and rumors that have toppled powers have been blamed on the harpy. They can land in the trees or on your window and whisper all sorts of gossip without you realizing where you heard your information or who planted the idea in your head."

"How impish."

Amaris nodded, returning her attention to the passage.

Nox pressed. "I don't want to take too much of your time away from the tome, nor do I want to downplay the importance of learning about owl-men, but I really need to talk to you about our mission to the south."

"Owl-women, I believe."

"Amaris."

She closed the bestiary rather dramatically, lifting one side, then allowing gravity to slam it shut. "Yes, fine, I'm listening."

Things between them had been strange for a long time. They no longer fought, nor had they moved forward. As much as it pained Nox, she remained firm in her conclusion, just as Amaris maintained her promise to break the curse so that they might see if there was a future where they might be together by choice, rather than fate.

Amaris gestured for Nox to join her on the bed.

She moved forward into the unfamiliar energy, as if they were playing the role of strangers in a theater in which neither of them had realized they'd been cast. They had spent their lives loving and knowing one another, and now cordial indifference wrote their strained lines as they regarded one another. This game of pretending they meant nothing to each other had grown tiring.

"What did you bring me?"

Nox sighed and unwrapped the handkerchief, focusing her attention promptly on the business at hand. "It's Yggdrasil's apple, from the Temple of the All Mother. I think you should eat of it. It showed me your birth and gave me a lot of the information I needed in order to understand the world and my place in it. I think if you're meant to be the goddess's curse breaker, you might benefit from it."

The last time Nox had offered Amaris the apple, it had ended in a chucked fruit and tempestuous fight. It had survived the impact without a single bruise. Its flesh was still as firm and juicy as if it had been freshly plucked that very hour, though two bites still remained taken from it.

Amaris accepted the fruit with a curt nod. "We're going through with it, then? We'll head south?"

Nox confirmed, "We have to. Ceres was wrong to force you into his mission of vengeance, but he did understand what we all know: you're the key to breaking the curse. You've been given gifts that no one else has for exactly this reason. It has to be you, Amaris."

Amaris kept her eyes on the apple. Her tone wasn't that of friend or partner. She spoke like a reever gathering intelligence. "What are the others doing to prepare?"

"Zaccai is connecting with their outposts, and we're gathering intelligence on how to get into the castle, and also identifying what spelled object Moirai possesses that made her resistant to your ability."

"Am I to go with the reevers?"

Nox hesitated before answering.

"What?"

"There may be a problem."

Amaris lowered her brows. "What problem?"

Nox exhaled slowly. "For all we know, you and Malik are the only two who will be unaffected by reentering Farehold. Neither Ash nor I had ever gone north of the border before now. I'm not certain whether or not we'll be in our true form or if, because of our northern fae blood, we'll be subjected to the perception curse. I know you would still see the two of us fine with those lilac eyes of yours, but no one else in Farehold could."

"Are you implying that Malik and I might be on a two-man mission to assassinate the queen?"

"No, I'm just saying there are problems we need to troubleshoot before we know for sure who can go south. And in the meantime, it's really important that you arm yourself with all manner of knowledge and information. If the apple could be as useful for you as it was for me, it's worth a try."

"Fine," she said coolly. "I'll try it tonight."

Nox supposed it was as satisfying a response as she was going to get. She stood as if to leave but hesitated a bit by the door. She felt the pressure of the wall between them. Her love for Amaris had shaped her very character since she was a child. She had done unspeakable things in the name of love. Love had fueled and sustained her not only as a reason for being but on her based magic level. Now this shaping force in her life had been locked up behind iron. Some part of her wondered if her sexual ruthlessness of late was born now out of need in the absence of her lifelong love.

She missed Amaris more than words could say.

"Is there something else?" Amaris looked expectantly.

She winced at the question. "No, there's nothing. Please let me know in the morning if you've learned anything."

Nox closed the door behind her and leaned briefly against it, hands still clasping the knob as it shut. She took a calming breath and grounded herself.

She was queen. It was time she acted like one.

A fitful night bled into the following day. By the time she made it to the dining room, she wasn't surprised to learn that most of the castle's residents had already finished lunch. She caught Gadriel just as he was leaving, a small dinner roll in his hand.

"Gad, will you do me a favor?"

He looked a bit startled, as she had rarely—if ever—initiated requests of him. "Of course."

"What are Gwydir's resources for magical manufacturing?"

He blinked while he considered her question. The hallway outside of the dining room wasn't the typical location for questions regarding the kingdom, but there was no time like the present. "We have a few smiths and tailors who have trained at the university, both humans and fae, magical and sans magic. Is there something specific you're looking to craft?"

She sucked in a lip. "Until now, we lacked the specifics of Moirai's curse. Now that we know everything from its location and motive to its source and intended recipients, do you think there might be objects that could be crafted to nullify the perception?"

If he had been startled before, now he was truly speechless. "You think we might be able to create a...what...a magical antidote?"

"More like a shield. We have plenty of objects for dampening and neutralizing that usually work by containing. Why couldn't we make one that deflected rather than entrapped? Or, if a manufacturer could collaborate with Amaris and her gift to rightly see, we may have untapped resources."

He nodded, gears in his head rapidly turning behind his thoughtful eyes. "Yes, I'll send word and have several of our best manufacturers at the castle by this evening. There's no reason for any of the curse's specificities to remain secret, so it couldn't hurt to put all hands on deck. In fact, this may be a clever grassroots way to begin to get word out regarding Daphne as Ceres's lover and you as their child. Once people understand the story of the curse, they'll know why their princess was in hiding. Not only will this rally Raascot for its resources in fighting the curse, but it may also prepare the people to accept you as queen."

Excitement crept into her words. "You think it might be possible?"

"I think this is great work, Nox."

"If there's even a shot at this working, we need to postpone southbound missions until our manufacturers have had a chance to collaborate with Amaris and her gift for true sight."

"I'll get on this right away." He took off with a bit more purpose in his step than she'd seen in some time.

Nox attempted to find Amaris in her rooms, but the reevers must have been off training, as they were nowhere to be found. Later that evening, the inner circle was gathered in the war room to discuss Gadriel's findings. He quickly explained Nox's idea, and everyone seemed to buzz with a bit of excitement at the possibility. The manufacturers hadn't sounded particularly confident that they'd be able to accomplish what was being asked of them, but a team of seven had been summoned to work tirelessly until they were able to either craft something useful or announce with some certainty that it couldn't be done.

Nox waited anxiously for her chance to ask what was truly on her mind. The moment Gadriel finished his report, she asked, "Amaris, what did the apple show you?"

Amaris's mouth turned downward. "I'm sorry; I don't want to disappoint you. The fruit did nothing for me. I ate of it before bed and woke up this morning without seeing anything."

Zaccai spoke from his usual resting point against the wall. "I wasn't there in the town house when the news first came, but this was the apple from the Tree of Life that gave you dreams of the past, correct?"

Nox confirmed.

He spoke slowly, as if choosing each word with care. "And these dreams were not just visions. They were memories?"

"Yes, I was looking from the perspective of the tree. They were Yggdrasil's memories."

Gadriel straightened his shoulders. "What is it, Cai?"

The spymaster shook his head, waving a hand as if to dismiss his thought. Gadriel continued to stare at his second in command for a while longer before accepting that the man would not be elaborating.

"Have we made any progress with Tanith?" Nox asked. She was discouraged by Amaris's report but had to remain focused.

Yazlyn confirmed, "She's been quite lovely."

Ash made a single, disgusted noise. "She's lovely to the pure-blooded fae and whatever Amaris is, you mean?"

Yazlyn ignored his attitude, examining her nails as she said, "We can't all be perfect."

Nox made a tired face. "If she's being cooperative, then I'm going to need you to push her further. The things she's shared have been interesting but not actionable. Get more specifics regarding the names of her Sulgrave companions and where they've gone. See what she'll tell you about their abilities. If she came on a skiff of five, then we may have four other zealots running loose on the continent. I doubt we can handle another vakliche invasion."

"I'll talk to her tonight."

Malik smiled from where he'd been resting his elbows on the table. "Is it just me, or are these meetings getting easier?"

The room relaxed a bit in agreement. Gadriel smiled. "Thank your queen for that."

Malik winked. "I intend to."

✦

She left Zaccai and Gadriel behind as the war room emptied.

Amaris apologetically returned what remained of the apple to Nox, who once again stashed it where she'd kept it wrapped in her handkerchief. Perhaps its magical potency had worn off, but it seemed impertinent to discard something so sacred. Nox returned to her room to do what she did best: put her thoughts onto paper. Her writing desk reflected the one she'd owned at the Selkie, covered in a collection of sketches from her memories.

The empty parchment filled like an inky cup, like thought poured onto the page as she kept drawing arrows from thought to result, working her way systematically through everything they needed to successfully move on Queen Moirai. There were a few unanswered questions that remained scrawled across the top. How could they test the efficacy of a spelled object without showing up in Farehold and frightening someone with the face of a demon? What part could Tanith and her cult play to either aid or destroy their efforts? What was she meant to do to help the mission succeed aside from strategize from the armchair of the throne room?

Nox looked up from her desk as someone knocked. "Yes?"

The door cracked, and Yazlyn entered. "Did you want any company?"

She sighed, returning her gaze to her desk. "Not tonight."

The fae's cheeks pinked as she shook her head with poorly concealed embarrassment. "No, no, I shouldn't have assumed. You were otherwise occupied last night as well, and I just thought you might think more clearly if you'd had a little help. You know, help detangle your mind by tangling your sheets." She attempted to diffuse the discomfort with a smile, but it had the opposite effect.

Nox frowned, setting down her pen. "I think we need to talk."

Yazlyn paled. Her eyes darted to the door as if contemplating escape. "Oh. That's never how pleasant conversations start."

Nox gestured for the fae to sit and left her desk to perch beside her on the bed.

She took Yazlyn's hand. Each labored breath was intentional as she allowed the weight of the moment to press upon them. "This was so much fun when we hated each other, wasn't it?"

Yazlyn's brows furrowed. "Are you trying to tell me you don't hate me anymore?"

She shrugged. She offered a small, sad smile. "I guess so. Who would have thought? And without that mutual hate... it just doesn't feel right."

The sergeant was quiet. She kept her eyes on the bed. "Because now that you don't hate me, you've realized there's no emotion to replace it."

Nox's fingers tightened around the hand in her own. It was a single squeeze in concession.

Yes. Yazlyn understood. While the company had been passionate and pleasurable and life-giving for months, in the absence of hate, she was realizing the only thing she felt was indifference. When she hadn't been able to give her heart to Emily, she had blamed it on the belief that only Amaris could possess it. The care that had formed in their relationship at the Selkie had been doomed from the start, and that knowledge had felt honest enough.

Whatever existed between her and Yazlyn no longer felt honest.

"I feel like if we aren't on the same page, then I'm using you. I'm not comfortable with that."

Yazlyn's hazel eyes were as large as a doe's. She looked like someone trying to catch a stream, thinly veiling panic as water slipped between her fingers. "I don't feel used, Nox. I know we aren't partners, and what we have isn't a relationship, but I come here because I want to be here. I want to be in your bed. In the interest of honesty, yes, it would be far easier to want someone else. It would be wise to wake up in my own bed. It's ill-advised for me to tumble with the ascending queen to the Raascot throne, and if I meet a nice farmer's daughter, I'll be the first to let you know that I'm not coming back. But as much as I want to want someone or something else, I don't."

Nox attempted a half smile. "Well, I have been told I'm rather spectacular in bed."

"And so humble."

Her smile was genuine this time. "What use is humility when you're in the presence of a sex god?"

"I'm pretty sure Amaris is the goddess. You're just the queen."

She pushed her gently. "As long as you still feel okay with everything…"

Yazlyn nodded a bit too eagerly to be believable. "You're not the only one who gets something out of this. Granted, your perks are a bit more rooted in your very center of power,

215

but I do think I climax three hundred times more frequently than the average fae as of late, so I've had worse problems."

Nox rested a hand on the side of Yazlyn's face. The gesture was meant to be comforting, but it only made her sad. Yazlyn leaned into her touch, and she felt like she'd been in exactly this position before. She was holding the face of someone who wanted more than she could offer. Still, Nox would have to respect the woman enough to take her at her word. If she said that she was mutually benefitting and happy with the arrangement, who was Nox to say she knew the woman's emotions and intent better than she did?

"I really am tired tonight," Nox said finally.

Moving in unconscious response, Yazlyn pushed a kiss into Nox's palm. It was clear from the way her back went rigid and her eyes flew open that she regretted doing it the moment her lips touched Nox's hand. It had been the wrong move. The gesture was far too affectionate and intimate to convey the appropriate distance needed for them to continue down whatever path they were on.

"Yazlyn..." Nox said, dropping her hand.

Yazlyn shook her head, and nothing more needed to be said. She got to her feet and left, chewing her lip against any final word. She closed the door behind her.

Nox felt terrible, not just emotionally from their exchange but with the physical weariness of an impending flu.

She grimaced against the feeling, hating that she knew its source. It was the terrible price of understanding herself. Now going even two days with neither love nor oxytocin wore on her. She knew she could call on Malik if she needed to, but she felt even worse about using him than she did of Yazlyn. Her loneliness was a prison of her own making. The affections were there at her feet, but she'd rejected them all.

Her castle was breaking.

Nox wanted to throw all her papers off of her desk in a tantrum, but she lacked the energy to do so. An icy void seeped into what remained of her fighting spirit.

She crawled into bed and hugged a pillow to her chest, at long last allowing herself to fully feel the weight of her heartbreak. Distractions had kept the crippling anguish that accompanied it, wholly absorbing what she had lost when she had pushed Amaris away for so long. She hadn't just lost the fragile gift of potential romance. It wasn't only a lifelong friendship that had hit the wall along with the apple. It couldn't even be boxed into something as easy as a familial constant.

She had lost her entire reason for being.

Amaris hadn't just owned her heart; she had *been* Nox's heart.

Something tore from her belly, clawing through her throat. Try as she might, she couldn't contain it. It was the wounded, primal cries of long overdue mourning.

Nox buried her face in the pillow, hoping the feathers would muffle the loud, miserable sounds of her grief. Salt stained her face and the creases of the pillow she clutched to her face, weeping into it with every drop she'd left unspilled for months. A sharp knife plunged into her, carving out everything she had. She had never known that so much intense, physical pain could emanate from one's heart, but this felt exactly like dying. If the All Mother was good, Nox would be taken from this cruel world now and spared ever having to feel again.

She cried until she ran out of water. Her mouth was desert-dry from the muffled pulls of ragged breaths. Her muscles ached. Her body trembled against the exertion. And the longer she cried, the more certain she was that if the night claimed her, she would have no desire to wake up in the morning.

Chapter Twenty

N OX WAS DREAMING.
There was a weightless quality to the air, as if each sip sent her closer to the stars.

She recognized the stone and ivy of Farleigh, but this was no childhood memory. Amaris, also fully grown and adorned with her two pink slashes of scars, was exiting the manor to walk toward the stables. Nox jogged to catch up with her, gravity holding little of its typical efficacy as she moved. She looked over her shoulders for other signs of life, curious as to what else had swirled in this surrealist version of Farleigh. There were no children running around, nor were there matrons.

They were alone.

The air grew heavier when she reached Amaris. This was not the pleasant sort of dream that she often found when she escaped to the clutches of sleep. In fact, this didn't feel like a typical dream at all. Something about the edges of the world was wobbly and unfamiliar as it shimmered in and out of focus.

Amaris saw her but didn't seem concerned.

Nox asked, "Where are you going?"

"I've always wanted to ride the horses in the forest here." Amaris shrugged, dark, weighted air rippling behind her as she walked. "The matrons taught me to ride sidesaddle, but we just went up and down the lawn. I thought it would be fun to feel free and see what's in these woods."

Nox followed Amaris into the stables and watched as she produced an apple for the horse. She was feeding him the apple from the Tree of Life, now three bites distinctly taken from it. The horse ate it happily and whinnied, crunching into the sweet, firm fruit. "This is Cobb," Amaris said.

Nox petted the dapple gray's nose. "I don't remember you at Farleigh, Cobb."

"He was Odrin's horse. Well, Odrin gave him to me, so I guess he was my horse." She continued petting the horse's nose. Cobb nuzzled into her, and she smiled happily back at the friendly beast.

"Odrin," Nox repeated quietly. Amaris hadn't spoken with her about the man following the events at the castle. Were it not for Malik, Nox would never have known what his loss meant, nor what pain Amaris was hiding. "I'm truly sorry about everything that happened with Odrin. I'm sorry I never got to know him. I did meet him briefly, you know. Both at Farleigh and at the town house in Gwydir. He seemed so lovely."

Amaris's eyes lined with silver. The sinking emotion formed a void, like that of a stone threatening to puncture paper. The dream trembled. "He was."

She didn't dare say anything further and risk the fabric of the dream. Amaris led Cobb out of the stable, but when they exited, they were no longer at the orphanage.

"Where are we?" Nox asked, eyes scanning the mountains and rocks that surrounded them. A hawk screeched somewhere in the distance, but the only other sounds were the clattering hooves of the gray horse and the gentle scuffing of their shoes over stone.

Amaris led Cobb over a stone bridge with no walls. One

wrong step and they'd plummet into a valley below. The bridge connected the granite rock faces of two sheer mountains. Into the very edge of the mountain, a castle was hewn.

Amaris said, "This is Uaimh Reev. I always wanted you to see it. I thought of you all the time while I was here."

The horse was gone before she had the chance to ask anything further. A distant, haunting sensation stitched through her as Nox continued to follow. Amaris walked absently through the doors of the reev, wandering aimlessly through the keep. Nox did her best to soak everything in, but every new sight caused the confusion within her to swell. She racked her brain for points of reference. She tried to remember a single conversation wherein Ash or Malik had described the reev. She wondered if there had been pictures in books or sketches on parchments, but nothing came to mind.

Puzzlement began to feel more like unease as they wandered down halls, through a large dining room, past a training arena, and across various studies and libraries. The sense of wavering crowded her peripherals, as if she were teetering on the edge of the bridge they'd crossed together.

Nox swallowed the stone in her throat, wincing as it filled her belly with anxiety-touched questions. "Amaris?"

"Yes?"

"How am I seeing this?"

Amaris frowned, ignoring her as she led her into a new space. "This is my room. This is where I slept. This is where I studied animals and politics and tactics and the history of the reevers. This is—"

"How am I able to see the reev?" Nox remained near the entryway as fear forced her to repeat her question. This was wrong. The air was wrong. The sights, the views, the place were all wrong. She challenged herself to think harder about all she knew to be true of lucid dreams, but she couldn't piece together the jigsaw.

Amaris rippled like the surface of a pond, as if the disruption were interfering with the very fabric of the dream.

220

"Look, it's us." Amaris showed her a drawing she'd made of the two of them. She didn't have Nox's talent for drawing, despite her years of lessons at the manor under the matron's supervision. The sketch was of two girls in a kitchen pantry with one's arm around the other. "I tried not to let myself miss you then."

A high-pitched ring cut through Nox.

"These are *your* memories." It was not a question.

Amaris looked up at her then and extended her hand. Nox took it wordlessly. Amaris continued talking in the matter-of-fact, impassive way of distant dreamers.

"I try not to let myself miss you now."

For the first time in months, they touched. Amaris slipped her arms around Nox's waist, resting her head against Nox's chest and tucking it beneath her chin. Nox inhaled juniper and melting snow. Her heart wrung itself dry, blood and pain coursing through her arrhythmic beats as she clutched at Amaris.

"This isn't my dream," Nox said, choking. When Amaris didn't react, she said, "Amaris, these memories don't belong to me. These are your thoughts. I'm in your dream."

Amaris looked up at her and inclined her chin the same way she had when she'd sought out Nox on their first night at the castle. Now panic-laced adrenaline pounded through her.

Frosted lashes fluttered to a close as Amaris leaned in. She was one small movement away from brushing Nox's lips with a kiss, the same way Nox had wanted so many times before in her own dreams. Her heart thundered painfully as she struggled to understand what was happening or what she should do.

She blinked her eyes tightly, shaking her head against the nightmare.

There was an earthquake then. No, it was a storm. It was a pounding, a thudding. What was that sound? It filled the room, bouncing off the walls, and punching through time and space. It was—

Nox shot up, gasping for air. Daylight. Sheets. Blue-black walls.

Sweat drenched her, soaking the clothes she'd fallen asleep in the night before. She clutched the salty pillow that had spent the night absorbing her tears.

Confusion roiled into sticky, miserable nausea. Fiction and reality blurred as she rubbed the grogginess from her eyes.

The door. The noise was someone knocking on her door.

"What?" she rasped. She clutched her stomach, certain she was going to be sick.

The moment the door opened, she understood why the knocker hadn't let themselves in. She blinked blearily up at Zaccai, too polite and unfamiliar to barge into her bedroom.

"I'm sorry to disturb you," he said. "I received an urgent raven from our outpost in Yelagin. I think we've found Sulgrave's forces."

She tried to nod, but the motion sent her vision spinning. "I'll be right out. I just need a minute. Go get Gadriel and Yazlyn. I'll meet you in the war room. Fetch Tanith…which means, don't allow Ash or Malik to come. My half-blood presence will be hard enough for her."

"Is that wise?"

Nox arched a brow.

"Accommodating her, I mean. Should we be changing our lives to work around her religion?"

The headache behind her eyes bloomed, competing against rational thought for her attention. "This will not be standard practice. Because no, she does not deserve accommodation for her religious prejudice. But right now, it's a temporary means to an end. I need an authentic reaction out of her if these are her men, and we won't get that if she's fully closed down."

He nodded once. Neither of them appeared entirely satisfied with the solution, but they both understood if Tanith's presence in the meeting told them anything useful that might help save the continent, it was worth the gamble. He asked, "And Amaris?"

She did her best to clear the fog from her head, conjuring her queenly fortitude as she said, "The fae bitch likes the little godling, doesn't she? Sure, round up everyone. Send my apologies to the other reevers. Once they know Tanith is there, I'm confident they won't want to be there either."

The moment Zaccai disappeared, Nox was on her feet, stumbling to the bathing room. She barely made it to the chamber pot before emptying what little contents her stomach possessed. She washed the bile from her mouth, locking eyes with her reflection as she did so.

The whites of her eyes were laced with prominent, bloodshot vessels. Sweat plastered her limp, lackluster hair to her neck and face. She splashed water on her face and scrubbed at the bright red pillow creases that pressed themselves into her once-plump skin, but it did little good.

A second wave of cold sweat misted across her forehead. It took her twice as long to put her hair in a braid with the tremble in her hands, but she had to pull herself together. If they'd located Sulgrave, then this was as serious as death.

She finished in the bathroom and changed into fresh clothes before making her way to the war room. She gritted her teeth against the hope that the others would be too distracted to notice how ill she looked and grimaced to find she was the last to arrive.

Tanith stiffened as she entered.

"Welcome to the meeting, Tanith," Nox said dryly.

Tanith's lips pulled back in a quiet snarl. "Raascot has allowed a mixed-blood fae to take the throne where a pure fae king sat only days before."

Too taxed and miserable to listen to fanatical bullshit, Nox said, "Well, if you hadn't attacked the gully, there'd still be a pure fae king on the throne. We have *you* to thank for my title. Now, Zaccai, what's happening in Yelagin?"

She watched the spymaster's face as he carefully avoided looking in Tanith's direction. "You'll recall Yelagin is built around a lake?"

Nox sunk into her chair. She gripped the edge of the table to keep the room from tilting. "If this is going where I think it's going, all I've learned is that nothing good can come from water. What happened?"

All eyes were on Zaccai. His brows puckered, shaking his head as he pointed to the city on the map. "It's hard to know, precisely. There are no bodies. It's a ghost town. We had a few men at our outpost at a farm in Yelagin who heard scuffles and screams. Reports say a number of citizens escaped to the woods. To the best of our knowledge…it seems as though the civilians were dragged into the lake."

If there had been anything left in her stomach, it would have come up at his words. She had expected an attack. Monsters, blood, fire, swords, battles, carnage were all nightmarish outcomes she could understand.

"What?"

"There are several things it may have been, though nothing has ever happened on such a mass scale. Sirens and kelpies have reputations for luring and drowning someone who's already on the water, but this creature would have to have the physical ability to walk into homes and take people from their beds."

"We need the reevers," Nox mumbled.

"You have a reever," Amaris said from the far side of the room. "The nakki snatch those close to shore and bring them under water, but those stories were rare and isolated incidents. They're little more than folklore, really. It's the ghost story of a lonely lady of the lake who desired companionship so badly that she'd drag others beneath the waves to be with her forever."

Zaccai's downturned face was not encouraging. He went on. "Wraiths or sea serpents might be an answer if the civilians had been swimming or already on boats, but the fact that these things exited the water, had the dexterity for abduction, and returned to the lake makes me think it has to be the nakki."

224

"Are they demons?" Yazlyn asked, looking at Amaris.

"They're said to bleed red, if they exist at all."

Zaccai said, "A huge problem with this theory is that these monsters are not, and have never been, creatures who live in communities of more than a few dozen, even in myths. No lore supports a coordinated attack like this. For a city the size of Yelagin to be taken from their beds in their sleep, the number of creatures would have to have been in the tens of thousands."

"Nakki?" Tanith asked curiously.

A bolt of surprise crackled through the room. Nox studied Tanith carefully as the spymaster chose his next words.

"They have names in other dialects, but there are more consonants than I know how to pronounce," Zaccai clarified. "Perhaps you know them by another name. They're corporeal water sprites. There's a sort of...hypnotic effect they're said to have on humans. They could have entered the homes and brought the humans back to the water with them without a struggle. They live in freshwater lakes and rivers and are generally perceived as beautiful faelike monsters. I've never met anyone who's seen one."

Amaris said, "I assumed it was little more than the wishful thinking of lonely fishermen who wanted to believe beautiful women lived in the water. That, and telling yourself a monster lured your beloved into the waves is easier than accepting that your child fell into the rivers and lakes and drowned, if it was preventable."

Nox wiped at the sweat on her brow. "I'm confused. Are they real or aren't they?"

Amaris turned to Nox. "There were just as many entries in my tomes about mermaids as there were about nakki. And we all know mermaids aren't real."

"The reevers also said vakliche weren't supposed to be real either," Yazlyn muttered.

Several pairs of eyes remained trained on Tanith, who seemed to be appreciatively absorbing the information.

"And your men?" Tanith finally asked.

Zaccai appeared confused by the question. "My men? You mean, the Raascot fae at the outpost?"

She arched a brow. "Yes, what happened to them?"

"They can fly, so they were able to escape."

She nodded solemnly. Tanith opened her palms, spreading them wide as if revealing a picture. "Precisely. Any fae would have been able to stop or escape the attack. Those of pure magical blood are at no risk."

Yazlyn paled. "How could you do this? To be clear, I don't mean morally, since now is not the time to debate your fucked-up religion. In the most technical sense: how could a fae bind so many creatures to themselves and coordinate such an attack?"

Tanith eyed them speculatively and then made a face at Nox. "I would prefer to speak without it in the room."

Nox was too tired to be angry, but fortunately, she didn't have to be. Others were there to do the job for her. Gadriel's eyes flashed with ice. There was no mistaking his tone or posture: he was ready to snuff out what remained of the Sulgrave fae's miserable life. "She is our queen, and you are on borrowed time, Tanith. We have been more than benevolent throughout your stay, in spite of the blood on your hands. Choose your next words very carefully, as they may determine whether you live or die."

"I am prepared to die for my beliefs. As are all of us."

Zaccai asked tentatively, "Tanith, what would you tell a true believer on how one might summon such powers so as to...purify the land?"

Nox was glad for the spymaster's diplomacy. The hot tempers of the others would get them nowhere.

Tanith smiled appreciatively. She held Zaccai's eyes as she said, "All fae are born with inherent power. Shall we think of it like water? Yes, I think that would be nice. Picture water, if you will. The ways our powers manifest are like freshwater springs that come out of the grass and moss and rocks. For example, I have this very neat gift." She wiggled her fingers as if to show something between her hands before remembering that her abilities had been rendered useless by her engraved cuffs. "Well, you're missing out on an exceptionally charming electricity display. I learned how to make my energy into the loveliest of shapes. Have you ever seen a lightning bolt shaped like a rose?"

Zaccai made a gesture to prompt her to continue. "Our gifts are like freshwater springs and...?"

"Oh, yes. A spring is simply an opening where underground water emerges. The water is there at all times; the spring is just how it breaks through the earth and reveals itself."

Gadriel began to speak, but Nox made a shushing motion with one hand. He withheld his thoughts and Zaccai continued.

"So, Tanith, one of my gifts is the ability to manipulate sound. I typically use it as a dampener. You're saying that this gift is just my freshwater spring?"

"Precisely. A lovely, useful gift, might I add."

He went on, "And that below me, is...what?"

She tilted her head. "Don't you see why we need magical purity? Can you understand why this continent is desperate for unity? How sad is it that you, a pure fae, could be born into this world and so separated from magic that you don't know the truth of what you are? This is what hundreds of years of living with humans will do."

He sucked his teeth carefully before saying, "Please tell me, Tanith."

"We are all connected to the well. The water is in all of us—what are our bodies but red water? You have the gift of flight and the ability to throw sound, which is quite useful in espionage and distraction. I will have to try it one day. But if you knew how to tap into the groundwater, you wouldn't be limited to only your freshwater springs. You could have a pump. Or a spigot. Or a waterfall!"

Gadriel finally spoke. "What you're suggesting is far

beyond primary and secondary powers. Are you saying you can access any power?"

Her lower lip puckered. Her tone betrayed her patient, if not disappointed, feeling that she was speaking to children. "I'm saying we can *all* access the power. Fae are conduits for magic. It is a river in all of us, and the current that flows through us is only as limited as our understanding of the magic. I feel so sad for everyone in the lower kingdoms. We all do. Our heart breaks for you. There's no reason that so many people should be cut off from the very source that gives us life."

"But I'm not fae," Amaris said skeptically.

"No, godling, you're a direct link to the All Mother. You are her living will. In the interest of our beautiful metaphor, if our fae power comes from the waters of the earth, yours then comes from the waters of the sky. It's water all around us."

Gadriel's forehead creased. "Nox is magic, though. She has power. Isn't that her freshwater spring?"

"The halfling is a thief who's built an aqueduct to redirect water meant for another field. After a few generations of diluting and sullying, they simply identify as humans who have the small magics. We've heard these humans called witches. Isn't that sickening? They're humans, taking credit for whatever fae six generations prior had defiled themselves and offered magic to their lineage."

"She does love her metaphors," Nox mumbled.

"Humans are weeds." Tanith glared. "They suck up the water, they sap the soil from its nutrients, they spread, they sully, they dry up every drop of the magic in the ground. It's time for the fae of the continent to have a fresh, pure rebirth."

Nox smiled with some sort of humorless self-satisfaction. "See, Zaccai? Told you it would be useful to have her here."

"Wait." Amaris paused. "You keep mentioning unity. If this is about cleansing…"

Tanith's frowns were always born of some distant confusion. While they all spoke the same common tongue, it was as if they operated with entirely separate vernaculars.

She said, "Uniting the continent, of course. Uniting Sulgrave with Farehold and Raascot. We're paving the way for a new, more perfect world."

Speechlessness followed, energy strung taut as a bow string. Nox's eyes had fluttered shut.

She heard Gadriel say to someone, "Take her, will you?"

Shoes scraped against stone as the prisoner was escorted from the war room back to her chambers.

In the river of seasick time that followed, someone had fetched Ash and Malik. Nox knew she should greet them, but she needed to keep her eyes shut for just a moment longer. She listened while the reevers were caught up on the nakki. Nox felt a tiny shard of her heart cut a splinter into her chest cavity as she pictured the long, black hair of sweet, kind, intelligent little Tess, the Yelagin girl who had invited her into her home for dinner. She closed her eyes against the horror as she pictured wet hands dragging her parents from their farmhouse into the lake's murky waters.

"Nox, are you not feeling well?" Yazlyn's voice cut off whatever the fae men had been saying.

She felt the room's eyes on her as if for the first time. Between Tanith's display and Zaccai's news, her illness had gone undetected until now.

Malik crossed the room and put a hand on her forehead. "She's burning up. Let's call the meeting adjourned. Can one of you find a healer?"

The room sprang into action. Yazlyn was the first to leave, doubtlessly on her way to locate whatever healer the castle housed. Nox looked up long enough to catch Gadriel's grim expression. Her power was no longer a secret. They both knew exactly what a healer would say.

Malik scooped her up and carried her back to her room. Gadriel scattered the others, trailing behind as Malik helped Nox into bed.

Gadriel's question came out as a demand. "What happened? There's no reason it should have come on this quickly."

Her voice scratched against her dry, cracked lips like sandpaper. "I think I used a power last night that I didn't know I had. I think...I think it drained me."

He gritted his teeth. "Malik, can you go to the kitchen and ask the cook for fire tea? Tell her not to go light on the ginger."

Malik nodded and jogged down the hall.

Nox swallowed again, fighting against the dryness in her throat. "What's fire tea?"

He shrugged. "I made it up. Listen, after our meeting yesterday Zaccai and I had a discussion. We absolutely should have involved you sooner, but we wanted to be sure. Nox: your father, Ceres, could dream-walk. It's a gift that's run through our family, though it doesn't surface in everyone. I think that's why when Amaris ate the fruit, she saw nothing. For you, it was a tether directly for you to be able to walk into the tree's memories in your dreams. Is this what happened last night?"

"Dream walking?" she repeated numbly.

"Have you ever done this before? Visited dreams?"

Nox began to tell him that no, she'd never done such a thing, when she halted amid her dizzying shake. Something strange scratched at her, forcing her to turn her thoughts over before she answered. "I...maybe. I mean, I've always been able to tell when I was dreaming, but last night felt different. I've had so many moments where dreams felt like reality. There were times in my life with Amaris...but I guess part of me always assumed I was seeing what I wanted to see. Last night was the first time I was certain that the dream was not my own. I was in someone else's memories."

"Something must have changed. What did you do to trigger it?"

Nox wanted to laugh. She had opened herself up raw and bare to her shattered heart for the first time in her life. She had allowed abandonment and reality to torment her like never before, raking her across the coals. "I cried myself to sleep."

"Great pain is often what instigates our powers. The apple may have just been a conductor between you and Yggdrasil that made it easier for this to break through the surface."

"And," she said quietly, "for the first time in my life, I fell without a net."

She didn't elaborate, and he didn't ask her to.

After a while, she said, "Ceres could dream-walk. But magic isn't supposed to be passed down in lineages, is it?"

He exhaled through his nose with a puff of frustration. "That's true, and it isn't. It's not as simple as that. We can talk more about it when you aren't dying. Now, do you need me to get someone to—" He gestured to where she lay.

She stopped herself from gagging. "That's repulsive, Gadriel. Look at me. I'm not going to let anyone fuck me in this state."

He made an apologetic half gesture.

"You're a terrible general."

He tapped his foot. "I'm a great general. But apparently my ideas regarding health aren't as brilliant as my military strategies."

Malik returned with a mug of fire tea, his hands pulling back from time to time against the scalding-hot cup.

"Um, thank you, Malik," Gadriel said, hedging uncertainly. Clearly, he hadn't expected his made-up concoction to be fulfilled quite so quickly.

Nox barely had the strength it took to remember being sick in the dark after burying a hatchet in the chest of a spider. The healer had given advice then that she knew she had to take now. To Gadriel, she said, "Just let me drink the tea and sit with Malik for a little while. You can check in on me later and see how well the tea has worked, okay?"

Gadriel looked between the two of them and nodded. Malik held her hand, kneeling on the floor next to the bed. She attempted to sip the fire tea but was confident that she was drinking juiced hot peppers, apple vinegar, and ginger. It scalded her taste buds, numbing them as it burned its way into her stomach. She'd have to make a mental note to tell Gadriel that next time he was going to invent a fictional medicine, it should be some mysterious miracle cure involving chocolate truffles.

"You're going to be okay," Malik said, pressing a kiss to her knuckles.

And with Malik with her, she felt like maybe he was right.

Chapter
Twenty-one

MALIK REFUSED TO LEAVE HER SIDE. His anchoring weight was a comforting force beside her that night, falling asleep with her hand in his as he watched over her. Within a day she was looking much better, and after two, she was up and about. Three nights later, she was almost back to her old self. Nox caught her reflection in the mirror as her skin began to shimmer once again. Life twinkled behind her eyes as she returned from the brink of death.

Over the course of the next several days, Malik moved a number of his things into Nox's room, setting up camp semi-permanently beside her. He knew both what she was and what it meant for him to be with her as a reever, as a friend, and as someone who'd become so much more.

By the end of the week, she looked into the lovely, healthy face that stared back at her and was hit by the weight of how many forms love can take. He wasn't Amaris, no. But in their own way, she and Malik loved each other. And for now, that was enough.

Change had a domino effect on the castle.

The atmosphere in the war room was the next to undergo

its shift. Gadriel and Ash no longer stood at the edges, yelling over the map at one another. Nox stopped spending meetings with her head buried in her hands, a curtain of hair protecting her from the world around her. Zaccai remained poised by the door, but everyone else found much more relaxed positions around the table.

Nox leaned into the meetings with the intensity of authority.

Zaccai reported, "My men have returned from Yelagin, and their descriptions seem to confirm our theories of the nakki. It was ghastly, but not in the way that teeth and venom and pinchers are terrifying. They recorded movement after midnight of what seemed to be slow-moving, naked women roaming the streets, entering homes, leading people into the lake. The way they tell it, my informants say it was too bizarre for comprehension. They couldn't intervene—they're seen as ag'imni and were outnumbered by the thousands."

"Thousands?" Amaris echoed.

"So much for not existing," Malik said.

Zaccai finished, "There has been no further activity in the city, though those who have escaped have returned to their homes and haven't seen any more disturbances from the lake. Early numbers sound like ten to twenty percent of the population survived. What remains of Yelagin is little more than a graveyard. People are afraid."

Ash leaned back in his chair. "Maybe if we wait long enough, you'll simply be able to walk into Aubade and pluck the crown from an empty castle. Sulgrave seems to be doing our work for us."

Nox bristled. Her irritation bled into her voice as she said, "Our work is not to kill innocent citizens. Our quarrel is with Moirai. Though I'll admit, I wouldn't mind if Tanith wanted to summon one of her demons for us and take care of that particular problem. Maybe we should start making her a regular fixture in these meetings. Win her to our cause."

It elicited a small chuckle as they thought of the tiny

package of fury and prejudice. While she'd made no attempt to escape, she also hadn't made any progress toward tolerance. Nox knew Tanith would not be willingly aiding the halfling queen anytime soon.

"Do we have any allegiances in Farehold that might be useful?" Nox asked.

Zaccai confirmed, "Our outposts grew organically from existing allegiances. The kingdoms have shifted as civilians have been shuffled around the continent over the past thousand years, but old loyalties die hard."

"And what of Tarkhany? The Etal Isles? Does Raascot have outposts or allies in other parts of the continent?"

"Tarkhany uses the sands as Sulgrave uses the Straits. I don't believe there's been a royal ambassador from Tarkhany in Gwydir for more than a thousand years, though we consider them neither friend nor foe. Whatever resulted from the summit a millennium ago left the west wing in rubble, and what seemed to be a treaty that the kingdoms of Raascot, Farehold, and Tarkhany would leave one another alone—at least, that Tarkhany would be left alone. If the documents of their summit are to be believed, the desert kingdom desires only separation and sovereignty. Though if Sulgrave succeeds in toppling Farehold and Raascot, Tarkhany is sure to follow."

Nox's thoughts drifted, and she wondered if she'd be able to tell which parts had been reconstructed without being told. Returning to the task at hand, she asked, "And what of the Isles?"

"What of them, indeed."

It was an unsatisfying answer but seemingly the only one she'd get.

Their daily meetings had become a bit less fruitful as they found themselves in the waiting stage. Zaccai and Gadriel had both offered to go into Farehold themselves, but with Nox's seat of power being so new, they knew their role at her side was too vital.

"Have we made any progress on the perception shields?" Nox asked.

Even the most basic of wards were precious, challenging to create and troublesome to tune to their intended subject. Gadriel shared that the manufacturers set on the task had begun to spread word throughout their homes, taverns, and churches about the curse, Ceres and Daphne, and the love child who had remained hidden from Moirai's prying eyes. While Raascot was in tatters following the fall of so many men in the massacre, the one loss no one seemed to mourn was that of their late king. The people were ready for the tide to turn and the northern kingdom to know peace and stability again.

"They're still hard at work, and it's become more than just the seven manufacturers. There's a team of twenty working on our project now. Several archivists and scholars of the magics have gotten intimately involved in the process. At the moment, they're not in any crafting phase. They still need to see how such an object would be possible. Amaris," he said as he looked to the reever, "they may need your help. You aren't fae, so no one is sure if it'll work. But the contribution of someone who can see through enchantments may need to be written in runes. It's a guess at best, but we need to try."

Amaris quirked a brow in wry amusement. "Because you still haven't made an effort to learn about manufacturing?"

"I lead armies, witchling. Would you also like me to learn how to bake chocolate pies and tame wild horses, or can I stick with my strengths and focus on military strategy?"

She grumbled before agreeing. "Of course. I'll help however I can."

"Great. Why don't you go train in manufacturing and then stop asking me about it."

"Maybe I will."

Nox didn't care enough to pick apart their banter. She was too focused on the hope that a spelled object might deflect the curse. The optimism was infectious.

Still riding the high from her manufacturing idea, Nox turned her attention toward the red-haired reever. "Ash, I have homework for you."

He looked to either side as if she'd forgotten his name and intended to call someone else. He was rarely addressed in these meetings. The others turned their attention curiously to the demi-fae.

"Yes?"

She leaned forward. "I'm putting you on babysitting duty. From now on, wherever you go, you'll bring Tanith with you."

He balked. His honey-colored eyes turned a dark, flat shade of amber as he glared. "Am I being punished?"

"Not at all," Nox said, waving away his horror. "We've seen her abilities. Tanith could be an incredible asset, but right now she's only talking to us under the conditions of her religious outlook. I think if she spent enough time with someone of mixed heritage, pure exposure therapy would force her to see your humanity. She has all of these ideas that I blame on her limited access to the real world."

Ash's temper flared. "Why can't Malik do it? Or you?"

"Malik is fully human, and though she doesn't like humans, as long as they don't interbreed with the fae, she doesn't seem to have a direct quarrel with them. And me? I'm the queen. I have more important things to do."

Only the general found her final sentence funny. She appreciated that her humor had an audience. Maybe it was a family thing.

Nox gestured toward the other women in the room. "Amaris: you or Yazlyn can act as a buffer in the beginning if you think it would be helpful, since she seems to like you. Eventually, I think that Ash and Tanith should be putting in as much one-on-one time as possible."

Nox had known Ash wouldn't be happy about her decision, but he was showing a lot more resistance than she'd anticipated.

"And what is she supposed to do with me every day? Eat together? Brush our teeth together? Braid each other's hair? Do we risk her coming with me to training and to making her even more dangerous?"

"I'm sure you'll figure it out." Nox waved a hand as if putting the matter to rest.

"Do we have anything else on the docket?" Amaris asked.

"Yes, there's one more thing. I don't think you're going to like it."

Amaris tilted her head expectantly.

"Right now, we're playing the waiting game, but once we've gathered the intelligence required on Moirai, we need to be ready to move in. Amaris, we're operating under the impression that you're on some divine mission to stop the queen. That means we need you at optimized strength. I know you and Ash have been training together and that you're a formidable reever, but Gadriel and I have been speaking about it and decided that you need to start training with him. He was able to help you unlock a shock wave before, and it would be a mistake if you couldn't access it when the moment of need finally arrives."

Her eyes bulged. "Are you saying you want Gadriel to strangle me?"

The room saw how Gadriel fought and failed to control a smirk as he muttered, "I think that's exactly what she's saying."

Amaris's eyes shot to the floor. Pink spread from her cheeks to whatever was visible of her neck and chest.

Deciding she didn't need to give anyone a chance to argue further, Nox clapped her hands to conclude the meeting. "Okay, if that's everything, I need to talk to Gadriel and Zaccai. Ash, go have fun with your new charge."

Ash was decidedly pouty as he and the other reevers left the room, Yazlyn in tow. Once the room had emptied, Nox said, "While we're speaking of training, I'm ready for you to tell me more about dream walking."

Zaccai left his regular post against the wall and approached the table to sit near Nox. He cleared his throat. "I suspected it the morning after you gave Amaris the apple and she found it ineffective. Ceres has been the only dream walker either Gadriel or I have met. We don't know a lot about how he controlled his gift, though he did visit us on multiple occasions in our sleep for meetings and strategy."

Gadriel agreed. "It was exceptionally useful. Now, Zaccai and I discussed this while you were ill. I told him you had unknowingly used your ability and that's part of what had drained you to the point of leaving our throne empty once again. We've been going through records and looking for information on anything Ceres had, but he didn't really write or keep up on any duties in the past twenty years."

The spymaster eyed her closely. "This is the first time you've walked?"

She looked at Zaccai, lips turned down. "I...don't think so. I think I've always been dream walking. I never would have said so. But when I look back at my dreams..."

Zaccai and Gadriel exchanged a curious look.

"You've never fallen ill before this experience?"

She shook her head.

Lines formed on Gadriel's forehead as he concentrated on the pieces of the puzzle. "Forgive me, but did you say you cried yourself to sleep that night?"

"What of it?"

Gadriel looked uncertainly to Zaccai, then to Nox again. "If I'm out of line, please stop me. But given what we know of your regenerative abilities—"

She made an exhausted sound. "You can call me a succubus. I'm learning to live with the word. Besides, I'm confident Zaccai already knows, or else he isn't a very good spymaster. We're protecting no one if we dance around the truth."

"All right," Gadriel amended. "I do think succubi abilities play into this, particularly if you have in fact dream-walked before and not fallen ill. Can you tell us more about where you went and what you saw when you walked?"

Nox's face crumpled. She rubbed her temples the way she had in her first few weeks in the war room. Once again, she felt very out of place. "It was an accident, and definitely an invasion of privacy. I don't feel particularly good about it. I went into Amaris's dream. She knew I was there, as she was speaking to me, but she didn't appear to know it was a dream the way I did. The thing is, I think I've visited her before. I think I've been visiting her for a long time. But I always thought it was a dream. Just *my* dream."

Gadriel appeared unbothered. He rubbed his chin thoughtfully. "Invading that privacy is part of the gift. Ceres used to use his ability for more than just meetings and information. It was a useful tool for spying. He wasn't able to cast himself into the dreams of anyone unless he'd met them in real life, which proved frustrating for him. I know he spent years scanning the minds of everyone in the kingdom for traces of his child."

Zaccai considered this. "I wonder if that contributed to his madness? He spent so much time in the minds of others that he had very little time to be in his own."

"We should assume the worst and tread lightly. It's a useful ability, but we can't have our second monarch losing touch with reality. It would reflect poorly on the kingdom."

Nox leaned back in her chair, crossing her arms. "I'll do my best to stay sane."

Zaccai shifted a bit uncomfortably. He looked to Gadriel then back to Nox.

"What?" she demanded. "Spit it out."

Zaccai made a reluctant face. "Staying with Malik has been…working?"

She understood the implication. Her exhale was tinged with guilt.

Gadriel spoke for her. "We know there have been plenty of instances where succubi have thrived off parental and familial love as children. A mother's love, in theory, is tireless and non-damaging to the source of affection. There's no reason to believe that love can't fuel her in a variety of forms. Come to think of it, can you imagine if she were beloved by the people? Nox, you may be sitting on a treasure trove of opportunity."

She choked on a laugh. "Are you seriously putting 'be beloved' on my to-do list?"

"Well, I think you're off to a great start," the commander said cheerily.

"Thanks, Cai."

"He's not wrong. All you have to do is stay sane and be even a marginally better ruler than Ceres, and the people are going to adore you. Royalty inspires a love of king and country that most of us will never truly understand. There are so many theories and beliefs about royal hearts, but to think that it might beat with the love of its kingdom as wholly as yours..."

"I don't know what to do with what you're saying."

"That's fine. I'm thinking out loud. It's more speculation than anything. I'll touch base with someone more knowledgeable in the subjects of magic. But it's curious... What do you know of primary and secondary powers?"

"Assume I know nothing."

"Well, your primary power is clearly your gift as a succubus. You're able to regenerate and absorb life in a very real way. If I'm to understand it correctly, you've even passed along life from one vessel to another. It challenges the way I've understood succubi and incubi entirely. It seems almost like relocating life from one place to another—from a first vessel to a second vessel, whether that second body is you or someone else of your choosing. That's incredible, Nox."

Discomfort heated her. She'd certainly never thought of her curse as incredible. Though when she thought of Malik and the spider...

"Secondary powers can be more treacherous," Gadriel said. "Secondary powers often take from us, rather than give. This has to be what made you so ill. I do think that, due to

241

the nature of your primary power, as long as you don't find yourself alone or without a nutritional source, you may be spared the negative consequences of your secondary power. In theory, you could use it without any fallout."

"Very helpful, guys. Anything else?"

Zaccai rubbed his chin. "Well, I ask about Malik because, as long as it seems to be producing desirable results and prevents you from being overtaxed, I think we should do our best to get you to practice dream walking again. Last time you were in distress while focusing on one individual, and then you were able to enter her dream. Do you think that's replicable?"

"Are you asking me to cry myself to sleep again?"

Gadriel shook his head contemplatively. "Not at all. I think we could try a variety of tactics. We work on unlocking magic in our war camps all the time, though it's often violent or uncomfortable. There's a tonic that puts people to sleep. I think perhaps if we did something like have Zaccai or me cut or hurt you as you were falling asleep, then you'd go under while thinking about us."

Her laugh was loud and clear and came from a place of true delight. Her eyes watered with her amusement. "You want me to fall asleep to you *stabbing* me? That idea was so bad that I'm officially replacing you as general. Zaccai, how would you like a promotion?"

Gadriel was immediately defensive. "So, it's not a perfect plan, but we were all subjected to some pretty ridiculous trials when we were learning about our own abilities."

"As your queen, I am officially striking 'drugging and stabbing me' from the list of options. No more ideas from you today, as you've clearly lost your mind. Perhaps it's hereditary. I'll think of something else and give it a try. Emotional distress might work just fine. In the meantime, I would like to hear more about how you think I could have inherited this ability."

While Gadriel remained put out for having his proposal

shot down so thoroughly, Zaccai spoke. "What Tanith said last week has challenged a lot of our beliefs about how magic manifests, but it also makes a lot of sense. We think one of the reasons that the northern fae seem to be born exhibiting similar powers might just be that they're the same expressions of energy we sense around us. To use her aquatic illustration: if magic is groundwater, it makes sense that the earth around us in kingdoms and among families would be weak in similar ways, allowing for complementary gifts to reveal themselves as their springs. Gadriel and his mother both have the ability to warm their body heat to scald like an iron in the fire, though hers is a physical fire, whereas his is internally contained. Perhaps proximity and relation to her didn't give him an inheritance of her magic but just a familiar outlet for the power to express itself."

"I'm only half fae, though. Shouldn't that limit my magical potential?"

"According to Tanith, yes. But I think there's a good chance you're more than half fae."

Nox's face folded skeptically. "Princess Daphne was human."

"Was she? Moirai clearly has a great power. Her gift for illusion seems singular, and when humans are born with a singular power, they usually call them the small magics. Moirai is channeling a much deeper well of strength than I've ever seen from a human. Besides, royal blood has been a common ingredient in blood magic for years. You might be harboring a lot more power than any of us realize."

Skipping over the blood magic entirely, Nox circled back to Moirai. "Moirai is a witch. Are you implying the southern queen is fae?"

Zaccai looked quite sure of this. He nodded. "Witch is just a word. I don't think she's fae—not fully, but her fae lineage may be closer to her than the Farehold royal family has ever let on. This would also help us understand why the Tree of Life was so receptive to Daphne's prayer. If she possessed access to the magical well—as Tanith has called it—she could have tapped into whatever stream of power ran between her and Yggdrasil."

"And why do they make us sick?" Nox asked, looking between Zaccai and Gadriel. "What are your secondary powers? Do they make you sick?"

Gadriel's brow furrowed. "Yes. I fall very ill if I use my secondary power. Sometimes it takes days to recover. Some fae never recover at all. It's believed to be a form of blood magic, but one wherein you're offering your own blood as the exchange. The ability draws on your life to trade for its access."

"Well, shit."

"I don't think you need to worry," Zaccai said reassuringly. "You have more protection than any other fae in the kingdom. You have an innate way to heal. It really is astounding."

She considered the information. After a while, Nox stood and the others followed suit, rising from the table as she walked them out of the room. "Cai, great first day as general. Outstanding work. I'll be sure to tell the others."

Zaccai laughed and kept walking.

Trailing behind them, Gadriel said, "Wait, I know you're joking, but can you just confirm that you're not serious?"

"I'll see you again tomorrow, boys." She wandered down the hall with a smile on her face.

Gadriel called after her, voice pitched louder than necessary, "Nox, can you please just state for the record that you're kidding? Nod once if I'm still the general."

She waved a hand goodbye without turning around, grinning to herself.

Chapter
Twenty-two

CALLING TANITH UNENTHUSIASTIC ABOUT HER NEW NANNY would have been the understatement of the century. The Sulgrave fae had shown great strength and inner peace throughout the majority of her stay in Gwydir, but being forced into constant proximity with Ash seemed a fate worse than death for them both. Amaris didn't know why she'd expected Ash to be the bigger person.

A crash and clatter reverberated off the stones in the courtyard as Yazlyn jumped out of the way, barely missing shrapnel. She crossed into the corridor just in time to bump into Amaris.

"Do you ever watch where you're going?" Amaris demanded.

Yazlyn's eyes were wide for a moment until Amaris's face cracked into a smile. She relaxed, appreciating the joke. Yazlyn apologized for tapping out from supervision earlier than she'd planned. She claimed watching the reever and the zealot claw at each other's throats like stray cats was only tolerable for so long.

"Good luck," Yazlyn said. "You're going to need it."

Amaris grimaced. She stepped into the courtyard that

previously had been used for training. Now, it seemed to serve as a place for Tanith to hurl insults and heavy objects at Ash while he chanted some mantra to himself about murder being wrong.

"Leave me be, mutt!" she cried, lofting what appeared to be a wooden training sword.

"If you don't stand down," Ash snarled, grabbing the wooden sword mid-descent, "then this stick won't be the only thing I break in half."

Tanith relinquished the training sword only to grab the next nearest blunt object.

Amaris settled against the wall near the entrance. She shook her head in disbelief.

Though Tanith had been provided with a number of dresses and outfits, she'd opted to wear red on a daily basis, which seemed appropriate for her bloodlust. Ash returned more than his fair share of tossed objects but was a bit more careful in selecting things that would neither maim nor kill.

"So," Amaris shouted over their mess, "things seem to be going really well."

Ash dodged what remained of the shelving unit that had once held all the practice weapons. It careened to his side. His lips were pulled back over his teeth in a growl. "Oh, things are great. Thank Nox for me."

Feeling decades older than her true age, Amaris walked up between them and crossed her arms. "Tanith. You are responsible for cleaning up the messes you make."

She wondered if Tanith understood the heavy weight of her implication as the Sulgrave fae's features darkened into a scowl. "I will happily clean once your beast leaves."

Amaris remained impassive. "Calling him names will do nothing but waste everyone's time. He's not going anywhere. I'm starting my run, and by the time I finish, I want all the equipment back where you found it. Hurry up and get it done, or else I'll see to it that we have the books taken out of your room."

Tanith's eyes flashed, and Amaris knew she'd struck the right chord.

Though she'd initially protested at Amaris's choice in stories, their ward had quickly found herself somewhat addicted to the escapism of romance novels. Her consumption of the books had proven ravenous, going through more than the castle could sustain. It made for an excellent bargaining chip. Being a prisoner was one thing. Being a prisoner forced to stare at a wall alone with your thoughts and absent any entertainment was an entirely different form of punishment. It was one Tanith had already endured and presumably had no eagerness to return to.

Amaris began her warm-ups, stretching and getting her blood flowing. She watched out of the corner of her eye as Tanith and Ash remained in a stalemate. Neither of them wanted to be the first to bend and pick up the evidence of their fight. Amaris could practically see Tanith's hackles raised, as if Ash were a viper and she were tensed for him to bite.

By the time Amaris began running, the ill-tempered pair was finally moving.

Nox hadn't been wrong to hope to expose Tanith to faelings, but Ash happened to be the least sportsmanlike half fae on the continent. Perhaps if Nox had talked to her about it ahead of time, she could have said as much.

Amaris ran a bit longer than she normally might have, pushing well past the point of exhaustion and exerting the remnants of her stamina in order to give the two time to finish their chore.

Amaris's face was hot and sweat-slick by the time she finished. She called Ash over to her where she was still panting from her exercise, doubled over on her knees. "You're going to have to be the adult here, Ash."

"No, she has to get over her magical bigotry."

"I agree. And how are we supposed to achieve that? Do we torture a change of faith out of her? Do we lock her away and let her stew in her preconceived notions? Nox is right.

The only shot we have at turning her is showing her that all of her beliefs were built in a void through exposure."

His lip pulled up in a half sneer. "Well, I don't like her."

"That's fine. I don't think any of us do. She's brainwashed. Anytime you match her energy and respond with hate, all you're doing is confirming whatever suspicions she has about you. You represent all demi-fae to her. You have to be the bigger person."

He flexed his hands. A muscle in his jaw ticked in irritation. "What do I do? She's impossible."

Amaris shrugged. "Sparring was always my favorite way to let out my anger. Why don't you give her the option to throw some punches? Turn her animosity into friendly competition?"

"Should we really be making her better at fighting?"

Amaris wiped the sweat from her brow. "I don't think she's shown any evidence of combat training. She's too powerful to have needed to rely on physical skill. I think if you help her build up her strength, she'll start to see you as a good thing in her life. Why not try making yourself an asset to her?"

"What do I have to threaten her with if she won't listen? Romance novels?"

Amaris's eyes narrowed, frustrated at having to explain that having the homicidal maniac on their side was important. The stitch in her side from her run was beginning to abate. "Any chance we have at understanding Sulgrave's next moves is in that head of hers. You'll catch more flies with honey than with vinegar. So you could try threats, sure. Or you could do what you did with me when I arrived at Uaimh Reev."

"And what did I do with you?"

She tilted her head slightly. "I was in a new place. I didn't know shit about the world. I was scared. And you were kind."

Ash's expression softened. "When did you get so smart?"

"I know you can do this." Amaris grinned.

She patted him on the back as she left the arena, hoping Ash and Tanith wouldn't kill each other.

"You handled that a lot better than I did," Yazlyn said. Amaris supposed the sergeant's posture was meant to look casual, but something about the way she leaned coolly against the wall seemed a bit forced.

"How long have you been waiting?" Amaris ran a self-conscious hand over the free-flying strands that had escaped from her braid.

"I was looking for tips for the next time I'm on nanny duty. Hey, I was wondering..." Yazlyn paused and fidgeted with her fingers.

Amaris eyed the sergeant somewhat impatiently.

"Any chance you'd be interested in going into town tonight? I don't know if you've ever seen Gwydir beyond the castle and the town house, but you've been in Raascot for a while now... I thought it might be fun to change out of our training clothes and maybe see if we can find live music?"

Amaris was stunned. "You want to go for drinks? With me?"

"Just as friends." Yazlyn's eyes widened in panicked clarification. "I don't know about you, but it would mean a lot to me to have a friend around here. And Gwydir is actually quite beautiful if you're open to giving it a chance."

They started walking again. Amaris nodded slowly as she considered it. Other than grabbing pints in Stone with her reever brothers, she hadn't done anything like this. "Yeah, that actually sounds pretty nice. But...what should I wear?"

✦

There come intervals in one's life when they realize how profoundly different their experience is from that of those around them. A child who has grown up in poverty may not realize their family's status until visiting the home of someone wealthy. After a lifetime of drinking liquor alone, it might take the observations of strangers telling someone that turning bright red from the alcohol is abnormal before they understand they're allergic to their favorite drink. The inner circle knew Nox had hoped that Tanith might have one of these moments when spending time with someone of mixed blood, encountering her own biases and internalized hatred. Amaris was having exactly such an experience now as she matched Yazlyn's pace, awkwardly fumbling for conversation as she realized she'd never had a woman for a friend.

Not only had Nox been Amaris's only friend, but Farleigh had cultivated such an alienating environment that Nox had become her only family, her beloved, her peer, her lifeline, her lone exposure to the world, her everything. Her friendships since escaping the orphanage had been exclusively male.

The walk through Gwydir truly was breathtaking, which gave her somewhere to direct her nervous energy.

Amaris had seen a few towns, from Yelagin and Stone to Priory and Aubade. But the labradorite of Castle Gwydir shimmered throughout the city. The very cobblestones glimmered with the twinkle of the captured night sky. While most of the buildings were composed of a similar stone, the lively painted signs, glows of firelight, variety of windows, and colorful cloaks and furs of the northerners kept the city from feeling anything but gloomy. While Yazlyn could have flown them, they'd walked so that she could soak in the sights, and soak them in she did. Her eyes had darted with childlike wonder as she took in every nook and cranny.

"I can't believe neither you nor Nox has even asked about leaving the castle," Yazlyn commented on their walk.

Amaris's face twisted contemplatively. "I went from an orphanage to an isolated keep in the mountains. I've been primed to stay put. And I suppose with Nox…"

The Selkie had been a keep of its own, though both Amaris and Yazlyn let the topic drift on the turn-of-the-season wind.

Amaris's legs burned from her earlier run. Gwydir was a rather hilly city in and of itself. It sprawled over steep inclines and roads with one large, dark river separating the castle grounds from the surrounding city. It created a natural moat between the royal family's property and the citizens of Gwydir. Yet Amaris had a sense that the moat was unneeded. The city's energy was one of warmth and acceptance, even if the temperature was anything but.

Raascot's capital city was fresh with the pines and evergreen brush dusted with snow blossoms that decorated the streets and lined the fronts of shops. Amaris had borrowed a heavy gray fur-lined cloak from Yazlyn as they set out onto the town, walking until snowflakes began to twinkle down from the cloudy night sky. The damp, falling snow pressed a lovely hush over the city, adding to the otherworldly feeling of wandering in a fairy tale. Beneath the cloak was a rather daring sky-blue dress that Yazlyn insisted on lending her for the evening, which was the first time Amaris had put on a dress in years. Yazlyn was quite a bit curvier than Amaris, but the ties and buttons of the dress's waist and bodice had made it adjustable enough to fit what she considered to be her boyish frame.

The snowflakes reflected the fae lights and glows from the fires of the buildings they passed, creating a glittery, snow globe effect of the world around them. Thanks to the exceptionally magical walk, Amaris was busy enough looking around at the sights that she hadn't felt pressured to make small talk. Yazlyn was a happy tour guide, allowing for long stretches of silences born from admiration.

But just as she adapted to the joy of a long, early winter walk, it was time to learn something new.

A peculiar spike of nerves pinched Amaris as they neared their destination. She wasn't afraid to fight a dragon, but she felt a stab of fear at the thought of entering the crowded bar. Yazlyn left little time to argue, grabbing her hand and leading them to what seemed to be the only vacant table in the pub.

The pub was packed to the seams. It overflowed with the warm, buzzing energy of humans and fae alike. Many of the bronzed Raascot men and women had the black, angelic wings common to the northern fae. Others, like Ash, were dark of coloration compared to those of Farehold blood, but they lacked the telltale wingspan familiar to the northern kingdom. Once seated, Amaris was acutely aware of all the stares she drew. Everyone continued chatting, drinking, dancing, or gambling, but no matter what activity was in front of them, everyone spared a glance or two at her.

Amaris shifted uncomfortably in her seat. She was hit with an astounding wave of relief when Yazlyn returned with two mugs of hot mead.

"Yaz, am I crazy or is everyone looking at me?" Amaris asked, rubbing the back of her neck.

The sergeant let out an honest, happy laugh as she clanked the mugs down on the table, sloshing the warm liquid slightly.

"I'm sorry, do you not know what you look like? Of course, they're staring! You're a strange silver creature with two prominent scars and a dress cut both down to your belly button and up to the middle of your thigh. They'd be crazy not to stare. You've been in more of a bubble than I'd realized if you've managed to elude prying eyes for so long."

Amaris drank too much too quickly in an effort to soothe her nerves but found a great appreciation for scalding, too-sweet mead.

"You're going to need to slow down or you're going to hurt tomorrow." Yazlyn laughed.

Between gulps, Amaris said, "That sounds like tomorrow's problem."

She tugged uncomfortably at the slit on her thigh, attempting to adjust the plunging neck that exposed too much of her sternum.

"Knock it off!" Yazlyn insisted, reaching across the table and indelicately yanking Amaris's hands away from where she pulled at her dress. "I know what you're trying to do, but it's having the opposite effect. Stop fondling yourself."

"Yaz!"

"I'm being honest." The sergeant shrugged. "Just relax.

This is your first time outside of the castle. You deserve some attention."

"Have you ever *tried* to relax?" Amaris hissed. "It's an oxymoron."

Yazlyn rolled her eyes good-naturedly and dipped Amaris's cup up, encouraging her to drain her first glass.

It helped.

She was able to focus on the music, which was a festive mixture of fiddles and song, half of the patrons joining in at intervals whenever they found a familiar verse. The tavern was a pleasant combination of both arched ears and pointed canines, and human teeth with small, rounded ears. An eruption of cheers came from a winged table engrossed in a card game, while others milled about sharing drinks and pots of stew and stories. The head of a white stag was mounted on one wall of the alehouse, with swords and axes and other decidedly masculine things adorning the opposite wall above the night-dark windows. Men and women of various classes and professions toasted one another amicably while they sang and chatted. They'd cast looks at Amaris whenever they thought they could get away with it, but she opted to believe Yazlyn, feeling that the looks were truly stares born more from curiosity than judgment.

They were well into their second round when Yazlyn said, "It might not be a bad idea for Nox to start making appearances in public. Don't you think the people should get to know her?"

Amaris rolled her shoulders. "You'd have to ask her. We haven't really been talking much lately."

Yazlyn's face betrayed her internal battle.

"What?" Amaris asked over the steadily swelling music and revelry. "Do you want to talk about Nox?"

"Oh, goddess, can we? Is it that obvious? Is that too much?"

Amaris's laugh was mead-fueled and honest. "Let's hear it. How are things between you and Raascot's new queen?"

Yazlyn took a few deep swallows. "Is that an uncomfortable question? I know you two were...important to one another."

Amaris made a show of rolling her eyes. "Everyone in the castle knows you're fuck buddies. Nothing you can say will shock me."

"We weren't subtle, were we?"

Amaris chuckled into the dredges of her glass. She scanned the tavern, meeting more than a few curious eyes. "You have to know how loud you are, Yaz. It's hard to tell if I'm happy for you or jealous."

Yazlyn twisted her fingers. "When I say I know you and Nox have a special relationship, I mean to remind you that I was there at the reevers' town house the night of your reunion..."

"Goddess, I just meant jealous that you're getting laid. I think the mood will stay a bit lighter if we don't bring up the town house. Can I have another one of these?" Amaris shook her mug a bit and Yazlyn grinned. Before she could even summon a barmaid, the server was there with a pitcher refilling their hot drinks. Yazlyn thanked her and returned to the conversation.

"I just don't understand her at all. She was supposed to have been with you. Then she and I were sharing a bed. Now Malik is in her room every night. I know she and I aren't together. I have no claim to her. I just don't know what to make of it."

Yazlyn took a few swallows, perhaps to stop herself from sharing more than she already had.

Amaris rested her elbows on the table, enjoying a delightful buzz. She looked down at the shimmery, light blue fabric of her dress and smiled at how pretty she felt. She caught the eye of a winged man in the corner who glanced up from his cards to cast her a rather devilish look. Amaris did her best to listen to the Yazlyn's complaints, but so far nothing had really registered as particularly problematic. "You're a monogamist, then?"

Yazlyn frowned. "I wouldn't say that..."

"It's okay if you are," Amaris amended. "Monogamy can be lovely, from what I understand of it. You might be disappointed if you're looking for it from a succubus." Amaris shook her head, enjoying the way her curled locks brushed over her shoulders. "I'm sorry, that's not fair to her. Her power doesn't define her or her actions. But whatever I know or believe or feel about Nox, I've never known her to be dishonest—even when she's being a royal bitch. Did she not have a conversation with you?"

"She did."

Amaris took another swallow, savoring the warming effect the mead had as it spread through her limbs. She was quickly depleting her third mug. "Then, there you go. I think we need to believe people when they tell us their intentions. Like, if a woman tells you that she only wants to fuck you, maybe it's a mistake to expect more than that."

"How did you..."

Amaris grimaced, cursing the mead for loosening her lips so quickly. She shrank into the music, wishing it would whisk her away from the embarrassment she felt at the coming admission. "I'm sorry. I heard you talking to Tanith a while ago in her room. I know I shouldn't have listened. At first it was an accident, but then when I realized who you were talking about...well, it wasn't an accident anymore. Fuck, I really am sorry."

A man wandered over to their table and tore their attention from their conversation, which served as a perfectly timed distraction. It was the same fae who'd been making eyes at Amaris from the corner table. He was a rather pretty winged fae with chestnut hair, similar to Yazlyn's but cut short like Zaccai's. His wings were tucked neatly behind him. "Hi, ladies. Sorry to interrupt, but would my friends and I be able to buy your next round of drinks?"

Yazlyn's eyes sparkled as she eyed the soldier who'd approached. "That depends. Would you send the pitcher over and leave us alone? Or do the drinks come with obligations?"

His laugh sounded genuine as he offered, "How about this: we send over your next round. Once you finish those mugs, if you'd like yet another round on us, you can feel free to join us at our table. I'm trying to teach those sorry asses how to play rummy, but Uriah has had one too many glasses to do much more than sing."

"Uriah's here?" Amaris craned her neck to look for the fae she'd met outside of Aubade. She tried to catch his attention, but he was too far gone to the ale, singing happily along with the tavern music.

"You know him?" The man arched a curious brow.

Amaris grinned. "Yes! Well, no. We've met once, briefly. But I don't know you. What's your name?"

"I'm Lucas, and I will consider myself particularly lucky if I'm able to learn your names later. I do hope you'll join us. You know, so you can get reacquainted with your long-lost friend." He winked and departed.

As the fae man headed toward the bar to fetch their next round of drinks, Yazlyn whispered a fun bit of information. The enlisted men were troops a few ranks beneath herself. She winked after them at the prospect of them not realizing they were buying their sergeant her rounds. Perhaps it was her markedly feminine attire and the fact that she wore her hair loosely, along with paint on her lips and the smudge of charcoal on her eyes that kept them from recognizing her. Her chestnut curls bounced as she whipped her gaze between the men and Amaris, keeping her voice lowered conspiratorially.

"Do you fancy men?"

Amaris was drunk enough that she could feel her answering tone may have been a bit of a mocking stage whisper. "I do."

"But what about Nox?"

She giggled as she drank the final drops of yet another full glass of mead. The server arrived just in time to top them both off with their fourth round of the night. "Yes? What about her? I don't feel the way I do about her because she's a woman—or even in spite of it. I love her because she's Nox. And you? Have you only ever been attracted to women?"

Yazlyn blinked as if it were the most absurd question in the world. "Of course! Women are art! Look at Uriah over there." She gestured to the drunken warrior bellowing his heart out to the festive tune being strummed by the lutist. "I'm sure he'd be exceedingly useful if I needed to lift a heavy object. I certainly wouldn't mind fighting beside him. But I shudder to think that someone would willingly take him to bed! Men are large, hairy, and don't smell particularly pleasant." She blanched.

The smile that bubbled over Amaris's lips sourced from the sparkle in her belly as the drink soaked through her innermost parts. "That must be nice, always knowing who you are and who you love. I'm sure it's a lot less confusing."

"Did you say 'love'?" Yazlyn's head turned a bit suddenly.

"Hmm?" Amaris buried her face in her drink, nearly choking bubbles into the liquid.

"Just now, did you say—"

"I said we need more drinks! Should I go get them?" She raised her hand to summon the barmaid to their table once more.

Yazlyn lifted her hand to pause Amaris before she took another swig, "As much fun as we're having, maybe we should take a water break before we've pounded our fifth mug in our first hour? Then, if we're still having fun, we'll show those boys a thing or two about rummy."

"I have no idea how to play rummy."

"Yes, precisely: act like that. We'll bet the castle and sweep them clean."

"No, I really don't know how to play rummy."

"Save it for the table. Your tone is perfect. They'll never see it coming."

Amaris hadn't the slightest idea how many pints they'd

consumed that night, but once the other table started paying for their drinks, the mead, shots, and ale had flowed freely. Yazlyn was good enough at rummy to clean out their pockets despite her state of drink. It was a blur of cards and bubbles and fire and fiddles. Neither of the girls would remember how they'd loudly announced to the men playing rummy that Amaris was a virgin, nor how Yazlyn had proudly recounted her favorite conquests and a particularly saucy story about a threesome between herself, a duchess, and a bladesmith. They'd both come across blacked-out walls of emptiness where memories about their singing and dancing had been omitted by their ninth or tenth mug of mead, all locked in an eternally absent vault of drunken nights where all memories flittered off and disappeared.

They may have fallen asleep at the tavern table if Gadriel and Zaccai hadn't eventually come looking for them after the four o'clock morning bell, which Amaris more or less remembered as an assortment of colors and blurs. Yazlyn was too stubborn to allow herself to be chastised. If Amaris could have recalled the view of Yazlyn's drunken belligerence as she attempted to take flight with Zaccai on her heels to prevent her from crashing into a pole, it would have been one of her favorite memories.

Amaris was simply too intoxicated to argue as the general approached her. Their game-mates had been flushed and embarrassed to learn they'd been playing with members of the castle, and none, save for the friendly, soused Uriah, had been able to meet their general's eye when he walked in.

✦

"General!" Uriah said cheerily. "It's been too long."

Gadriel did his best to put a polite smile on his face.

It was true. The surviving men had been on leave ever since Ceres's failed attempt to march his troops south. Gadriel had kept himself otherwise occupied with a multitude of responsibilities within the castle, leaving Zaccai to oversee the military. The people were terrified about what had happened to the troops, but as far as anyone was aware, the story remained that they'd unwittingly camped in a demon's nest. There would be no further discussion about who had orchestrated the massacre, or anything to indicate that, following the death of their king, Raascot was not in times of peace.

The survivors deserved whatever happiness they could find.

"Boys." Gadriel nodded, sighing at the sorry state of the table. His hands planted on either side of Amaris, leaning over the drunken ball of silver and blue who had tucked her head to rest on her arms. With his palms flat on the table, he'd enveloped the small, drunken reever in a single, forward lean. He eyed his men.

Lucas swallowed, forcing himself sober as he spoke for the table. "I'm sorry, General. We didn't realize she was your girl."

"I knew!" Uriah grinned. "But can you blame the boy for trying? Look at her!" Then he turned his very drunken attentions away once more to the music.

Gadriel's eyes glided from Uriah back to Lucas. He laughed a bit, but the sound was humorless. "You're free to have your fun when on leave," he began before lowering his voice. He looked Lucas squarely in the face before his tone took on a chilling quality. "But if I find out any of you touched her, I will return to rip your tongues from your throats."

Lucas's face was plastered with shock, which Gad found particularly satisfying.

He lifted his hands from the table and proceeded to appear good-natured toward his troops for all the bar to see as the men let off steam in their free time. Regardless of his opinion of his enlisted troops, the general and commander had another thought or more for the two who'd vanished from the castle without letting anyone know, despite them being in the throes of espionage and on the brink of war. Drunkenly disappearing into the night without a word was perhaps an act best saved for times of peace.

Gadriel had to sweep Amaris up and carry her out of the alehouse along with low rumbles about how she'd be paying for this later. He'd intended to be angry with her but struggled when she rested her head so trustingly against his chest. The tavern cheered warmly at the mighty general, come to rescue a pleasantly drunk damsel from the tavern. Gadriel did a mock salute to the patrons. He cast another cool, parting glance at the troops at the table before exiting the bar.

"My fur cloak..." came the quiet, slurred mumble from the bundle in his arms.

If he'd been in charge of dragging Yazlyn back to the castle, he would have let the cold sober her up. Instead, he sighed as he warmed himself until her shivering stopped.

He was quite certain Amaris wouldn't remember that he'd landed once to hold her hair, stroking her back patiently while using his wings to shield her from the falling snow as she vomited into the evergreen bushes outside of the castle. Hopefully, the only thing either she or Yazlyn would remember is that for the first time in a very long time, they'd had real fun. After he picked her up from the wintry ground, she'd closed her eyes once more, napping with a small smile tugging up the corners of her mouth until Gadriel pulled off her shoes and tucked her into bed.

He put a glass of water and a small healing tonic by her bed and informed her that he'd be shaking her awake at dawn to start her training, to which she'd tossed up an encouraging thumb with one hand and a vulgar finger with the other from under the sheets.

He'd bit his lip against the sadistic laugh, feeling particularly excited for the punishment she'd incur when her hangover hit.

Chapter
Twenty-three

GOOD MORNING, WITCHLING!" GADRIEL WAS POSITIVELY grinning as he threw open her curtains.

"Fuck off and die, demon." She pulled the covers over her head more tightly. Her head pounded as if someone were nailing icepicks into her temples.

"It's time to wake up." He yanked the comforter from her bed.

She reached for the duvet, desperate to return herself to the safety of its warmth. "What is it, seventh bell?"

"It's noon. And it doesn't shock me at all that you haven't touched your water or the tonic. I'm giving you thirty minutes to take a bath and drink down the healing potion, or I'm throwing you off the roof."

Amaris tried to sit up, but as soon as she moved, she felt her stomach turn. She ran past him toward the bathing room, where she emptied the contents of her stomach into the chamber pot. By some small blessing or curse of the goddess, everything that came up tasted precisely of the sweet mead that had gone into it the night before.

"You wouldn't," she hurled from her hunched place over

the pot. Her angry words floated from the bathing chamber to where the general loitered by the door.

"You're right. I'm throwing you off the roof regardless of how long it takes you to get ready. However, if you're finished in thirty minutes, I promise to catch you before you hit the ground."

She was barely able to glare before her stomach rolled once more. She spun back for the chamber pot. Between retches, she said, "You're not throwing me off the roof."

He followed her casually into the bathroom, handing her the tonic as he said, "Twenty-nine minutes and counting, witchling. See you on the roof."

For thirty seconds she was positive she was going to regurgitate the healing tonic, but it began working before her body had the chance to reject it. The tonic's magic knit its way through her body, soothing her stomach and alleviating her headache. By the time it settled, it was as if she'd had a proper night's sleep. Though now sober and physically whole, it was a ghoulish tangle of hair and smeared cosmetics that looked back at her from the washroom mirror.

Yazlyn had talked her into putting charcoal liner on her eyes the night before, all of which was now malevolently smudged both above and below her lids. She scrubbed furiously at her face to clean it and raked her hands through her hair in the bath. By the time she emerged from her room and made her way to the stairs, she had about four minutes to spare.

She sped down the corridor and ran up the twisting stairwell to the final door that stood between herself and where the general claimed their training would begin. She cracked open the door and regretted it immediately.

"Goddess! It's freezing!" Amaris loitered at the doorway, ready to launch herself back into the warmth of the castle. She eyed the winged general from where he stood like a stone gargoyle overlooking the castle ledge.

"Oh, you don't have the ability to warm your skin? How sad for you. Come here."

"No! Let me go get a coat first!"

Gadriel didn't budge. Raising a single brow, he said, "Are you going to make me count to three?"

She blinked at him, hating how she heated under his gaze. What was it about this man that constantly sent her into a total state of confused, embarrassed arousal? Struggling to make eye contact, she let the door to the castle shut behind her as she joined him where he stood on the roof's ledge. She crossed her arms tightly, desperate for any residual warmth. The snow had been relentless through the night, leaving a thin, icy coating on the world around them. Though the moisture had stopped, the wind continued. Its frozen fingers raked across her skin, and her teeth began to chatter.

"Are you going to tell me what we're doing out here?" She was barely able to mutter through her tremors, her teeth clattering together against the cold. Though she couldn't see herself, she was quite certain her lips were turning as blue as the castle's stone.

"Come here." He extended a hand.

Given his ability to heat, being near him didn't sound half bad.

She approached him, standing beside him as they overlooked Gwydir. He put an arm around her to warm her with his gift for heat as she eyed the glorious stretch of the city below. Shops and homes and churches and buildings sprawled even more beautifully than they had the night before on her walk with Yazlyn. It was much easier to see the mountains and forested areas from up here. With his warmth, she was even able to relax enough to enjoy the view, if only for a moment. She was barely within two steps from the ledge of the castle's outlook when Gadriel did the unthinkable and used the arm that had been warming her to give her a hard shove into the open air.

Shock.

She barely had time to scream as the cold whooshed past her hair, her face, her clothes. The ground was closing in

263

faster than she could think. She couldn't breathe. She couldn't even panic. She winced, preparing herself to die, just as strong arms grabbed her and pulled her up from the fall. He used his warmth to sooth her tremors.

"You didn't even try! Come on, witchling! Where's your survival instinct?"

She glared up at him from where she was shuddering against the cold in his arms. She found her voice now that her stomach was no longer in freefall, and she was roiling with anger. Despite being caught in the tight space between his strong arms and the hard wall of his chest, she wriggled enough to throw a few punches. "I can't believe you really tried to kill me. Are you insane! Goddess damn it, Gadriel! Fuck! Fuck you!"

"Such a filthy mouth you've developed. Is this Yazlyn's doing? I'll have to have a word with her. Are you ready to go again?"

She watched the castle as they approached the lip, but just before they landed on the stones of the overhand, he released his arms. She gripped for him uselessly, arms flailing toward the empty space where he'd released her. She managed a scream this time, her terror a sharp, shrill high note as she fell. Her eyes widened as he became smaller and smaller. She knew she was falling backward toward the ground. She scrunched her face against the impact only to be rescued again at the last second by the general. Whatever momentum his wings possessed seemed to allow him to propel at triple the speed of her gravitational pull.

Though blue and utterly frigid, she was burning with her anger. "I hate you."

He was positively sparkling. The sadist was enjoying this far too much. "Ready to go again? Face the ground this time—I think it will help." He spun her a bit as he dropped her from mid-air, higher and higher each time.

"No!" The sound of her shrill yelp was stretched into the long, gravitational pull of her fall.

They made about seven useless plummets toward the ground before Gadriel announced definitively that she had no will to live and would rather let herself splatter against the snow than access her powers.

She was livid as she pushed her way back into the castle. Amaris stormed down the hall without turning to look at him. "You're not getting any gifts for the winter solstice."

He was still sparkling with his own amusement, but he made a face of mock-wound. He jogged after her. "I don't know why you're acting so shocked! I told you repeatedly that I would be throwing you off the roof. I always make my intentions excessively clear, witchling. And what's more, time and time again, you *agree*. Obviously, you just don't listen very well. Honestly, all this has taught me is that I'm going to need to find more creative ways to try to kill you."

She paused for a fraction of a moment in the hall, feeling a resurgence of whatever boldness the mead had offered her the night before. "I seem to recall a method that worked quite well last time."

A muscle in his jaw ticked with interest. "Go on?"

She blushed again and abandoned him where he stood near the tower. Amaris couldn't believe she'd been so bold as to attempt flirting after he'd tried no fewer than seven times to murder her. If he had missed by only a second, she would have been smushed on the frozen earth outside of the castle doors. She'd have to talk to Nox about the madmen she was employing to lead her military. A regime change called for a turnover in leaders.

"Come back here." He continued smiling, but she intended to put as much space between herself and the general as possible. He gave up, still lightly chuckling as she escaped around the corner.

Amaris found her way to the kitchen which the attendants seemed to keep relentlessly stocked with fresh, delicious foods. There was a buffet at nearly all hours of the day or night seeing as how all of its residents appeared to have set and maintained their own schedules. Yazlyn was sitting at the table with her head resting against her forearms. If it weren't for the occasional tuft of coppery-brown hair indicating she was breathing, Amaris may have thought the sergeant to be dead.

"Aren't fae supposed to regenerate more quickly?" Amaris asked pleasantly, entering the room.

She groaned without raising her head. "Why are you shouting? How are you up and talking? Never mind, don't tell me. No more speaking."

"Hold on." Amaris disappeared for several minutes before returning with a healing tonic. She was running low on her personal stocks of the brown glass bottles and would have to learn how to either replenish her private collection or else find a healer on call for these sorts of things. Yazlyn grabbed for the tiny bottle without raising her head, one exploratory hand slapping around the table until her fingers wrapped around the container.

Amaris went about her business, dishing up a plate of lunch foods and allowing the fae time for the potion to absorb throughout her various parts before Yazlyn raised her head. Though her face didn't look as ill as Amaris might have anticipated, her hair was still a mess, and she was definitely in the same smoke-scented clothes from the night before.

"How were you up so early?" Yazlyn grumbled.

"It's far past the noon bell. And I'm only up because your general dragged me out of bed to throw me off the roof."

Yazlyn's eyes widened, her mouth curling in a smile despite herself at the visual. "You're training? Already?"

"Why do you look happy?"

"I'm not!" she insisted, still smiling regardless of her best efforts to maintain a serious face. "I just remember exactly how it felt to be tossed into the snow in my panties by my commanding officers. So? Did it work?"

Amaris sighed. "Nope. According to Gadriel, I seem to possess no will to live."

Yazlyn grimaced. "Oh, shit. I'm sorry to hear that.

266

Honestly, you're going to wish this had worked. He's going to need to get more creative in things that elicit a response from you. Being tossed from the lookout might be the least of your worries."

Amaris's mouth tugged to the side as she allowed her mind to fleetingly wander to just how creative the general would have to get.

Yazlyn spoke again, "Hey, last night..."

Amaris looked up. "I had a great time. We'll definitely do it again, though maybe we limit ourselves to four?"

"I was going to say three."

"I'm so sorry, but I pretty much don't remember anything after agreeing to play rummy with those soldiers."

Yazlyn smiled. "That's for the best. You're terrible at rummy. By the way, you owe me roughly four silvers. I'm willing to accept it in trades and favors."

Amaris hedged a bit as she was standing to clear her plate. "Did we say anything..."

Yazlyn waved a hand. "What happens by the mead stays within the mead."

They exchanged smiles as Amaris returned to her room to ponder what fates might befall her to get her powers to emerge. It felt good to have a friend.

Chapter
Twenty-four

S HE FELT GADRIEL'S PRESENCE BEFORE SHE HEARD HIM
enter.

Amaris had been standing by the armoire, hanging
Yazlyn's blue dress, which had remained crumpled on her
floor. It smelled distinctly of smoke and spilled alcohol and
would need to be sent off to be cleaned before she could
return it. She looked over her shoulder and made a helpless
face at the figure looming in the doorway. "Here to plunge
me to my death again? Can't we retry tomorrow?"

He closed the door behind him, and she heard a lock click
into place. "Unfortunately, Farehold can't wait for you to get
your shit together. For all we know, we might receive word
as early as tomorrow on Aubade's weak points and Moirai's
schedule."

Amaris straightened. "Why? Has there been word—"

"No." He leaned against the door.

She fidgeted when he said nothing further. "Are you
going to tell me why you're here? Or should I be bracing for
throwing stars from across the room?"

Gadriel continued eyeing her as if waiting for something
to register. He hadn't moved, or spoken, but everything

changed. She felt it: the small prick of fear that fills the deer in the meadow when watched by a wolf. Her eyes widened ever so slightly.

He took a step toward her, and all she could think of was how Yazlyn had told her she was going to wish being thrown off the roof had worked. Her eyes fluttered to her peripherals to see where she could possibly move to escape.

His question was a low, controlled rumble. "Do you want to hear the things I've done to my troops over the centuries to help them access their abilities, witchling?"

She opened her mouth to make a smartass remark, but nothing came out. Her breath hitched as she responded to his movements. She mirrored each step with a step back of her own, then another. She had nowhere to go. The moment her back hit the wall, he took the final step to close the space between them. He placed a large hand beside her head, relaxing his weight into the wall so he was mere inches away.

"What have you done?" She could barely breathe.

One corner of his lips ticked up just enough to reveal the sharpened point of his teeth, presumably as he reveled in unsavory memories.

"I've broken bones," he said, tone cool. "I've lit fae on fire, once or twice. I've held heads under water. I've watched one of my men realize that his wine had been poisoned as he summoned the power he needed to heal. There have been knives, and ice, and ropes…"

"And rooftops," Amaris rasped.

"And rooftops," he agreed, leaning his mouth close to hers. If she didn't know better, she could have sworn he was tilting his head to hear the way her heart pounded within her chest.

"So, have you always been a sadist?" She tried to swallow, but her mouth felt dry.

"Do you know something I would never do to one of my troops?" he asked, ignoring her question entirely. The leather scent of his fighting clothes reminded her of combat and adrenaline. His lips were so close to hers that she could practically taste black cherries and pepper. The proximity elicited a familiar bloom in her lowermost stomach. She shook her head, scarcely able to manage the movement.

He raised his free hand, tracing a line from her throat to her collarbone, gently edging her tunic off her shoulder. Amaris shivered, unsure if she should fear the sensation or savor it. She didn't know if he was using his ability to summon heat or if it was just her that made his touch feel it left a trail of fire. Her eyes fluttered shut. Maybe she was meant to be on high alert, but as the heat spread, the only thought on her mind was the hope that he wouldn't stop touching her.

The general's voice was a low growl as he answered his own question, one she'd forgotten altogether. "I would never cross the line between personal and professionalism with my troops."

She swallowed again as his hands hovered over her exposed upper half, landing on her sternum and slowly sliding its way up her collarbone. Goose bumps rippled across her skin as she fought for her breath. "But I'm not one of your troops."

His teeth glinted in the firelight as he smiled. "Precisely. Amaris, do you—"

"Yes," she said in a whisper.

"You don't even know what I'm going to ask," he said, his gentle chide tasting heavily of peppers as she inhaled him fully.

"Whatever it is," she said, mind flooding with their stolen moments, their combatant, electric exchanges, their volcanic push and pull, "the answer is yes."

Her eyes closed once more as he pushed in close. The heat of his exhale warmed her neck. Her chest tightened as he drew slow, exploratory lines from her exposed shoulder to the other, running his finger along the fabric.

When his hand stopped moving, the anticipation grew painful. Fighting the ag'drurath had required less bravery than admitting she wanted him to touch her. She tried to nod but wasn't sure if she was successful. A single, low chuckle let her know that he understood. Gadriel dragged his fingers down, slowly tugging her breasts loose from her shirt and watching as the fabric gathered around her waist, catching on her hips.

She remained in the dark, terrified of jinxing the moment with a single movement. The muscles in her stomach clenched. This was either a cruel or particularly delicious brand of torture.

He leaned in for a kiss, pausing a hair's breadth above her lips. Her eyes fluttered open to confirm she wasn't imagining things, but there he waited, allowing anticipation, greed, and lust to crackle between them. Rather than press his mouth against hers, a large, strong hand traced up her side, grazing her breast, and slipped into a perfect cuff around her neck.

Her eyes opened wide. Her hand shot to his forearm but not to pull him away. She dug her claws into the firm muscle of his arm and waited for him to look at her. When he did, she held his gaze and raised her chin slightly, allowing further access to her throat.

An offering.

The tension between them snapped. His grip tightened as he avoided her mouth altogether, pressing his lips against her jaw. Fire trailed everywhere his mouth landed, scalding her from jaw to ear.

She wanted to groan, but nothing escaped her lips. She choked a brittle, pleasurable sob as she tried to inhale. Her hips rolled, pressing into him as light-headedness took her. His hand was an immovable vise as he choked her, moving his mouth farther south. He dragged his teeth along the tender space where her neck and shoulder met, biting down, letting her squirm beneath him as she realized she truly couldn't move. She moved against the wall again as he skipped her shoulder and collarbones altogether in favor of kissing the tender spaces around her breasts. Stars began to dance in her vision and a ringing sounded in her ears as he constricted the blood flow on either side of her jugular.

271

Pleasure mingled with the rush of alarm as her fight-or-flight unlocked.

Amaris began to struggle in earnest. Her hands tightened around his muscular forearm, fingernails carving into the flesh of his skin as she tore at him. He ignored the fight she put up, his teeth dragging along her breast. He bit down on her nipple, sucking it into his mouth.

She erupted in fire as delicious heat soaked her. She wanted to wrap her legs around him, for him to kiss her mouth, to be carried to the bed, to *anything*, but was rendered helpless. His free hand found the arm that had been clutching him and pinned it to the wall behind her, joining her throat as she was held firmly against the immovable blue stones of the Castle of Gwydir.

The carnal haze made it difficult to remember her training. She could break free from his hold. She could disarm him. She could...*oh, goddess.*

Every motion was met with the squeezing intensity of his ever-tightening grip as he moved over her, his mouth exploring her exposed neck and breasts. His hot tongue, lips, and teeth worked their way up her throat. She heaved as every muscle tensed and spasmed. Her entire body went as taut as a bowstring, with nowhere to release.

She was going to lose the game before she understood it. Her toes curled, her fingers tore until they drew blood. She was going to lose consciousness, and he was going to let her. She attempted to lift her knee, to bring her elbow down to break his hold on her, but she couldn't. Years of training fell to little more than static.

She should know this. She *would* know this if it was anyone else. The general had wiped her mind, and she was out of options. Panic roiled through her.

Black dots speckled her vision. If she didn't do something—if she couldn't even gasp out their safe word—she'd collapse lifelessly to the floor. She didn't know if she could remember the word he'd drilled into her or if it had abandoned her along with her years of reever training. Adrenaline, oxytocin, and fear clouded her in a drunken cocktail as she twisted against his grip with her entire body. She drove feet toward him, trying to shove her knees into his stomach, into his thighs, searching for his manhood, but found no purchase.

The ringing in her ears grew louder. The stars grew brighter.

Come on, come on!

She thrashed using every drop of strength in her body, summoning her shoulders, her legs, her lips, her head, her throat, but nothing came to her answering call. This was it. She was going to go under. He'd won before she even knew they were playing. She was helpless, disadvantaged, and failing. She felt herself going lifeless as one, final, panicked tremor tore through her, shattering the world around them.

It happened.

The very dust that formed the world shattered as the earth itself exploded.

Amaris was set free as the general was thrown backward against the room. She stood at the epicenter of a sonic boom as the room erupted. She dragged in a frantic gasp for blood and air as the furniture in the room shuddered and toppled on all sides. Gadriel missed the desk by a fraction but was able to jump to his feet in time to catch the four-post bed from clattering to the stones. Before she realized what she was doing, a second shock wave of frenzy and power as she threw both fists behind herself onto the castle wall. Amaris barely had time to register its power as the window shattered. Ten thousand silver shards glittered their threat from the corner of her eye as Gadriel threw himself toward her, flaring his wings to shelter her from the glass as it sliced through the room. His feathers caught the jagged shards as they fell around the bedchamber like snow.

The musical tinkle of glass on stone joined their ragged gasps for air. Hands and arms sheltered her head and back of her neck beneath the canopy of Gadriel's wings. Amaris realized she was still half-naked. She tugged at her shirt, dragging painful breaths into her lungs as she looked up at Gadriel.

He was positively sparkling. He braced her shoulders. "Breathe, Amaris. Take a deep breath."

Her back continued rolling with the force of her gasps as she struggled to find her equilibrium.

"You're safe," he said through a bright, white grin. "You did it."

He swept her into his arms, pulling her against him as he held her. She was still too distressed to do little more than heave. She attempted to check in with her body but struggled. She felt little more than muscles, feathers, and the cold air that rushed into her room as wind and snow poured in through the void where once a window had been. Gadriel relaxed his wings and gravity pulled a second snowfall of glass shards to the floor. He used his supernatural body heat to warm her as he gently attempted to help her with her tunic.

She pushed off his hands, rolling onto him in a way that forced the general onto his back. Surprise at being knocked from his footing bought her the second she needed to kneel over him. Her mouth found his, and he accepted her wholly. He wrapped his hands around her body. Heat enveloped her as her hips moved against him, her breasts brushing against the hard wall of his chest. Their lips parted, tongues moving together as she tasted black cherry and power.

She had the vantage point for all of three seconds. He clutched her as he spun them from the ground, pushing her into the wall once more where she was safe from the glass.

He cradled the back of her head as he echoed, "You did it, Amaris."

Still panting from their kiss, she asked, "What did I do?"

He gestured to the ruined room around them. Kindling remained where her furniture had been. Picture frames had clattered to the floor. Her desk had fractured into splinters upon impact. Glass was everywhere, as fine and sparkling as the early winter snow beyond the castle walls. Gadriel had caught her bed before it collapsed, but ice particles and snowflakes were already collecting on the duvet.

His tone didn't match her primal turmoil as he mused, "Maybe I'm the All Mother's favorite. This is...not what I expected. You are not what I expected."

"What?"

He continued to cradle her. "It was a theory at best. Wishful thinking, maybe, when I gave it a shot. But... you seem to have merged survival instincts with arousal. Truthfully, it's my best-case scenario. I guess that's what you get for spending your formative years around a succubus."

Amaris blinked up at him, still pulling ragged breaths from where she pressed her back against the stone wall, sheltered underneath his wings. "Don't call her that."

He frowned, pulling her in tightly against the cold. "It's what she is. I need you to shake whatever negative connotation you have against these words. But we'll get to that later. Don't begin creating shame where none should exist, for any of us. For now, you should be proud of what you accomplished today. Let's get you somewhere warmer."

Whether because she was too shocked, tongue-tied, or tightly wound to protest, she complied. She couldn't very well hunker down in the ruins of her own room, after all.

Amaris took Gadriel's bed that night, as he claimed he had a bed in the barracks that he should visit while he checked on his troops. She'd spent every night in Castle Gwydir alone. Tonight should have been no different, yet his absence had left her more confused and alone than she understood.

Minutes ticked into hours as her arousal cooled, leaving a disassembled jigsaw in its stead. Between the wind's howling rattle, the rippling effect of her power, and the disorienting information that Gadriel had presented to her, sleep struggled to find her.

They'd kissed.

No, they'd done far more than kiss.

She'd given herself over to her wants. She'd offered him everything, on more than one occasion. Her mind's eclectic joining of pleasure and brink of death had stirred whatever gifts slept within her belly. By the time she'd summoned her shock wave, she'd been bare-breasted and enraptured by the terrifying, incredible power of someone she wanted, trusted, and hated in equal proportions.

She curled herself against a pillow that smelled like him, insisting on breathing through her mouth so she could focus on her reflection. She asked herself if Gadriel's feelings were romantic or was he merely trying to help unlock further abilities. He said it himself—he'd gone to extremes to aid in unleashing the magic of others.

But this…this was intimate.

She tossed in bed, still feeling the tingle of where Gadriel had pressed his hands, mouth, and tongue on parts of her that no one else had. Memories dragged her back to the taboo, tantalizing entanglement in the town house where she'd shattered against his touch. Leather remained on her nose, pepper on her tongue, fire and ice tracing wonderful, terrifying lines down her skin.

The sheets twisted with her restlessness as she struggled with how much had been for desire and what had happened in the name of training. She wasn't sure if she wanted to laugh or cry. Instead, she felt conflicted, hurt, and decidedly foolish.

When she was finally pulled under, she dreamed of him.

✦

Amaris didn't remember how she got outside, only that it was nice. Wonderful, even. Gadriel was close. She felt safe. Everything was right.

His wings flared above the two of them as the first true, heavy snow of the season fell around them. She relaxed into the tall, frost-coated wild grasses of the meadow. She extended her fingers toward Gadriel, brushing them against his warm

276

face, admiring the contrast of her winter skin against his summer complexion. Her eyes followed the line of her arm, falling over her body. She realized she was completely naked, from the tendrils of her unbound hair that pooled at her shoulders to the curl of her bare toes, though she felt no cold, no wind, no snow. Maybe it was his gift for heat keeping her warm. She didn't know. She hadn't asked.

Her hands tugged through his hair and she frowned, noting for the first time that he was clothed. She was stripped bare before him while he hadn't reciprocated with any vulnerability of his own. She attempted to tug his shirt from the hard wall of his chest, but he pressed into her, barring her access. Her eyes fluttered close a moment later as his lips brushed from her brow to her cheek to her chin. The stark white forest was perfect and belonged to them alone.

"I'm going to be honest. I preferred the dream of the reev."

Amaris jolted up at the unexpected noise. She spun to gauge Gadriel's reaction, but he had vanished. She squinted through the falling snow to see Nox standing with her arms crossed in the glen.

"Nox?" she asked, suddenly aware of the snow in the general's absence. Her skin turned from white to bluish gray. She chaffed her arms for warmth.

"Goddess, Amaris, summon yourself a blanket or something."

"What?" Amaris blinked numbly at Nox as she crossed the glen, frowning at her. Her teeth chattered as she summoned whatever droplets of vitriol remained. "Is it uncomfortable when I refuse to cover up after you've entered my encounter with another?"

Nox made an impatient sound. "You can't just sit naked in the snow."

Amaris would have fought her off, but the cold had become unbearable. Nox knelt beside her, put her arms around Amaris, while doing her best to avert her eyes just as Amaris had done many moons ago. Shivering, she tucked herself against Nox. Whatever anger remained could wait until she wasn't freezing to death. When she opened her eyes, they were no longer in a snowy glen. They were in Nox's room. A soft, wool shawl was wrapped around her shoulders, protecting her from whatever might come next. Nox still held her while their reflections moved. As if regarding a mirror to the past, they watched their reflections fight the night after the massacre, when Amaris had attempted to turn their friendship into something else.

The young women followed their past selves, locked in the heat of battle, passive observers of their own painful memories.

Nox's ghost threw an apple after the echo of Amaris.

She winced at the memory. "I don't want to see this," Amaris murmured.

Nox frowned at her side. "What happened?"

Amaris's heart ached as she watched herself storm away, shoving past the winged sergeant as their paths crossed. Amaris had heard Yazlyn pick up the apple before she turned the corner. The first few words between Nox and the fae had cut down the hall, piercing her, forcing her to pick up her step. She wiped tears from her eyes, every bit as bleary-eyed as she'd been that night as she tore past the rooms and corridors. She made it to her chambers before screaming into her pillow, fragmented heart scattered to the wind.

"I..." Nox swallowed, words heavy with dry-throated sadness. "I'd never considered what happened to you that night. I was hurt, yes. But, I never meant to hurt you."

Amaris shrugged while looking down at the memory of herself as wailing on the bed. Her voice was quiet and matter-of-fact. "You spoke your mind, and I heard you. You spent your life loving a fantasy. I'm not who you thought I was."

"No," Nox denied. Nox nuzzled into Amaris's temple, tears dampening her cheek.

"It's okay," she said, whether or not she felt it.

Nox tightened her hold. "I miss you so much."

Amaris returned the hug, leaning into how right everything felt. After months of abandonment and turmoil and confusion, for this brief moment, everything was exactly the way it was meant to be. "I miss you too."

"We don't have to be at odds like this," Nox said. "When you wake up..."

"This is the way things are until I break the curse," Amaris responded. Her voice was little more than curious as she asked, "Do you ever think about how different things could have been? How our lives might have looked if we had run away together that day?"

It was with a whirring, driplike quality that the sights and colors changed.

The earth shifted with her words. When the trickle of light and sound settled, they were in Farleigh. New phantoms appeared before them, ghosts who hadn't existed for a long, long time. Younger, innocent versions of themselves held hands as they raced down the back stairs, brushing past a stunned, wordless Odrin as they escaped through the kitchen and ran for the woods.

Amaris's breath caught at the sight of the man. But he didn't recognize her at fifteen, nor she him. The girls were carefree as they ran, fingers interlaced. Twigs and branches tore at their clothes, but with every snag and stumble they laughed, as if reveling in wild proof that they'd run from orphanage and toward freedom. She was barely a teenager. The childish phantom couldn't have known north from south, up from down. But she and Nox watched with sad smiles as young, hopeful versions of themselves escaped into the trees, never to be seen again.

"Do you know where we are?" Nox asked.

Amaris looked around at the yard sandwiched between the manor and the pond. She frowned up at Nox. "We're at Farleigh."

"That's not what I mean. I'm asking if..."

Amaris looked around as the world shimmered slightly,

earth and horizon wobbling together as the trees quivered with curiosity.

"Never mind," Nox said quietly. "Can I try something?"

"Of course."

"Close your eyes with me."

Amaris complied. Nox's hand tightened around hers as she inhaled deeply through her nose. When she opened them, they were in a small farmhouse on a lakeside just before sunset. Gold bathed the humble, comfortable cottage. Overstuffed furniture filled the cozy sitting area beyond a sturdy wooden dining table. Books decorated the shelves and green plants thrived within the shelter of the cabin. A fire was crackling in the hearth. The sounds of farm animals echoed somewhere beyond the walls of the home.

This wasn't right. Nothing felt right. Amaris hedged uncomfortably as she asked, "Where are we?"

Nox's voice was raspy as if she might cry. She spoke into Amaris's hair, breath tufting it into a cloud, obscuring Amaris's vision with her own silver locks as Nox said, "I didn't know if it would work. This was your dream but—goddess, I think I would have been better off never having seen this."

"Seeing what?" Amaris asked, uneasiness growing.

"It's not your dream anymore. This is something new. Something shared. We're in Yelagin. This is a house I visited once when trying to..." Nox's sentence drifted off, joining the glittering bits of sunlight on the water. She redirected her thought, saying, "I saw this farmhouse and I thought of some different future. Some life where you and I shared this home together. I suppose none of it matters now."

"Did you call this a dream?"

Nox released Amaris long enough to cover her mouth, brows creased with worry. She nodded slowly. "I didn't know if telling you would make a difference. I've visited you before, but—"

Discomfort faded. All the curious wrongs about the unfamiliar sights and smells and sounds seemed unimportant.

Amaris smiled, interrupting Nox's ramble as she said, "Then it's a good dream."

Nox laughed a single, broken laugh.

Amaris looked over the chairs, the books, the table, the life that never was, and never would be. She looked at the hand in her own, then back up at the face that hadn't been this close to her in months as she asked, "Do you have any idea how badly I wish things were right between us?"

Nox's lip quivered as she said, "That's all I want."

"They will be." Amaris nuzzled her face in closer, resting her cheek beneath Nox's chin as she used to do. "Will I remember this in the morning?"

The tears that streamed quietly down her face bypassed her sad smile as Nox said, "I guess you'll have to tell me."

Chapter
Twenty–five

I'M SORRY. I THOUGHT YOU'D STILL BE ASLEEP."

Gadriel hadn't knocked, as he hadn't wanted to wake her. He dropped his voice to suit the gray hours of first light. It had been a surprise to see Amaris sitting up in bed with her knees pulled to her chest, but when she didn't move, he recognized the half-asleep, half-awake position he'd seen in his men who'd dozed at their posts. Her head rested on her knees, facing the window as she drifted in and out of consciousness. When she answered, her voice was quiet and distant.

"I was dreaming. It was hard to fall asleep afterward."

Her face remained angled toward the snow and ice pellets that clanged against the glass. Wind whirred through the city beyond the castle walls. It was challenging for Gadriel to differentiate the bright white outline of her hair from the snow blindness of the white light beyond the window as the cold morning daylight filtered through the gray clouds overhead. He reached out to touch her bare shoulder and grimaced when he realized the pale skin that remained exposed to the air beyond the sheets was chilled to the touch. Her shoulders, arms, and cheeks were like ice.

"May I?" he asked.

"It's your bed."

He frowned. She hadn't even looked his way to understand what he was offering, but he couldn't very well let her freeze. He slipped his arm around her, hoping she might relax into him. When she remained in her groggy, upright position, he said, "I'm the reason your room is in shambles, Amaris. This room is yours for as long as you need it. I'm still very proud of you for accessing your powers. That's an incredible feat."

She remained silent. The wind filled the quiet between them.

"Can I ask what you dreamed about?" he asked, keeping his voice as gentle as he could.

She took a deep breath. Enough time passed that he thought perhaps she'd fallen back to sleep. His arm settled around her, calling on his easiest magic as he warmed her.

"At first," she said, "I dreamed of you. Then Nox was there. It was an unusual dream. It was like we had a chance to say things we'd left unspoken."

He moved his hand across her back slowly, doing his best to comfort her. He wished he knew the right thing to say. He never seemed to do the right thing when it came to Amaris, no matter how clearly he tried to ensure they were on the same page. He forced his jaw to unclench, keeping himself calm, doing whatever he could so that she might feel safe. He asked, "Would you tell me a little bit more about your dream of Nox?"

Amaris looked at him then. Her posture stiffened as she asked, "What's it matter? It was a dream."

He bit back what he wanted to say. There was no honor in ingratiating himself to Amaris by betraying Nox's confidence. He pursed his lips in silent denial of his thoughts. Whatever had happened, her dreams should belong to her and her alone. Redirecting his attention, he said, "I'd like to talk about what happened last night, if you would."

Her face was impassive. Even though Amaris was now looking in his direction, her eyes did not meet his. They were the complex bouquet of light and dark flowers, their petals intermingling in shades of lavender and strands of deeper purple woven together. He didn't have to look over his shoulder to know that there was nothing to see. She was simply unfocused, her voice far removed from how close she was to him.

"I accessed my shock wave."

He nodded slowly but didn't force her to look at him no matter how badly he wanted to. Gadriel felt as though he were treading onto the thin, clear ice of a lake in early winter. Ice like this might support his weight, or it might plunge him into frozen waters. Every step needed to be made with careful deliberation. "There was more to it than that. I'd like to discuss it, if you're up to talking."

"You want to talk about what triggers my ability?"

His thumb moved absently against her spine where his hand continued to rest on her back. Before realizing he was moving, he brushed a strand of hair away from her face. When she didn't react, he lowered his hand slowly to her back once more.

She turned toward the window, watching the gray fingers of tree branches scrape the sky. Her voice remained detached from feeling as she said, "You said it yourself: my power seems to be interwoven with arousal. Is that what you want to talk about?"

He wished she would turn and look at him. "Amaris, I'm worried about what's going through your head. Refusing to discuss something is a breeding ground for assumptions and miscommunication. I know that shame builds walls, and I understand the comfort of constructing those walls for safety and protection. But I'd like to be let in. Talk through this with me."

"What's there to talk about? I did what I was supposed to do, and you did what you had to do to elicit that response."

284

He tensed. The battle between wanting to pull her into a crushing, reassuring embrace and to throw up his hands at how far she was from the truth was a bloody war with casualties on both sides. The wind continued to blow beyond them, creating a symphony of sorrowful, snow-swept music to score his emotions. He closed his eyes as he searched for the right words.

"Amaris—"

She snapped into the present moment, stretching her legs and raising herself to the side of the bed. She didn't meet his eyes again as she straightened stiff muscles.

"Thank you for letting me use your bed last night," she said to the open space as she walked toward the bathing room without casting a glance toward the plea scrawled across his face.

Frustration overcame him.

He'd spent years priding himself on clear communication. He thought he had conveyed to her that this was not something he did with those under him in the military, because he did not see her in any such way. The two of them had consented to training time and time again. He'd wanted to elicit a powerful response—to trigger her feelings and her survival response and her adrenaline and her emotions—but he'd also approached it in a tactic unique in the world to only the two of them.

He was no saint. He'd had partners and lovers and submissives in the past—all of whom had mutually scratched itches belonging to the other. In the fae lifespan, it was easy to take your time, clarify your intentions, and feel comfortable and confident in the mutual respect exchanged between equals. He had been—perhaps against his better judgment—wooing a demigoddess who, though far more powerful than she realized, had no concept of her own potential. She was not his subordinate. She was his equal. As she shut the door between them, though, he was confident she didn't know the truth that hung between them. He waited tensely as he listened to the sounds of running water. He tried, and failed, to relax.

An eternity passed.

When she opened the door to the bathing room, her hair was damp and clean from the soapy bathwaters. She clutched at the towel wrapped tightly around her. He blocked her path with an arm stretched onto the doorframe. "We have to talk."

"We spoke."

He adjusted his bodyweight to halt further movement. It was her tone that was killing him. She was not speaking with the stubbornness he'd come to appreciate in their banter. There was an undercurrent of pain in her voice. It was a hurt she was doing her best to maturely conceal. Her misplaced stoicism was shredding him.

"Please listen. Listen for the next thirty seconds, and then if you never want to speak to me again, I will respect your wish."

He waited for her to acknowledge his offer. Once she dipped her chin to take the bargain, he continued.

"In this moment, I feel as though you think whatever this is between us is a product of who I am professionally. I admit, I've let the lines blur, because it has been a win-win in every sense of the meaning. Not only can we be together intimately, but we've been able to work together to help you access incredible gifts. Before you brush past me with your intent to pretend like last night never happened, I need you to know that it was special for me. What happened was important. I didn't *just* enjoy last night immensely, though; don't get me wrong—it was incredible. I want to be in this with you, in whatever capacity that takes. Whether or not you just want to utilize our power exchanges for training, or if you're interested in more, that's something I'd like to discover together. I'd like to explore it as equals."

It wasn't until his final sentence that he saw how her shoulders relaxed. She finally lifted her eyes to his, tension melting from her as she met his steady gaze. He hadn't realized he'd been holding his breath awaiting that very moment.

Quietly, she said, "You're interested in more?"

Relief coursed in a curious flood of emotions. On the

verge of what had moments ago been anguish, he now fought off a smile. He didn't want to appear too eager. Gadriel needed to let this be her decision. Controlling his face to the best of his ability, he said, "If you want to train and use the intersection of power and sexuality, I'd be grateful to be your volunteer." He caught her chin with his hand before she looked away. "But, just speaking for myself, I'd very much like to be more than someone who trained you. I'd like to be more than someone you traveled with. I'd like to be more than a court advisor or a Raascot general or—"

She lifted her hand to his face and stood up on the tips of her toes to bring his mouth to hers, stopping him in his sentence. This was the kind of kiss they'd never shared. This wasn't the tornado of lust or possession or domination that had ripped them to pieces time and time again.

This was tender.

This kiss was reassuring, precious, and distinctly new. He released the hand that had been clutching the doorway and brought it to her back, holding her to him as her small frame disappeared against the body and shoulders and wings of his stature. For a moment, he forgot himself. He lost his words, mind, and body in the gentleness of their kiss.

Amaris broke free first, looking up at him. Their faces were terribly close as she spoke, lips moving only a hair's breadth from his. "I'm interested in more."

He smiled, relief dimpling at the corners of his mouth. Both his arms wrapped around her then, pulling her tightly to him, enveloping her. His lips grazed against hers again, this time letting hunger bleed into his intent. She wrapped her arms and hands around his neck and head, drawing him in as close to her as she could.

By the time she broke free, he'd forgotten how to breathe altogether. He didn't want to pull away. She looked up at him under hooded eyelashes, a low, soft sound passing between her lips as she released herself from the entanglement of his grip.

His throat bobbed, flexing the tendons in his arms, hands,

and neck as he detangled himself from her hold. He rested his forehead against hers.

She beamed. Through her smile, she said, "We'll still need to find me another bedroom."

His fingers flexed where they rested on her lower back. "Or we won't."

As the wind blew its frosted ice into the window and the winter howled outside the castle, Gadriel and Amaris disappeared for all the world in the special, private moment of their kiss, where both felt safe, wanted, and accepted.

✦

Amaris spent the next three days in a dreamlike state.

While she and Gadriel had yet to explore their romantic relationship, she'd been able to regularly access her shock wave with his help. Unfortunately, practicing such a destructive power had required some great distance from the castle. Gadriel would pick her up for training, bundled in her warmest things, and they'd fly outside of the city to an outcropping of rock and low-lying brush. Early winter was especially cruel in Gwydir, which created an interesting challenge in how to force a response from Amaris.

She'd made it clear that she would under no circumstances subject herself to frostbite. Unlike Yazlyn, she would not be thrown into a snowbank in her underthings.

The wrestling alone as Gadriel had fought with her to get her coat off had successfully summoned her first wave in the clearing beyond the city. Gadriel appeared rather pleased with himself that his mere presence seemed to be keeping Amaris in a heightened state, so that all she needed was the added element of struggle.

Practice took on a familiar rhythm. They'd circle each other, silhouetted against the painful ice and gloomy overcast skies as he flexed his hands preparing to pounce. By the third day, her mere anticipation of his lunge was enough to call forth her shock wave.

They trained during the day, met with the war council in the afternoon, shared meals at night, and had fallen asleep in the same bed three nights in a row. On the fourth morning, Amaris had tried to initiate something more intimate when she'd awoken with his arm around her, feeling his hard manhood pressed into her. She'd reached around encouragingly, running her hand along his shaft through the fabric. He'd growled in a sleepy mixture of pleasure and semiconsciousness at first. Gadriel had stilled her hand as quickly as he realized what was happening, though he kept his restraint as gentle as possible and his tone light.

"I don't think it's wise to risk destroying another bedroom in the castle," he murmured into her hair. She began to protest when she realized he was gripping her wrist loosely to avoid turning her on.

Had she really become that predictable?

He wasn't wrong. She'd already left one bedroom in shambles. Amaris's room had been cleaned out by the servants following their raucous event. The furniture had been replaced, and they'd used wood to board up the broken window until they could fetch a manufacturer for a more permanent solution.

He returned her hand to her side of the bed. She wiggled her hips backward against his.

"Don't do that," he warned. His voice was unconvincing, which pleased her.

"Or what?"

She continued to move against him, and he had to fully reposition his body so that he was out of her reach. He stifled a growl, fully rousing from sleep as he did his best to reposition himself away from her. "You're playing with fire, witchling."

"I'm sure I can have sex without turning the castle into rubble, demon," she protested.

"Are you?" He chuckled. "And what makes you so sure?"

He had a point. She'd still never experienced the fullness of sex, though they had gone up to the precipice once before.

289

She remembered how he'd slowed down, softening his touch when he realized it would be her first time. Perhaps it had been that gentleness that had kept her power at bay. Now they'd reached such heights where even his scent heated her blood. Every day it had become easier and easier for her to call upon her gift. They were certainly playing with fire—or, perhaps more accurately, playing with sonic booms.

They walked to the war room together from Gadriel's chambers and had absently been clasping hands without realizing they'd engaged in such a casual intimacy. Amaris dropped her grip on the general as soon as she heard the sound of the others' voices and was surprised to enter the room to see a very uncomfortable-looking Tanith joining the group. Amaris absently wondered how many red shirts the fae must have commissioned from the seamstress to always be in a new shade of crimson. Tanith had her arms clasped firmly in front, face twisted in a contentious pout, while Ash continued his guardian duties.

Gadriel and Amaris forked as she joined the reevers and he took his typical place in the war room. He frowned, looking between Nox and Tanith as he asked, "Are you sure it's wise to have her present?"

Nox's eyes twinkled. "I think Ash is meeting his duties with spectacular gravity. With Tanith nullified and under constant supervision, she isn't at any risk of sharing anything we might discuss. What do you say, Tanith? Do you want to be here?"

Tanith looked up briefly from where she'd been staring at the floor. Her head whipped away, breaking contact almost immediately.

"How is it going between the two of you?" Nox directed her question to Ash.

Ash sighed. "About as well as one might expect."

Amaris had been impressed with Ash's recent adaptation to his life in Castle Gwydir. She knew it hadn't been easy, but reevers were left to their own devices to solve problems as they saw fit. She, Ash, and Malik had been sent to Aubade to deal with the queen. The journey had taken a rather spectacular detour, but deal with her they would.

When it became clear he wasn't going to elaborate, Nox brushed past them onto the next topic. "Zaccai was informing me about some rather serious news. A spy I'm told was on the frontlines of reconnaissance for years, Silvanus, has been missing for some time now. Word has confirmed that Moirai has him successfully under lock and key within her castle. If she's had him for months, I think it's best to assume that he's told her what he knows."

Gadriel shook his head. "My men wouldn't break."

Nox's expression was an attempt at soothing, but she remained firm. "You forget Moirai's power. With her ability for illusion, who knows what she could conjure or make him witness to get him to turn. I think we're safest if we assume that whatever Silvanus knew, Farehold now knows."

Gadriel deflated. "He was on the same mission we all were. Once we captured the priestess and learned that Ceres's son was dead, all efforts were focused on locating Amaris. We didn't know her name at the time, but once we found someone who fit the description, Silvanus would have known as well as Zaccai or I that we have her in our possession."

Nox pushed, "And what exactly did he know about Amaris?"

"He'd met her in our encampments outside of Aubade. Silvanus knew only that she could see through enchantments and that she fit the description of the goddess's promised curse breaker. I have no reason to believe that Moirai would know of her persuasion."

Amaris grimaced. "I was intensely focused on issuing commands to her. Don't you think she has suspicions?"

He rubbed his chin. "She might suspect, but that would be all it was: suspicion. You may just as well have been using a perceived authority granted by the reevers to attempt to issue commands. Persuasion is an exceptionally rare gift, so there's no reason to believe it would be on anyone's mind. Besides, if she's fae or possesses any spelled objects as a ward, she wouldn't be concerned about such a gift."

Zaccai gestured for everyone's attention. He abandoned his regular post by the door and approached the table.

"And on the note of wards," he said, distributing small rings, "conversations with the manufacturers are going well, but testing is going to be challenging and rigorous. If you could all do us the kindness of wearing these and not taking them off, we'd be able to measure a lot in terms of magical progress."

Amaris inspected her ring. It was a rather stunning, simple, peppery-black diamond on a single, white-gold band. She slid it easily onto her center finger and admired how it looked on her hand. "This is supposed to help with the perception spell?"

Zaccai responded, "This is important progress in helping the manufacturers understand magical connection over space and time, so if we all promise to keep ours on—" He slipped his ring onto his center finger, the masculine equivalent being a thicker metallic band with the stone set firmly within. Everyone in the room, save for Tanith, tried on their black-gemmed ring and inspected it on their finger.

"How will we know if it works?" Yazlyn asked, turning her hand over to admire how the gem caught the light.

"Well, at first, we won't. But I trust the people in our employ, and they're working diligently toward a solution. This is an invaluable first step."

"Gadriel?" Nox drew his attention. "How is Amaris's training going?"

He cleared his throat. Amaris fought a smile as she watched him battle to keep his composure, as she felt the early pink of blush on her neck at the mention. It was improbable that they could make eye contact over such a sensitive topic without making the room uncomfortable. "Very well. She's nearly able to summon it without prompt. Every day has gotten easier."

Nox nodded. "That's great. I'm not sure what led to her section of the wing nearly toppling in on itself, but I appreciate that you've managed to take your training somewhere less destructive. Please keep me updated on her progress."

He coughed. "Will do."

Amaris sucked her lip inward, closing her smile as she concealed the urge to laugh.

"Tanith?" Nox's voice was gentle as she called to the Sulgrave fae.

Amaris sobered up, instantly curious about what could have required Tanith's attention. She wasn't the only one. All eyes were fixed on their ward.

The small fae's head snapped up, mirroring the surprise worn by everyone in the room.

"I was wondering if there was anything you might like to add?"

Tanith's lips parted. She watched Nox for a long moment, then shook her head numbly.

Nox asked, "If you were at a meeting with your advisors, what would be something you would deem important in the conversation?"

The room waited, taut with curious anticipation.

Tanith seemed to genuinely be considering the question. "I guess..." she began, then shook her head to stop herself. Nox nodded in an encouraging nudge before Tanith continued. She twisted her mouth and fidgeted with her fingers, keeping her eyes down at her thumbs while she responded. "I guess we'd reiterate objectives and what's being done to achieve them?"

Nox made an appreciative noise. "That's excellent, Tanith. So, everyone, if our objective is to break the curse and dethrone an evil queen, can we summarize what's being done to nullify the threat?"

Zaccai echoed what he'd been saying earlier. "Yes. We're working on protective wards to deflect her curse for those who travel south. Amaris is making strides in her abilities, should she be the curse breaker the goddess intended. We're gathering intelligence on what's going on in Aubade and with Moirai."

Nox nodded. "And what of the threat from Sulgrave?"

Tanith looked up again, flinching at the question.

Zaccai continued, "Other than the attack on Yelagin, we haven't seen any evidence of Sulgrave fae south of the Straits."

Ash chimed in, "I'd like to hold a meeting with my father and Grem on what they're doing in response to the influx in magic."

Nox made an appreciative noise and nodded approvingly. "That's great, Ash. Bring Tanith and the other reevers with you. See if we need to be calling on Elil for war room meetings when discussing the threat of Sulgrave." She eyed the room. "Is that everything?"

The room cleared out with Gadriel echoing some words of encouragement for Nox and her leadership, but she seemed to no longer need his validation. Amaris had known it for weeks, and now it was undeniable. A mechanism had clicked into place within Nox. For so long, she had acted as though she was an imposter, a stand-in until a better solution was located. Once she accepted herself for who and what she was, she refused to look backward. And perhaps Amaris wasn't sure what they were to each other, but for now, she knew what Nox was to Raascot, and she believed with every stitch of her being that they were lucky to have her as their queen.

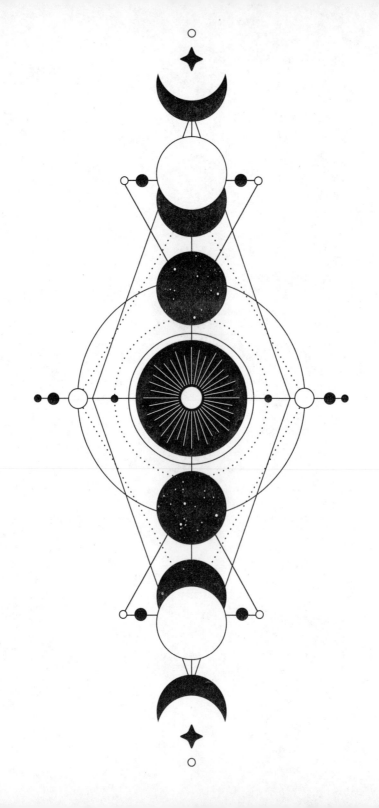

PART FOUR:

To Know and Be Known

Chapter
Twenty-six

A MARIS AND THE OTHER REEVERS KNEW TANITH WAS unhappy.

The first irritation came when Tanith realized if Ash visited Elil and Grem, she would have to go too. Her second agitation was that she hadn't received her own horse, but as everything seemed to bother her, no one felt that this tantrum was of any special significance. The horses stabled within the castle's grounds were all glossy black and outlandishly large. Amaris nearly required a boost up to mount the enormous beast. She missed Cobb greatly and was sure to inform everyone as much at every opportunity. The powerful Gwydir stallions were meant to pull kingly carriages through the snow, not transport three reevers and their ward on saddles, but a ride was a ride.

Amaris, Malik, and Ash were bundled against the cold. Tanith had been given proper attire, but her refusal to wrap her arms around Ash precluded her from considerable warmth. Amaris supposed it was a small blessing that Tanith's preferred display of temper was to suffer in brooding silence. If she was going to be miserable, at least she was quiet.

Malik led the crew, with Amaris bringing up the rear, just in case Tanith tried anything on their trip across town. Given the way she shivered, Amaris was quite certain she wouldn't be making a break for it anytime soon.

Gwydir had seemed so much prettier in the windless snowfall of Amaris's night out with Yazlyn. Now as ice pellets bit her skin, gray wind lashing her hair painfully, and arctic temperatures burning the tip of her nose, she was quite certain she hated the cobblestone streets and their icy storefronts. It was as if the hills intentionally funneled the wind toward them as they journeyed to the reevers' Raascot outpost on the city's edge. One hour into their horseback trek, Malik made a comment regarding his surprise that Ash hadn't made an effort to see his father sooner given their proximity.

Ash shrugged. "He didn't come to see me when my mother died. I'm more comfortable with his absence."

His comment cast a dampening quiet on what remained of their ride.

They arrived and tethered their mounts. It was unwise to sneak up on a reever, so they did the polite thing and announced their presence. Malik pounded on the door. They shivered on the threshold, muttering something or other about how they were meant to be on dispatch to the warm, sunny coast. When the door remained unanswered, Ash tried the handle to find it unlocked.

"It doesn't look like anyone's been in today," Amaris said, walking over to the black cinders of the cold hearth. She took a lap around the house to ensure the elder reevers were nowhere to be found while Ash and Malik set to lighting a fire. They'd spent less than fifteen minutes warming themselves when the front door opened.

"Well, look what the vageth dragged in!"

Malik was the first to his feet. He grinned from ear to ear as they clasped one another in an embrace. "I don't think that's the expression. How are you, Grem?"

Grem made a curt, grunting response. "I'm cold! Now, what brings you to our humble home?"

Amused, Amaris said, "You're holding out on the keep if you call this humble."

Grem's eyes sparkled, surveying his brethren until his eyes landed on Tanith. His face faltered, becoming carefully expressionless. "What have you brought me?"

Tanith stiffened slightly. Ash made a calming gesture toward her while he turned to Grem. "We wanted to talk to you and Elil about Sulgrave. Is my father around?"

"She's harmless," Amaris said, knowing it was equally parts true and false. Tanith was perhaps the single most dangerous fae on the continent. She was, however, wholly contained and a model prisoner.

Grem kept a cautious eye on the unsuspected guest. He poured drinks for everyone and set to work on cooking dinner while they waited for Elil. He did his best to catch them up on the events of the season, but his words remained carefully guarded given Tanith's presence.

Although she wasn't sure if Tanith deserved it, Amaris couldn't help finding that part of her sympathized with the small fae who remained far from the others, huddled against the fireplace. After all, Amaris knew what it was to feel unwanted.

She would have continued pondering these things if her first bite of dinner hadn't gagged her into the present.

Grem was not a particularly skilled chef.

The gruff, bearded reever made some dish that was essentially three-quarters composed of charred onions and one-quarter made up of remnants of meat. He had salted it generously, which hadn't helped. She choked down a few polite bites of the onion-seawater-meat concoction, all the while noting that Ash and Malik were moving the food around their plates to make it appear as if they'd consumed more than they had. Even Tanith attempted a forkful, but her wrinkled nose gave her away.

Amaris was saved from dinnertime thespianism a moment later. The door opened with a dramatic slam, cold air and wildly drifting snow rushing in against the warmth of smoke and onions. Dusted from head to toe in snow, Elil scanned the room and nodded at everyone. Amaris and Malik didn't have the repertoire with Elil that they did with Grem. As such, they waited for Ash to take the lead.

Ash stood to greet him, but their attempt at a hug devolved into an uncomfortable handshake. Amaris found it particularly jarring to regard fae parents and children who stood side-by-side. Though Elil was at least a century or more the young faeling's senior, they could have been brothers. Fae seemed to hover in their twenties until destiny fated them to pass on to dwell with the All Mother.

Grem muttered a hello, standing to clear the mostly full plates as he did so. Amaris missed Grem instantly, wishing he'd stayed at the table as a buffer. If Grem's reaction to Tanith had been stiff, Elil's was downright terrifying. He ignored the offers for warm drinks or whatever remained of the mostly untouched onion dish.

Elil did not bother with chitchat. He did not ask about their travels, their lives, or their meals. He regarded the girl in red and spoke in stiff, formal words. He kept his eyes on Tanith while he spoke to his son.

"In your limited time in Raascot," he said, each word colder than the one before, "it seems you've managed to gain more exclusive access and knowledge to Sulgrave than I have in my more than ten years north of the border. Are you here to hand her over to us?"

Amaris's cortisol spiked as alarm ticked through her. She moved an arm to block Tanith, but she saw that Ash was already repositioning his body to shield her. He'd stepped to obscure her from his father's line of sight while she shrank.

"This is Tanith, and she's my charge and mine alone. I can't allow you access to her."

Amaris's heart stopped as she watched the oldest reever in the room.

Elil appeared to neither inhale nor exhale while he

processed Ash's statement. He eyed his son, and Amaris felt for the first time that perhaps she'd been lucky to have been raised without parents. It was more pleasant to imagine a happy family than it was to have access to a parent only to have them fill you with whatever woe now drowned the room.

"You do know why I've spent more than the past decade on dispatch in Raascot." It wasn't a question.

Malik got to his feet, remaining as casual as possible. He'd always been good at dissolving tension. Amaris watched on bated breath as he interceded. "We know that Raascot was left particularly vulnerable under King Ceres's neglect. Has word spread about what has happened in Farehold?"

Grem and Elil exchanged looks.

Eager to keep the topic off Tanith, Amaris spoke. "Yelagin was abducted. I do mean that quite literally. Our sources in Gwydir and their outpost in Yelagin witnessed nakki in the thousands emerge from the lake and drag civilians into the waters of the lake. Numbers haven't been confirmed, but it sounds like less than twenty percent of Yelagin's civilians escaped."

Grem shook his weathered head, beard catching in the firelight. "That first requires us to believe there are thousands of nakki in one lake. Even a hundred of the creatures in a single body of water would be a stretch."

Malik agreed, "We'd be inclined to side with you on this, but we were present for the massacre that occurred in the Raasay Gully. What have you heard of it?"

Amaris fought the impulse to look at Tanith. A quiet inner voice prevented her from entirely exposing her role in the slaughter. She kept her peripherals trained on Tanith's ever-shrinking form as they waited for the elder reevers to answer. It seemed Ash and Malik were doing the same.

Grem said, "The soldiers who returned from the war party had horror stories of what occurred. What they described was something like a two-legged scorpion rising out of the river."

"Vakliche," Amaris confirmed.

Malik continued, "We were present for the attack. No one at the reev has seen a mud demon before this. Even if they had, there shouldn't have been more than one or two in a gully—never attacking or so much as emerging without provocation. Mud demons don't nest. They don't congregate."

Elil's eyes narrowed. "We know that Sulgrave is summoning them."

It was as if a void opened up with Elil's words, sucking the air toward him. Amaris had spent years among reevers, but he had never encountered the energy that Ash's father emitted. His shoulders did not carry the companionship or camaraderie she'd felt in her years in Uaimh Reev.

Ash spoke. "Summoning, sure. But how can they summon what isn't already present? How can a fae bond to what doesn't exist? The fact remains, there would have to be tens of thousands of nakki for a Sulgrave to summon—or dozens of mud demons in a single gully for a similar fate."

Grem's voice was three times the volume of anyone else's in the house. It wasn't out of anger, simply a lack of awareness of his own booming diaphragm. "What are you implying, boy? They're conjuring demons from thin air? Is Sulgrave the goddess, now?"

"No," Malik interjected, "no one is talking about manifesting. This is indicative of a greater problem."

Ash kept his eyes trained on his father. "This is why I wanted to meet. I was hoping you might have insight on how so many monsters could congregate. You must have some knowledge from your years of studying, and it seems like the kind of thing that would benefit us to discuss. As reevers."

Amaris swallowed a lump in her throat at his final words. As tension grew, she found herself scanning the room for something that might alleviate her anxiety. Firelight was generally so cheery. Tonight, it flickered with vague, ominous shadows as it licked over the faces of those present at the table. Nothing in the home brought her comfort. She had to keep herself from wincing when Elil spoke again.

The man's voice was low with a vague undercurrent of threat as he said, "I've been the northern kingdom's guardian for more than ten years, child. I've monitored the influx of monsters. I know of the increase in attacks. It has been my sole purpose. I'd appreciate the opportunity to interview the Sulgrave fae you've brought with you tonight."

If Amaris had felt helpless before, the sense was amplified as she looked at Malik—his congenial spirit was fully unwound. Both turned to Ash.

He extended an arm as a barrier between Tanith and his father as he said, "Of course you can speak with her. Ask your questions."

Elil shook his head once. "I'd prefer to speak alone."

This was not the unprejudiced egalitarianism of a reever. Amaris heard her pulse in her ears, and she knew she wasn't alone. Trepidation was scrawled on the faces of everyone in the room.

Ash tried, and failed, to keep his face clear of emotion. He turned to regard Tanith, controlling both his posture and his tone to present a face of neutrality. "The new queen of Raascot has given me a quite specific objective not to leave her unattended. Tanith, will you answer his questions?"

Her eyes widened. Her body remained in a perpetual flex as she seemed poised to scramble backward from the table, should the occasion arise.

While Amaris knew Tanith to be compliant and amicable, she was well aware that the fae was powerful beyond measure. Tanith was not ignorant to man's sinister edge. However, with engraved cuffs containing her access to abilities, she was as defenseless as a human child in a room full of combat-ready enemies.

Elil was markedly displeased with the compromise. Teeth gritted and jaw clenched, he spoke. "Sulgrave's infiltrators have been steadily increasing over the past ten years with your creatures showing force throughout the kingdom. Now the attacks are coordinated, systemic eliminations of entire cities and forces. What has changed to create this spike?"

Tanith moved her head from left to right, her razor-straight black hair moving slightly with her failure to give a satisfactory response.

Elil tried again. "Are orders coming down from the comtes?"

"No," she said.

He breathed through flared nostrils. While he seemed to accept the answer, he was clearly dissatisfied with the stone wall he was hitting.

"Who is issuing the order for your forces to increase?"

Tanith moved her weight uncomfortably.

Elil drew close in a movement so lithe, it shocked everyone to see the instantaneous change. The preternatural grace of the fae was easy to forget. Even Grem jolted at the unexpected motion. Amaris's eyes fluttered to her belt, eyeing the empty sheath on her hip. No reever left his bedchamber without a weapon, but they'd disarmed when they'd taken off their cloaks in the company of brothers.

"I need the name of your commander," Elil said.

Tanith blinked. She looked to Ash quickly before responding, "We have no commander."

Ash planted his feet as Grem positioned himself further from the table. Amaris struggled with whether or not to stay seated or get to her feet, but she didn't want to leave Tanith alone at the table.

Ash rose to the occasion. He was every bit as tall as his father, with slightly broader shoulders and a stronger build. He matched the authority his father commanded as he said, "She belongs to a religious movement. This is not an issue of government or military. You won't get anywhere while threatening her, so why don't we sit down and civilly discuss our options."

Elil began pacing near the fire. "Your Sulgrave pet did not act of her own volition. She did not come down from the mountains alone. Coordinated attacks don't happen by coincidence. No one crosses the Frozen Straits on a whim."

Ash maintained a sense of calm that Amaris did not feel. She was quite certain that Ash didn't feel it either. He said, "Tanith told us she crossed on a skiff of five. And as I've stated, this was not a whim. This is a matter of faith. There are others on the continent—"

"The other fae on the continent are merely the body of the snake, boy. They do us no good until we know who sits at the head."

Anger pumped through the room with a steady pulse.

Ash flexed his hands. The tendons that ran down his arms and into his fists ticked. The faeling looked down at Tanith, softening his voice. "Is there a leading member of your church?"

She looked up at him with terrified eyes and communicated everything she needed to.

Tanith was a fae of faith. Amaris knew it. Ash knew it too. Tanith would sooner die than betray the beliefs that had sent her across the arctic wastelands. Any persecution she faced at their hands would only further the barbarism she believed to thrive on the continent.

"Why bring her if you won't make her speak?" Elil asked.

Elil appeared to be implying that physical force would be an essential means to an end, as if he'd forgotten that they were the sword-clutched arm of the All Mother. Torture was not an expression of virtue. Though they were effective, they were not cruel.

Grem's face scrunched with displeasure, which surprised even Amaris. Elil's hostility was unmistakable, but there was power in numbers. And it seemed no one was on his side.

Malik tapped the table. "Well, I think this is a good sign for another drink. Amaris? Grem?"

With his simple invitation, everyone, save for Tanith, had an excuse to be on their feet. Malik moved into the kitchen to fetch a pitcher while Grem and Amaris remained in the

307

room. When Malik returned, he did so to refill drinks that had scarcely been touched.

Ash's voice dropped. He made a final pitch for diplomacy. "I thought it would be a good idea for all of us to come together and discuss options for dealing with the threat on the kingdoms. We're all reevers sworn to peace and balance. I won't presume to imagine what you've come upon over the last thirteen or so years, but I think we might also have some helpful information. Collaboration would be wise."

Elil rubbed at his temple, and as he moved his hand, Amaris became aware of the weapons he had kept strapped to his belt as he'd entered the town house. His short sword and a dagger reflected the light of the fire from where they remained sheathed against him. Amaris wasn't the only one who noticed.

"Yes," Elil said finally, painting a calming smile onto his face. "It's wonderful to have access to a source of information. You were right to come here."

However terrifying she'd found his open hostility moments prior, this eerily calm smile was much worse. From the corner of her eye, she noted how Malik's mouth moved to find a new way to diffuse the tension, but no sound came out. He was depleted of distraction techniques.

Grem spoke for them. His wrinkled face creased in something like worry. "Elil, let's hear the boy out and have a civil conversation. All we talk about is the damned monster presence. Why don't we give the opportunity for some new perspective? It would be right helpful, wouldn't it?"

But the time for comfortable diplomacy had come and gone. The smell of onion and fire paled into comparison to the metallic stench of tension. Whatever goodwill had initiated their visit was dashed to the wind. Amaris looked to Tanith, only to find she hadn't so much as flexed a muscle, frozen in perpetual fight or flight.

Ash made the first move to attempt to disband the meeting. "It was good to see you, Father, but it was a mistake to come as a group. I'll return on a better evening to discuss what I've learned of the demonic presence in the kingdoms. I think we need to be on our way."

Malik concurred, saying, "It's quite late already. It'll be dark by the time we get back to the castle. Don't want to freeze to death on horseback, do we? Come on, Amaris, Tanith; after you—"

With two smooth movements, Elil was in front of the door. Amaris kicked herself. She hadn't realized he'd been navigating to put himself between them and the exit. "I know it's getting late," he said, thinly veiling the intensity in his voice, "but I'd really like to speak with your ward tonight."

Through tightly clenched teeth, Ash asked, "Is there another question you'd like to ask her?"

His father released a long, slow hiss of air. "I've said my piece, but there are other ways in which I'd like to ask it."

In response, Ash wrapped his hand around Tanith's arm. He gave her a gentle tug to her feet, guiding her out of where she'd remained vulnerably exposed at the table. She took a partial step behind him. The silver cuffs nullifying her powers were as reflective in the firelight as the weapons at Elil's belt. Tanith's feeling of helplessness was an absolute presence, as prevalent as a seventh party in the room.

"I will speak to Tanith about the hierarchy of her religious organization. I will return with my findings," Ash offered with a note of resolution. He extended his arm, and Tanith's light steps scuffed the wooden floor as she inelegantly stumbled behind him.

Elil's brows fell to a straight, unamused line. "I'm afraid that your offer is roughly ten years too late. I've buried enough bodies to learn to appreciate that the life of one is not greater than the lives of those left in its wake."

"Elil," came Grem's placating attempt, "the boy will be back. Let's—"

Elil spoke over him, eyes still trained on his son. "I apologize for the unpleasantness this will bring you, but I can't allow you and your short-sightedness to interfere with my dispatch. We do not serve the agenda of the newly ascended queen of Raascot. We are reevers. Our only interest is in the truth."

From Amaris's position, she could still see Tanith's expression. Tanith knew at the same moment as everyone else in the room that she wasn't going to be allowed to leave.

The time for subtly had come and gone. Amaris took three swift steps to stand at Ash's side. She'd let Ash take the lead with his father until now. Amaris said, "We have the same dispatch, Elil. We're all invested in the continent's peace."

He seemed bored with the conversation. "Your lives are short, and your understanding of consequence and effect equally lacking. Your youth betrays your ignorance, and the continent can't afford patience. None of you are qualified in this task. Accept my apologies, as I will need to keep the Sulgrave fae under my care. Please, move aside."

Ash took a step toward where his weapon rested near the door. "I can't let you do that."

A tendon in Elil's neck flexed, and time seemed to stop.

Grem seemed to know what was coming before the others. The heavyset man lurched to push the other reevers out of the way as Elil raised a hand. The whites of Grem's eyes matched his soundless cry as he jumped to prevent the inevitable.

It happened in a sudden burst, like a clap of thunder on an otherwise cloudless night. One moment the room was intact, and in the next, everything disappeared. Shadow emanated from the very tips of Elil's fingers as darkness swallowed the room.

A tidal wave of black engulfed Grem first, but not before two large hands gave Amaris a shove. In turn, she grabbed Tanith in a single movement, yanking her along. Thick, tar-dark clouds nipped at their heels as she and Malik launched up the hall, climbing the stairs on all fours. They hit the landing to the second floor, and Malik moved on powerful legs to throw open the first door.

"Go, go!"

Tanith needed no encouragement, matching her step for step as they sprinted down the hallway, a tidal wave of shade swallowing the room behind them.

Amaris ran to the far window, eyes widening as she realized she'd led them into a dead end. They were on the second floor, and the window had no latch. She looked helplessly at Tanith for the barest of moments. Without a further thought, Malik threw himself shoulder-first into the glass. The sound of its shards joined the high, angry whir of wind and snow as winter raged beyond the town house walls. In a single, swift movement, Malik removed his shirt. He wrapped it around his fist, punching the cruel, jagged edges of glass from their frame, then laying his tunic over the remaining shards. He didn't hesitate before leaping from the window, fingertips tight against the windowsill until he was ready to drop.

Thirty precious seconds had passed as darkness began to lick like rising tides into the room.

"Go!" Amaris urged, shoving Tanith forward. Malik's arms were outstretched to receive her as she fell to the ground, absorbing her fall. Amaris snagged Malik's shirt from the shards of glass, knowing he would brace her fall as she toppled toward the ground. He tugged what he could of the shredded tunic over his head before shouting, "Get to the horses! I'll get Ash."

Amaris stopped him with the grip of his arm. "You're human. I'll go! Stay with Tanith!"

She didn't give Malik the option to respond as she took off toward the front door. She grabbed the handle a second later. She had expected to see the landing room, dining room, and fireplace, but instead, Amaris opened the door to reveal a solid rectangle of night.

The sounds of scuffle and metal emanated from somewhere inside the void, but there was no light or shape to be seen within the blackened depths. She held her breath as if plunging underwater as she launched into the dark. She

311

called on memory as she felt her way to where the cloaks and swords had rested. She kept quiet as she grabbed their weapons and clothes and felt her way through the nothingness along the wall to the door. The sounds of struggle filled the room, though she remained blind to the world until her fingers found the frigid lip of the doorframe to the outside world. All at once, she went from seeing nothing to breaching the surface of the deep, dark lake and emerged into the harsh winter night. She gulped in the painfully cold air.

She spotted Malik and Tanith instantly, each dragging the horses with stiff, disjointed movements from where they'd been tethered. She ran to them, seeing red, chapped hands and bluish lips. Amaris pushed the clothes into Malik's arms, all swords save for her own clattering to the ground as she turned back toward the void and yelled for Ash.

"I have your sword! Follow my voice!" she called to the black.

There was the banging noise of a table and the toppling of chairs. A struggle and angry words were exchanged. A thump reverberated as the sound of total bodyweight missed the door's opening, landing against the adjoining wall.

"Ash!" she screamed into the dark, clutching her sword as she readied herself to strike if it wasn't her brother who emerged. There was a flash of an elbow, then a splash of red hair as someone threatened to surface from the shadow of the opened door. Ash toppled out, falling into the snow. Amaris was quick for his weapon and cloak, but Elil was faster.

Ash was on his feet a moment later as Elil burst forth, throwing jagged pieces of darkness from his fingertips, wielding shadow like a weapon.

"I can't let you leave with her!" Elil bellowed.

"Go!" Ash's face was wild as he turned for Amaris and Malik.

Malik was the first to obey. He mounted his horse, sweeping Tanith in one scoop without a moment's hesitation. Tanith's dark eyes stared after them, her face twisted in some horror, growing ever smaller as their stallion galloped toward Gwydir.

"I'm not leaving you!" Amaris called through the wind as it lashed chipped ice and strands of hair at her face. She squinted against the unbearable cold, holding her weapon in front of her as they positioned their bodies against his father.

Ash looked over his shoulder, and they exchanged an unspoken thought. They didn't have to harm Elil. They only had to create enough time for Tanith to get away.

Elil seemed to realize this at the same time they did, his gaze turning to watch Malik's silhouette dot against the mouth of the city with Tanith clutched against him. In the moment of distraction, Ash charged toward his father, his shoulder hitting the man in the chest.

Shadow rippled around him as he absorbed the blow.

Amaris ran for them and raised her sword to bring the pommel down into Elil's head, hoping to make a blow that would render the threat unconscious. He raised his hand to catch the broad side of her sword, stopping it in its descent. Blood leached from his hand as he gripped her blade, pointed teeth glinting against his rage as he stared into her shocked eyes.

Elil threw out shards of shadows from his fingertips, blowing the two onto their backs, cut by a thousand splinters of shade while he continued to hold Amaris's sword in his bloodied hand.

"Stop!" Grem shouted from the threshold, finally finding his way from the darkness to the door. He clutched the doorway, anguish heavy on his face as he burst from the black. "There are only twelve reevers left in this world! You can't hurt each other. This needs to stop!"

Grem slammed into Elil, tackling him into the snow. The shadows evaporated in an instant.

"He's your son!" Grem pleaded, face still savage with rage. "Think of Odrin! Think of your wife! Think of Samael."

Amaris stumbled to her feet. She reached for Ash but found it difficult to see. Blood obscured her vision. "Come on," she grumbled to Ash, throwing the last cloak over his shoulders. She wiped at her eyes, and her hand came away crimson.

"Lives are temporary" came Elil's voice, quiet and fierce. "The mission has no timeline. Justice knows no familial restrictions."

Grem looked to them, his eyes stitched with pain as he pinned Elil to the snow. "Leave!"

Amaris grabbed Ash's forearm, knowing they wouldn't receive a second clean opportunity for escape. They seized their window, swinging themselves onto the Gwydir stallions. They urged their mounts from canters to gallops and pointed the beasts toward the castle.

The wind gnawed at her wounds, numbing her exposed skin and freezing her joints as they put as much space between themselves and the wreckage as possible. She pulled her horse to a trot before Ash did, slowing it for the remainder of the journey lest their beasts burn out on the cobblestones of Gwydir.

Time blurred as her vision vignetted. Amaris knew only cold and pain as even the sticky blood that clung to her cooled.

The city lights smudged together as they trotted over the cobblestones, neither of them meeting the gaping stares of Raascot civilians who had pushed their faces against the windows. The torches that lined the castle grew brighter. By the time they crossed the dark waters of the river and heard the clatter of their horse's hooves on the bridge, a small crowd was waiting for them outside the castle.

Servants were standing at the gates, ready to take the horses to the stables. An anxiously awaiting healer extended her hands for them, and Amaris knew who she had to thank. Malik had doubtlessly summoned everyone in earshot the moment he'd crossed the bridge and raised alarm bells.

Gadriel was in the foyer in a heartbeat. He ran to meet her, barking an order at the healer who dabbed at Ash's bloodied wounds.

"I'm fine," Amaris mumbled.

"You're not fine," Gadriel said, face tight, teeth clenched. To the room he demanded, "Someone get me another healer!"

Amaris didn't know what had stirred his reaction. Ash looked terrible, but he had been in a physical fight. The healer had been right to see to him. All she needed was to nap...

Commotion filled the entryway as words were exchanged and orders were shouted, each reever being relocated to their resting place. Tonics were called for, people scuttled in and out, rags and water rushed from one place to another. Tanith's small frame followed the action as she stood in the doorway and watched droplets of blood drip from the wounds of the reever who had been attacked by his own father as he'd defended her.

✦

The wounds they sustained from Elil's razor-edged darkness had been superficial, though even shallow head wounds were known for their bloodied drama. Between ten thousand tiny cuts and the onset of hypothermia, she almost understood why Gadriel had seemed so upset. But with the immediacy of the treatment and efficacy of the healers, neither reever was expected to so much as show a scratch from their altercation.

While the castle had initially bustled with urgency after their arrival, the quiet that pressed into them after the chaos died down was deafening. The warmth of the castle, along with its soft beds, bright fireplaces, and comfortable rugs, seemed to mock them at every turn when contrasted against their evening with Elil.

The next night, Amaris rested her head against the wall as she sat on the floor of Ash's room. She'd followed Ash back to his chambers, and he had not protested when she entered. She'd asked, "Did you know your father could do that?"

"I was six when he left," he said.

She nearly chuckled. "I knew you two weren't close, but

goddess damn it, that was the worst father-son dinner I've ever heard of."

She had hoped to make him smile, but her attempt fell flat. She let the moment linger, regretting her joke as it clattered hollowly against the walls around them.

"I thought it was a good idea." His response was sullen.

"It *was* a good idea," Amaris insisted. "Combining information and efforts is prudent and wise. You had every reason to believe that this meeting would be beneficial. And at the very least, even if we didn't learn anything, it should have been an amicable meal between reevers. No one could have predicted how poorly that would go."

He raked a hand through his hair. He normally liked to keep it pulled back, but tonight, it was wild and unbound. "Really? Because I feel like all the evidence that he's been single-mindedly obsessed with this mission has been right in front of us. I don't know what I was thinking, bringing Tanith there."

"Nox told you to bring her."

He made a face. "Even if she hadn't told me to, I would have brought her. It made sense. We've learned so much from her in the war room. She's been communicative to almost everyone in the castle. And even with my father, I at least thought she'd like him more than me, as he's full fae."

Amaris insisted, "You did everything right, Ash."

When he didn't look up, she spoke again. "I don't have a lot of experience with families, but I can tell you that the only thing you have in common with that man is the color of your hair."

He rubbed his face, covering his eyes. His voice was muffled by his hand as he said, "I need to speak to Tanith."

"You haven't talked to her since you got back?"

He dropped his hand. "It's not exactly like she and I were having riveting conversations. She hates me, and to be quite frank, I'm not her biggest fan either. But I'm worried that the events of last night will have set back any progress we may have made. Nox is not going to be thrilled if our only source from Sulgrave goes on lockdown."

"So what?"

He looked up at last. "Huh?"

"So what if Nox isn't thrilled? She's not your queen. You're a reever."

He laughed. "Don't let her hear you say that."

Amaris shrugged. "She knows as much. Both kingdoms know that we're neutral. We just happen to be in a very fragile place in the timeline where the south has declared us enemies of the crown and the north seems to have dragged us into her inner circle. Our missions are aligned for the time being."

"Come on." He eyed her.

"What?"

"We have not been dragged. Nox took off into the sunset to go north when she thought you were here. And I know you, Amaris. You would have fought all odds to be at Nox's side. Aren't you destined by the goddess to be with each other for some grand prophecy?"

Amaris pressed the heels of her hands into her eyes. "Don't remind me."

"Look," he said, physical and emotional exhaustion flooding his voice, "I don't know what happened between the two of you, but it seems incredibly stupid. I won't lie to you: I've had a similar conversation with her. I've tried to think about how I would feel if I met someone that I loved, and then learned not only did I love them, but that the All Mother had designed us for one another. Isn't that the purest definition of soulmate?"

Amaris turned away, looking into what remained of the dull fire in his hearth. "It's not like that."

"Isn't it?"

She used the wall to help herself to her feet. Six steps later, she reached for the doorknob, but the handle began to turn on its own. Amaris frowned down at the door as it opened. Their small dark-haired fae in a red tunic stood in the opening.

"Oh, I'm sorry."

"No!" Amaris nearly choked on the word. She couldn't push past Tanith fast enough. "I was just leaving. Please, he's all yours."

She wished there had been someone else in the hall to exchange the flared, excited look she was giving to the empty corridor at the fact that Tanith had sought Ash out on her own, but unfortunately, Amaris would have to patter her way to the kitchen and see if anyone was around the dinner table to exchange gossip.

Chapter
Twenty-seven

NOX WOKE UP AROUND NOON AND SMILED AT THE GLIMMER of the peppery diamond gracing her otherwise unadorned fingers. She enjoyed the lazy feel of a late morning and bed to herself. The sheets were so wonderful and warm against her skin, particularly when contrasted against the chilly day outdoors. Her stomach told her that it was time to eat, which finally incentivized her to get out of bed. She kept such odd hours that she was usually surprised to see anyone else in the dining room, and today was no exception. She was entering the empty room that had remained set in a buffet of food for anyone who should wander in and out. A pretty servant girl with light-brown hair wandered in to clear the plates from whoever had eaten in the dining room before Nox's arrival, keeping her eyes down.

"Hello?"

The attendant looked as if she had been tripped, skidding to a halt. "Your Highness? Can I help you?"

Nox blushed at the title. She considered how odd it was that the girl before her was not much older than she was, and only a few months prior they would have been in very similar class statuses. In fact, working in a castle would have been a huge step up from her station at the pleasure house. "I'm Nox. What's your name?"

The kitchen attendant looked around as if perhaps someone else were being addressed. "Leona, but my friends call me Lee." She cleared her throat then repeated, "My name is Lee, Your Highness."

Nox felt herself growing a bit embarrassed, "Please, it would mean a lot to me if you would call me Nox. Lee, can I ask you a question?"

The girl blinked at her while shuffling under the weight of the dishes she had been carrying to the kitchen.

"Oh, are those heavy? I'm so sorry. It's okay if this is a bad time. I can come back."

Lee shook her head, setting the plates down and clasping her hands in front of herself, wringing her fingers with nerves. "No, your H—erm—Nox. Now is fine. You can ask anything you like."

Nox smiled. "I just haven't had the opportunity to speak to many people in Gwydir aside from the general and Cai and Yaz. I was wondering, if it isn't too much to ask, if you would tell me...are the people happy?"

If discomfort had a portrait, it would be the eternally captured oil painting of an awkward Leona standing in the dining room wishing she could vanish. She was still too surprised to spit out coherent thoughts, so she choked out an echo. "Ma'am?"

"I'm sorry. I know you can't speak for the people, but I just thought it would be nice to hear from someone who's from here. Are the people of Gwydir happy? Is there enough to eat? Are there jobs for the citizens?"

Lee was blushing terribly, but she nodded. "Well, the weather is terrible, so we always find something to complain about, but we've mostly kept to ourselves. Ceres wasn't involved—I don't mean to criticize him, Your Highness—"

Nox brushed it away, prompting the girl to continue.

"But that also meant he didn't hit the people with any

320

unusual taxes or focus his energy on our regulation. The soil has been good, and people have been able to keep their family businesses. I would say that people are mostly happy, if it weren't for the creatures."

Nox had been waiting for mention of demons. "There has been an influx of creatures?"

Lee twisted her fingers in her apron. "There were always stories of monsters and things in the forest, but those may have been things mothers just told their children to make them mind their manners. Then folks started seeing things, and others went missing. First the hunters, then the country-folk, and now sometimes you'll hear about someone in town who sees or hears something that shouldn't exist beyond nightmares."

Nox considered this, acknowledging the girl's fears. "The general and all of his best men are helping me to find a plan for the monsters. I'm glad to hear that the people are gener-ally happy."

Lee nodded quickly and grabbed for the plates she had set down. "Oh yes, Your Highness, plenty of food on the table and that's all one can want. And of course, I'm incredi-bly grateful for my station in the castle, at your service, Your Highness." She was taking off for the kitchen as Nox tried uselessly one more time to tell Lee to call her Nox, but overall she seemed pleased by the exchange. It was a relief to know she wasn't ascending to the throne of an angry kingdom or a starving people. Raascot seemed to self-govern relatively well. If she could find a way to neutralize the Sulgrave fae, eliminate the curse at the border, and otherwise stay out of the business of Gwydir's citizens, she may easily go down as the best monarch in two hundred years.

She was surprised to find she was one of the last ones to arrive in the war room. She looked over her shoulder as if there might be an indication to a summons that she had missed.

"I'm sorry, Nox," Zaccai said apologetically. "I was

speaking with the reevers about what occurred last night, and it's bled into our meeting time. We should have called for you sooner."

"No, please." She sank into the chair at the head of the table. "I know it went terribly, but I haven't yet heard the specifics as to just how poorly. Do you care to share?"

Ash and Malik took turns explaining how horribly the altercation had gone while Tanith remained quietly holding her knees to her chest in her chair. She remained lost to silence as the active mind behind her eyes relived the night.

By the end of their story, Zaccai spoke again. "We're sending Malik to Uaimh Reev to discuss the turn of events with Samael. We would send a raven, but I know that Elil will have his eyes peeled for correspondence."

Nox's mouth twitched in protest. "Shouldn't Ash go?"

But she already knew the answer. Ash had Tanith as a charge here in Gwydir, and Amaris was in the midst of readiness training for her match with Moirai. It could only be Malik. She regretted voicing her question, knowing it was betraying her favoritism. Ash was perfectly lovely and deserved only good things, but she couldn't help the small stab of panic she felt at hearing Malik would be taken from her. They hadn't spent a night apart in weeks.

"You won't even notice I'm gone." Malik smiled reassuringly at her, but his green eyes didn't sparkle as he spoke. Perhaps he was also doing math. He hadn't spent more than twelve hours away from her from the moment they met in the dungeons of Aubade.

If travel was uneventful, he could be to Uaimh Reev and back again in under ten days. She pretended to smile as if it were a short length of time, but she felt her heart stutter with worry at the thought of what ten days could mean for her, not just as a person who cared for him but as someone who relied on his care for her life force.

"Do you want us to send one of our fae with him?"

She shook her head uselessly. "I know the reev belongs

322

to no kingdom, but it's still not in Raascot. I don't think it will do us much good to have someone else accompany him. Unless the ring is meant to be a shield? Should we test it?"

Zaccai furrowed his brow. "No, the ring is not a shield. It's merely a test of magical efficacy of our spelled objects. So, it would be ideal if you kept yours on, Malik."

"In that case, I'll treat it like a wedding ring. I assure you, I'm quite capable of a little road trip," he said, keeping his tone as light as he could.

Nox tried to regain her composure. "There's something else. I was speaking with one of the kitchen attendants, and I realize that we've been so focused on the big picture that I might be missing out on the day-to-day life in Raascot. The girl I spoke to made it sound like the people are generally happy?"

Gadriel grimaced. "They're happy because they don't know we're on the brink of war. Obviously, whoever you spoke to didn't have a brother or lover lost in the massacre."

"She did mention the influx of creatures. The people are afraid. Is there a way we can spread any message of hope? I want them to feel like their fears are acknowledged. They've spent a long time being ignored."

Gadriel nodded. "That's a great idea. Yazlyn, you haven't had a project in a while. Do you want to oversee some sort of benefit?"

"Are you asking because I'm a woman? I punch people and kill bad guys. I don't know why you think I know jack shit about planning a party."

"No." He narrowed his eyes. "I'm asking because you're lazy and haven't been pulling your weight. Why don't you visit a few establishments and put up signs saying that you'll be giving away loaves of bread and pies and pastries made by the castle's kitchen staff on such and such a day, something like that? Use the opportunity to mention that the new queen on the Raascot throne is benevolent and loving and—"

"And beautiful and wise and magnanimous," Nox finished for him.

Yazlyn stifled a yawn. "Stand out in the cold with bread and spread lies about Nox. Got it."

"I'd like an opportunity to..." Everyone turned to Nox and watched her twist the fabric of her dress. "I don't know how to be queen to a people I neither know nor understand. There's so much educating that I need to shoulder, but it really needs to be overseen by one of you." She looked to the Raascot fae. "Or, by any of your scholars, or someone from your war camp, or even the town candlestick maker who just wants to tell me old folk tales. I just can't shake this feeling of guilt."

Zaccai's expression softened. "You have no reason to feel guilty."

Something in Nox's chest twisted. It wasn't just Malik's impending absence, or the tenderness in the eyes of the commander, but the crushing sense of being undeserving. She'd accepted that she would rule. She'd be a fair, decisive, and intelligent leader. In order to live up to the demands she had of herself, she needed to learn more than just the history and politics. She needed exposure to what it truly meant to be from Raascot.

"Get her a tutor," Amaris suggested. "We had lessons at the orphanage. When my specialty changed, so did my mode of education. I was tutored while at the reev. I think all of us were, though my lessons were a bit more rigorous since I—like Nox—was in over my head and needed to work twice as hard for twice as long in order to learn what it meant to be a reever. I'm sure there would be plenty of men who would jump at the opportunity to drool over you."

Gadriel seemed to enjoy the joke. "I think we'll pair you with a woman. Your education will probably be more thorough if we keep the drooling to a minimum."

Amaris and Yazlyn laughed every bit as hard as Nox did. The women enjoyed the chuckle until the general understood his mistake.

"Oh, that's right." Gadriel cleared his throat, reddening ever so slightly. "I'll find you a grandmother. A clever, elderly, intelligent seventy-five-year-old human professor complete with gray hair and wrinkles. How does that sound? Is everyone at the table happy now?"

"I think our meeting is adjourned," Nox said, clasping her hands in front of her. It seemed pertinent to avoid wandering down the road of her sexual preferences at the war table. "Before we go, there's just one more thing. I was hoping to have a word with Tanith alone."

Gadriel ushered the others out of the room. It wasn't the first time Nox was glad to have him so resolutely on her side. She caught the uncertain glances Ash shot Tanith before Gadriel closed the door behind them.

Tanith clutched herself more tightly and watched after the reever as he left.

"I'm sorry for putting you on the spot," Nox said. She had to stop herself from speaking to Tanith as though she were a child. The girl was timid by circumstance, not by capability. Nox cleared her throat before asking, "How are things going between the two of you? You and Ash, I mean?"

Tanith twisted her mouth to the side and looked toward the door where Ash had gone.

Nox made an attempt to spur a response. "Does he treat you unkindly?"

"No," she answered quickly.

Nox had hoped as much. She suppressed a smile over the speed with which Tanith spoke her resolution. This was certainly progress.

"Because," Nox pushed, "if you wanted me to assign someone else to you after what happened last night, that could be arranged. I'm very sorry for putting you in that situation with his father and everything that occurred at the town house. I don't want you to feel unsafe."

Tanith looked instantly disconcerted at the suggestion, though she kept her eyes on the floor. This wasn't the refused eye contact due to the anger or distrust she'd felt so long ago but one born of a shy discomfort. "I don't feel unsafe."

Nox nodded and made a motion with her arm to ask permission to sit closer. She moved cautiously, choosing a chair near the young woman. Nox hadn't realized how gaunt the girl had been when they'd first captured her until seeing it contrasted today against her healthy cheeks. Her hair was nearly as dark as Nox's, though her ears poked through her curtain of hair. When she did speak, her sharpened canines looked capable of drawing blood like the vampires of lore.

"Do you have everything you need? Do you have access to the books you need?"

Tanith deflated ever so slightly. "You know about my books?"

"Amaris mentioned that you really like to read. She isn't one for fiction. She always has her nose in one of those tomes about creatures and habitats. I tend to be more of a writer than a reader—mostly journaling. What do you like to read?"

Tanith adjusted her weight in her chair, but there was a shift to the tension. Nox noted that Tanith was no longer holding her knees as tightly. Nox wasn't trying to be patronizing, so she did her best to keep her tone conversational. Still, this was the most they'd ever spoken.

Tanith answered carefully. "I've been enjoying love stories, I suppose. I think I've read all of the books in the castle. At least, all of the fictional tales."

Nox dared, "Would you like to go on an outing to the library? I haven't visited it either, though Zaccai says Gwydir has a gorgeous library. It might be nice to journey out into the city. We could ask Yazlyn to go?"

Tanith twisted the fabric of her shirt. "Ash could come."

Fighting a smile, Nox said, "Certainly. I'll see to it. Will you let me know if there's anything you need or want to talk about?"

Tanith dipped her chin once in lieu of any verbal confirmation. Nox contained the beaming pride of her achievement. Tanith used to recoil at her presence. Now they were practically chatty.

"Let's head out, shall we?" She got to her feet, and Tanith followed suit. Nox led them out of the room and was glad to find Ash waiting to resume his guardianship. As pleasant as the conversation had been, no one was willing to leave the fae unsupervised in the castle.

The moment Nox returned to her room, the joy from her progress with Tanith extinguished. Malik was already in her chambers gathering his items.

Dismay filled her. "Are you leaving tonight?"

He met her frown but kept his face happy, even if the smile didn't touch his eyes. "Wouldn't that be better? The sooner I leave, the sooner I can return. You just go to sleep and before you know it, the first eight hours have already gone." He snapped his fingers to indicate the passage of time.

"Could you wait until morning?" She tried not to imagine how pathetic she must look.

Everything about him softened, from his broad shoulders and kind eyes to the tilt at the corner of his lips. Malik stopped the packing he'd been attempting and set down his bag. He took a seat upon the bed, patting the space beside him for her to join. She curled into a small ball next to him.

"You can just say you're going to miss me. I won't tell anyone."

"I think they know."

She rested her head on his chest as he agreed that yes, his departure could wait until morning. After all, he said, one more night holding Raascot's queen couldn't hurt.

Chapter
Twenty-eight

G O BACK TO SLEEP." MALIK PRESSED A KISS TO HER TEMPLE.
"Come back to bed," she grumbled under the sheets.
"It's too cold for a trip to Uaimh Reev. Go in the spring."

His low chuckle spurred her to roll toward him, but he
shushed her. "The castle will worry if they see you up before
the seven o'clock bell. If you sleep until noon, that's five more
hours of time that will already have passed. Please, sleep."

"The watch—" She waved a hand from where she
remained tucked under the sheets. "It's in my top drawer.
Take it so you can always find your way back."

Malik obeyed and found the pocket watch quickly with a
grateful nod in her direction. He didn't allow her the opportunity for the protests that she wanted to make. She supposed
he knew that no good would come from his deliberation. She
might even talk him out of going altogether. She was pretty
persuasive, after all.

He winked at her from the door before closing it
behind him, and she felt as if her heart was breaking all
over again. He had been her security blanket. He was the
buffer between her and the world. She didn't want to do
this without him.

Despite his urges to stay in bed, Nox left the comfort of her mattress and put on a warm sweater over her night dress as she shoved her feet into furry slippers before wandering down to the kitchen for tea. Regardless of his teasing, she knew she'd never be able to fall back to sleep. If she was alone with her thoughts, she knew she'd start to cry.

She regretted not fully dressing when she entered the dining room and found nearly everyone present and ready for the day. She knew her hair was still mussed from the sheets. Between her smudged eyes, her slippers, and the bottom half of her nightdress poking out from the oversized sweater, there was no hiding she had just rolled out of bed.

"Is something wrong?" Gadriel asked, the first alerted to her presence. He had been sitting very close to Amaris at the breakfast table. Nox could have sworn he removed his arm from where it had draped around Amaris's back when she entered.

Nox stifled the urge to feel offended. She leaned against the frame of the dining room. "You mean because I'm awake before noon? I don't always sleep in."

"Yes, you do." Amaris laughed into her pastry. "Try these—they're great."

Nox crossed to where they were sitting and bit into an apple pastry dusted with sugar. "Oh, goddess, that's good. Why aren't these out when I come for breakfast?"

"Because you don't come for breakfast. You come for lunch. The best food is gone by then. Zaccai was here an hour ago because he likes the almond pastries the best. None of us ever get to try them."

Yazlyn still hadn't said anything. Nox slid into a chair and scanned the others. When she raised an eyebrow inquiring as to what was wrong with the sergeant, Gadriel responded in a stage whisper, "She's not very pleasant before her second cup of tea."

Ash entered the dining room, closely followed by Tanith in yet another red tunic. This one hung off her shoulders, which seemed like a very chilly choice for the late season, even if it was very flattering on her delicate features. "Nox is here? Is something wrong?"

"Goddess, everyone. I wake up early sometimes." She took another apple pastry from the pile. "I didn't realize you were holding out on me."

Amaris waved a nonchalant hand. "You could probably ask the kitchen to make breakfast pastries for lunch. You are their queen."

Nox grimaced.

Yazlyn broke her silence to say, "No! Pastries are for people who wake up early. If she wants a damn apple pastry, she has to get out of bed before lunch."

Nox was too entertained to be offended.

Gadriel sparkled with amusement as he slid another hot cup of tea toward Yazlyn. Amaris snorted into her mug.

Ash loaded a plate of food for Tanith before dishing up his own. The pair sat quietly in the corner, gnawing on salted pork and sticky rolls. Yazlyn grumbled into her tea, and Amaris and Gadriel went back to whispering about whatever they were whispering about.

"Has Malik left yet?" Ash asked.

The room shared a collective wince at his question.

Nox dipped her chin in acknowledgment but wouldn't be elaborating. Waking up early had not been enough to distract her. Coming to breakfast early had not taken her mind from their separation. She was quickly realizing that she had no hobbies. She wrote notes, drew from her memories, spent time with loved ones, and conspired in the war room. The days would be long and miserable enough as it was unless she found something to do.

"Tanith?" Nox asked, looking up from her second apple pastry. She sucked the powdered sugar from her finger before asking, "Would you and Ash like to go to the library with me today?"

She heard the surprise ripple through the room but kept

her eyes on Tanith, who nodded with a bit more enthusiasm than she'd expected.

"Why aren't I receiving an invitation to the library?" Yazlyn pouted.

"She'll be more pleasant in about fifteen minutes," Gadriel apologized.

"Will you two be joining?" Nox directed her question to Amaris and the general.

"We're still a bit preoccupied with Amaris's training," he said.

"I'd love to see her abilities. Do you think I could see a demonstration soon?"

Amaris threw Gadriel an elbow and cleared her throat, choking on whatever crumbs had fallen down the wrong tube as she inhaled. Her pale face blotched with crimson as she gagged on her food. "I'm sorry, goddess; excuse me, um, I don't think it's ready for public viewing?"

Nox chewed contemplatively. "Yes, Yazlyn did mention it can be a little unpleasant to conjure those gifts. I'm glad you are making progress."

Gadriel's face changed, and Nox repressed her reactive displeasure. He'd identified her emotion, and she knew it. She hated how transparent she was. Undoubtedly in an attempt to alleviate her anxiety in a life without Malik, he said, "How about you have Yazlyn take you to a few of the shops in town after you go to the library? Start meeting your citizens around the city?"

"Wear something nicer than your nightgown," Yazlyn muttered.

An hour later, a much more pleasantly caffeinated version of Yazlyn was at Nox's door. She'd already brushed the tangles out of her hair, washed her face, and stepped into a clean silk slip. While Nox had never required help dressing herself, she was a tad anxious about making a good impression on the people of Gwydir and grateful for Yazlyn's input. Nox opted for a deep-amethyst dress of crushed velvet beneath a fur-lined black cloak. Yazlyn wanted her to wear her tiara, but she politely refused. The crown would be something she'd wear only on the throne, should the occasion arise.

Her first outing was seamless and laid the groundwork for routine adventures beyond the castle wall, whether with Ash and Tanith as they explored the library, Yazlyn as they toured the shops, or even an outing with Gadriel where he showed off Gwydir's military base. The days that followed were as filled with activities as possible, which was great for Nox but less wonderful for the others.

She didn't miss the poorly concealed irritation of those around her regarding her constant need for distraction. Nox made at least three more trips to the library just to look around the gorgeous rows of colorful books. While the outside of the library building had been the similar blue-black stone from which the city was built, the inside shimmered with white gold from its floors to its shelves. The first day, Tanith had left with more books than she could carry, giving at least eight to Ash to hold. Nox had promised she would return to collect the other selections and made good on her word.

"Do you want to try somewhere other than the library and the seamstress?" Yazlyn asked. She'd become Nox's unofficial escort over the last several days.

"What do you have in mind?"

Yazlyn led her to a few of the jewelry shops, tailors, leather smiths, bakeries, antique shops, and even a mystical shop filled with spelled objects.

The space was like nothing Nox had ever seen.

The shop was so crowded and cluttered that it was challenging for one's eyes to land on anything in particular. There were shelves, glass cabinets, display cases, and piles nearly everywhere. More than one clock seemed to be ticking, and there was definitely the sound of something fluttering about the room. Despite the curious medley of piled items, everything in the shop was utterly spotless. No cobwebs, dirt, or speck of dust was anywhere to be found.

"People can just buy these?" Nox whispered, horrified as her fingers dared to graze an intricately carved rose quartz crystal.

Yazlyn wandered deeper into the shop. "Anything truly wicked or dangerous is confiscated. But for the right price, pretty much anything can be bought."

A beautiful pair of ballet slippers was displayed with the ability to gift the magic of dance to its wearer, though a sign in careful handwriting stated the shoes could only be used once per owner. The accompanying plaque said they were a commonly purchased and resold item for brides on their wedding day. There was a small array of empty books that claimed to fill with beautiful calligraphy when it heard words, as if a scribe were rapidly writing the owner's each and every spoken thought, saving them the need to exhaust their hand. A small wine goblet had been enchanted to never spill a drop, no matter how it tumbled.

A mid-sized blue bird that sat near the register was chirping kind words to Nox as she approached. It clucked with the confident, cheery voice of a household parrot. "You're so beautiful. Your hair is lovely. You are a good person."

The shopkeeper approached. He was a kind-looking—though a bit eccentric—human man in his later years with wispy facial hair and an oversized mustard jacket. "I wish I could tell you that she really likes you, but she's a charmed bird. She only speaks encouraging words to whoever's nearest. I like to keep her by the counter. She's good for my self-esteem."

"What a wonderful colleague." Nox nodded in agreement.

"Are you searching for anything in particular? Or maybe you're looking to sell?"

Nox flashed the whimsical old man a smile. "I have a few neat objects. One of them is with a friend at the moment. Have you ever heard of a pocket watch that points in the direction you want it to go?"

He clucked his tongue. "It's a shame such an object is

with your friend! I would be glad to take it off your hands, should you feel so inclined."

Nox's heart warmed. "I think I'll hold on to it."

He had one of those voices that seemed permanently delighted, as if perhaps he was always laughing at his own private joke. "Wise enough, wise enough. I have many spectacular things in my shop of curiosities. A lovely lady like you doesn't need much use of these charms for luck or love. Hmm. Let's see. Can you cook? I have a spoon that will make your husband taste something delicious anytime he eats from it, even if you've burned the dinner."

Yazlyn leaned against the counter. "This is Nox. She's the late King Ceres's daughter. Woefully unmarried, I'm afraid, but delightfully less insane than her father. I wouldn't be surprised if she couldn't cook. Nox, you look like you'd burn water."

Nox wished Yazlyn hadn't said anything but knew that they had been taking trips into town specifically to spread goodwill and show her face among the people.

"This doesn't seem like an appropriate time for your weird sense of humor." Nox made an apologetic face at the shopkeeper.

He nodded gravely as he realized who was standing before him. "I have just the thing for you. Come with me, Your Highness."

The shopkeeper led them through piles of papers and oddities to the back of the store. He opened an armoire that had been curiously hidden behind a standing mirror. Within the cabinet was a locked drawer that he opened with a key that had been hanging around his neck. In the locked drawer was a little box. This tiny treasure chest was opened with another key that was cleverly hidden on his ring. Nox absently wondered how many keys the shopkeeper wore on his body at any given time. He lifted the lid and revealed what appeared to be a cut of emerald silk.

Yazlyn and Nox exchanged confused looks. Nox had been

quite certain from the layers of secrecy that the object in the box would be more akin to skulls and bones than something so delicate.

"It's a ribbon?"

"Go on then." He gestured with weathered, age-spotted hands for her to pick up the item.

"Do I just...hold it?" Nox frowned at the bit of fabric.

He nodded encouragingly. "It's armor. Go on: tie it in your hair."

She lifted it uncertainly and felt it between her fingers. It felt like a perfectly normal strip of green ribbon. Thick with skepticism, she obliged, tying her hair back from her face with the jewel-toned strip.

"Let me see what I have here...just one moment..." He fished in his seemingly bottomless jacket pockets until locating a small pin. He was delighted when his fingers wrapped around the sharp object. "Here, if Her Majesty wouldn't mind! Offer me your finger."

Yazlyn shifted nervously. Nox hadn't been anxious until this moment. Her heart skipped as the sergeant lifted a hand to intervene, saying, "If this has to do with a blood spell—"

But it was too late.

He'd already taken Nox's hand and pressed the sharpened tip of the pin into her outstretched index finger. Yazlyn flexed to stop him, but to their mutual amazement, the silver needle glanced to the side as if there were a small, invisible layer of clear skin hovering just above Nox's own.

"See for yourself," he said, offering the pin to Yazlyn.

It took her a second to recover from her shock. Wholly impressed, Yazlyn was far less gentle with her trial. Nox thought she seemed a bit too eager to stab her. Yazlyn attempted to jam the object into Nox's upper arm with more built-up angst than she could conceal, but once again the needle veered mysteriously to the side.

"Well, I'll be damned," Yazlyn muttered. Nox didn't miss the subtle twitch of Yazlyn's hand near her leg as she'd secretly tried to stab Nox with the dagger. She cleared her throat before saying, "I was just making sure your armor was effective against more than pins."

The shopkeeper's face crinkled in a grin. "It's only effective for objects that intend you harm! See?" He grabbed Nox's hand comfortingly and clasped her on the shoulder to prove his point. She could be touched with friendly intent; she simply couldn't be pierced.

"Well, that is quite the trick," Nox breathed. "How much would you like for the ward?"

He scoffed and began walking toward the front of his shop, disappearing around his cabinets and stocks of dolls and toys and books. "To be fair, this is no ward: it's armor. Any fear caster would be capable of sending just as many demonic terrors into your thoughts while wearing it, and powers of the like. The ribbon will do nothing for you if you're met with magics, only if someone comes upon you with weaponry."

"How much would you like for the armor?" Nox amended.

"What if, in exchange for the ribbon, you promise to be a kind and fair queen? Does that sound like a deal?"

She faltered. "I can't take this from you."

"Believe me, you'll be doing all of Raascot a far greater favor than I."

The young woman followed after his oversized mustard coat with the blue bird chirping, "The ribbon is lovely. You're quite clever. You have beautiful eyes."

Yazlyn grinned. "Any chance the bird is for sale?"

"I'm afraid I can't part with it. Who would tell me how handsome I am?"

They thanked the shopkeeper profusely, but he merely waved them off, eyes sparkling with delight as he walked them out of his shop and waved to them as they departed down the cold, cobbled streets.

With the ribbon in Nox's hair and four more romance novels for Tanith under her arm, they set out on their return toward the castle. They stopped once at a quaint tea-and-scones shop to enjoy mugs of hot cider and to warm their feet by the fire while sitting in oversized chairs. As Nox looked at the winged fae woman sipping from her mug, she found herself feeling terribly guilty once more. Yazlyn was being a friend. A companion. A whole-hearted citizen of Raascot.

Yazlyn held her hands out to the fire. Nox couldn't help but feel bad that the very woman she'd rejected only a few weeks ago was escorting her around the capital.

"Hey," Nox began, running her finger around the lip of her mug, watching steam curl from her cup as she averted her gaze. "I wanted to say I'm sorry."

Yazlyn rolled her eyes. "Are you trying to ruin a perfectly lovely winter day with talk of feelings? You've said sorry already. I don't accept it because you have nothing to be sorry for. Nobody likes having to repeat themselves, so don't make me tell you again. Drink your cider."

The rest of the walk back to the castle seemed a lot shorter and Nox's weight significantly lighter. Struggles raged on, difficulties persisted, but when she stopped to look around, she realized her life had become something unfathomably lovely. She'd reigned over a kingdom of power and souls in Priory. She'd contented herself to rule as Queen of the Damned, her army of mindless lovers getting precisely what they deserved.

Yet, here she was, falling in step with an unlikely ally who'd truly become her friend.

She'd found herself in a beautiful city with a wonderful home, food on her table, and people who cared about her. Even the narratives she continuously tried to craft in her mind about her unworthiness or their dislike for her seemed to be chapters in novels that were repeatedly slammed closed, no matter how many times she reopened them. If Nox could stop feeling sorry for herself, she might just realize that she was the most fortunate person in the world.

Chapter
Twenty-nine

WHAT IS SHE DOING?"
Ash made a patient gesture. "She does those stretches every day before she'll spar with me. She's had me try them with her a time or two. They're rather difficult."

"Because they require balance," said Tanith calmly from where she twisted herself into a position on the sparring ring. Her eyes were closed against the bright light of day. After Amaris finished her run, she'd joined Ash on the ground to watch a few of the balance poses and contortions that Tanith did. She wasn't sure how it was possible, but the ivy of the courtyard retained its leaves and blossoms even in the cold winter months. Perhaps it had been enchanted to grow this way. She'd have to ask someone next time she got a chance, but for now she greatly appreciated how the emeralds and violets of the plants and their flowers broke up the colors of the stone around them.

"What's the hardest stretch you can do?" Amaris asked curiously.

The sun shone overhead, which was a nice change from the gray clouds common to their climate. The walls kept the arena perfectly windless. They were dressed in exceptionally warm, fur-lined leathers designed for tactical movement in the north. Tanith had expressed her approval that these did not restrict her ability to twist and knot herself into her daily positions. She'd even been comfortable enough to request a set of leathers made in red.

Tanith kept her eyes closed while she lowered herself into what appeared to be a plank pose. Slowly, she shifted her bodyweight forward and bent her arms at the elbow until her legs came up off the ground. Her right knee stretched over her shoulder, curling her body into a perfect half circle, tucking the leg deftly behind her head while her left knee twisted and extended behind her as a counterbalance. After hearing impressed murmurs from the reevers, she unraveled herself from the challenging balance pose and resumed her typical regimen.

"I will pay you four hundred romance novels if you can train Ash to do that," Amaris called to her.

Tanith placidly answered while arching an arm overhead, eyes still closed. "If I hadn't already located the city's library, I might have taken you up on that deal."

Amaris chuckled lightly. She'd be the first to admit that, for better or for worse, she'd come to like Tanith. She and Ash ignored Tanith while she continued her stretches, chatting amongst themselves.

"How long has Malik been gone now?" Amaris asked.

"Nearly seven days. I expect he's on his way back."

Amaris twisted her lips into a tight bunch in the corner of her mouth. "I thought maybe scouts would send a raven from the border when he crossed back into Raascot."

"I think they're trying to keep his journey as discreet as possible."

Amaris considered the implications of their meeting. "What could Samael do after he and Malik conclude their meeting? Will your father be punished?"

Ash shook his head. "You know as well as I: reevers are a challenging organization to police. Peace and justice are subjective. Given that they're up to our discretion regarding how we best see fit to restore balance, I suspect Samael will see the fact that four of us stood against Elil as casting our vote of dissent."

"Maybe there's something in the air up here that predisposes people to obsession," Amaris mused. She meant it as something of a joke, but sadness leached through her as she thought of all Elil had sacrificed in dedication to his cause. He hadn't been a husband, nor had he been a father. Now Elil was hardly even a person. He'd become as consumed with his desire to eliminate the threat of Sulgrave as Ceres had been with his desire to reunite with his child.

Amaris chafed her hands against her leg for warmth and felt her ring snag on her pants. She shook her hands against the small hurt. "It keeps doing that! I forget I'm wearing it. I'm not used to jewelry."

Ash brandished his. "Maybe Zaccai will let you swap for one of the men's rings. Our stone is much flatter since it's embedded in the band. See?"

Amaris held her finger up to compare. Her ring had a feminine loveliness, with a generously cut, two-carat gem. "Oh, but mine is so much prettier. It's even shinier than yours. Look how it sparkles! See, it has all of those peppery flecks in it."

Ash held his closer to his face. "Mine is solid black. I wonder why yours is so different?"

With the same quiet serenity that she'd had since she began her exercises, Tanith interjected from the mat, "It's because Amaris's is a siphon, and yours is not."

She continued stretching as if she had never spoken.

✦

"Zaccai, I need to talk to you," Amaris seethed.

She had tried his bedroom first, then stormed through the dining hall before eventually finding the second in command in the war room with Gadriel, leaning over the map.

Zaccai's brows bunched in concern. He paused over wherever they'd been gesturing to on the map below. "Amaris, you seem angry. Is everything okay?"

She flipped her middle finger upward, accomplishing two goals at once as she displayed her gem and used the vulgar gesture to convey her displeasure. "Do you want to explain what the hell you gave me?"

Zaccai and the general exchanged grimaces.

She stormed closer, grabbing for their respective hands. She yanked large fingers up from where they'd rested on the table and lofted them in front of her to examine their rings. The gems set in their pieces were the same black that Ash's had been.

"So, it's just mine, then? Do you care to explain?"

Zaccai's expression was pained. "How did you find out?"

Incredulity washed through her. It had been one thing to hear it from Tanith but an entirely separate thing to hear Zaccai confirm it. "Is this a punishment? Am I in some sort of secret prison? Why are you siphoning my power?"

She began to twist it off her finger, but Zaccai reacted with instant alarm. "No, don't!"

"Give me one good reason I should leave this *lie* on my hand for another minute. What was that story about testing magical distance? Or your story about the manufacturers trying something out? Why would you give them to all of us? Why would you lie to me?"

Zaccai's calming gesture only infuriated her further as he said, "I understand that you're angry, but I think you clearly misunderstand the ring."

She shot her look of distrust from the spymaster to the general. "Gad, did you know about this?"

He sucked on his teeth in a way that confirmed her fears. Her blood boiled. If she didn't calm her temper, she may just call upon her shock wave and use the distraction to stab both lying bastards where they stood.

"Give him a chance to explain. I don't think you'll want to take it off."

Her lips pulled back in a sneer. "You have ten seconds."

Zaccai slumped into a chair. Gadriel joined him in a seated position, and they clearly hoped Amaris would disarm herself by doing the same. She stood for a long while until it became apparent that they weren't going to speak until she relaxed. She sat down and crossed her arms on the table, glaring.

"It is a siphon, yes, but it doesn't siphon your power. And it *is* meant to test magical efficacy over distance...*and* it is a trial. My lie was one of misdirection, and a necessary one."

"Are you going to stop talking in riddles?"

His expression remained troubled as he looked to Gadriel. "Is there a best way to go about explaining this? Every way I think to word it, it's going to sound bad."

Gadriel sighed. He looked up at Amaris and said, "It's for Nox."

"What's for Nox?" she bit, frustration swelling by the minute.

"Do you recall how sick she was recently? And then how she started to feel better again after Malik stayed with her?"

Amaris's eyes narrowed. "Yes."

"Nox and Malik, to our knowledge, aren't necessarily sexually intimate. His affection for her has sustained her. You have to understand that with succubi, love really is a matter of life or death. A lot of demonization of so-called 'dark powers' comes from tales of malevolent succubi or incubi taking a human to bed only to drain them of their life force. While that's certainly one way to stay alive, it's only the case in extremes. Love takes many forms. And since Nox doesn't seem to be the kind of villainous queen who wants us disposing of dead bodies, we've worked through solutions with the manufacturers."

Amaris took a backward step. "I don't understand."

Zaccai offered, "He's saying that if Nox were more comfortable with murder, she could probably go months between nourishment. Instead, we're blessed with a queen with a moral compass. One that has her on a more precarious road and that needs a more constant stream for low levels of oxytocin."

Gadriel brought a hand to his chin. "You, Malik, and Yazlyn were given siphons that have been tuned to Nox's ring. We didn't tell any of you because we had no reason to believe it would work. Now with Malik gone, it's really the perfect opportunity to test the theory. Does she seem sick to you?"

"No, but—"

"And have she and Yazlyn slept together recently?"

Amaris's shoulders slumped. "I don't believe so..."

Zaccai tried again. "The gift wasn't meant to be malicious in any way. It doesn't affect you, your strength, your abilities. Honestly, for you, Yazlyn, and Malik, it's little more than a fashionable accessory. It was an experimental project. We didn't want to say anything until we knew it was effective."

"And you gave them to everyone so that the three of us wouldn't be suspicious?"

"To be honest," Zaccai said through a breath, "we didn't want Nox knowing either until we'd learned whether or not they worked. We weren't sure she'd be comfortable with the experiment."

Gadriel twiddled the ring on his index finger. "I do think they're quite dashing though, don't you?"

Zaccai nodded appreciatively.

Amaris frowned at her peppery diamond. "Why give one to me?"

She didn't know why she asked, because she already knew the answer. Gadriel said it anyway, his voice low and quiet, echoing exactly what everyone knew.

"Because you love her."

✦

Amaris looked up from her hiding place in one of the castle's many alcoves. She'd needed time to herself following the afternoon's tumult. Cool light illuminated her parchment, spilling in from the iron-latticed window. She'd curled onto a settee with her bestiary tome open to the vakliche. Her hands tightened around her notebook as she turned to see who'd discovered her.

The corner of Zaccai's mouth tipped apologetically. He left his hands clasped behind his back with polite curiosity as he asked, "What are you doing?"

Amaris frowned at her notebook, then set it next to the text. She'd scratched and scrawled and shaded her own depiction of the monster, including as many horrid details as she could remember. She'd crammed notes and commentary into the spaces surrounding her drawing. "I'm making a few amendments and additions to what we know of the mud demon. It would have been useful to know they were blind. Maybe future reevers will benefit from the knowledge."

"May I?"

She gestured for him to help himself as he took a seat. Zaccai touched a finger to the tome, tapping the sketch of the beast.

"I know the author of this particular tome," he said, eyes unfocusing slightly as if looking into a memory. "She would have loved to have been there."

"She would have wanted to have been present for a massacre?"

The skin around his eyes crinkled in some distant nostalgia. "Probably," he said. "But that's not why I'm here. I'm still sorry about the ring, and grateful that you've kept it on."

Amaris relaxed against the chilled stone wall. "You didn't need to come find me for that."

"No," he agreed, "but there is a second piece of jewelry I've been meaning to give you. It never seemed like the right time. But I suppose the time will never be right for something like this."

Her palms prickled as she watched the sad discomfort on his face, the slope of his shoulders, the heaviness he'd brought with him. He did not carry the energy of someone about to

344

give a lovely Yule gift. She folded her arms over her chest, protecting herself from whatever was coming next.

Zaccai procured a closed fist, fingers unfurling to reveal the reds and browns of a thin, frayed leather strap. A grooved, triangular ivory pendant rested in the center of his hand. Amaris's eyes widened. Her hand flew to her mouth to stifle her gasp. She looked at him with pained alarm as recognition flooded her. It was Odrin's necklace.

"It was left behind when he was collected from the throne room. I want you to know he was given a warrior's send-off. But...I thought you should have this."

Her breath snagged as she extended her fingers for the object. She'd never seen him without the token. Her eyes went to Zaccai once more, understanding the crimson stains for what they were. Her throat knotted as she lifted it with excruciating tenderness.

Zaccai touched her arm in a brief comforting gesture before he got to his feet. He didn't force conversation, nor did he tear her from her reverie, which she appreciated. He didn't even say goodbye. Instead, he left her in the alcove with Odrin's ghost and an ornament engraved with the letter *e*.

"For *everywhere*," she said quietly, speaking to his memory as she slipped the piece over her head. She clutched it against her chest, and in that moment she knew she would never take it off. "Because I know you'll always be with me."

Chapter Thirty

ASH OPENED HIS EYES.

Though his room was dark, his internal clock told him that it was well after midnight.

He wasn't sure what had woken him, as he heard no noise apart from the winter winds that sang beyond the castle. The fire in his room had died in the night, leaving only inky blackness where a warm light might have been. While normally he'd roll over and pull the sheets farther up over his head, an unfamiliar uncertainty pricked at his ears.

He listened to see if perhaps there had been noises coming from Nox's chambers down the hall, as Malik had returned the night before. He was more than happy to ignore the pair and give them whatever privacy they required. Malik had seemed more than a little enthusiastic to be reunited with Nox after his time on the road, and Ash wasn't sure if he wanted to eavesdrop on whatever they might be doing.

It had been decided from Malik's visit that the current reevers at the Castle of Gwydir held an acceptable presence in Raascot, and Grem was to escort Elil back to the keep. Samael decided that Elil was to focus on the scholarly aspects of studying Sulgrave. Even in what might very well turn out to be his ag'imni form, how Elil appeared wouldn't interfere with his academic pursuits.

But no, there was no indication that either Nox or Malik was awake. Instead, he heard only silence and winter.

He wasn't sure why, but he couldn't let himself go back to bed. Instead, a small adrenaline motivated him to slide out from under his covers, stand, and light a small handheld lantern. There was no reason for him to believe that anything was amiss, so he told himself he'd simply go to the kitchen for a cup of valerian root tea. The walk toward the kettle would give him an excuse to pace the corridor.

He did his best to silently open and close the door behind him, not wanting to disturb the others. Ash padded down the hall with as much stealth as possible, pausing outside of every room to ensure all was as it should be. His handheld lantern created warm puddles of light around him, pooling at his feet and crawling up the walls, casting shadows. If anyone turned their head from their bed at this hour, they'd no doubt see his flame and come looking for answers.

He began to feel quite guilty, as if he were invading the privacy of the others in the castle wing where they slept. He quickened his pace.

The chilly night soon had Ash wishing he had put on a shirt and slippers, but the tingle of urgency had rushed him from his room in the pants he'd slept in. He was fine against the plush rugs that ran through the corridor, but every time he stepped on the stone floor, chill jolted through his bare feet.

He turned the hall and was on the final corridor to the kitchen when he paused outside of Tanith's room and frowned. Her quarters had been set apart from the others. The location pinned her a bit farther into the castle than its other inhabitants, positioning her between the common bedrooms and the dining hall. Ash lifted his lantern slightly, moving it from side to side to see the yellowish puddle of light move against the floor. Something was odd about the way it hit her door. He bent down to touch the space beneath it to see if something dark had spilled, but his fingers came up clean. Holding his lantern closer for a better inspection, he realized it looked as if the lantern was unable to absorb the space. Rather than his warm light going in through the cracks beneath her door, the shadow of her room was coming out.

Icy fear filled him from head to toe. Ash jerked upright and tried her handle, but her door was locked. The others had been able to lock it from the outside, but she shouldn't have been able to do so from the inside.

"Tanith?" he called through the door.

A noise sounded as if it were coming from under water. Ash twisted the handle again, but he already knew exactly what was happening. Without wasting another second, he set the lantern down and began to throw his body weight into the door. He banged his free hand against her door as his shoulder made repeated contact with the wood. "Tanith!"

The creaks of the doors to other rooms in the adjoining corridor began to open as people stirred. Sounds of curious feet joined the noise of Ash's continued thumps against her door. His arm was already beginning to ache at the force of the unmoving obstacle before him. His focus remained solely on Tanith's door as he threw his shoulder into it again and again.

Gadriel was behind him in a flash in only sleeping shorts.

"It's locked!" came Ash's panicked voice.

The general asked no further questions. The alarm on Ash's face said enough. Gadriel pushed him out of the way and rested his hand against the handle until it clicked. They threw the unlocked door open to meet a solid black rectangle of shadow. Gadriel had taken a backward step, still blinking in confusion as Ash plunged into the darkness.

"Where are you?" he growled. He was not speaking to Tanith.

Somewhere in the hall beyond, a commotion was sounding as others rallied. No one knew how to break the impenetrable shadow being cast into Tanith's room. Orders were shouted and things were being fetched as others stirred into action, but Ash paid them no mind. He focused his faeling ears, tuning out the sounds of others to feel his way forward in the ink. An intense rush of cold pressed upon him, and he knew the glass to Tanith's window had been removed. He began to swing his hands, praying they hadn't already escaped the castle through the window. He brushed a desk and tripped on what must have been an overturned chair. The bedrooms—including Tanith's—were on the second floor. Neither Tanith nor his shadowy bastard of a father was a winged fae. They would never survive the leap onto the snowy ground below.

Ash heard the push of air as an item cut through it at the same time something struck him. A high-pitched ring hit as the thud of a blunt object knocked him squarely in the face. The stars in Ash's eyes were the only spots of color and light in the sea of dark. His father's voice accompanied the thump of the impact. The elder fae was angry as he spoke into the tar of his own making.

"Tell Samael I'm sorry, but the mission must go on," Elil growled.

"Leave her alone," Ash shouted. "Your dispatch is over."

Ash swung in the direction that the object had come. Anxiety pumped through him as he knew exactly how badly his father wanted to take Tanith alive. The man was so consumed with his mission that he would not let his last opportunity at progress be snatched from his fingers. He would not be returning to Uaimh Reev. Between his unhinged actions, his infiltration of Castle Gwydir, and the attack on his only son, it was clear Elil would find answers at any cost.

Again. The painful, cracking thump. The high, loud noise.

Ash fell to his knees. He was loosely aware of a small, drowning sound and realized that if they were still both in the room, then Tanith must be gagged somewhere in the shadow.

He couldn't let himself panic. She needed him.

Ash found his way to his feet, worried if he continued to throw fists into the void, he'd be just as likely to hit her as he was his father. The room was too large and too small all at once. There were as many obstacles in his way as there was dead space.

Urgency came in the form of rapid, unanswerable questions. Could Elil see through the dark? Did his powers affect him as they did the others? A shout and clatter told Ash that Gadriel was now also in the blackness of the room, for better or for worse. The second sound scarcely had time to join Ash's own noises before the general let out a groan of pain as the contact of a blunt weapon found a new victim.

Gadriel's snarl was truly feral as he lashed into the dark, toppling into furniture. The muted smack of flesh and bone told him that Gadriel had landed a blow. Hopefully the distraction would buy him the time he needed.

Ash used the cold like a rope, pulling himself on the icy temperature toward the window, knowing it must be how Elil planned to escape. If he could put himself between his father and his exit strategy, he could stop whatever the man intended for Tanith. He realized that if Elil had been able to sneak in and out of the castle undetected, no one would have noticed the girl was missing until morning. By the time they discovered her empty bed, he could have been halfway to the Frozen Straits.

"You're defending the enemy of the continent!" Elil barked, still locked in a blackout brawl with Gadriel.

Ash shouted toward the deranged proclamation, "It's over, Father!"

The whooshing tipped Ash off this time. He hit the floor just in time as his father's swing missed its mark. Enraged, Elil said, "It isn't over until Sulgrave has been contained! It isn't over until their forces on our continent are dead!"

With a final leap, Ash found what he was looking for. His fingers clutched at the arctic blast of the night beyond as he successfully located the window. If he dangled his upper body out of the frame, perhaps he would be able to see the moon and stars, but from where he stood, he was still firmly within the darkest tar. He grazed along the sill to find where a grappling hook was clinging to the corner of the window. This was how the man had entered, and it was undoubtedly how he planned to leave. If the hooks were engraved with dampening spells, Elil's infiltrating tools may have crashed through the glass soundlessly. Ash realized Tanith wouldn't have even known Elil was in her room until the frigid air met her skin.

Ash pressed his back against the open window where the pane had been removed. The cold helped to briefly shake him awake from the dizzying threat of unconsciousness. The blow he'd sustained threatened to drop him to the floor, but if he went down, there was no hope for Tanith.

Another swoosh. He braced himself for whatever impact was coming, expecting Elil to grab Tanith and make a run for his lone means of escape. The sounds of scuffle gave away Elil's position, as Gadriel had found the man once more. If the general could keep Elil distracted, it might buy Ash the time he needed to find Tanith. Ash felt along the ground, fingering the seam between the floor and the wall until his hands landed on flesh and thin fabric.

"Tanith!" he gasped.

She cried out in frantic protest through her gag. He pulled her to him, clutching her with one arm while the other stayed raised against the wielded threat in the dark.

"It's me! It's me. I'm going to get you out of here."

Though his equilibrium was bobbing uncomfortably, he forced his eyes wide open. He could not fail. Not now. He adjusted his grip on Tanith, refusing to let her stumble. He wasn't entirely certain he'd survive another blow to the head, but perhaps if he could drag her to the doorway...

The object whirred through the air the second before its impact, giving him the barest of moments to lift a defensive arm to take the blow. Elil's weapon avoided Ash's arm altogether, striking him in the jaw with ear-popping intensity. Ash's entire body tensed in an angry scream as he absorbed the blow, feeling fury and energy and fire tear through him where the wound pulsed. Every cell within him went from limp to flexed; every muscle strained as his scream tore from his throat.

But a cry wasn't the only thing he emitted as the killing blow shuddered through him.

As Ash screamed into the night, a piercing white light erupted from his mouth, his fingers, his eyes; his entire being seemed to explode in sunlight. The light cut the darkness around it like knives slashing into tattered linens, the slices of shade crumbling and falling wherever his beams emerged. This light was not the heat of fire, nor was it the pulsing current of lighting; it was the piercing, carving light of day intended to banish all darkness.

He saw the face of his father then in the path of the light and used his free arm to strike, Elil too bewildered to react. Ash threw a fist, satisfied with its crunching impact as his father buckled against the blow. A second later Gadriel had the man in a hold. Elil was a trained fae reever with hundreds of years of experience, and against any other opponent he would have escaped from the hold with instantaneous ease. But Gadriel was no normal opponent.

The places where light had carved through the darkness had created a path for Malik and Zaccai to pound through the bedroom and aid in their hold of the crazed reever, but Ash left detaining to the others. He had only one task as he dragged Tanith out of danger's path and into the hall.

"I've got her," Yazlyn said, eyes wide. She extended her hands.

Ash couldn't fathom what he must look like.

"She's safe with me, Ash."

He relinquished Tanith into Yazlyn's arms before he reentered the room. Ash approached the crowd of men just as they were binding a struggling Elil. Malik's entire weight pinned the crazed fae to keep him anchored to the ground while Gadriel and Zaccai forced his hands and legs together.

Ash's voice was quiet, but it was not broken. "I've known for a long time that your mission was more important than your family. I knew it when my mother died. I knew it when you failed to send letters or an encouraging word as I became a reever. I knew it when you fought against us to capture and interrogate Tanith. But even I couldn't have thought you so far gone or that the mission was so important that you would try to murder your own son."

Elil lost none of his intensity as he snarled, "What importance is blood against a calling? What does one life matter against the lives of the continent? Is your Sulgrave fae's life worth more than the countless who remain vulnerable because you're too weak to do what needs to be done?"

Ash shook his head. "Maybe not. But it's sure as hell worth more than yours."

Ash didn't look over his shoulder as the others escorted his thrashing father to the dungeons, where they would be undoubtedly fitting him with engraved manacles before stuffing him behind the same rune-etched iron bars that had once held Tanith. Yazlyn was still holding the small fae, as everyone had been too shocked to move in the moments that had followed the scuffle. Ash knelt, gently tugging the gag off from Tanith's mouth. Yazlyn held her up while he unbound the ties around her wrists and knees, freeing Tanith from everything, save for the silver cuffs that safely nullified her power.

Tanith pulled in oxygen as if she truly had been drowning, gasping at the free air in the hall around her as her hands braced against the floor of the corridor. The tear-soaked gag hung loosely around her neck.

"Are you okay?" Ash asked, voice soft. "Did he hurt you?"

Her shoulders shook as her fears crashed over her, audible tears coming from the strong, stoic fae who wore red nightdresses even to sleep. She had not cried when they'd captured her in the gully. She had not cried when she'd sat in the prison. She had not cried when she'd been forced to collaborate and spend time with those she had deemed unworthy. Only now, after escaping the terrors of true dark, did her fear find her at last.

"It's freezing," Ash muttered to the women in the hallway. Nox and Amaris stood with wide eyes, unsure how best to help. "Can we find her a new room?"

"She could stay in Amaris's old room," Nox offered. "There's still no glass, but the window is boarded up, which would make it safer."

"No," Tanith said quickly, the word filled with her distress. She was shrinking against the idea of being left alone and vulnerable, shuddering at the monsters that must lurk in every shadow. Tanith lifted her tear-soaked face to Ash. "Can I stay with you?"

He blinked his surprise but nodded quickly. "Yes, of course."

Yazlyn followed them, fetching a few of Tanith's things from the shambles of her room. Amaris helped them light a fire in Ash's hearth while Nox announced she was tired of the staff cleaning up glass and would prefer if, from now on, everyone in the castle could stop ruining perfectly good bedrooms. There were orders to be issued, plans to be made, and plenty to do in the small hours of the night.

Ash shut the door to mute the sounds of the others bustling through the hall.

Tanith still wasn't speaking. She was a cocoon of huddled blanket in the middle of Ash's bed, part of the duvet pulled up over her head to truly create a warm cave of bedding for her to sink into where she sat. He realized he had still been shirtless and apologized, pulling a shirt over his bare back. After drinking the contents of a small brown bottle of healing tonic to help with the wounds and almost certain concussion he'd sustained, he sank into the chair near the fire.

"I'll be three arm's lengths away if anything else happens. You can sleep, okay?"

From her shrunken place in her swaddle, he just barely saw Tanith's nod. He had been most certain that there'd be too much excitement to even consider sleeping, but after the adrenaline started to leech from his body mingled with the alleviating properties of the tonic, sleep dragged him with it, along with the knowledge that within him had been the long-slumbering gift of light.

Ash wasn't sure how long he'd been asleep when a noise caused him to jolt awake. His heart exploded within him, at the ready to battle once more. It took a moment for his eyes to calm, his amber gaze settling on the sound that had stirred him.

Tanith was no longer bundled in blankets. She had shifted out of her wrapping and had begun scooting toward the end of the bed. Her feet were tucked beneath her while she held the bedpost, eyeing him cautiously. Ash wasn't sure if it had been a sound at all that had woken him. Perhaps the sense of being watched had been enough to shake him from his slumber.

"What happened?" he asked, voice quick.

"Nothing," she said quietly.

"Are you okay?" He blinked rapidly, leaning forward in his chair. He scanned the room again for threats. The fire had waned substantially, leaving only the barest glow of embers at the base of its earth. "Are you cold? I'll get the fire going."

"No, don't—" She stopped him just as he began to move from the chair.

He frowned at her expectantly.

"I am cold," she said carefully.

He looked to the dying fire, the untouched pile of wood, and then to the bed. The first thoughts that dripped into his mind were questions, then curiosities, then the slow spread of realization. Ash did his best to control the surprise in his expression. He swallowed but found his mouth suddenly dry. "You're cold?" he repeated quietly.

She nodded, unmoving.

His lips parted in a silent question.

Wordlessly, Tanith began to move back to where she'd been tucked beneath the covers. She slipped her legs under the comforter before pulling it up over her lap. Still sitting up, she turned down the cover on the far side of the bed. The gesture was equal parts permission, risk, and hope.

Ash had never felt so paralyzed in his life.

He'd made efforts with nearly every maiden who crossed his path since his sixteenth year of life. He'd gained something of a reputation in Stone—whether for charm or promiscuity depended largely on who was telling the story. Now he looked into the dark, wide eyes of a woman who'd hated him with a repugnance and ferocity that should have been reserved for serpents in a child's crib. She'd burned with her prejudice for faelings, crossing the Frozen Straits, binding demons, hurling insults, weapons, and furniture alike at him as she'd trashed the training ring when they'd first been paired.

Now she was quite unmistakably asking him to sleep beside her.

"I'm sorry," she said quietly, her whisper thick with emotion.

He knew she wasn't apologizing for his father's attempted siege. Ash remained silent, for there was nothing he could say. He didn't tell her he forgave her, because her sins were not his alone to absolve. He didn't tell her it was okay, because the wrongs of the past could never be undone.

But maybe the future…

He swallowed against the lump in his throat, knowing it to be something that had been growing within him for some time.

He'd chosen Tanith the moment he'd moved his body between hers and his father's in the town house. He'd been willing to die for her earlier that very night, and she knew it. Their shift had occurred with the glacial slowness responsible for transformation.

With Tanith, this flower had planted its seed in his heart before he'd had a chance to understand what had taken root. It wasn't a fragile orchid or a pure lily or a simple daisy. This was something beautiful that had grown from the mud. It was a lotus from the warmest regions on the southern shores, the plant that emerged from silt and ponds and swamps, bringing unspeakable beauty where none had existed.

It had only taken him three steps to cross the room. He didn't drop her eyes as he slid into the bed beside her. A small smile twitched the corners of her lips as she relaxed into his acceptance. Her shoulders released a tension that he hadn't realized she'd held while she'd waited for his response. Tanith lowered herself to her pillow and turned away, facing the window. Ash draped his arm over her, holding her in the crooks and grooves of his body, and knew his heart would belong only to her.

Chapter
Thirty-one

G OOD MORNING!" NOX CHIRPED CHEERFULLY, DRIFTING
along the scents of food and tea as they carried her to
the dining room. The sun had woken her, its warm rays and
promise of cinnamon rolls nudging her out of bed.

"What's wrong?" Gadriel's fork clattered to his plate as he
looked up at her from his place at the table.

"So help me." Nox's joy soured as she glared at them.
Everyone was present at the table, save for Zaccai. "If one
more person asks me what's wrong just because I'm awake
before high noon, I will have you all in the stocks."

Yazlyn's auburn curls danced around her shoulders as she
shook her head, clearly on her second cup of tea from her
amiable attitude.

Nox drummed her fingers against her bicep. "No stocks
in Gwydir? What's the equivalent? Tried and quartered in
the square?"

Gadriel laughed over his breakfast. "How much more
medieval is Farehold than Raascot? Goddess, getting you a
tutor might be a more pressing issue than I'd thought." He
looked to Amaris. "Is this why you're such a barbarian?"

"You sure know how to charm a girl," she muttered.

"Why *are* you here?" Yazlyn asked Nox, draining her tea.

"Well, damn, I thought I was going to invite everyone to go out on the town, but now I don't think I want to bring any of you. You're rude. I will go find new friends. Except for Malik. He can come." She began to fill up a plate and looked to Malik, who was already creating space beside himself at the table.

"And what will we be doing?" Malik asked.

She shrugged. "Amaris and Yazlyn went to a tavern the other day, and that sounded fun. We could all go for drinks? Maybe get dinner? Leave the castle for something other than the library? We'll say we're celebrating Tanith's rescue from the brink of death and Ash's access of sunlight, or whatever it was you did."

"That was pretty cool, wasn't it?" Ash agreed.

The other reevers smiled appreciatively at their brother. If Nox wasn't mistaken, she also thought she noticed a faint flicker of pride on Tanith's face.

"So?" Nox looked to Yazlyn and Gadriel. "What do people do for fun around here?"

A silent conversation happened between the general and his sergeant in front of all of them. The winged fae made eye contact. Nox watched their faces carefully. It was Gadriel with the first telling expression. His mouth twisted into something of a mischievous smile. Yazlyn's eyes flared, an eyebrow cocked in warning as if to shoot down his unspoken suggestion. When his face remained unchanged, she tilted her head as if to ask if he was serious. His grin only deepened.

Yazlyn finally shrugged and turned back to Nox. "Ask the sadist."

Gadriel clapped his hands together. "Nox, how are you with a bow?"

✦

"I hate all of you," Nox grumbled, fumbling with her bow string against her fur-lined gloves. They were lined up outside

359

of the castle in the bright, sunny winter day. The regal architecture of the city sprawled just beyond the river on one side, and the enormous castle loomed on the other. Sunlight set everything twinkling, from the glitter of the snowbanks to the shimmering of the stones. Even the mountains were sparkly today.

"Come on," Malik said. "Stay near me."

"No!" Yazlyn's voice was loud as she overheard his words of comfort. "That's cheating! There are no teams."

Nox shot daggers with her eyes. Yazlyn stuck out her tongue in response.

Zaccai took over. He'd been far too enthusiastic to hear they were going to play his favorite game, immediately abandoning whatever task had been in his hands so he could gather supplies for their event.

"Okay," the commander began, "the rules are simple. We have to stay on the castle grounds." He made a sweeping gesture to the large, snow-covered lawn with Castle Gwydir cutting a stark figure behind them. "We can't cross the river, but anywhere else is free rein. Behind bushes, around corners, anywhere you can find to hide. Yazlyn," he admonished as he looked to her, "don't think we've forgotten the year you built an ice shelter. If you manipulate snow to hide—"

"I learned my lesson," she barked.

"Firing squad." Zaccai raised his bow with a smile. He mocked a release as if to hit her where she stood.

The arrows in their quivers were not tipped with any sort of metal or stone. Each arrow had a thick, blunt, powder-filled pouch of thin tissue at its tip, stuffed with a vibrant color. Each of them had been assigned a hue. Lavender was given to Amaris, green to Malik, royal purple to Yazlyn, red to Tanith, yellow to Ash, sky blue to Zaccai, pink to Gadriel, and orange to Nox.

"I'm the only one who can't shoot a bow," Nox argued. "This was supposed to be fun."

"This *will* be fun." Yazlyn's teeth glinted wickedly as she aimed her bow and arrow playfully at Nox.

"Goddess help me." Nox narrowed her eyes with threatening competition at the sergeant.

"No, that's okay," Gadriel said in defense. "We're giving Nox an advantage to level the playing field. She's the only one not trained on the bow and arrow, but she should still get to participate."

"You did not bring the child's bow," Yazlyn said, giving a characteristic roll of her eyes, but even amidst the gesture, it was clear her attitude was all for show. Her tone and her posture indicated that the sergeant was just spouting yet another grumble in a long list of one-liners as if she were always performing to entertain an audience of one: herself. She smirked with her own amusement.

Nox frowned at the bow Gadriel offered. It looked no different from the others, save for a reflective band around the center. "This is a child's bow?"

He nodded. "It's enchanted to assist with aim."

"Why doesn't everyone use these in battle?" Nox asked, turning her bow over in her hand.

"Because it's a child's bow. They're harmless by design. It's little more than a toy. You can't hit your target with violence."

"What would keep an enemy from having all of their archers possess bows like this?"

Gadriel sighed. "Because, like I said, it's a toy."

"But couldn't manufacturers—"

"If they could, I suspect we'd all have them. Manufacturing isn't something I have a knack for, but I know it's taxing, tedious, and expensive. Harmless things like toys and knickknacks are usually some of the few things that get made successfully. Other things…well, it's hit or miss. You'll have to ask your tutor."

She mumbled, "This is humiliating."

"We'll teach you how to use a bow later, how's that sound?" Malik asked, patient as a saint as he looked at her hopefully. He was practically bouncing with excitement, ready to get to action. Nox looked at him to inform him that no, she did not find his comment particularly helpful.

"First one hit buys drinks." Gadriel beamed. He hadn't stopped glowing with wolfish delight since the idea first filled him over breakfast. He scanned them as if he were a hound eyeing prey.

"Okay." Zaccai hadn't finished with the rules. "We get until the count of one hundred before we can begin. If anyone shoots early—"

"Yes, yes, firing squad," Yazlyn grumbled, hands on hips as she recalled whatever unsavory memory accompanied her incident with the ice fort. Her tone perked up as she began to count. "Ready? Set?"

At once, the mismatched crew took off like hares sprinting through the woods, all bounding in various directions, save for Nox. She was as frozen as the ice beneath her boots. She looked to one side, then the other, having no idea what to do. She was the only one with no weapons training, and she was meant to take on three of Raascot's military, three reevers, and a murderous zealot.

At least ten counts passed before she took off into the snow, angling for a tangle of bushes near the stone bridge. The others had sprinted around the castle and seemed to be heading for the back, which would hopefully give her the opportunity to hide before they ascertained how little ground she'd covered. Fortunately, there were enough footprints carving their way across the yard that hers wouldn't stand out too prominently.

She was glad to be bundled against the cold. Her toes wiggled comfortably within her fur boots, enjoying the way excitement pumped through her blood with matching warmth. The blue-green coniferous shrubs twisted and crouched in a perfect conciliatory perch. She picked her way through two of the large plants until she was certain she was little more than a small splotch of black hair that could be mistaken for a branch.

She didn't need to hunt the others.

She just needed to avoid getting caught.

The count had scarcely reached one hundred before an eruption of noises informed her that someone was already responsible for buying drinks. A loud shriek led her to believe with some delight that Yazlyn was the first victim. She hid her smile, enjoying the curse of obscenities that floated from somewhere around the castle's back. Gadriel whooped in victory, but his happy declaration had apparently given him away. A commotion of curses, yells, and laughter bubbled from around the castle wall.

Nox ducked further as Amaris tore around the corner of the castle, skidding to a halt with such immediacy that she almost slid through the snow. Nox watched with wide, appreciative eyes from behind the branches. She'd had no opportunity to watch Amaris in action as reever and was impressed with her speed and competence with a weapon.

Instead of continuing in her run, Amaris pressed her body into the castle wall and drew her bow taut. She had an arrow nocked, knees bent, chest unmoving as if she didn't dare take a breath. A second burst of sound came as someone new came sprinting past the castle's outermost wall. Nox saw Ash's red tuft of hair as he bolted into view. He was barreling toward the bridge. He'd passed Amaris without ever realizing she was there.

She raised her bow and released it in a fluid motion, but Ash dropped to his stomach with inconceivable speed and grace. He lay in the snow just in time for the lavender pouch to whir past him, burrowing into a nearby snowbank. Ash wasted no time. He was up on one knee within a beat, twisting his bow as he aimed for Amaris.

In the seconds it had taken Ash to drop, Nox seized her opportunity. While he knelt and lifted his bow for Amaris, Nox's small orange pouch poked from beneath the boughs of the wilting pine. She pulled back her bow and released her arrow in an instant. It hit Ash squarely between the shoulder blades, exploding in a cloud of brilliant tangerine powder, adding to the gingers of his flamelike hair. He yelped as he spun to see who'd taken him down, eyes as wide as saucers when Nox stepped into view.

Amaris angled her arrow for the queen.

"Don't you dare!" Nox yelped.

"No teams, remember?" Amaris cried back with a mischievous smile.

Nox took off to the right but made only three long leaps until she was confident Amaris was tracking her pace. She didn't even wait for the wooden sound of nocked bows. Amaris released her arrow, anticipating Nox's trajectory, but Nox faked her next step in time to twist, skidding in the other direction.

"Hey!" Amaris shrieked. "Get back here!"

Nox giggled as she scrambled through the snow over the castle grounds. She was running for a large tree near the center of the yard when a thump hit her in the arm. She gasped at the sudden pain as she was enveloped in a verdant cloud. Her eyes went wild as she searched around for its owner.

Malik mouthed a silent "Sorry!" so as not to give his position away.

She continued gaping at him in both shock and humor, watching as he took off after the only other remaining reever. He ran for Amaris like a hound after a rabbit, but Amaris zagged with such agility that he couldn't anticipate her movements. She twisted onto her back mid-dive, spinning with such so much grace that she had angled her bow and arrow for Malik before she hit the ground. The greens and lavenders that accompanied their standoff made it difficult to ascertain who had hit whom first, but their exchange of colors made it clear on no uncertain terms that they were both out. She'd hit him in the center of the chest, while his green pouch had erupted in her face.

The initial game was over within twenty minutes of its onset. The anarchy that followed took another thirty minutes.

"Gadriel cheated," Yazlyn said definitively.

"I did not. It's not my fault you're terrible at the game."

"You hit me in the back of the head!" She turned, revealing the shocking shade of pink where cherry-dark hair had been. Amaris looked unsympathetic to Yazlyn's plight from where her skin had completely disappeared behind the vibrant green caked over her face.

Nox smiled at her rainbow of friends, everyone covered in loud splotches of color.

Zaccai had been the winner, but after he hit Tanith—the last one standing—she'd shot a defeated, retaliating arrow in his direction. Her red, giggling explosion of poor sportsmanship had resulted in a flurry of arrows, colors, and bursts of powder until they were a kaleidoscope of battle and amusement. No one was safe as everyone emptied their quivers, shooting arrow after arrow at anything that moved. Even Nox had managed to hit a few more of her friends in their free-for-all, but they'd taken a bit too much delight covering her in clashing colors in response. The once-pristine castle yard was now a chaotic disaster.

"So, to the tavern?" Gadriel asked.

Amaris's unamused, arm-crossed silence was as loud and telling as if she'd hit him in the head. He hadn't been spared from her wrath during their post-game anarchy and was sporting a rather intentional lavender coloration on his jugular, as if she'd needed to remind him that she could kill him.

"Okay," he amended, "so first we clean and change, and then Yazlyn buys everyone drinks."

"I think the queen can afford it," Yazlyn said with some wry amusement. "Doesn't she pay the military salaries anyway? Let's cut out the middleman."

Nox grinned through the greens, pinks, and reds that decorated her hair, skin, and clothes. "I'll buy the drinks, as long as we all remember from now until the end of time that I'm the one who eliminated Ash."

✦

It was only a few hours past lunch, meaning their raucous day of drinking had earned a tavern almost to themselves.

Afternoon drinks were generally a result of one of two possible extremes. Either it was an occasion so jolly that only daylight would do it justice, or it was a tragedy so sad that no hour could stop the need for the numbing comforts of alcohol. Fortunately, the first round of wines, ales, and mead was firmly a result of the former.

Tanith requested wine, but after Yazlyn forced her to try the mead, she'd quickly abandoned her order and switched to the sweet mug instead. Ash and Malik had also started with beer, before deciding that it was a honey mead sort of day.

There would be time for politics. There would be time for war and curses and plans. There would be meetings and war rooms and plots in the days that followed, just as there had been every day prior.

Today was about childhood memories. Today was for favorite foods, horrible jokes, drinking songs, and whatever level of alcohol consumption had convinced Nox to order a round of drinks for every human and fae in the ever-filling tavern. By the time dinner rolled around, they'd decided to stay at the tavern for the aromatic stew and fresh sourdough bread.

Gadriel shared a story wherein he and Ceres had once attempted to convince women at a pub that he was the king and Ceres was the general—to mixed success. Ceres had bedded a woman under the guise of a military man, but Gadriel hadn't had the believability to convince her friend that he was a king. Zaccai added with some amusement that he specifically remembered that story because he'd heard it weeks after the incident being loudly told at a party that some winged fae had tried to pass himself off as a monarch.

"What about you?" Amaris looked to Zaccai. "Any tales of false identities or wild lovers?"

He lifted an eyebrow and took a drink in a way that told them that yes, he was a man of many tales, and no, they would not be hearing any of them.

Ash taught the others an interesting drinking game wherein everyone set their hand on the table as if it were a standing spider, and then they each had to lift a finger at the same time when Ash said a combination of words in an old dialect. Whoever lifted an identical finger to the speaker had to drink. It was a fun game, as it was quite easy to figure out and relied solely on luck. Nox generally preferred to sip her drinks, but the spider game had her guzzling red wine like it was burning spirits.

Evening faded into night. Music, alcohol, and patrons' laughter filled the air, giving everything a jolly, humming quality. Drunk enough to chime in with the sort of memories that were recounted only with a belly full of ale, Malik did his best to recite a few of the poems they'd heard during their stay in Henares for the table. Ash helped him with the punchline of several of the duke's dirtier limericks, much to Nox's chagrin. Thoroughly enjoying the lovelorn duke's vulgar poems, Gadriel declared that the Duke of Henares was destined to be his very best friend, should their paths ever cross.

"Did I ever tell you about my threesome with—" Yazlyn started.

At the same time, Gadriel and Zaccai completed her sentence with a similarly disinterested "A duchess and a bladesmith."

"Well, it was a great story," Yazlyn grumbled.

"Your first threesome does stick with you," Tanith agreed. The table went silent, eyes and mouths bulging and gaping like she sat at the table with six drunk fish in need of air and she as the seventh had been the fisherman. If it weren't for the cacophonous sounds of a now-lively tavern, they might have remained frozen in time.

"What?" Tanith said, shrinking from the table.

Nox nearly choked. "It's just…"

Yazlyn clapped her on the back. "We assumed you were a prude, TanTan."

"Why would you assume that?" Tanith looked at the sergeant, then made a face. "And I don't care for that nickname. Please don't repeat that."

"You're just so pious!" Amaris said, gagging on her mead.

Tanith looked to the reevers. "Are you three not also the sword arms of the All Mother? Celibacy isn't expected of any of you, is it? I don't see what battle readiness and magical servitude have to do with sexuality. We're not bishops or priestesses wed to the All Mother. You all know so little of the church. Such poor, primitive savages of the southern kingdoms…" She said it with something of a wry smile.

"Fair enough." Nox coughed into her wine. She jerked her head up from her cup as she looked to the Sulgrave girl again. "Wait, wait—did you say your *first* threesome?"

Tanith shook her head. "I'm quite certain I'm not drunk enough for this conversation."

"We can change that!" Yazlyn raised her hand excitedly to get the barmaid's attention.

To Nox's buzzed amusement, they wouldn't get any more out of Tanith that night. Nox wasn't sure that Tanith had shown any distance from her radical religion or repentance for her war crimes, but with every day that passed, it felt more and more that Tanith no longer considered them enemies.

They may even cautiously have begun to consider her a friend.

Chapter Thirty-two

"SO THAT'S IT? WE'RE READY?" NOX FOUGHT THE HOT COALS of emotion that threatened her diplomacy. She leaned a single elbow on the war room table, covering her mouth with a finger as she processed the information. She wasn't the only one on edge.

She'd known the day would come. Their comfortable days in Gwydir couldn't last forever.

Queen Moirai had been sowing dissent for a while. They'd had speculated that she'd make a formal call to arms soon. When Zaccai arrived with the news that his network had intercepted an invitation meant for the lordlings of Farehold so that Moirai might gather forces, they knew what needed to be done.

Nox would send word for the Duke of Henares to prepare for the arrival of a few Raascot ambassadors to ride with him into the palace. As if the All Mother had blessed their timing, the manufacturers had at long last announced their confidence in the shields they'd crafted. The efforts toward the spelled objects had increased from seven, to twenty, to fifty of the brightest minds in magic, history, academia, metalworking, and fabrication before two cuffs were forged.

"Who goes south?" Ash asked, eyeing Tanith from where she sat in the corner of the room. They collectively knew they couldn't bring their Sulgrave contact into battle. It had become very clear over the passing weeks that neither of them wished to be separated from each other. If Tanith wasn't going to Farehold, neither was Ash.

Nox closed her eyes and inhaled through her mouth. Invisible fingers throttled her, biting back her fury with destiny as she said, "Amaris must go, but we knew as much."

"I'll go," Gadriel said, quick to volunteer. "If I fly her, we'll cut our travel time substantially."

Yazlyn frowned. "If your arms are busy carrying Amaris, then no other wingless reever could journey south. It's clear Ash will remain here with Tanith, but is it wise for Malik to also stay behind? He has no wings, but Amaris is trained as a reever, as is he. Shouldn't they fight together?"

Nox stiffened, ready to intercede on the proposition, but Malik was already nodding.

He said, "No one understands our fighting style better than those in our brotherhood. I know you two have been training together," he said, gesturing between Amaris and Gadriel, "but she's going to need her swordsmanship and combat skills just as much as any power. I'll go."

Yazlyn agreed. "Then Gadriel will need to fly with you. Either Zaccai or I will have to carry Amaris."

Zaccai's expression crumpled. "I can't leave the castle. With Gadriel gone, someone needs to stay behind with Nox."

"I'll be here," Ash offered uselessly.

Zaccai corrected, "A Raascot fae needs to stay behind with Nox. Her title is too new, and our armies have been shredded since the massacre. She can't be left alone on the throne."

Nox settled both elbows on the table, hands in fists as she used the physical barrier of her folded fingers to prevent her mouth from saying everything she wanted to say. Because that's all they were—wants. She was incensed by the knowledge that Amaris was fated to go south. Rage cut through her at the prospect of Malik leaving for Farehold. She didn't even want Yazlyn to be put in harm's way. But she saw the wisdom in the divisions as their plans to infiltrate the Castle of Aubade fell into place. Visions of her own arduous journey from one kingdom to the other flashed across her mind. She knew the dangers that stood between the two castles. She cleared her throat and lowered her hands, forcing her mind to stay on the task at hand.

"What of the spelled shields? How do we know the collars work?"

Zaccai had brought the objects to the meeting and passed them between Yazlyn and Gadriel. The military fae eyed the silver ringlets. Hearing it described as a collar, Yazlyn lifted hers to her neck and gasped as it snapped into place around her throat. She began to tug at it and was dismayed to find it wouldn't release. She clawed at her neck, fingers digging for a ledge beneath the silver ringlet and her skin, but she found none. Her face flashed from annoyance to panic as she tore at the silver band that had become a fixture of her throat.

Gadriel winced at his frantic sergeant, holding him at a distance like a snake.

Zaccai answered Nox with a frown. "We don't. This is part of what has taken so long. As you can see with Yazlyn— and by the way, Yaz, I'm not sure why you wouldn't wait for instructions, this is your own fault—the collars appear to tune to an individual and then become challenging to separate. Their fusion has made trial and error nearly impossible. While their primary purpose is to shield you from the curse, they'll have the added benefit of acting as generalized magical shields. You should be safe from all charms and powers of the mind or perception while you wear them."

Malik lifted a finger. "Wouldn't I be able to tell whether or not the collars have worked once we cross into Farehold?"

Zaccai shrugged helplessly. "We honestly don't know. It isn't just fae who've been perceived as ag'imni; it's all northerners who cross the border. Our spy network in the south have been exclusively winged fae due to their ability to fly and quickly escape life-threatening situations. Raascot humans were sitting ducks when they crossed the border, so they haven't for more than twenty years. And though you aren't technically from Raascot—"

Malik's mouth twisted into a frown. "I get it. We can't be sure."

"It if helps," Zaccai said with a broken smile, "all of our bets are on you remaining your normal, charming self to the citizens of Farehold, as you are fully human and were born and raised in the south."

Nox examined the silver objects from across the room, watching how the light caught on Yazlyn's new accessory. "Will I be getting a protective ward?"

Zaccai made a face. His careful wording made her bristle as he said, "Yes, of course. We just need a little bit more education on how to make one for you."

Curiosity was more powerful than disappointment as Nox asked, "Why would I be any different?" She would have thought nothing of it, had Amaris not visibly flinched from across the room.

"You have to understand," Zaccai said delicately, "we're being overly cautious with our only remaining monarch."

While the reevers and military fae discussed the permeation of the curse and Nox waited on an answer that wasn't coming, Gadriel provided enough distraction for the topic to be dropped. He bent his arms over his head and gripped his shirt from behind, pulling his long-sleeve tunic off from the back. His glossy black hair mussed slightly as the shirt slid over his head, his bare chest revealing his muscles to the room. He brought the collar to his upper arm, and it snapped in place seamlessly just as Yazlyn's had with her throat. Everyone was blinking at the half-naked general, but he shrugged.

"I don't think collars particularly suit me."

Yazlyn's eyes narrowed in a glare while the general

returned his tunic, magical device now securely hidden beneath his top as it encircled his bicep. "You had to take your shirt off for that?"

"My muscles are too big for me to shove up the sleeve," he said teasingly.

Amaris offered a sympathetic pout to Yazlyn. "For what it's worth, I think it looks really nice on your neck."

With an eye roll, Yazlyn said, "I've heard you have a thing for throats, Amaris. Not everyone wants a choker."

The room erupted in a combination of wide-eyed laughs and claps as Amaris turned crimson and shrank into her chair in humiliation. Nox couldn't keep herself from giggling, though she did her best to cover her mouth.

Perhaps it had been the tension of the news or the anxiety of their impending battle, but they were all ready to snap. Amaris tried to bury her face in her hands. Perhaps she'd thought her proclivities were more clandestine than she'd hoped. Gadriel tried to pat her comfortingly on the back, but she shook him off. Even Tanith clasped her hand over her mouth in shy appreciation of the joke.

"Okay," Zaccai said, trying to gain control of the cackling room, "let's go back to the issue of testing the efficacy of the collars. We need someone from Farehold who's never been north to be willing to meet with us. Ideally, we would have stayed hidden until Yelagin and then our contact at the farmhouse could have intervened as our assessor, but after the invasion of Yelagin, I don't know any humans or fae south of the border who would be receptive to meeting with us. Our strongholds are exclusively composed of Raascot fae."

Nox's brows knit. "I may be able to write to someone in Farehold. I have a…contact."

Amaris pivoted from embarrassment into authority as she spoke, face still a shade of pink. "Do we know who commands Moirai's troops? Ever since the captain of the guards found himself in the belly of a dragon, I haven't heard word of who's taken his place."

Zaccai nodded. "There are two in his stead, a man and a woman who've been promoted to captain. We don't have names, but they're referred to as the Hand and Hammer. Word has passed through our sources that make them sound particularly fearsome. Whoever Moirai has appointed doubtlessly possesses skill surpassing those of her former human captain."

Amaris frowned. "The Hand and Hammer? That sounds ominous. I think I would have preferred Eramus."

"Trust me," Nox said, shaking her head as she remembered the murderous captain of the guard and his torture chamber, "you wouldn't."

Malik spoke. "When do we leave?"

Nox pulled herself back into her body and away from her memories of her former life and espionage beyond the Selkie's walls. "Zaccai, when is this meeting with the lords of Farehold? Those traveling south need time to test the shields and then get to Henares before the gathering."

"The date is two weeks from now, which would be nearly an impossible distance on horseback, but if Gadriel and Yazlyn are flying our two reevers, the four of them should be able to get to Henares in ten days."

Nox closed her eyes. "And it's another two days from Henares to Aubade. This means the travelers need to leave tomorrow if they hope to make it on time."

The room quieted as they appreciated the seriousness of their situation. The day was truly upon them. There would be no more communal meals or talk of pastries or adventures through shops of antiquities. The libraries and taverns and cozy winter days would soon be a memory of the past. All that was left was to hope that their training had prepared them for the task at hand to make their move on Moirai.

"Are you ready, Snowflake?" Nox said, dropping her queenly authority as she looked at Amaris. For the first time in a long time, she didn't feel as though she were looking at her through the wall they'd built. She was not a queen

374

regarding a reever. They were not acquaintances who shared an enemy. They were Nox and Amaris.

Nox didn't see the scarred and battle-ready white-haired combatant before her. She looked into the big, bright eyes of the girl she'd held in the pantry. She saw the pale, snowy face of the one who'd hid with her on market day, who'd run from the bishop, who'd curled up in her arms in the forsaken walls of the mill. Behind Amaris's lavender eyes, she saw a pained, tumultuous crackle.

"I am," Amaris said.

Her statement didn't come out with the strength of the sword arm of the All Mother. Instead, it was strangled with nostalgia. No matter who she was or what she'd become, she wanted Nox to know she was ready to fight.

They called the meeting to a close with the promise that everyone would set about packing for departure, doing whatever necessary for food, water, clothes, and weapons. Nox knew she needed to write to Farleigh's Gray Matron, but her feet seemed to disagree. She found herself in the practice arena.

The open sky of the late-winter evening was a clear, cold brick above her. The four walls of the training area shielded her from the wind as she stood within its security. Her hands wrapped around Chandra as she grunted and thrust the axe time after time into the target. It embedded itself without fail with every angry toss. She had neglected to put on a coat after coming directly from the war room. Cold air bit at her flesh, but she ignored it, warmed by her own anger.

Fury lit her from within.

She was angry at her mother for abandoning her at an orphanage and her father for failing to find her. She hated the Matron for misleading her, convincing her to believe she was second class. She was enraged by the Madame who'd purchased her and the world that had made her cruel. She was bitter that the softness she'd found ever since leaving the Selkie was slipping between her fingers.

Life had been too perfect. Too much had gone right. She had grown too comfortable. Maybe this was what she deserved for allowing herself to feel happiness. The All Mother had torn it from her.

She crossed the space and used her foot as leverage each time she yanked the axe from where it had stuck, moving farther and farther with each throw until she was landing tosses from incredible distances. The day's chill made her muscles tense, solidifying the target, making each fetching more challenging than the one before.

Nox had backed so far that she'd practically pressed herself to the far wall of the training room. When she stepped as far as she could away from the target, she tossed the axe and it missed, hitting the target with its broad side and clattering to the ground. Marching across the arena with frustration, she picked up Chandra and tried again, this time missing the mark entirely. She flinched as it hit the vines, hoping its blade had avoided the stone wall. Nox stormed over to the axe and examined it, relieved to find it unaffected. She returned to the far wall and let out an angry snarl as she threw it again, once again hearing it thud against the target and clatter uselessly to the ground. She shouted a string of vulgar curses at Chandra for being a worthless traitor.

She hadn't noticed Malik leaning against the doorway to the training arena with the shadow of an amused smile on his lips. She caught his gaze as she retrieved her axe, pausing by the vines where she had bent for Chandra. She didn't think she could speak to him without yelling or crying.

"What are you looking at?"

"Oh nothing, Your Majesty."

She jerked her face away and attempted again to toss it from the farthest distance in the arena, but this time she used too much thrust and threw her axe into the ground with a nearly immediate force after it traveled an embarrassingly short distance. She fumed as she retrieved Chandra, cleaning the blade of the dirt and earth from the wintry archery range off on her pants. Malik continued to eye her, his lily-pad eyes tinged with sadness.

Nox growled at him without turning to face him.

"Are you going to help, or are you just going to watch?"

Malik pushed off the cool stones and approached her. A moment later, she heated at his nearness. She didn't want to cry. She craved violence. She wanted the target to represent Moirai and the curse and the distance between Gwydir and Aubade. She set her stance, and Malik stood behind her. His emotions were as level as ever, kicking her feet farther apart with his own, using the force of his kicks to widen her stance. He used his large hands to adjust her grip on the axe's shaft.

"You're overthinking it," he said. "The distance between you and the target is not the obstacle you're making it out to be. Relax and allow it to happen."

Nox swallowed, choking on resentment, on mourning, on the double entendre of his words.

Malik didn't step away from her as she took a relaxing breath, clearing her head of whatever compulsion she'd felt to analyze every movement, every step. Anger would not fix this. Frustration would not stop them from traveling south. Feeling helpless and pathetic was not going to turn the tide or save the ones she loved. She knew that if she trusted Chandra, her weapon would find its bullseye. Perhaps there was a deeper symbolism in the trust she needed on the cusp of the mission. She allowed her body to go practically limp, her spirit exiting her body as she found the closest thing she could to peace amidst the turmoil, stepping and releasing without a second thought. The sharpened edge of her axe embedded itself in the target.

She spun to Malik with a grin, but he was already smirking at her. She left Chandra stuck where it was as she threw her arms around him, and he spoke into her hair.

"See? Things worth doing don't need overthinking."

Tension blurred as frustration became passion. Stone and ivy dripped into velvet and silk.

Nox couldn't quite remember how they'd gotten from the ring to her chambers, though it seemed to have included a few knocked-over weapons and a lantern that nearly caught fire to the rug. The anger and frustration and fury and helplessness had manifested in a tear of clothes and the fiery trails of kisses and mouths. There had been the bang of bruised elbows and a shove or two against a doorway.

Malik was everywhere and everything as she tilted her head back and allowed herself to be enveloped.

His masculine energy was such a remarkable contrast to Yazlyn's soft, beautiful lines. Where Yazlyn was curved, Malik was cut and hard. Where Nox's most recent lover had been silken, he had stubble and muscle. Love and lust took so many forms, and it was bliss to experience their rush.

He'd guided her into her room, but it was Nox who flipped the stance, stepping nimbly around him. He'd been steering her toward her back as he had in their night in the woods when she redirected him, catching him completely off guard. He didn't fight her as she lifted his shirt off over his head. She ran her hands slowly over his muscles as they stood pressed into the wall, appreciating the dips and curves. She shoved him onto the bed so hard that he lost his footing, thudding backward onto her mattress. He flashed a bewildered, breathless smile. She crawled atop him, a fury and pain mixing with need and passion as she let herself mount the bed like a hungry cat on the prowl.

Malik continued to kiss her, his hands moving along her body, touching, appreciating, honoring.

She stripped herself free of her tunic as his hands moved from her hips to her breasts. Her pants followed quickly, eager to free herself from their restraint and embracing the feeling of being ripped free of everything that had held her back. It hadn't mattered how many nights they'd slept in comforting proximity fully clad in their night clothes; he had never beheld her nakedness in its entirety. This was his first time truly regarding her in the full light of day as the cool winter light poured in through her window, hiding nothing behind darkness or shadow. Every inch of skin, every raised bit of gooseflesh as she responded to his touch, every freckle and dip and curve.

His mouth parted reverently, and her eyes softened lovingly. While Nox and Yazlyn had once enjoyed spending the majority of their nights passionately hate-fucking each other, Malik worshipped her.

She lowered her mouth to his and kissed him tenderly at first, backing off the moment there was a shift in intensity. This was not about thirst. This was not need or hunger or consumption. This was intimacy.

Nox dragged white-hot kisses along his jawline, down his neck, over his chest, tracing fire along skin. When she raised her dark eyes to see the effect she had on him, he had his hands fisted in his own hair, eyes closed with his chin arched toward the ceiling in disbelief and ecstasy.

She tugged down his pants over his hips, and for the first time, she felt his hesitation. He very clearly remembered the warning she had given him on the first night they'd kissed. He knew the consequences of intimacy. He looked up at her from his place on the bed. They met eyes for a moment, and neither of them had to say what they were both thinking.

Choosing to echo his words from the ring, she returned her kiss to his abdominals and murmured, "Don't overthink it."

As he relaxed, his consent told her one thing: he trusted her.

She shimmied his pants further down his hips, tugging them from his tree-trunk thighs, caught in genuine admiration at her first exposure to the golden-haired man and his incredible girth. She'd been exposed to her fair share of men in her time at the Selkie and was rarely impressed.

Malik was already fully hard from her kisses as she straddled him, hovering just above him. It was a familiar position but one that would have an entirely unfamiliar ending.

While it was hard to feel nostalgic for her days in Priory,

379

she missed this deliciously powerful feeling. She hadn't had a man beneath her like this in a long time. Despite whatever memories it conjured, this man was entirely different. This one truly, completely trusted her, and she him.

She grabbed Malik's left hand and guided it over her breast, cupping it against her. He opened his eyes as he absorbed the view again in the daylight that cascaded in through the window, hiding nothing. Drenched, she dragged herself along his length, stopping just shy of his tip.

Nox navigated his hand along her lines, gliding over her waist, her hips, clenching his calloused fingers against her bottom and making an appreciative noise as they dug into her. She brought his right hand to his shaft, and as he gripped himself, he understood. She helped him with the first few movements as he stroked himself while she stayed on her elbows and knees, enjoying the sight of the warrior beneath her. His breathing hitched with intensity as he matched his strokes with her movements. She rocked her hips to the rhythm of an unheard song as she remained above him, returning her mouth to his jaw, his cheeks, his forehead, his eyelids. Her hand settled on her most sensitive place, working in tight circles as she rocked above him, enjoying the pleasure of his hand as it moved beneath her.

Malik's groan of pleasure was one over each brush of lips, each touch at the tenderness and intimacy of gentle kisses. Nox folded her weight back on her knees, focusing on their mutual pleasure. As he stroked his shaft, he rubbed against her entrance in hard, rhythmic pumps while she continued to move above him, allowing her breasts to drag over his chest, gently sinking her teeth onto his collarbone, her hand working toward her own indulgence. Her kisses matched his intensity, exploring his chest, neck, and face, sucking his earlobe into her mouth as she felt his speed increasing.

His breathing changed, and she knew he was nearing climax.

She sat up straight and arched her back, struggling against

the haze of pleasure as she worked in rotation to keep her eyes open and meet his heavy gaze. His lips were parted against his rapid gasps for air, working in tandem until he reached his breaking point.

She saw the glorious moment on his face the moment it happened. A tendon in his neck flexed, and he went rigid with his release.

Nox lowered the moisture of her lowermost lips very lightly over the bottom of his shaft as he shivered, allowing the drag of soaking contact as he completed his climax. She wanted to feel his final pulsations as he unleashed every drop onto the clean cut that divided his abdomen. She examined the product of their handiwork, eyeing the complementary cream that frosted his muscles. Her gaze went impish as she scanned him from his stomach and chest to the small puddle in his navel. She smiled with deep, full-belly pleasure at the only man who had ever climaxed with her and lived with his mind intact to tell the tale.

Nox rose with pride, allowing her hips to sway as she felt his gaze still on her naked body as she walked away. She fetched a towel from the bathing room and made the tender gesture to clean him up, chuckling lovingly at the sight of a man truly spent. Her ego fluttered as she watched the first signs of sleep tug him under. This was not the fleeting life force of a victim to a succubus. This was a man who had been satisfied and relaxed within an inch of his life in every human way.

He fought against full-bodied exhaustion as he mumbled, "Let me take care of you."

She stifled an amused giggle. Nox was in no need of such generosity, as she'd had more than enough oxytocin. She did appreciate that even on the brink of oblivion, the only thing standing between Malik and sleep was his unrelenting need to take care of her. She tsked and planted a slow kiss on his cheek, her words a whisper near his ear. "I can be a giver too."

Completely naked, Nox curled up next to him.

Into his neck, she mumbled, "I don't want you to go."

The intensity that had filled the room ebbed as she tucked herself against him more tightly.

"I've left before. I came right back, didn't I?"

She closed her eyes. "I don't want any of you to go."

He stroked her hair, and she fought the torrent of what it meant to love and be loved. Malik loved her deeply. He understood the complicated waters of her heart. Nox was not a lake with set shores and familiar borders, or even the sea with its knowable tides. She was a river, carving paths down valleys and through mountains, running from glaciers to oceans, forking and twisting and complex in its interconnectivity while always remaining one, true river. One of her streams loved him in return. And now he, and everyone who cared about her, would be leaving for battle while she sat uselessly on the throne.

Eyes closed, he said, "The continent can't have the new queen of Raascot going to battle. The turnover rate for monarchs needs to be slower than two per year."

She looked up at him through the puddle of black hair that had pooled on his chest. "But I'm so good with an axe. Are you sure your forces don't need Chandra and me?"

"You are great with your axe." He kissed her hair again. "Why don't you and Chandra focus on keeping Gwydir safe?"

She answered with a disgruntled grumble. "Zaccai will keep the city plenty safe. Ash is practically useless, since he's on eternal nannying duty, but he's fit in a pinch. They're fine without me."

Malik smiled. "Do you think Ash and Tanith—"

"God, I hope so. It would be really convenient if he could flip the enemy with his magical lovemaking."

Malik nearly choked. "I'll have to tell him that you suspect he has an enchanted cock."

"I'd prefer if you didn't."

He rocked against the lure of sleep. "No, no, they aren't having sex...though you're right. They'd probably do us all a favor if they did. Ever since the attack on the castle, she's been by his side by choice, not by obligation. And after her comments in the tavern…"

She swatted playfully at Malik. "When I tell you my soul left my body! I cannot believe those words came out of her mouth! We really don't know her at all, do we?"

"She does seem less likely to kill us, so that's something."

Nox rested her head on his chest again, relaxing as she said, "I had thought Elil might really drive her away from any progress we'd made with her. Who knew Ash's crazy father was our missing puzzle piece?"

He dragged his fingers up and down her spine in long, soothing strokes. "Cheers to insane fathers. His found him an intimidatingly powerful, relatively insane, possibly sexually deviant Sulgrave fae, and yours found you a throne."

"And what of your father? Was he mad too?" Nox asked.

"My dad? No." Malik smiled fondly. "He's the best man I've ever known. He'd give the shirt off his back to any stranger in need. He'd really like you." He folded his hands behind his head as he looked at the ceiling, as if watching the scenario play out in his imagination.

She allowed the dreamlike warmth that touched her to pull the corner of her mouth upward at the thought. "Your dad would like me?"

"Of course" came his calm, steady reassurance. "What father wouldn't clap his son on the back for bringing home the most beautiful creature in the kingdoms? And that's before he learns you're clever and funny and artistic and talented and can occasionally throw an axe. Oh, yeah, and that you're the Queen of Raascot."

"I am something of a catch, aren't I?"

He exhaled on a single, low laugh. "You're not so bad."

"Will I be the Queen of Farehold?" she asked more to the ceiling than to Malik as she rolled onto her back. They both chewed over the question.

383

"You could always put the Duke of Henares on the throne and be Farehold's queen by proxy."

Their shared humor was warm, but it didn't last. The afternoon faded into evening as their stomachs told them dinnertime was approaching. Nox still needed to find her quill and write to Agnes. She didn't want this moment to end. She didn't want tomorrow to come.

Malik could clearly see the thoughts as they played through her head as he said, "You have a lot to do to prepare for tomorrow."

"So do you."

He stroked her hair again, looking down at her with shining eyes. "Are you sure you don't want me to take care of you first? Trust me—it would be my pleasure."

She smiled. "How about we put a pin in it until you come back home to me alive?"

"You're cruel." He made a wistful face, apparently hoping she'd changed her mind, but Nox was firm. He moved from the bed, pulling on his pants.

She turned away, preparing to forge her heart in iron.

"Nox?"

She turned, her eyebrows asking the question.

He came back into the room, grabbing her hands into his own. "Don't go anywhere."

Her lower lip lifted in a slight frown. "Where would I go?"

He ran a hand through his hair, dropping it as he looked for his words. "You disappear sometimes. Into yourself, that is. You're here, but you aren't. When things get hard, or bad, you've found so many ways to be strong. You've found so many ways to survive. You're stronger than all of us. There isn't a person here who doesn't admire you."

She swallowed, turning to face the window with the sheets bundled around her.

"Nox," he said her name again. She continued watching the naked tree branches in the darkening afternoon as his final words came. "I am so devoted to you."

The message was fire and water, balm and cut, pain and healing all at once. She heard the love in his words, just as she heard goodbye.

The blush flooded from her chest to her neck, then her cheeks. She felt the sting in her eyes. It was all-consuming.

"I just needed you to know, if we aren't going to..."

She lifted her eyes again, still hot with the threat of emotion. "We will. When you come back. Because you will. You will come back."

He pressed a final kiss into the space where her hairline met her forehead. Malik dressed and left her room. With him left any sense of peace she'd gained from their time together. Her rage had left her. Her passion had abandoned her. Her comfort and sense of ease had departed with him. All she felt now was true and bottomless emptiness.

She moved to her writing desk without bothering to redress. She dipped the elaborate black quill in ink and wrote on a piece of paper.

It's Nox. There is an urgent matter between the kingdoms of the north and south, and I require your assistance. Your help would be minimal, and it would take no effort on your part. If you agree to help, you would merely need to visually assess two troops on their journey south. Please write back as soon as possible. Your aid is urgently needed.

Perhaps the impending day's gravity pressed on them, but everyone found themselves in the dining room around the same time that evening. There was no jovial energy to accompany the tender, fatty pork and greens and pies and potatoes. Everyone ate with the task at hand on their mind. They exchanged enough knowledge to find the four departing were packed and prepared. Nox explained that they would be heading for Farleigh, protective guilt flooding her as Amaris's expression deflated at the word. Nox knew Amaris had hoped to never return to the orphanage that had planned to sell her for her weight in crowns, and she wished she could protect her from it, even now.

The calm resolution in Amaris's face told her that it would not be up for discussion. She would do what must be done.

The others crowded in on the southbound crew in the hours after dinner, chiming in for better or for worse as the team packed as many weapons as Gadriel and Yazlyn would be able to carry while remaining airborne if traveling with the reevers. They shared tips, complaints, jokes, advice, and well wishes, but they knew there would be no relaxation.

After all, they were on the verge of breaking the world.

Chapter
Thirty–three

H EY, CAN I TALK TO YOU?" NOX'S KNUCKLES RAPPED LIGHTLY
against Gadriel's bedroom door. The greeting was polite
and perfunctory as the door stood ajar. She had not come to
see the general.

Nox was as aware as everyone in the castle that Amaris
had been sleeping in Gadriel's chambers ever since she'd
shattered the window in her own rooms. The window had
been long since repaired, but Amaris hadn't returned to a life
alone between the sheets. Nox knew she was hardly one to
pass judgment. She'd preferred the comfort of a warm, affectionate presence to lull her to sleep for some time.

Some people used exercise or meditation. Some used
alcohol or tonics. Others used sex, love, or the deep, steady
breathing of a trusted human to help them sleep.

She met Gadriel's eyes for the briefest of moments. He
dipped his chin in acknowledgment, knowing without being
addressed that her visit was not for him. He made his exit,
wordlessly greeting and departing all in the same movement
as he slipped into the hall, presumably to make himself busy
sharpening weapons or studying maps or doing whatever else
it was that generals do the night before an impending mission.

Nox slouched against the doorframe, waiting for an invitation.

Amaris had already put on her night dress and was sitting on the bed.

"Are you going to come in? Or will you just be standing there?" Amaris asked.

"Do you want me to come in?"

Amaris made the facial equivalent of a shrug, tugging the sheets back as Nox slid onto the duvet beside her. Amaris may have been feigning indifference, but Nox knew the weight wore as heavily on Amaris as it did on her.

Nox pulled the duvet over her hips, resting her temple against the headboard as she looked at Amaris, thinking about how different their story might have been.

If Nox hadn't rejected Amaris's advancements on their first night in the castle, they might be two different people living very different lives. The mission southward would remain, but the pain, the stony glances, the dismissive attitudes, the lovers, the fights, and the uncaring characters they'd painted themselves into would have never come into existence. They could have spent months sharing a bed, breathing out as the other breathed in, growing closer, learning the sounds and curves and touches. Nox could be the one beside her, wrapping her arm around Amaris on the cusp of battle.

If things had been different, the women would be in the soft, loving arms that had been intended to hold each other from the moment they'd entered this world.

But things weren't different.

Through a bit lip, Nox managed to say, "Ash made a comment to me some time ago that I haven't been able to get out of my head."

Amaris kept her face impressively neutral. Nox had looked at her blank expression for years in Farleigh, calling it naivete or blissful ignorance. She'd hoped Amaris was sheltered from pain, and that was what kept her from poignant reactions. Watching her now, Nox wondered if Amaris had developed a different strength entirely. Something beneath the surface that she had yet to discover.

Nox swallowed, saying, "He was not sympathetic to my reasons for wanting distance from you. You know Ash; he isn't truly mean—even if I deserve it—but he's honest. I trust him. He has no motive, no incentive to gain favor with me. While I was stewing over feeling robbed of our authenticity by the prayer that initiated your birth, he said that if the goddess had crafted someone specially for him, he would have found it unspeakably beautiful. He said that you and I have the chance to be soulmates with the certainty that no one else on this earth will ever experience. That we really were made for each other."

Amaris closed her eyes without moving her posture. She was not relaxing, nor was she inviting. She breathed through her nose as Nox spoke, absorbing the speech. When Nox finished, she leveled her gaze.

Nox lost her breath. She'd looked into the gentle purples of Amaris's eyes for a lifetime. They seemed like such stormy shades of careful violet now.

"What are you trying to tell me?"

Nox gnawed on the tender flesh of her inner cheek, struggling to look at Amaris as she said, "Maybe nothing. Maybe everything. I don't know."

From beyond her peripherals, Amaris exhaled. The sound was one of quiet resolution as she said, "You feel bad for rejecting me now that I'm about to go off and die, is that it?"

Nox's face was serious. She straightened her posture, cupping Amaris's face in one hand. She held Amaris's eyes with scalding gravity as she said, "You're not going to die."

Amaris nodded slowly, chin brushing against her hand. "I certainly don't plan on it."

Nox's free hand found Amaris's opposite cheek. She shifted her weight to lean in closer. "You are *not* going to die. You are going to kill Moirai. You are going to break the curse. And you are going to come home to Gwydir. You are going to come back to me."

Amaris's careful, emotionless facade cracked. Her throat bobbed, and for the barest of moments, Nox recognized the person she'd known for so many years.

"And once I break the curse?"

Nox wrapped her arms around Amaris and pulled her in tightly, crushing her as she said, "You don't need to break the curse for me to know that what we have is real. I'm a goddess-damned fool. I'm so, so sorry for ever doubting it—for doubting us. I don't know if you'll forgive me. I don't know if I'd ever deserve your forgiveness. But it will never ease how sorry I feel for what I've done to us."

"Nox—"

"Shh." She stroked Amaris's hair, struggling against the prick of white-hot tears as her fingers intermingled with long, unbound tendrils of silver.

Amaris pushed her bodyweight into the hug, tightening their grip on each other. They hadn't been this close in a long, long time. "Why do we always wait for tragedy to bring us together?" she asked, her voice hoarse.

Nox choked against her laugh. She was right. They were ready to run on the eve of an assassin's arrival in Farleigh. They'd kissed through the iron bars of the dungeon of Aubade. They'd spent a beautiful, painful, complicated night in the town house on the edge of Gwydir in the moments before Amaris was dragged off to see the king. Their only chance at peace and normalcy had been the months Nox had squandered in the castle with her uncertainty. She spoke into Amaris's hair, creating tufts of pearly white against her breath as she spoke.

"How about you come back in one piece, and we do our best to lead an exceedingly normal, boring life?"

Amaris's smile didn't reach her eyes as she pulled away. She touched Nox's cheek in an unfamiliar gesture, as it had always been Nox who comforted and cupped her. Nox wrapped her hands around Amaris's wrists, securing the hand that rested against her face, appreciative beyond words that she had instigated this small intimacy.

"You know as well as I that nothing about us has ever been boring."

Her heart had cracked so many times. She wasn't sure how many fractures might remain before she ceased to exist. Nox was quite certain she was going to cry. Their cocktail of emotions swirling with pain and frustration and resentment, anchored in one thing alone.

They loved each other.

They loved each other even when they hated each other. They loved each other when they weren't sure how, or why, or in what capacity. They loved each other even when they needed space, needed the solace of others, needed to avoid speaking at all costs lest they hurl apples at the back of each other's heads. They loved each other when another's chest rose and fell beside them in their sleep. And they loved each other now.

"I—" Nox began, but Amaris moved her hand to cover Nox's mouth. Their eyes rimmed with twin, silvery tears. So much had changed from who they had been as powerless orphans, and yet in some ways, nothing had changed at all.

"Don't tell me now. Tell me when I get back."

Nox nodded as two traitorous droplets of saltwater ran down her face. "I'll tell you then."

"And I'll be ready to listen."

✦

Nox was still wiping the remnants of tears from her face when she returned to her room. Back on her writing desk, a question was written in Agnes's penmanship below her message.

What do you request of me?

Nox returned with a response explaining the barest bones of the situation before them. Keeping her message as brief as possible, she delineated to Agnes that in a few days, Amaris would be there with three companions, two of whom traveled from Raascot. Agnes was to write back with their description and nothing else. This was all that was required of the Gray Matron. Before Nox fell asleep that night, Agnes had responded with a short sentence in agreement.

The moon came up between the branches, bathing her room in silver. And despite swearing to Malik that she wouldn't sleep a wink, he tucked her against himself and held her until the night claimed her.

The goodbyes that followed the next morning were not tearful. No one allowed themselves sorrow or dread. Pessimism would not serve them well on their journey to Aubade. Their hugs stretched on a bit too long as Nox held each of them, feeling the entirety of her heart as it was torn from her and sent into Farehold. Even Zaccai hugged everyone, including muttering something or other about making everyone promise to wear their rings.

Ash, Tanith, Zaccai, and Nox stood at the doors of Castle Gwydir as the southbound travelers became dots indiscernible from dark birds in the sky. Long after her eyes could no longer see them, Nox continued to strain her gaze against the bright gray of the overcast morning.

"At least they're going somewhere warmer," Tanith said, turning into the building. Everyone stiffened with surprise that Tanith had spoken of her own volition, particularly with something mildly encouraging.

Tanith was the first to disappear behind the castle doors, followed closely by Ash, who had more or less become her shadow. Zaccai put a comforting arm around Nox's shoulders, which was every bit as funny as it was sweet. She'd never truly been able to pin down the spymaster, and perhaps now was not the time to start. The reassuring weight of his arm tugged on a memory of the first night she'd met the ag'imni in the forest holding out a blanket to a cold, lost girl he'd never met before, long before he could ever know she'd be his ruler.

"They'll be back."

She was a queen. She shouldn't cry. But that didn't stop a few wet drops from silently leaving her lids as she rested her head on Zaccai's shoulders.

All they could do now was wait.

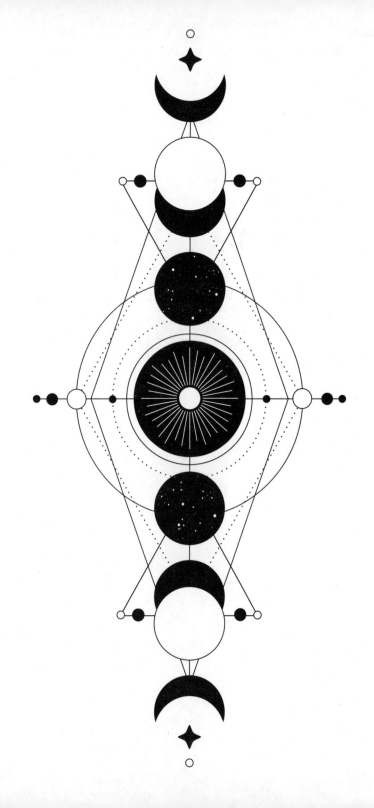

PART FIVE:

The Fall of Everything

Chapter Thirty-four

AMARIS FELT THE WORRIED, SIDELONG GLANCES EXCHANGED by Malik, Yazlyn, and Gadriel. Far too much time had passed since they'd landed in the woods outside of Farleigh House. She meant to get moving. She'd intended to lead them forward, but she remained frozen to the ground. Her body was trapped in a half step, her arms rigid and immobile. The manor had stopped her in her tracks the moment it colored into view.

At least it was warmer. Sort of.

The trees had gradually changed from conifers to the leafless deciduous trees that populated the southern kingdom as they descended from the mountains. Naked, gray-brown branches offered no shelter from the wind. Perhaps if it had been any other season, the others might give her the patience to sort through whatever complex emotions plagued her as she stayed frozen in full view of the orphanage.

Gadriel touched her back, and she jumped as if she had completely forgotten where she was or who was with her.

"Are you okay?" he asked.

Amaris blinked rapidly. She had fought monsters and demons. She had faced a wicked monarch and escaped on the back of a hell-dragon. She had gained an orb, held the love of a queen, and uncovered incredible powers. She bore the two bright scars that had announced her unwillingness to go to Priory and live a life against her will. Yet as she stood facing Farleigh, she didn't feel like a powerful reever. She didn't feel like a curse breaker, and she especially didn't feel like a tool of the goddess. She didn't even feel like an adult.

She was a child again, powerless and small.

Farleigh was not the mystical night sky of Gwydir, nor was it the sparkling granite of Uaimh Reev. It wasn't the warmth of the custard- and cream-colored stones of Aubade. Farleigh was made of flat, lifeless gray rock that spoke of the emptiness of the self-contained world within.

Gadriel gave her shoulder a comforting squeeze.

"I'm fine."

She took another step forward and felt the weight of the three behind her as their feet crunched into snow, dried leaves, and fallen branches. Amaris stopped in her tracks once more, this time throwing up a hand to the fae behind her.

"Oh, this isn't a good idea. In case the cuffs don't work, I don't think the children should see you. You two stay here, okay?"

Malik frowned. "Are you sure you want me to come with? What if—"

"You're a Farehold boy. I feel like gambling," she said, wondering if she was as transparent as she felt. The truth was, she didn't want to face the matrons alone.

Yazlyn and Gadriel relaxed against the trunks, settling in to wait in the tree line behind the stables. Malik matched her steps as they crossed the yard, and she found her strength as she did so. They rounded the lawn and made their way to the front door. Pale, chubby circles popped up like daisies in the window as a few small, curious faces peeked through the glass at them.

Amaris straightened her shoulders and Malik muttered an

encouraging word behind her. Her knuckles rapped against the door with three loud knocks. Her mouth went dry as she waited.

She tensed when the door opened, prepared to face the horrors within. Instead, she looked into the kind face of Sister Mable. The woman hadn't aged a day.

Mable looked like she had seen a ghost. She scanned Amaris from head to toe, taking in her fighting clothes, her winter cloak, her weapons and scars. Mable's eyes flitted briefly to the man who stood behind her, who was undoubtedly doing his best to look nonthreatening.

Mable's voice came out in a small, disbelieving squeak. "Amaris?"

"Sister Mable." She tried to smile. "I think Matron Agnes is expecting us?"

Mable opened the door widely and urged them inside. Amaris hesitated on the landing, but Mable insisted that they were letting the winter in with every moment they hedged on the front step. Amaris and Malik stepped into the foyer and saw several small faces poke out from the various rooms, both on the ground floor and the balcony above. The familiar smell of baking bread filled the manor.

Mable scuttled off to find Matron Agnes, leaving Amaris and Malik alone with a tiny galley of gasping, whispering children. Many were too young for her to recognize. Still, a few of the faces had familiar features as young girls from her dorms or small boys she'd seen at her prayers and lessons gaped at the two tall strangers.

Not knowing what possessed her to speak, Amaris looked to the children at the balcony, speaking to no one in particular. "I grew up here, you know. I lived in this orphanage from the time I was a baby until I was fifteen."

An older, freckled girl with curly, mousy hair poked around the younger children from where she'd been waiting upstairs. She must have been cresting sixteen. "Amaris?"

Amaris recognized her freckled features immediately. She

was nearly her elder sister's reflection. "You're Emily's sister, aren't you? Ana?"

The girl descended the staircase, opening her arms for an uncertain hug. They had never been friends. They hadn't even been close. Emily and her sister, like Nox and Amaris, had been inseparable. She knew what it was like to be torn from the only one you loved.

"Do you know what happened to my sister?" Ana asked.

Amaris shook her head. "I'm so sorry. I heard that Nox was living with her in Priory. Now, Nox and I live in Gwydir."

The freckled girl met her eyes, nearly taller than Amaris. "Everyone thought you died. Some said you killed yourself in the kitchen. Others said you were kidnapped."

Amaris's expression was something between a smile and a frown. "I guess it would be easier for the matrons to say I had died than it would be to tell you the truth. I escaped. I ran off to become a reever."

"What's a reever?" piped a boy who'd been quietly listening by the door.

Her mouth spread into a slow smile. She looked up at Malik, appreciating the warmth on his face as he regarded the children. She absently hoped his princely face would encourage a few of the children to look for good in the world beyond these walls.

Amaris said, "Reevers are like warriors for peace. You might hear people call us assassins, but that's not quite accurate. Tell the other children here. Tell everyone here. If you don't want to be an orphan, if you don't want to be sold to the highest bidder or live in Farleigh, all you need to do is make it to the village of Stone. It's about two days from here by horse. From there, you need to climb the mountain pass and ask for Samael. He can train you to fight. You can live a different life. You can be strong. You can be whoever you want to be. You can make a new family."

Ana stepped out of the hug. She looked at Amaris with a haunted expression. "Samael?"

"That's right. I know Farleigh seems like the whole world right now, but you can leave. You all can. It will be hard, and it will be cold, and you'll probably want to quit, but no one can tell you who you must be. Your life is yours."

She pulled the freckled remnant of her past in for a second hug just as Agnes tutted down the hall, shoes slapping against stone. Amaris wasn't sure why time and perspective changed things so greatly, but the once-grand Gray Matron now looked astonishingly feeble, as if she'd shrunk, somehow.

Regardless of how small she looked to Amaris, her expression was no less fierce as she regarded the reevers.

"So, here you are," she bit out. "After all the years I clothed you and housed you and fed you."

Amaris opened her mouth in protest, but the matron spoke over her.

"Never mind that. Are you out of your goddess-damned mind using the front door? Let's fulfill this request and be done with it. Bring the others to the entrance near the kitchen. Shoo, shoo." Agnes pushed Amaris out of the front door with Malik close on her heels.

"She seems like a treat," Malik murmured as the door closed behind them.

Amaris exhaled, leading them to the kitchen door as she told him that he didn't know the half of it. She shot a glance into the tree line, where she could just barely make out the shapes of Yazlyn and Gadriel. If the shields had failed and they were still perceived as ag'imni, she didn't want to risk the children seeing two demons in the woods and never leaving the manor again. It would ruin any chance of them running away and leaving this horrible place behind.

Agnes had her arms crossed against the cold, tapping her foot impatiently as they made it around back.

"So? Who is it I'm supposed to see and describe? Your blond tower of a companion? Are we finished?"

Amaris checked to ensure the matron was wearing shoes.

"Can you come with us? They're just waiting beyond the stable. I thought it was best if the children—"

"Fine, fine." Agnes shut the door in their face before she had the chance to finish her sentence, disappearing for several minutes.

"Well," Malik said, "at least she didn't greet you with a pitchfork."

Amaris crossed her arms. "For all we know, that's what she's off to fetch."

"Maybe she should," he mused. She widened her eyes at him, but he stood his ground. "I think it might be cathartic for you to have reasonable cause to pummel her."

Amaris's smile had just begun to fade when Agnes reappeared with a warm cloak. She pulled her hood up and made a hurrying gesture for Amaris to lead the way.

The moment Gadriel and Yazlyn came into view, Agnes skidded to a halt.

"How could you bring them here?" Agnes demanded.

The blood drained from Amaris's face. At her side, Malik looked like he was going to be sick. Yazlyn elbowed Gadriel to get his attention. They were too far to be a part of the conversation but near enough to make out their features. They took three careful steps out of the threes, drawing closer to Agnes. She backpedaled and they halted, holding up their hands to reveal they clasped no weapons.

"What do you see?" Amaris asked, her tone urgent.

"How could you bring demons to the place of the All Mother!"

It was like being hit with bricks and doused with ice water all at once. No single sentence could have been more discouraging or hopeless than this. It had all been useless. The manufacturers, the scholars, their efforts had been wasted. The time had come, and they had failed.

Malik spoke to the matron for the first time, reiterating, "You see ag'imni?"

Agnes wrinkled her nose. "What? No! I see you brought

demonic Raascot rabble to our home for children. How could you bring the dark kingdom to our doorstep, Amaris? Do you hate us that much?"

Amaris stiffened in confusion. "You see fae?"

Agnes's hands flexed at her side as if she were fighting the urge to slap her. Amaris sincerely wished Agnes would take a swing, so that she could have an excuse to block and blow.

Malik tried again, "Can you please describe them? Nox said she asked you to describe Amaris's traveling companions. Could you do that for us?"

Agnes bared her teeth in disdain. "When Nox said she was sending two people from Raascot, I didn't realize she meant bats out of hell. What is it that you want me to describe? What holy creature has wings? What human or fae of the south has wings like that?"

Amaris made a face. "Just to be clear: you don't see ag'imni—you're just racist?"

Agnes's scathing look could have melted flesh and bone. "I don't know what vile path turned you into the ungrateful, worthless, conspiratorial—"

Amaris waved a hand. "You see a fae man and a fae woman? One black hair, one auburn?"

"I see Raascot—"

"Answer the damn question, Agnes, or you'll leave this meeting with fewer teeth than when you arrived," Amaris said through a growl.

Agnes went rigid. Her eyes opened and closed rapidly against the disrespect. She hadn't been spoken to in such a horrid, acrid way in decades. "That's what Nox wants? Yes. Are you satisfied? If Princess Daphne stole into the night only to know that her daughter would grow up to consort with demons—"

"Not consort with," Amaris corrected. "She's their queen."

Agnes looked distinctly troutlike as her eyes bulged.

"Oh, yes. The little princess you hid in your orphanage? She wasn't just Daphne's daughter. She was King Ceres's as well. The girl you had fetch your errands and run your chores is now sitting on the throne of Gwydir. And me? The babe you bought for fifty crowns and tried to sell to a whorehouse? As it stands, I'm the deadliest weapon on the continent. We know who you are and what this place is, Agnes. Regarding how you treat these children, I would think long and hard about Farleigh's next steps if I were you. If Nox holds the titles in both Raascot and Farehold, you could either have a powerful friend or an enemy beyond your worst nightmares."

Amaris wished that a childhood version of herself could have watched the exchange. She would have loved to have hugged a waifish youngling who'd felt so pathetic and vulnerable in the face of the matrons. A small piece of her inner child healed as the weight of her words settled over Agnes. She smiled as the Gray Matron took on an entirely new posture. The woman no longer tilted her head to look down her nose. Maybe Amaris had been little more than a commodity, but the woman truly had favored Nox, and for good reason. Now if it was required of her, Amaris knew that Agnes would comply.

"The one on the left, I see a tall, broad man with black hair and unnatural raven wings. The girl on the right has reddish-brown hair and her wings are every bit as ugly. I haven't missed their pointed ears. I know you're with the dark fae."

"Was that so hard?" Amaris asked.

Agnes eyed her in a way that conveyed she was truly seeing her for the first time. Not seeing just her scars and weapons and clothes but seeing her as an individual rather than a sack of crowns. Agnes released a sigh that felt like decades of weariness wrapped into one single exhale.

A sound cut through the wintry day. Over their shoulder, Mable called to them from the door to the kitchen. The friendly, pious sister from Stone, who had always been too lovely for such a horrid place, waved an arm to gain their attention. "Would you and your friends like some food for the road?"

Under different circumstances, Agnes might have protested. Instead, she turned her head somewhat slowly and acknowledged Mable's request. "You four may enter through the kitchen. Take what provisions you need."

While they had packed plenty of food, they did not dismiss the offer to warm their bones and sip on hot broth by a fire. Agnes abandoned them the moment they crossed into the manor, hopefully to write to Nox about what she'd seen. Mable remained positively enraptured by their stories. As a girl from Stone, she'd grown up with knowledge of the guardians who lived in the mountain and acted as though she were in the presence of gods—which, technically, she was, with Amaris sitting at the table.

Gadriel and Yazlyn were amiable and polite, which was a relief, though she suspected no one could be rude to Mable. By the time their muscles had thawed and their bags were refilled with provisions, they wandered back into the woods with Mable waving excitedly behind them, her life dream of meeting the mountain guardians having finally come to fruition.

Amaris felt sad about leaving Mable in such an awful place—the pious, genuinely good woman who deserved so much more than service in a mill. But part of her realized that this might be exactly why Mable was where she was meant to be. She was the sunlight in a dark room. The children needed her.

Amaris was lost to her reflection on Mable, practically under the cover of trees once more, when a voice caught her attention. She turned to see Agnes jogging after them without a coat, hugging her shoulders against the cold.

"Here," she said, pressing a black quill into Amaris's hand.

"What is this?"

Agnes chafed her arms as she said, "It's a spelled quill. I had assumed that Nox would have told you. We do not speak by sending ravens. This is how we communicate across kingdoms. She is in possession of its twin. If you have the quill, you'll be able to write to her and she'll see your message no matter where you are."

Amaris's mouth opened as if to thank the matron, but the old woman merely made a dismissive gesture and began her walk back to the comfort of the manor. Amaris eyed the quill carefully, looking to her companions. None of them seemed to have known about Nox's secret correspondence. Amaris stashed it in her traveling bag, and before long, they had taken to the sky once more, this time with the knowledge that they were two reevers and two intimidating winged fae warriors— nary an ag'imni in sight.

✦

Amaris hadn't brought any paper, but she'd peeled a particularly large piece of thin bark from a white birch tree and rested it against a stone by firelight that night. It may be generally unwise to light fires when traveling by night, but the icy temperatures of winter didn't offer much of an alternative. If the heat from the campfire went out, so would they.

> *Nox—Agnes gave me her quill. Neat trick. I don't know if she had time to write to you before handing the quill over to me, but the collars have worked. Also, Farleigh is horrible and how dare you make me return. Though it was a bit fun to yell at the Gray Matron. We're safe, all is well, and I miss you.*

Each of them had awoken at regular intervals from their interrupted sleep to throw gathered logs and branches onto the fire, ensuring their survival through the wintery night. They pressed rather tightly against Gadriel, disregarding any broad sense of social norms in favor of his gift for warmth. He wrapped his arms around Amaris as he slept, with Yazlyn curled against his back. Amaris was sandwiched between the general and Malik, who bundled his blanket in a tent over Gadriel's heat for residual warmth.

After several hours of broken rest, they deemed themselves travel ready. Amaris found a note written in cramped letters below her own.

Yes, Agnes told me—she's quite the bitch, isn't she? I'm glad the shields work, and equally glad she gave you the quill. I miss you too. Don't die.

She intended to live, though if Yazlyn was to be believed, getting to Aubade was just as terrible as fulfilling their actual mission.

Despite Amaris being the smallest person in the castle save for the absurdly tiny Tanith, Yazlyn still complained about how carrying her made her arms ache. Yazlyn required a lot of stretching and encouragement before takeoff. Each day that passed was another day closer to Henares. Every day of travel and every cold, miserable night of broken sleep brought them nearer to Moirai. The sooner she was dead, the sooner they could return and get on with the happy lives they were owed.

Chapter
Thirty–five

I S THIS IT? WE JUST SIT AROUND AND WAIT EVERY DAY?" NOX slouched into her chair. She'd unraveled three cinnamon rolls, only eating the gooey centers and abandoning the exteriors. Ash made a comment about her wastefulness, and she told him that when he was queen, he could eat rolls however he wanted.

The four of them had taken to meeting for at least two of the daily meals. It had seemed pointless to hold afternoon meetings in the war room as long as they regularly found themselves in the same place at the same time.

Plus, the dining room had wine and a window to look out if the spymaster was reporting on something particularly boring.

Zaccai continued chewing on the sandwich he'd made, speaking between bites. "I stay apprised of any information that filters in from my informants. And now that you have a direct line of communication with Amaris, we have a particularly advantageous connection to the party. Other than that, we continue to train, we stay in shape, we keep the castle safe, and we stay sane."

"How will we know when the curse is broken?" Nox asked.

Zaccai polished off his sandwich and reached for another. "I guess we don't. We have every reason to believe it will die with the queen. So, either you'll hear from Amaris through her quill in one hand and the severed head of Moirai in the other, or news will pass through the traditional channels of information. I expect they're only a day or two from Henares at present."

Nox had thought she was bored when Malik left for Uaimh Reev, but it'd barely been a taste of how mind-numbing her days could be. Now she clawed at the walls. Nothing held her attention for more than a few moments. There was no food she could eat, no wine she could drink, no library or bakery or axe-throwing that could distract her from her constant, gnawing worry. She tried on several occasions to bond with Tanith, but even if the Sulgrave fae was no longer hostile, she was certainly aloof.

"Tanith?" Nox asked. "Would you like to go shopping with me? I was thinking we could go into town and maybe look for a thick red cloak?"

Tanith perked. "I'd like that. Thank you. And, Nox?"

The room gave its attention to Tanith.

"You're...you've been..." She cleared her throat nervously, looking into her food. "You make a good queen."

Nox bit her lip to contain her grin. She caught the impressed flare of Zaccai's eyes. Maybe the price of knowledge didn't always have to be so terrible.

Ash was quick not to draw too much attention to their progress, as if reluctant to startle a wild rabbit. He kept his smile easy as he asked, "I've never asked you this, but what makes you love the color red so much? Most of us have a favorite color, but you take yours quite seriously."

Tanith lifted her lower lip contemplatively. "My favorite color is blue-green, like the color of the shallow sea in crystal-clear waters."

This twisted everyone's face into a down-turned frown. Nox spoke for the room. "Then why do you wear red all day and all night? Even your nightdresses are red."

Between bites, she said, "It's my title. Everyone in the church wears the color of their station."

Zaccai set down his food. He leaned in with interest. "What are the different colors and their significances?"

Tanith took a drink of water. She looked up and to the side as she sorted through her memories. "Well, I guess my station is a bit like Ash's. He's told me that reevers are the sword arm of the All Mother. So am I. Though, the reevers are self-governed, and we most certainly are not. Red is for the battle-ready activists. The church recognizes us by our color and calls us Reds."

"And the others?" Zaccai prompted.

"Not everyone in Sulgrave is religious, you know. In fact, I'd say that it's part of what makes those of us in the church feel ever more closely knit. Dressing for our station helps us identify one another even when we're in the territories and villages, so we always know how to locate other believers. If you're a worshipper or general church attendant, you wear gray. I can walk into any village and find someone in all gray and know that I am safe with them. They're bound to the All Mother and would shelter and feed me. They're simply referred to as Grays."

Nox blinked several times at this. "Like the Gray Matrons?"

Tanith frowned. "What are Gray Matrons?"

Nox's tongue stuck to the roof of her mouth as she was flung into her past. She took a swig of tea before saying, "They're supposed to be servants of the goddess, but the ones who ran my orphanage were not religious. It was a sham, though it claimed to be affiliated with the church."

"Fascinating," Zaccai muttered to himself. "Are there other similarities between how the church is run on the lower continent and how the goddess is served in Sulgrave? Can you tell me about the other colors in your organization?"

Tanith obliged. "The bishops wear white and gold. They are generally the readers and those who hold church services across Sulgrave. When we gather, a bishop will address a congregation of those of us in gray, red, green, and black, as well as the faithful across all territories who gather in their typical attire."

"What are green and black?"

Her tone remained far-off as she recounted, "The Greens are the monetary arm of the church. They handle taxation, tithing, donations, and charities. There was a bit of trouble when nonbelievers learned they could wear green to rob the believers, but that's where those of us in red intervene."

"And black?"

"Our priestesses wear black. They are the closest to the All Mother and serve her most intimately. They do not live or reside in the church meant for public ceremonies but in the sacred temples. They're the highest in our organization, except for the Speaker."

"The Speaker?" Zaccai repeated.

Tanith began to sound fatigued, as if she were a mother who was tired of answering the incessant questions of toddlers. Nox attempted to empathize with how it would grate on anyone's nerves to be in what one perceived as endlessly ignorant company.

"Yes. The church doesn't always require a Speaker, but one is provided every few millennia, usually in times of great strife or change. The Speaker is the All Mother made flesh to tell us her word."

Zaccai flicked his finger toward where Amaris used to sit. "Would Amaris be considered a Speaker?"

Tanith shook her head, looking almost offended at the question. "No, Amaris is an acorn from the tree. The Speaker is the tree itself walking among us."

Everyone listened to Tanith's description of her church and their organization, though some were a bit more interested than others. Zaccai still wore a question on his face.

"How is a Speaker chosen?"

It was clear from Tanith's impatient tone that she was more or less done with the conversation. "They are not chosen. They arrive."

Nox took the hint and spared Tanith the further inquiries. She clapped her hands as she concluded her meeting. "Well, I don't know about the rest of you, but I'm going to be in the library studying theology for the rest of the day if anyone needs me." Nox put her hands on the table and pushed herself up to a standing position. "Tanith, why don't we get you a red cloak, and then I can keep asking you questions about the church while you look to see if there are any romance novels left in the entire city of Gwydir. How's that sound?"

"Will Ash come?"

Nox fought a smile. "How about if just the two of us go today? I'll have you back to him before dinner."

Ash appeared somewhat perplexed at Nox's decision, but she hoped he understood that his charge had been building up to small moments like this. If Tanith could survive one pleasant outing with the half-fae queen, it would be the closest they'd come to a breakthrough.

✦

Ash watched them go as the women abandoned the castle for shopping and research. Zaccai said something or other about needing to work on research of his own. Ash appreciated Zaccai's thirst for knowledge, as he decided that he would never be curious enough to enjoy the role of spymaster. The similarities between how the faith had manifested had been surprising, though time, distance, and isolation certainly created chasms in its practice. He appreciated the implication that their church had a single figurehead. It might be an important key in learning how to best stave the tide of monsters as battle-ready zealots in red continued their blood-soaked travel across the continent, but he would leave studying to the others.

Ash decided that he might also benefit from a day away from the castle, and after dressing against the cold, he wandered into town.

Though he hadn't needed to access any of his funds since

arriving in Gwydir, he still had the silvers and crowns that the Duke of Henares had sent with them those many seasons ago. He played with a crown between his fingers, practicing a trick he'd learned as a boy where he could move the coin along his knuckles in a smooth, easy movement one way and then the other, back and forth. He wasn't sure whether to smile or frown at the duke's money, knowing his friends were on the cusp of returning to Henares, where safety and crowns and resources awaited them.

Ash had been a little nervous about how he might be received in Gwydir. He knew he bore a striking resemblance to his father and couldn't imagine Elil had a very positive reputation among the people. As he wandered into shops for teas and spices and a warm hat, he found everyone to be perfectly welcoming and friendly. Perhaps Elil had been as reclusive to the city's citizens as he had been to his own son.

Ash passed a bakery and spotted the almond pastry that Zaccai always ate before anyone else could try, and he ordered four. He consumed his in the shop, making appreciative noises for the plump, pleasant baker. The other treats he planned to return with him to the castle for Tanith, Nox, and Zaccai. He was on his way back as he passed a trinket shop and spotted something in the window. It had cost him three crowns, but he felt quite pleased with his find.

Yet as he wandered back to the castle, it occurred to him how lost he felt.

✦

Nox wasn't sure if she'd lost a few marbles, but she was genuinely enjoying Tanith's company.

They chatted about their respective days, with Tanith talking excitedly about her new cloak and five more novels she'd found misshelved at the library. Nox had brought home nearly every record of Sulgrave theology she could find, as well as many of the older texts on the practices on the continent. She was no longer alone in her pursuit of knowledge, as a rather enthusiastic librarian had glued himself to her upon her arrival and piled her high with books. She vowed to fill her time cross-referencing religious practices and creating a map of similarities and differences so they might better understand how the faith branched out into two major deviations of expression.

"Are you having trouble finding what you need?" the librarian asked.

Nox sighed. "It seems every kingdom counts their days differently. I find it challenging to gauge how many years or centuries or millennia have passed depending on the text I'm reading."

He considered this. "I suppose it's inconvenient for everyone to count from significant historical events, but isn't that better than deeming any one event more important than all others that it might shape time itself?"

She supposed he was right and continued reading a text dated only five years after King Tempus's ascension. She didn't know who Tempus was or when he'd taken the throne, but supposed she'd add it to the long list of things she had yet to learn.

While nothing as clear as Reds, Greens, or color demarcations of the various branches of the church bubbled to the surface, her skimming and studying had found a few references to what Tanith had called the Speaker, though never with such a name. There was a recorded tale of Yggdrasil's mouthpiece arriving in the southern kingdoms nearly two thousand years before to bring restorative peace during a time of war between mortals and fae. The tales were contradictory, as some declared the arriving woman to be a prophet, while others insisted it was the physical Tree itself that had spoken. The texts agreed that she'd neutralized conflict, but everything else seemed like a story told from wildly conflicting perspectives.

"Are you a man of faith?" she asked the librarian on one of his many passes to check on her.

He strolled up with his third armful of books and plopped them down on the desk beside her. A small cloud of dust kicked up from one of the mustier texts. "My parents are devout," he said, "but I lost my faith when I attended university."

Nox looked at him with interest. "Studying under the Master of Literature turned you away from the church?"

The librarian dusted his hands on his tunic. "Nothing like that. It's just that I wasn't well read before I went to university, and by the time I left, I'd consumed nearly everything there was to know. It had more to do with the histories of the old gods and other paths of belief. Growing up, there had been a compulsive understanding that the All Mother was the only deity. She was the norm. Seeing cultures and pockets of people write of different encounters and various practices just made me examine the way I'd looked at life."

She chewed her lip. "I don't think I'm interested in studying the old gods—at least not yet. There's too much I don't understand about the existing religion to expand."

He rested on the precarious tower of books. "Some scholars believe the old gods and the All Mother are the same thing. There's a case to be made for the power of simplifying and centralizing belief. It facilitates control."

Nox's brows met in the middle.

He patted his body until he found a small, palm-sized book he'd tucked in a pocket. "I almost forgot that we have a handwritten collection of letters between theologians that you might find interesting. It's something of an antiquity and pretty niche interest, but you're the queen. You could order the library burned if you wished."

She was repulsed at the very thought of anyone having the power to erase knowledge from the face of the earth.

Nox thanked him and returned to the book in front of her. It was open to a passage on pivotal historical moments that were signified by the arrival of the Tree's harbinger—sometimes more literally, the All Mother made flesh—though there had been a few allusions from time to time to the All Mother's body being that of fruit, rather than the skin of human or fae. Her head ached as she considered the implication.

She closed the book and massaged her temples. Her eyes strained, and she wasn't sure that she had much more in her. She reached for the pocket-sized compilation of letters the librarian had left on her table and flipped through them. It appeared to be a collection of correspondence between a historian and a theologian, alternating in penmanship as if the authors had passed the booklet between one another to share their notes.

The historian wrote:

The mythos of the All Mother has disseminated differently throughout time, culture, and kingdom, but I've come to find a common thread running through the texts, much like a connective tissue or undercurrent. Dear friend, they'll call me a madman, but I don't believe the goddess to be more than a woman; maybe a collection of women, with greater power or abilities for creation than the others understand. Perhaps that's all it is to achieve godhood—to transcend comprehension. My friend, I do not believe her, or them, to be good, nor do I believe the goddess to be evil. She seems to want for nothing, and care for nothing. Please, do not tell the others I have said this, but I have suspicions that the peace she desires is her own—to be unbothered, unencumbered. Her desire for balance might not be one of altruism. These suspicions may need to die with us, my friend, for they are blasphemy.

The theologian responded:

Tell no one.

Back at the castle, Nox had attempted to discuss as much of this as she could, but speaking to Tanith about faith was like bouncing thoughts against a stone wall. The rantings of atheists, Tanith said, would stop at nothing to disprove the church and the goddess, regardless of her limitless miracles.

Nox showed the transcribed letters to Ash and Zaccai, who found them mildly interesting, if not largely useless.

"But what do you think it means? What if it is just a fae? What if there's a fae who can send messages through trees or fruit? What if there's a fae who—"

"What if?" Zaccai had shrugged. "Will it alter the way you do or don't worship? Will it impact your life in any way? Will it dissuade the zealots if you prove to them that they worship an omnipotent fae? And what is a god, if not omnipotence?"

"That's not what I mean. I'm just saying..."

"You're saying that you want to keep company with theologians, and I think that's admirable. We can see if we can rally up a few to add to your tutelage on Raascot. It's good to keep the mind active," Zaccai said in a way that told her that, though he wasn't trying to be dismissive, theology was not an area of interest for him.

Nox dropped the issue, deciding she'd force her conversations upon Amaris and Malik the next time she cornered them when they got home. Maybe Amaris would feel compelled to listen if she truly was some extension of the goddess.

When the four finished their dinner, Ash made an announcement.

There was something tranquil about him, as if his muscles had melted at the hand of his wine.

"I brought presents," he said with a crooked grin. He'd procured the almond pastries for everyone as a dessert, which Zaccai seemed to appreciate just as much as the other two, even though he'd had multiple helpings that very morning. Nox felt particularly betrayed that something so delicious had been withheld from her for so long.

Ash then turned to Tanith. He brought out a small box and passed it to her.

She took it from him and frowned. "What is it?"

He shrugged, pinking slightly as the others watched. "Everyone else has a ring, so I thought it might make you feel like a more included part of our circle if you got one too."

She opened the box and took out the small piece of jewelry.

A small, appreciative sound escaped her lips. She looked up uncertainly to Ash and waited for him to give an encouraging nod before she slipped it onto her hand. It was too small for her middle finger as the others had worn theirs, but it fit nicely on her ring finger.

"It's beautiful," she breathed, turning her hand over and watching the small stone catch in the light. Nox's jaw was practically on the floor as she gaped at the exchange. She wished Zaccai were more of a gossip, as she'd very much like to spend the entire rest of the night dissecting every move and breath and meaning that had transpired between the reever and the Sulgrave fae.

"It's aquamarine. The way I see it, if you must wear red, you should at least own something in your favorite color."

Chapter Thirty-six

AMARIS HAD LISTENED TO NOX ATTEMPT FOR DAYS TO prepare them for the Duke of Henares, but nothing he said could have truly readied her for the absurd lordling.

"This can't be real," Amaris mumbled, baffled at the dazed man who welcomed them.

"Apparently, Nox has quite the effect on men," Malik supplied.

Yazlyn made a comment about how she doubted the effect was limited to men.

The Duke of Henares welcomed them into his estate with the wherewithal of a cotton puff. Amaris strained to remember one other human male she'd encountered in the dungeons of Aubade. She'd encountered Nox's handiwork without understanding what had happened as the late Captain of the Guard launched himself toward an ag'drurath.

Having the time to regard the duke as he flitted about carrying bouquets of flowers and insisting that everyone listen to his poems about his night-haired angel was another matter entirely. Gadriel was endlessly entertained and kept prompting the duke to recite another, which earned him a number of irritated elbows from Yazlyn.

"Ow!" Gadriel grumbled, elbowing his sergeant in return. "This is the most fun I've had in months. Don't take this from me."

"Come on," Amaris said, ignoring their exchange. "We have a lot to do and not a lot of time to do it."

Their visit would not be particularly restful. They had one night to bathe and sleep on real beds before they set out for Aubade. For days, they'd spitballed plans on how to conceal four stowaways, but Malik was the only one who could almost definitely get in without being detected. They'd very briefly discussed the possibility of binding Gadriel's and Yazlyn's wings so that they could fit into somewhat normal clothing, but upon hearing the suggestion, the fae looked as if the reevers had proposed they march into the village and slice the hands off babies. They remained at the table, coopting the duke's dining room as they plotted the day before them.

Gadriel wanted to fly onto the balconies, but Amaris had to remind him that last time he tried he was captured, his wings were torn, and he'd been thrown into a coliseum to be either beheaded or eaten.

"I have a plan," Amaris said. "It's a bad one. But it's a plan nonetheless."

Gadriel steepled his fingers and dipped his chin. "Let's hear it."

"Malik can be our charming carriage driver, and the other three of us will just sit in the carriage with the duke. Anytime someone opens the door, I'll persuade them that we belong there and that they don't see anything suspicious."

Gadriel was unimpressed. "You're right. That is a bad plan."

"Hold on, now." Malik raised a hand. "You're thinking of this as a fae. The fae to humans in Raascot are four to one. Humans are the minority. Perhaps that's part of why so many humans preferred to move and stay south, to be amidst their own. In Farehold, however, only one in ten is fae."

Amaris was impressed with herself. "See? Ten-to-one odds! The gamble is in our favor."

Gadriel wasn't liking it. "But even if they're part fae—"

"Part-fae are resistant to her, but not immune. They'll still be perfectly charmed as long as the two of you do your best to conceal your tell-tale features."

The more they spoke, the more Gadriel pushed back. "Even Moirai was resistant. We're confident she's human. Our most generous guess might be that she has a splash of fae blood."

Yazlyn chimed in, "We all know Moirai is in possession of a ward. I'm confident that she wouldn't have been able to completely ignore Amaris's commands if she hadn't been wearing it."

Gadriel rubbed his chin. "But she will be prepared for your persuasion this time, Amaris. You won't be able to just shout your way through to her guards—"

"Why not?" Amaris asked. "We've said it before: she only knows of my ability to see through enchantments, even with Silvanus as a source. And if I'm to believe that I was born as a curse breaker, then doesn't it stand to reason that my power of persuasion was crafted for such a time as this? Why else would I possess such an ability if not to use it? Besides, if wards are so difficult and challenging to make, the probability of the guards wearing one is slim to none."

He huffed. "I don't like it."

Yazlyn seemed to have been won over. "I don't think you have to like it. It's the best idea we've got."

"Fine," Gadriel bristled. "Let's say we ride with the duke in his carriage, and at every check for papers and security, you're able to persuade the guards. What would we do when it's time to get out of the carriage?"

Amaris kept her words free of feeling as she said, "I get out of the carriage with the duke, and I tell them all that I'm his wife and insist that the carriage is empty and that they do not need to check it. Malik, of course, is our servant and will need to accompany us for…servant reasons."

Yazlyn clicked her tongue. "Damn, I wish persuasion worked on fae. That's one hell of a power."

Gadriel was impossible to please.

"You have white hair and very noticeable scars, Amaris. Silvanus not only had your description from Ceres's charge, but he'd met you himself at the campfire. The southern queen has seen your face. Once he offered up your appearance, it would have taken her a matter of seconds to put two and two together. She knows who you are."

"Then I'll wear a very big hat and a veil," Amaris huffed.

"It's not a masquerade!"

"I'll wear a fashionable, non-suspicious veil."

"See?" Yazlyn rolled her shoulders. "Her veil will be fashionable. It seems to me like she's got it all figured out."

A tendon in the general's neck strained as he controlled his temper. "Am I the only one here trying to keep us alive? Why aren't any of you acknowledging how terrible this plan is?"

Yazlyn propped her feet up on the table. "Because we're trying to be solution-oriented. I'm only hearing problems from you. Please, share your better suggestions."

"I fly in—"

Amaris slammed a flat palm on the table. "You flew in last time! It did not work!"

He leaned forward. "It did work! I entered via the balconies without any trouble. She didn't catch me until I was in the halls."

Just then, the duke cracked open the door to the dining room. A wolfish grin spread across his face as he greeted them. "Hello! I heard you were still awake. While I was in the bath, I thought of the loveliest limerick. Would you like to hear it?"

Gadriel grinned. His tension slid from shoulders like snow off a roof's peak. "Yes, very much. Do tell."

The duke cleared his throat and began, "There once was a beauty named Nox. She was as clever and lithe as a fox. I kissed her nose and nibbled her toes and then she licked my—"

"That's enough for tonight!" Amaris flushed, shooing the duke out, tone shrill. Gadriel hooted behind them, slapping his knee appreciatively. They decided that they would go with Amaris's plan for the time being, as the carriage ride would be at least two days' travel and give them plenty of opportunity to discuss better options.

"I'm only going with your plan because it means I get to ride in the carriage with the duke. He is an absolute delight."

✦

They'd decided that he and Yazlyn would head for the ocean, flying up on the cliffside of the castle and enter through the coliseum, as the front of the castle would doubtlessly be the most heavily guarded. Infiltration from behind was their surest bet at success, as one would truly need the gift of flight to enter over the sheer cliffs. Amaris and Malik had done their best to describe the passage from the coliseum's dungeon up to the throne room as they'd once been escorted, though Amaris proved of little use, as she'd been unconscious for half of it.

Ideally, the four would fight side by side as they took down Moirai. In a perfect situation, they'd all go in with their weapons and methodically plough through obstacles until they could eliminate the queen. In an even more perfect situation, Moirai would exit the castle, announce the curse to be broken, and step down from the throne before walking off into the ocean. As it stood, Malik and the fae would be doing their best to subdue the sentries and take down the guards to clear a path for Amaris as they worked their way in from various points of entry.

It was a glorious break after two days in the carriage. Yazlyn's childlike joy was infectious. Every new plant and interesting bird was worthy of gasps and inspection. She repeated her gratitude time and time again for not having to hoist Amaris through the air. She'd never seen the strange, slender trees with branches concentrated at the top. Amaris was impressed that the odd trees still had leaves, even if their fronds were brown with the lateness of the season. She abandoned her stress to join Yazlyn in pointing out lizards or the flap of yellow feathers that they wouldn't see in the north.

The duke had only been obnoxious for the first hour of the ride, until Amaris realized she could simply command him to be quiet. He'd sat in companionable silence, doing little beyond providing them opulent spreads of scones, jams, soft cheeses, hearty fruits, juices, wines, and whatever else a clandestine crew of four infiltrators might hope to indulge in as their last meal before a suicide mission.

They took their joy where they found it. Even Gadriel relaxed, playing hand games, telling riddles, and swapping war stories as they bounced down the roads that connected Henares to the capital. Malik taught them a curious song, and Amaris wasn't sure if she'd ever heard him sing before. Yazlyn taught them an interesting trick where she folded her tongue into a three-leaf clover, prompting everyone to share their own curious tricks.

But all good things must come to an end.

Amaris did her best to remain calm, but the fog of apprehension grew suffocating as the city neared. They laid out their plans once more. First, the duke was to take them to a finery shop where his tailors and seamstresses had prepared their attire for the evening. Amaris had quickly used her gifts to dismiss everyone in the store so that she could change and get ready. Malik was to head to the stables and enter through the servants' entrance. She wished her golden brother could escort her in playing the role of a cousin; Malik had once bowed before the queen, as she had, only he would not have the luxury of obscuring his face with whatever they might find at the tailor. Amaris was to walk through the front door on the arm of the duke. And Gadriel and Yazlyn were to, according to Amaris, "wing it."

"We're almost to Priory," Amaris said, turning to Malik. "We'll leave the coachman behind at the tailor, and you'll have to take his place before we head into Aubade."

"I don't see why I'll be the only one who has to sit out in the cold," Malik grumbled.

Conversation fell off as the road beneath them changed from compact dirt to the bumpy cobbles of the city. They remained in tense silence until the carriage jolted to a stop outside of one of the many cream-colored storefronts that had closed for the evening. A wooden sign swung on iron hinges, boasting what Amaris supposed was the tailor's name beside a sketch of a carved spool of thread.

After an hour behind the velvet curtain of the shop, there were only two things they agreed upon: Amaris looked positively breathtaking, and this was a very, very bad idea.

"I don't like anything about our strategy," Gadriel muttered for the hundredth time.

"Yes, but I look great and that's what matters."

"You are stunning," he emphasized, "but this is still the worst conceivable plan. I am deeply uncomfortable with you walking in there on display for Moirai to see."

"She won't recognize me." Amaris spun to examine herself in the mirror.

"Amaris"—he said her name almost as if it were a prayer— "all eyes will be on you. You are the most beautiful creature on this earth."

And for once, she believed it. She was a vision.

Everyone invited to the castle for Moirai's gathering was to attend in winter-formal attire, so she dressed to match her escort, the Duke of Henares. She was in a snow-white gown to honor the season as she prepared to play the role of Henares's duchess. Her dress was sleeveless and gauzy at the top, slowly gathering into silver crystals that looked like stars and snow had come to life as they cascaded down her dress. To conceal her tell-tale hair and scars, a gossamer scarf draped over part of her hair and half of her face, twisting in a curious fashion that only added to her mysterious allure.

Amaris wasn't one to stare at herself in the mirror. But tonight, she'd earned it.

She'd painted her mouth in a vibrant ruby, contrasting starkly against her pale skin and white dress. Beneath her dress was a skintight set of white pants for when she needed to abandon the part of delicate maiden and spring into battle-ready action. Her favorite part: the gorgeous, wintery gown had two deep pockets, perfect for concealing some of the slender weapons that she couldn't strap to her legs or tuck between what existed of her cleavage.

"Hey." Gadriel grabbed her hand and pulled her to him. Her heart pattered as he peered down into her eyes. He drew her closer, holding her body against the hard wall of his chest, fingers flexing against her back. "You are the most talented assassin I've ever met. You are brave, you're intelligent, you are quick on your feet, and you are incredibly capable. I'm so lucky to know you. If anyone can do this, it's you."

Her eyes fluttered, not wanting to ruin the makeup she'd painted on in the shop with the emotion that threatened her.

"Are you afraid?" Gadriel asked. His question held no condescension or accusation. His dark eyes held her purple gaze as she refused to look away. She soaked in his features, from his strong jaw and glossy hair to the tan of his skin. He was the most beautiful man she'd ever seen. He frustrated her. He thrilled her. He was the first man outside of Uaimh Reev who'd ever earned her trust. And now she had to leave him behind.

"I think I'd be less afraid if we had anything even resembling a real plan—"

Gadriel opened his mouth as if to comment on whose fault the lack of plan was.

"But no," she said before he might interject. "I'm not afraid of dying. I'm afraid of surviving if the people who make life worth living aren't there to experience it with me. Who will swap stories about our narrow brushes with death over campfires for years to come if I'm the only one who makes it out?"

There'd already been so little space between them. Her

breath left her as his hands grazed down her back. "A reever once broke my neck, you know."

A quiet laugh bubbled through her, eyes falling to the dip at the bottom of his neck before it spread into the broad expanse of his chest. She watched him inhale, vividly recalling their day in the forest.

"She was a really wicked little witchling with powerful hand-to-hand skills. Snapped it clean in the woods. Fortunately, I'm pretty hard to kill."

She scoffed at the memory.

"Life and death aside," he added, "you are the single most breathtaking creature in the world. The things I would give to be the one entering the castle tonight with you on my arm." He ran a hand down her arm as he added, "If any man in there touches you, I may have to deviate from the mission to do a little dismembering." He kissed her lightly atop her head so as not to smear the red paint on her mouth.

"Hey." Yazlyn poked her head in from the far side of the thick, velvet curtain. "Put a pin in whatever this is and make it incentive to survive the night. Gad, you and I have to go."

The fae would not be continuing in the carriage. While Amaris's confidence in her persuasion may work for her and Malik, the winged fae could not simply sit in the carriage and then exit undetected. By his logic, they'd be far more vulnerable and easier to spot if they were directly in front of the castle, fully exposed by the lamps and lanterns that illuminated all the streets and courtyards in front of Castle Aubade. They'd be shot down by prying eyes before they stepped their foot on the soil outside of the carriage.

"Besides," Gadriel had said, "if we're going to jump out of the carriage only to fly up to windows or outlooks, we might as well do it in the first place under the cover of shadow. Yaz and I need to push our efforts toward neutralizing the ones called the Hand and Hammer and their forces so that you can focus on the actual target."

The time at the tailor had come and gone. Amaris was dressed for royalty. And their plan would work, or it wouldn't.

She looked at Yazlyn and held the sergeant's eyes for a moment. There was fear there and bravery in spite of it. Yazlyn looked away from Amaris before further emotion betrayed her.

"I'm ready," he said to Yazlyn.

He squeezed Amaris's hand once more before the pair disappeared into the night.

It took three deep, calming breaths before Amaris was certain she'd found the cool, emotionless place within herself to do what needed to be done. Amaris walked over to where Malik and the duke waited with the horses, and Malik did his best to smile at the beautiful reever. "You and me, brother."

She returned the empty smile. "Let's give them hell."

"Worse," he amended, "let's give them the demi-goddess."

It felt like the lid closing on a coffin when Malik shut her into the carriage with the duke. Though Amaris's spirit was willing, she couldn't keep the tremble from her palms. While she didn't even want to breathe the thought into life, part of her felt like this might be the last time she ever saw Yazlyn or Gadriel alive.

Their first task came quickly. Her heart thundered with bruising strength when she attempted her persuasion on the guards at the wall, but the men obeyed without question. The carriage was stopped again at the first set of gates to the castle, and once more the human compliance was immediate. Amaris flexed and squeezed her hands into balls, trying to calm herself. She chanted Farehold's human-to-fae odds like a prayer with each stop, smile, and persuasion.

Everything was going according to plan. There'd been no resistance. The math was on her side. And no matter how she reassured herself of this fact, her heart would not cease its sickening pounding.

The carriage began to curve as they entered the rounded courtyard with a lovely, circular waterfall, frozen in crystalized ice for the winter. Malik brought their carriage to stop under the buttery illumination of large, overhead street lanterns. Other carriages were stopped or presently arriving as various lords and their ladies descended from their rides and wandered into the castle. Amaris made a gesture for one of the guards wearing Moirai's sigil to approach her and the duke, and he looked around a bit skeptically before obliging the young mistress.

"My horses require special care," she said to the guard, who wore a glinting, metallic breastplate. "You will escort them and my coachman to the stables and then see to it that he safely enters the castle. If anyone asks you why, just repeat that you're under direct orders from the queen to see him in."

The sentry nodded once as he led Malik off toward the stables on the castle grounds.

Malik dared the smallest of parting glances, and she saw the final "good luck" in his eyes.

She swallowed her relief knowing that at least one of her companions would be fine, and then an idea struck her. Every guard she passed as she entered the castle or as she was escorted through the corridors or while heading toward the banquet hall received the same whispered command from her. "If there is any fighting tonight, you will stand down. You will not draw your weapon, no matter what."

Each guard offered the barest of bows in acknowledgment, and she would carry on as if she'd never spoken. Queen Moirai could scream for their aid, and they'd ignore their monarch entirely, allowing Amaris and the others to do what needed to be done.

The soothing balm she'd expected evaded her as she systematically disarmed guards throughout the castle. Instead of feeling increasing calm, no matter how many potential threats she nullified, her anxiety swelled with every minute that passed. Amaris had spoken to no fewer than eight guards in the corridors alone before they made their way into the dining hall.

Opulence took on a new meaning. The angelic chorus of minstrels, the tinkling of champagne flutes and silverware, the glow of fae lights, the glitter of ten thousand stars as if the falling snow had been captured and scattered throughout the dining hall took her breath away. Amaris nearly twisted her ankle, so lost in her reverie that if she hadn't been using the duke as a human prop, she would have fallen entirely.

She supposed the goal was to blend in. And in many ways, she did. She matched the colors, the fashion, the gleam, and gild of the wealth around her. She didn't give herself away. Nor did she disappear amidst the crowd as one might hope.

Scarves, veils, and hats were certainly in fashion, though her choice was more daring than most. Many of the women in attendance wore elaborate headpieces to accentuate their hair or give them an aura of mystery, though none had opted for anything quite like the gauzy shroud Amaris wore.

An attendant escorted them to their seats at an enormous banquet table, which was one of twelve identical tables in the room. Each was richly ornamented in the frosty blues, whites, silvers, and evergreen cuttings of winter decor. At the front of the room was a small table only for the queen, the crowned prince, and their immediate guests. Even the guards posted on either side of the royal table glistened in the fleur-de-lis carvings of their decorative armor.

"I'll be right back," Amaris said, rising from the table.

The rather intoxicated couple across from them had just launched into introductions. She'd never seen so many ringlets piled high upon one head as she did in the woman's ornate hair. Enough jewels to feed the nation rested on the bosom that had been tightly gathered into a shelf to display her precious gems. She humphed, "You're leaving us already?"

"Nox?" The duke looked up at Amaris with doe-like eyes.

The middle-aged lord from some town she'd never heard of in a region she didn't care about scoffed. "He calls you 'night'? A sweet little moonbeam like you?"

It took Amaris every feat of strength to keep her eye from twitching. She knew precisely how far her hand was from her knife, and how quickly she could retrieve it. She reminded herself that she shouldn't commit murder in broad daylight before the time was right just because people were boorish. She hoped her painted smile remained placid. "Yes," she agreed. "You know how it is: lovers and their pet names. Now, if you'll excuse me."

Amaris abandoned the table to continue making slow laps, whispering to the guards that they were to stand down, no matter what, as she navigated the room. She drew eyes with every step, but not because wandering was unusual. Many titleholders mingled the hall, rubbing elbows with the other nobles of Farehold before taking their seats. The eyes on Amaris were solely because she was a thing of beauty. The curious veil couldn't have hurt her aura of mystery either. She heard hisses and whispers as she walked by that she was the fabled Duchess of Henares, by whom the duke had been so infatuated that he had spoken of no one and nothing else in a year. It suited her agenda fine that the duke had grown a reputation for being lovelorn over an unknown creature now that she circled the perimeter of the banquet hall.

And though she was on a life-or-death mission, she couldn't help but feel like she'd stepped off the world and into the heavens. She wished she and Nox could have been here together, the brightest stars in the gem-soaked sky as they went to see and be seen. Nox's acerbic wit and ease amongst humans would have been a sight to behold. They might have shared a bottle of wine, traded bites of their desserts, and she knew Nox would have had an excellent comeback to the lord's piggishness.

But Nox was not with her.

She was in the most stunning gown she'd ever get a chance to wear with no loving arm to hold. The tables were overflowing with frosted ivy, red berries, dripping candles on white-gold candlesticks, and seemed to be alive with the light of winter. The kingdom's nobility had not disappointed either. Everyone was spectacularly dressed in seasonal shades of blues, grays, whites, and silvers to pay homage to the weather. The loveliest white-gold harp was being played by an angelic musician who had been stationed so everyone could see her as a living work of art while she performed for the evening. The music that filled the hall was a mixture of the familiar, jovial Yule carols and haunting, heavenly songs that were the sounds of ice and wind and falling snow composed into a flurry of notes, breathed into life through the deft fingers of the talented harpist.

She'd have to commit it all to memory so she might tell the others about it later. She had to stop herself from the thought that pressed down on her, catching it and shoving it into the box, but not before five words clanged through her.

If there is a later.

She had nearly reached the last guard when she decided to do a bit more reconnaissance. Amaris had poised her body in such a way so that it looked as if she were merely walking past the sentry, pausing a half step beyond his face to whisper her questions as commands. The harpist's trill and the cacophonous conversations covered her words as she spoke to the guard.

"Tell me when the queen is expected at this banquet," she said, flexing her power.

"The queen and crowned prince will be here shortly," he obediently responded, staring forward. Of course, he would still be subject to the illusion of the prince, as would everyone else.

"Tell me what security for the banquet is like," she whispered. Her voice was so quiet, it was barely a breath above the merry burble and music of the room.

"Guards are posted at every entry, exit and window, m'lady."

She swallowed at that, wondering if there would be anything she could do to help Gadriel and Yazlyn as they attempted to ascend through the dungeon.

"What about—" She stopped herself, rewording her thought as a command. "Tell me: will the Hand and Hammer be guarding Queen Moirai tonight?"

"No."

She stifled the urge to step backward to examine him for signs of deceit. She wanted to press the issue further, but everyone began moving to their tables to begin the meal. Amaris issued one final command. "Go to the dungeons and subdue any guard or sentry who attempts to prevent two winged fae from entering. Use whatever force necessary. You will help them safely enter the castle."

He nodded and stepped away from his post as Amaris glided back to her table. Her hand went to her veil to ensure that it was still concealing her telltale scar.

Amaris glanced about the room and wondered at her next step. She had gotten into the castle. To her knowledge, so far there had been no commotion or ruckus regarding the stables or dungeons, though she was quite certain that the walls in Aubade were thick enough that she wouldn't have heard any scuffle or calls until they were on top of her.

She trusted her friends to do a thorough and precise job in their coming battle, but she felt the poignant terror of being deeply and utterly alone.

She would be on her own tonight. Malik was nowhere in sight, though in theory even if he were down the hall, he wouldn't make himself known. The northern fae were similarly absent, as they needed to be to avoid detection and capture. She counted on Moirai's guards to expect only ag'imni. Seeing a fae face should give the sentries enough of a pause to buy Gadriel and Yazlyn an advantage. Still, she had no verifiable way of knowing if any of her other companions had successfully made it into the castle.

Now, Amaris had nothing to do but wait.

She couldn't very well jump up and launch her slender throwing knives at Moirai as soon as the queen entered. Murdering her in front of all of her lords and dignitaries didn't seem like the best move. But then again, she had no moves. Gadriel had been right: their plan was very, very bad, because it was not a plan at all. This was no genius heist, nor was it a covert assassination. She was quite certain that this was the single, sloppiest infiltration and usurpation in the whole of history.

She settled back into her seat, barely feigning nods and smiles as the couple across from her yammered on. They were too self-absorbed to see the acute worry in her eyes or the vacant glaze varnishing the duke's absent mind.

The artistically plated food was served, but no one touched their meals. She wasn't sure about royal mannerisms but mirrored the dignitaries and nobility at the table around her. The roast pheasant, tied with string and decorated with twigs of rosemary, sat beside cranberries, greens, and festive dinner rolls upon the dishes in front of them. Less than thirty seconds after the massive influx of servants had arrived to set down the plates, they disappeared.

The room throbbed with the knowing pause that the night was about to begin. The musicians ceased. Conversation halted. The room quieted as everyone waited for the main event.

Side doors opened with dramatic fanfares as Moirai entered.

Amaris choked on the flood of repressed memories that flashed through her. She angled her face ever so slightly, ensuring the queen would see nothing but a white curtain of gauze if she looked in Amaris's direction.

While everyone in the room wore wintry shades, Moirai arrived in gold. Her dress was gilded and shimmering from its sleeves to its skirts, every inch of her sparkling gloriously under the twinkling lights of the banquet hall. Amaris had seen Moirai only twice before, but both times, the queen had worn her hair loose and long down her back, a style that had been striking and unusual for a woman of her age. Her brown-gold hair was nearly as metallic and shimmering as the sheen of her dress. Her crown, yellow gold, was set with rubies. Amaris shoved down a horrid memory of the queen and her crimson jewels as she'd glared up at her from where she'd stood on the arena's sands.

The ripple of murmurs about a handsome young man led her to believe that they were also witnessing the entrance of the crown prince, though Amaris saw nothing. One sentry stood off to the side and slightly behind each perceived monarch, though the guards accompanying the queen appeared to be the same rank and station as all of those she'd effectively disarmed throughout the night. Fear flashed through her as she eyed the sentries. If the new captains of the guard were not here with their queen, where were they?

Moirai wasted no time.

She made several sweeping pronouncements about the grandness of Farehold, the beauty of winter, and the glory of the All Mother. Each word grated over Amaris, forcing her blood pressure higher and higher as she wished she'd listened to Gadriel. She should have had a plan. Instead, when Moirai raised her mug to a toast, Amaris lifted her glass.

Her heart fell into her stomach at the unthinkable words that spilled from the queen's wicked, smiling mouth.

"To the expansion of Farehold as we reclaim what is rightfully ours!"

Chapter
Thirty-seven

THERE WAS A SHARP, OZONE FLAVOR TO THE ARCTIC WINTER
air. It burned Nox's lungs as she walked, savoring and
hating the calm before the weather turned. She was on yet
another in an extensive pattern of trips from Gwydir's archives,
arms clutching a small stack of books from the inordinately
helpful librarian in one hand and a small hot treat. She'd been
about to tip the paper cone of sweets back into her mouth
when she paused. A sound from somewhere beyond the rows
and rows of city homes scratched at the space just behind her
ears. She stopped in her tracks, looking at the streets and hills
of the city she'd come to call home, searching homes, alleys,
and buildings for the source of the noise. Her curiosity was
cut short by the wind's impatience. It whipped tendrils of hair
across her cheeks, forcing her to squint as its speed increased.
She forwent the treats, deciding she'd have plenty of time for
candied nuts when she returned to the safety of the castle.
Nox shivered, grateful for the extra layer of warmth. Having
long, unbound hair was a bit like eternally possessing a wool
hat and scarf, even when her hair fought against her.

She was nearly to the bridge that crossed the dark waters
and let her onto the grounds. Given the remoteness of the

city, she hadn't felt the need to bring company with her when she'd gone on her outings, nor had Zaccai or any of the fae so much as suggested it. She felt safe here, which was more than she'd ever been able to say for Farehold. Every day, she grew more and more comfortable in her community. People recognized her and welcomed her with open arms. She savored their warm smiles, loving how they beckoned to her from their doorways to come in and try their goods, despite the cold season. She'd be enjoying warm, spiced, sugar-coated almonds now if the odd, discordant noise hadn't pricked at her once more.

Nox came to a full stop in the middle of the bridge. Winter days were often windy and gray, but she had become familiar with the blinding, soupy white of overcast days. Today was the dark, ominous pewter of an impending storm. While she'd grown accustomed to the cold, she knew better than to be caught outside the castle before any blizzard began. There was nothing to see. The city was its normal, magical self. The world was as it should be.

And yet.

It was one of those noises that her gut knew was a scream before rationality reasoned that it was most likely a child playing, shrieking in some loud, distant game.

Children playing. That had to be it.

Still, she remained glued to the middle of the cobbled bridge, feeling the almonds cool in her hand. She stared at nothing as she scanned the rows of homes. She couldn't explain why, but no matter how much her mind tried to persuade her that she had heard the innocent noises of city sounds, she couldn't shake the prickling feeling that crawled up the back of her neck.

The wind increased as the first whips of dry, white snow snaked across the path. The clouds churned from flat, overcast shades to the dark, leaden shades of storms. The impending blizzard had seemed so far away only moments ago. She hadn't realized how quickly the threat could move this far north.

Nox held her books more tightly as she jogged over the long stone bridge and closed the distance between herself and the castle. The black waters of the river bobbed with frozen chunks like ever-moving stepping stones as it flowed quickly from one end of Gwydir downward to the southern shores. Her eyes remained on the slippery, cold stones of the bridge as she hastened her steps.

Ever-vigilant attendants were already opening the door by the time she reached the gates. Her gut forced her to stop one last time before she entered. She turned back into the oncoming storm, squinting into the rapidly rising wind speeds and the snow that had already begun to obscure her vision.

"Get in and warm yourself, Your Highness! It's awfully cold."

"Yes." She nodded limply without turning to see the servants. She was aware that they were standing in the cold, waiting for her movement, but her feet wouldn't allow her to shift. She was still squinting into the dark wall of the oncoming blizzard and the hazy view of whipping crystals as dry snow blustered through the streets beyond the river. She finally rotated to the attendants as they closed the door behind her and handed the contents of her arms to a pleasant-looking man.

"Please, can you take these for me?" she said, struggling to fix her gaze on the attendant as her eyes continued darting between him and the city beyond. "And where is Zaccai?"

The servant was too old for her to force his bones to be chilled by this weather. His kind eyes knit as he regarded her. "I believe I last saw the commander in the war room. Would you like me to fetch him for you?"

"No, no. Thank you for taking the books. Please feel free to eat the almonds and share them with the others. I'll go find him."

It was as if lightning crackled through, its jolt inexplicable and all-consuming.

She should have relaxed and rationalized with herself.

She should have taken a few calming breaths and settled into reason. But she didn't bother to remove her cloak or mittens as she jogged down the midnight-hued corridor. By the time she saw the half-open door to the war room, she was practically sprinting.

He looked up the moment the door flung open.

"Something's wrong," she said between pants.

"What?" He was already rounding the table, face slicked with alertness as he approached her.

She shook her head and dragged him out of the war room to the nearest window. She pointed in the direction she'd heard the noise, then nervously raked a hand through her hair. "I don't know. I don't know. But I'm not crazy. Something is wrong, Zaccai."

She waited for him to tell her to relax, to inform her that she just wasn't used to winters in the mountains, or that she missed Amaris and Malik and hadn't been getting enough sleep.

He didn't.

Zaccai took off down the corridor without a second thought. She watched his steps skid against the stones as he bounded down the hall and up the stairs toward the lookout tower.

She would not stand and wait.

"Ash?" Nox began to shout as she moved hastily through the bedrooms, throwing open the doors on all sides of the halls. Instead of calming herself, she felt her anxiety grow with the minutes. He wasn't in the bedrooms. He wasn't in Tanith's room. She made it to the kitchen, but he wasn't there either. She hadn't stopped moving, searching, panicking.

Zaccai's shouts mingled with her own just as she was passed the dining room. She ran toward the sound of his voice. They nearly crashed into one another as he rounded the corner, grasping her shoulders to stop himself from running headlong into the wall.

"They're in the city," he said breathlessly, snow clinging to his hair and the eyelashes of his widened eyes, dusted white from his quick overhead flight.

"Who's in the city?" she asked, eyes wild.

"Aubade."

Chapter
Thirty-eight

T HE AIR LEFT AMARIS'S LUNGS.
  The royals and lordlings around her cheered, reveling in Moirai's proclamation as she reclined into her chair. They lowered to their seats and began to merrily shovel the festive dinner into their mouths. She woodenly mimicked their movements but couldn't bring herself to eat.

She'd lifted her flute to Farehold claiming the north. Amaris stared at the queen, scarcely able to comprehend that this vile woman could be Nox's grandmother. Moirai's curly, unbound hair was the brown-gold that Daphne's might have been, and perhaps Nox's might have been had it not been for her father's blood.

Conversation bubbled throughout the banquet hall, but Amaris wouldn't touch her food. Her mind raced. Moirai had given no further proclamation. Did the queen intend to invade in the morning? Next month? Next year?

It didn't matter. She couldn't allow it to happen. Nox, Malik, Gadriel, and Yazlyn were here in Aubade. She would be left exposed with a skeleton team unless Amaris cut the head off the snake now. She could hear her heartbeat in her ears, the rush of blood drowning out her critical thinking as she paged through question after question.

How would she get from where she was to where she needed to be? She was certain she could strike the queen where she sat eating next to her invisible crowned prince if she simply stood at her table and threw a deadly, slender knife. What would she do about the multitudes of royals? Could she do it now? Might she win before the remaining guards intervened? And if they did, what value was her life contrasted against Nox and the future of the continent?

Focus, focus.

If she'd learned anything from her failure to command during her first visit to Aubade's throne room, it was that her persuasion needed to be direct. Shouting at Moirai to release her had not moved the guards in the slightest. She would need to be intentional about her commands, meaning that generalized shouts for every lordling to stand and calmly exit would probably be ineffective.

Her stomach cramped against the uncertainty. Her fingers crept down the table, grazing up her leg and settling on her hip. She slid her fingertips into her pocket, clutching the slender silver blade inside.

She had one goal.

Moirai must die.

The outcome was more important than her exit strategy. It was more valuable than her survival. The fate of the continent depended on her success, no matter the cost.

Amaris began to slowly pull the knife from her pocket when her eyes caught movement.

A guard had entered from the main door, closing and latching the doors behind him, and hustled to whisper to the sentries who stood behind the queen. She tilted her ear so as to receive the message when the sentry knelt to whisper to her.

This was it.

They knew she was here.

They had found Raascot fae within the castle.

Malik was dead.

Gadriel was captured.

Something was wrong.

Moirai did not scan the crowd to look for her, though her heart attempted to escape its place within her ribs, adrenaline pumping through her with every frantic beat as she waited. The woman's face twisted in a disgusted contortion as at first she attempted to dismiss the sentry. Agitation as clear as a stain, Moirai raised her fork to her mouth once more. At her dismissal, the guard who had first run in from the outside threw protocol to the wind and bent down beside her. Cold sweat beaded on Amaris's brow as her gaze fixed on the guard's rapidly moving lips. She wasn't the only one who had paused to watch the exchange. A number of prominent lords paused their chatter, ceasing their meals to eavesdrop on the fuss.

Inhale. Exhale. Inhale. Exhale.

Amaris counted the royals. She numbered her enemies. She clocked the sentries, the swords, those who might stand against her, and compared the number to those she'd commanded to stand down. She'd done all she could, but she might still be overwhelmed by sheer numbers.

She was alone in a sea of enemies.

Whatever the sentry said landed. Moirai finally gave her attention to the guard, facing him as he frantically relayed information. Her brows bunched, mouth turning as if whatever he said lacked comprehension, though she did appear to be trying. Moirai kept shaking her head, but he did not relent. The man would not leave her side. His voice grew louder with worry, though his words were indiscernible. If he hitched into panic, Amaris might just be able to hear what had brought the man to the verge of hysterics.

They're fine, she told herself, lie though it may be. *Malik is safe. Gadriel and Yazlyn are elite warriors. They're powerful. They're unkillable. They're fine. They have to be fine.*

Amaris's palms began to sweat, the clammy dampness

making it difficult to grip the blade that remained fastened to her thigh. She released the blade long enough to dry her damp hand on her dress, eyes never moving from the queen.

The queen stood, though the man urged her to remain quiet. The dining hall had grown utterly still, everyone's eyes wholly focused on the unnerving impropriety at the head table. Moirai refused the sentry's pleas.

The queen turned to the crowd. With a tight, fake smile, she addressed the now-silent audience. "There seems to be a bit of a confusing disturbance in the castle. Never fear! We have guards at every entry and exit. You are in the safest place in all of Farehold. Please forgive the interruption and carry on! Tonight, we celebrate the Yule Feast before we discuss our advancement northward!" Moirai raised her goblet again with her final words.

The lords returned her toast, if somewhat trepidatiously. Many shouted agreeably as they lifted their drinks to the prospect of northern expansion. Amaris wanted to focus her energy on Moirai but couldn't settle wholly into the target until she understood the problem. It was one of many panicked questions clawing at the walls of her mind. How long had Farehold been planning this? Why hadn't the Duke of Henares informed them?

There was a thump at the main door.

The guard who had entered drew his sword from its sheath.

The main door thumped again, but the sound was neither loud nor urgent.

Somewhere deep in the castle came a blood-curdling cry. The nobility and guests of the dining hall began to nervously murmur, everyone setting their food to the side as they regarded the door. The thump continued, methodical and low. After another thump, one of the centurions moved to open the door to look into the disturbance.

"No!" shouted the queen and the worried sentry in unison.

It was too late.

The man was already opening the door as another low, knocking thud landed against the main wooden doors. The moment it opened, Amaris's spirit left her body. All of her blood drained. It was no fae, nor was it Malik or any other face she worried might have been captured. It was not an armed guard, rushing in to tell them that they'd been compromised. The being at the door was nothing she had seen or expected outside of her bestiary tomes. The presence slowly thudding against the door was something—some*one*—she recognized.

The decaying, skeletal remains of Eramus pushed themselves against the door as he limped into the room. His mouth hung off of one jaw hinge, skin green and gray with rot as holes pocked his face and body. If it weren't for his golden breastplate, she never would have identified the ghoul. He opened his mouth, and a guttural, wet, sucking noise emanated from it. He limped forward, raising the rusty sword he clutched and bringing it down on the nearest noblewoman. The horrid, sinking sound of sliced, butchered flesh rose with the scream of pain, accompanied by shouts of horrendous disbelief.

Plans, training, bestiary tomes, years of running up and down the mountain, of sparring, of preparation slipped into a sticky puddle, pooling at her feet.

Ghouls.

Everyone had been too shocked, too terrified to believe their eyes. The room had been frozen as the dead man had entered. When his blade sunk into the flesh of a duchess, the world erupted.

The volcanic onslaught of screams happened all at once as the fabric of civility unraveled. Sentries flanked the queen and began to rush her from the room. Chaos shook Amaris with its angry hands, snapping her back to reality. She leapt from her table, pushing through the crowd as tables overturned, plates scattered to the floor, candles knocked sideways, and shouts filled the hall. Beyond the living corpse of Sir Eramus had been several other slowly moving skeletons, disjointedly

445

groaning their way forward through the cream corridors of the castle.

A ghoul raised his sword and thrust it downward, cutting into the skull of a guard as if it were splitting wet logs. Lordlings pushed and shoved in all directions, scrambling in vain toward the exits. Amaris realized with horror that she had commanded every guard in the room to stand down from battle. There would be no help. They wouldn't raise a sword in defense as the undead infiltrated the castle.

Amaris ducked and wove like a fish swimming upstream. She propelled through the flow of noblemen, carving her way after the exit the queen had taken.

The frantic guard who had first come with the news began to shout to the others, ushering the nobility and dignitaries down an exit on the opposing side, while the sentries who had entered with the queen were yelling and pushing their way through the crowd to get Moirai to safety. Screams and the crunch of bone mingled with the guttural noises of death, filling the hall. Amaris dared a glance over her shoulder to see that at least four more corpses in various states of decomposition had entered the room, all clutching their otherwise destroyed and discarded weapons and hacking at the defenseless nobility.

They were sheep, corralled for slaughter.

She elbowed past a duchess, and the woman stepped on her gown, tripping her. Amaris fell to the ground and grabbed her knife, cutting away the skirt of the elaborate, formal dress as she scrambled from her defenseless position and barreled toward the exit.

Other wings of the castle were alive with the sounds of horror. Cries and wails echoed off the walls from servants, guards, and royalty alike. The dead had infiltrated at every point of entry.

She ducked, she pushed, she scrambled, and she dug through her recesses of information for anything she knew about the reanimated. There had been tales of necromancers and horrible folk tales of the King of the Undying, but never before had there been a coordinated infiltration of ghouls.

They didn't bleed black, as they weren't demons. There was no killing wound, no vital piece of information, nothing that might save her, unless she were ready to set the castle and everyone in it on fire.

Amaris focused on her breathing as her feet pounded against the cream stones of the castle. She'd lost valuable time in the moments it had taken her to maneuver through the scrambling, hysterical noblemen. She couldn't worry about whatever Sulgrave fae wielded the army. She couldn't distract herself by battling the dead. She was here for Moirai.

Amaris nearly skidded sideways as she rounded a corner only to run into the putrid, sloughing flesh of someone who had bloated with death. The ghoul raised its weapon, and she slashed it across the throat in what would have been a killing blow to anyone capable of experiencing death. It swung at her, and she threw herself onto her back, barely catching herself with her hands as her head nearly collided with the stones in her backbend. She thrust out a leg to sweep the stance of the corpse before picking up and continuing her run. There was no use fighting that which was already dead.

As she rounded a corner, she caught the golden hem of Moirai's dress as it disappeared behind a door. One guard had followed her in while the other guarded the door, hands shaking from the nightmares made flesh that descended upon him from all sides. Amaris rushed for the man and shouted a command.

"Defend me!"

The guard's sword whirred, slicing through the air as she slid past him. Her hand flew to the handle. It opened easily as the man stayed behind, warding off the walking corpses that advanced. The sentry bought Amaris time as she searched the room, gasping, eyes wide, battling the panic that consumed her.

Groans bounced off the walls in a terrible symphony,

mingling with the sounds of the dying as lords and dignitaries ceased their screams. In a matter of moments, nothing living would remain. If she was going to die in the clutches of a fucking skeleton, she had to take Moirai down with her.

But the room was completely empty. There were no doors. There was no place to hide. Amaris ran to the window and threw it open, but they were several floors too high for the queen to have escaped. The wails of terror infested the castle, invading her every cell. She pushed it out, shoving it down, narrowing her eyes, and focusing her thoughts.

Moirai had entered this room. There was an escape somewhere. And if it was here, she would find it.

Amaris returned to the window and shouted for Gadriel or Yazlyn, but she saw no one. Surely, they'd already be inside. The ground below showed the advancement of even more dead as the ghouls clawed their way through the frozen earth and limped through the ice and snow toward the castle. They seemed to be pouring in at all points of entrance from the castle grounds. Whoever was commanding this army was coordinating their attacks directly on Castle Aubade.

She didn't have minutes. She had seconds at best.

Amaris spun as she saw the guard who fought at the doorway take a blow to the leg. Fresh, red blood pooled from the gash on his thigh onto the custard-colored stones below. He fell to one knee as he continued swinging, but the dead were closing in on him. Amaris began to throw pictures off the wall, tearing down the tapestries, looking for anything that might be an exit. She grunted, shoving, unsuccessfully pushing the armoire until something caught her eye. She had ten seconds—twenty seconds, maximum—before the ghouls were in the room with her. Her eyes snagged on the unusually large mirror.

It was enough.

She pulled on it, and though it did not give way, there was something unnatural about the way it shifted.

Surely, there was some trick to the space, but Amaris had

no time to figure out the latch. Shielding her face with one arm, she used the pommel of her knife to smash the mirror, crying out in victory when the cold rush of air and dark tunnel of escape greeted her. She leapt over the jagged shards, plunging into the shadows. The ghouls would be only a few moves behind her as they stepped their engorged, gray-green feet over the lip of the mirror and toppled down the stairs.

A new sound cut through the air just up ahead. She heard another scream, but this was not the blood-curdle of dying breath. This was the fight and high-pitched cry of battle.

Amaris pounded down the stairs and burst into an enormous, subterranean passageway of a curved stone room filled with barrels of whiskey and liquor. She whipped her head from left to right, but no ghouls had made it to the alcohol storage yet. Instead, she saw the glint of Moirai's gown disappear down a hall as the queen's guard was locked in battle...but not with a ghoul.

The iridescent flash of wings, the blur of hair, the scream of war let her know that she didn't have a second to spare.

"Yaz!" Amaris slid underneath the guard, slashing upward with her small knife. The guard was so shocked at the surprise attack that her slash distracted him long enough for the sergeant to make a dismembering strike.

"Here!" She tossed Amaris the additional short sword that had been strapped to her belt. The women shut out the dying cries from the passages above and beyond as they sprinted forward, matching each other step for step as they pounded after Moirai.

"Where's Gad?" Amaris asked between breaths, pushing them faster. There was no way Moirai could outrun them. They'd close the distance any second.

"Looking for you!" Yazlyn shouted in response, matching the reever's pace. They caught another metallic shimmer and rounded a corner in pursuit just before skidding to a halt as they came upon Moirai standing in the center of a circular room. Underground passages from throughout the castle intersected like spokes of a wheel. Moirai had come to a halt as ghouls populated each of the passages in varying numbers.

"Moirai!" Amaris bared her teeth as she snarled at the queen. "Do you remember me?"

Moirai's face twitched in a half smile, and Amaris knew that yes, she would never forget the girl she'd thrown into the coliseum. She relaxed with the ease of someone who had all the time in the world. With cruel power, she said, "The reever demon sympathizer, here to join the army of the undead? How poetic. You will die with the very winged dogs you love."

She flicked her hand up before her, wiggling her fingers.

"What's she doing?" Amaris breathed. She looked to Yazlyn for answers, only to see the sergeant's eyes the size of saucers. Yazlyn was scarcely breathing, her inhalations coming in rapid, shallow pants as her eyes flickered across the ceiling.

"They're everywhere…" Yazlyn said, voice hoarse with nightmares.

"Moirai!" Amaris shouted again, stepping away from the sergeant. "Your imbalance to magic—"

"Monologue later!" Yazlyn shrieked, clawing at the exposed skin of her arm. "Amaris. They're everywhere! They're everywhere!"

Amaris fumbled against the nails tearing gashes into her arm, fighting Yazlyn off as she demanded, "The ghouls?"

"No! Not the fucking ghouls! Look! You don't see them?"

"No! We'll deal with the ghouls in a minute."

The queen smiled. "It looks like you're all alone, reever." Her teeth glinted as she watched the fear grow on the fae's face. "Your winged bitch deserves to be put down with the other Raascot filth."

Amaris didn't have time to listen to the queen's slurs— she'd seen the curse and had felt the hate burn through the southern queen as she'd towered over Ceres. Knowing now that Ceres had been shielding Daphne from her mother's words, a hate of equal strength raged through her. Her vitriol needed no audience.

450

The sergeant turned to defend where they stood as Amaris thrust her slender knife toward Moirai. The blade cut through the air, straight and true as its killing blow barreled toward the queen's chest. Amaris blinked rapidly as she watched her knife ring glance off Moirai, like oil separating from water.

Amaris reached for another dagger strapped to her leg, racing toward Moirai. The queen turned to meet her as she darted forward, jumping and plunging her knife downward for the kill. But her knife found no purchase. Amaris couldn't even grip the queen as she thrashed to wrap her hands or legs around the royal woman. It was as if she wore a slick, unseen protective layer.

Moirai didn't wait for the reever to recover. As Amaris skidded to the ground, Moirai used the opportunity to continue running. She chose the passage with the fewest number of ghouls.

Yazlyn was struggling as the dead advanced, their wet footsteps and stench of rotting flesh filling the passages. Amaris turned in frustration and grabbed Yazlyn.

"Fly me!"

Chapter Thirty-nine

ASH SHUDDERED AGAINST THE WEATHER AS THE FRIGID day turned into something else entirely. Snow swirled throughout the ring in a tight, white tornado of ice and sound. His lungs burned, exhausted as he lowered his fists. His fingers were red and wind-chafed. They'd been training in the wintry sparring ring of the courtyard for hours. He had no idea how Tanith had kept up her stamina, but she seemed unaffected by the cold. She stopped in the middle of her move, frozen in her pose as if listening for something.

"What?" Ash prompted.

She tilted her head to the side, dark hair curtaining on her shoulder a moment before the ominous sound of a bell began to toll.

"What's that?"

Ash shook his head. "It sounds like a warning bell."

They looked overhead into the sky as the clouds went from dark gray to nearly black in the impending blizzard. "Shit," he grumbled. "I didn't know it was supposed to storm. Let's get inside." Ash grabbed Tanith's hand and began to guide her forward toward the exit in the event of a storm, but she paused to push both of them into the ivy that crowded the stone walls.

"Wait," she hissed.

The footsteps pounding through the castle were not the genial noises of friendly movement. It was the thundering sounds of strange, heavy boots punishing the ground beneath them with every powerful step. The rough barks of voices, the metallic clang of weapons, the cries for action told him one thing.

The castle was under siege.

Ash shoved them into the wall as hard and as quickly as possible so they'd remain undetected as the invading noises passed.

When he made eye contact with Tanith, he knew he didn't need to explain himself. She may be new to the continent, but she was no newcomer to danger.

They wasted no time in the brittle, long-dead ivy. Ash held Tanith's hands as they crouched low to the ground and kept their bodies pressed against the wall, hunched below the windows that allowed spectators to watch the gymnasium from the corridor. He released her hand as he raised his amber eyes to scan the hallway.

"Get weapons!" he breathed to Tanith while he kept his eye on the hallway.

She dashed to the training racks and returned with a handful of metal; everything from a practice sword and small throwing knife to Nox's axe was clutched against her chest. He didn't have time to argue with her choices and grabbed her hand again to tug her into the hallway, leading them in the opposite direction from wherever the invasive steps had been headed. They kept their footsteps as quiet as possible. Ash held the sword in one hand and axe in the other so that Tanith's added battle weight was minimal.

"Ash, what—"

"We've got this," he promised.

She looked back at him with wide, frightened eyes. "We?"

He hated that she'd questioned it even for a second. "I'm not going to let anything happen to you."

Ash had been foolish. In his time in Gwydir, he'd been too comfortable, too relaxed. He had not done his due diligence on hiding places, on exits, on weak points and strongholds, and now for all he knew, he was about to pay for it with both their lives.

The bell continued, each resonant vibration filling him with a dread deeper and more poignant than he understood. His mind raced for solutions, but every answer ended in their demise. If they'd been invaded, the clock was ticking on how long they had to escape Castle Gwydir. If they made it out with their lives, they'd be at the mercy of the blizzard beyond its walls. If the invaders didn't claim them, the arctic ice and fury of the blizzard raging beyond certainly would. Escaping the grounds would not be enough to ensure their survival. If they lacked the minimum survival provisions, their escape would be meaningless. A careless soul would die in under three minutes in true arctic conditions. Ash would not elude an enemy to become a chipped statue like those who littered the Frozen Straits, nor would he drag Tanith to such an icy fate.

A second stampede of feet sounded in the hall again. The wave passed and he opened the door to the closest room, guiding them forward as they slipped inside and quietly latched the door behind them.

He didn't have to know their enemy to know their outcome: defend, escape, or perish.

There was a new, quieter shuffle. He strained his ears, barely having time to discern the noises before Tanith shook his arm for attention as she alerted him to something. The feet outside the door were accompanied by voices. He recognized the woman.

Tanith reached up to twist the knob, and he joined her, pushing the door open to find Nox and Zaccai. With legendary grace and speed, Zaccai thrust out his hand to protect

Nox from the new unknown, identified their allies, and slipped them both inside in three seconds flat.

"Chandra!" Nox grabbed for the axe, clutching it to her chest as if it were a raft in a shipwreck.

"Who's here?" Ash focused his attention on Zaccai.

He'd never heard the spymaster so harried. "It's an invasion. Aubade must have known we'd go south for their banquet and leave the castle undefended. It was a trap."

The blood drained from Ash's face. "Moirai?"

"Her forces."

He couldn't think of Malik or Amaris or the south. They were alone in Gwydir. He looked between Zaccai and Nox as he asked, "What do we do?"

✦

Nox wanted to be strong. She wanted to do and say the right thing. But she had no idea what to do, and she hated that it was being asked of her. She didn't know how many stood against them, nor their odds for survival. She was going to lose her kingdom before she ever had the chance to serve it.

There would be a uniting of the north and south after all, but she would not be the one history remembered for bringing the continent under one, bloody banner.

Even on the brink of their utter annihilation, Zaccai took a calming breath and grounded them with his level-headed voice.

"We have almost no troops after the massacre. Only two of us are trained for battle. Nox, I know you can throw an axe, but between yours and Tanith's combat training, I think we're safe in saying armed forces boils down to Ash and me."

Nox didn't have it in her to argue. Nothing about Zaccai was belittling. He remained cool and practical in the face of their assured destruction.

"My father is in the dungeon," Ash whispered.

All eyes were on him, but she knew instantly that he wasn't saying it as a son who cared about whether his father lived or died. He was saying it as a warrior knowing there was one more reever who may be an asset.

"Will he fight with us?" Zaccai was quick to counter the proposal.

"I can't say. But I don't know what choice we have."

Zaccai nodded. "You and Tanith get to the dungeon. There's an underground route that will lead you to the forest near the river from there. I'll get Nox out of the castle."

Nox wanted to protest. "But the people—"

Zaccai closed his eyes briefly, shutting out whatever emotion may have clouded judgment. "The people can't have their queen die. Raascot cannot fall to Farehold. If you perish, so does our kingdom."

"I'll be fine!" She grabbed a handful of her hair before procuring a single braid that had been carefully tied with an emerald ribbon. "I have armor. This ribbon is enchanted against weapons. It's—"

"It's not enough," Zaccai said, worry and passion and plea in a single sentence. It won't stop them from capturing you and taking Gwydir. We have to get you out."

Frustration silenced her. She remained on the floor, kneeling with Chandra as she watched Ash and Tanith stand to leave.

"Ash, wait." Zaccai felt along his chest. He pulled out something that looked like a flat, smooth stone with three runes etched onto the surface.

"What is this?"

"It's a key," Zaccai said.

"What does it unlock?"

"Everything. It's the skeleton key Gadriel made with a manufacturer's help so that his skill with locks might be with me even when he's away. Hold it against your father's cell if you truly feel he'll fight with us."

"What if you need it?" Ash said urgently.

Zaccai shook his head. "We're going up. There are no locks in the sky. When I give the signal, get ready to run."

Zaccai pressed his ear to the door and nodded once to acknowledge it was clear. Ash and Tanith turned right to creep toward the dungeon with only his sword and her knife. Nox held her axe as if she had freshly birthed a child, muting her steps and swallowing her breath against her fear. Zaccai grabbed her hand and pulled her down the corridor, and she followed on blind trust as he steered them toward the outlook. In five minutes they could be up the stairs and escape into the storm. They were nearly to the first set of stairs when the sounds of boots descending forced him to correct course. On a hairpin turn, Zaccai switched back and pushed her through the nearest doorway.

Her vision swam as the world crashed down in on her.

It took her a second to understand where she was. They tumbled quickly into the throne room she'd spent so much time avoiding. Ceres's enormous, spindly wooden throne had gone untouched in the months that she'd been in Gwydir. She'd deemed the room haunted with the ghost of the man who'd left her in madness and ruin. While the very stones that had built Gwydir glimmered with captured starlight, the sunken feeling of the blue stones that surrounded the throne felt as if they had been built for a living sarcophagus. Rather than expanding into the night sky, these stones pressed down in a paralyzing tomb of iridescent death.

She would have hated it here under the best of times.

And these were not the best of times.

She'd barely had time to adapt before a noise at the main door forced Zaccai to give her another hard shove until they were both pressed against the back of the wooden throne, hidden by what very well may have been the petrified roots of a once-great tree. His wings flared around them as if they were little more than shadow slanting away from the throne.

Nox struggled to hear as the constant bell and her cowardly heart battled for attention. Zaccai remained perfectly still, not making a single noise as she strained to listen. It wasn't the sound of advancing troops but the appreciative chatter of two

457

victorious conquerors as they entered the room. The voices of a man and a woman filled the hall that they loudly claimed for themselves. As the invaders spoke of their new seat of power, it was clear they'd called the battle.

They'd won.

This was the afterlife. Nox was already in an aurora borealis–wrapped hell.

"I think it's Moirai's Captains of the Guard," Zaccai breathed, words so quiet she almost missed them altogether. He squeezed his eyes shut and reopened them as if to summon moisture to his ever-wide eyes. It seemed to take everything within him to refrain from stretching his neck around and exposing himself to peer between the outstretched roots of the extended throne so he could see the faces of those who had entered. But he couldn't risk giving away their hiding place.

Nox knew enough of games to understand when she'd been outmatched.

The ploy was brilliant, and she'd lost before she knew they were playing. Moirai had called her lords to the castle so all eyes would be on the south while she sent her forces north. If Nox hadn't hated the southern queen wholly, she may have appreciated the brilliance of the plan. Her mind shifted in a single, fractured second as the voices of the two intruders echoed over the stone. Nausea roiled through her. Nox stiffened so notably that Zaccai jolted at the change. She wasn't breathing. She wasn't even blinking.

"Nox?" His breathless whisper was worried, trying to get her attention without making any sound that might give them away. She knew he was scanning for their escape route, but she didn't respond.

The thick, choking scent of vanilla perfume descended on the throne room, drowning out her other senses. The scent triggered a memory of a glossy carriage, a silken lounge, of red velvet, of death.

Zaccai shook her softly. "Nox, listen. You may have to go without me. I'll buy time. They'll never look for you in the reever's old town house. Can you get to the edge of the city? If you exit the castle—"

"I know her."

Zaccai shook his head. "What?"

"I know her," she repeated numbly.

Zaccai seemed too horrified to react as Nox slowly stood from where she crouched in hiding behind the throne. He gaped as she stepped away from the spindly wood of Ceres's former throne.

He reached out to grab her, to yank her back into the safety of their hiding place, but he was too late. Nox straightened her spine as she examined the two figures who stood before her.

Clad in the golden metal of the queen's Captains of the Guard was a man the size of a minotaur. For as ugly and malformed as his face had been with drooping scars and gashes, he very well may have been mauled by a polar bear and earned his title by defeating the beast with his bare hands. From his height and breadth to his towering presence, he was the most gargantuan human she'd ever laid eyes on. As if he needed anything further to be terrifying, his weapon of choice was an enormous, spiked mace. A single hit would pierce any armor and crush any opponent. The man grunted as he viewed the northern queen from where she stepped from behind the throne.

The beast of a man was terrifying, to be sure, but Nox paid him little mind.

She understood their titles in an instant. The man grasping the weapon was clearly the one they'd called the Hammer.

Beside him were the small, golden, elaborately pinned curls that belonged to the unequal grip of death. The woman wasn't in the jewel-toned dress Nox had seen her in for so many years. Instead, she was in bright emerald fighting clothes with a smaller gold breastplate, undoubtedly fur-lined against the elements but allowing for lithe movement that the woman had never needed until her present station. The Madame of the Selkie had risen to the ranks of the queen's Hand.

459

Through the vanilla, through the preening smile, the lash of memories, the cascade of horror as the castle filled with enemies on all sides, Nox smiled. Fear fell from her like molted scales. She stepped into a commanding voice that knew neither fear nor hesitation as she spoke. "If anyone could create diamonds from coal, Millicent, I should have known it would be you."

Millicent's eyes flashed wickedly. "Well, well, well. Look who's finally living up to her full potential."

Nox's smile broadened. The fear that had filled her was gone. Perhaps this wasn't an unfamiliar game after all. She understood these players. She knew this role.

The powerlessness she'd felt dissipated, replaced with a rage so terrible it knew no bottom. However small or worthless or used she'd once felt evaporated the moment she laid eyes on the owner of the shriveled, wicked touch of death. Nox had once promised herself that if it were the last thing she did, Millicent would die.

Nox's eyes practically twinkled in cold delight as she said, "I heard they dragged you away by your hair."

"Well," Millicent said, taking a few steps away from her mountain of a companion, "people do love to tell a good story."

"To be honest," Nox said, matching her steps to maintain their distance, "I'd be disappointed if it had gone any other way. You're too resourceful to let that gift of yours go unnoticed."

Millicent cooed. "You flatter me, dear. You're the one who's finally used her power to claim a title, though I do think I should receive some credit. If it weren't for me, you never would have known what you were capable of."

The women exchanged dark, humorless smiles.

"I'm capable of more than you realize." Nox adjusted her grip.

Millicent's lip jutted forward in a mock pout. "And where would you have been without me? Still in the orphanage? Or still holed up in your bed with that freckled girl for comfort? What was her name again? You should know, you were the last thing on her mind when she died."

Nox felt the wind knock from her lungs as her lips parted. "What did you do to Emily?"

The Madame glinted wickedly, drinking in the thrill of unseating Nox from her certainty. "Her love was a weakness I couldn't afford. Running off to Yelagin in the dead of night while those in my house undermined me? She drew her loyalties. Take it from me: insubordination has to be pulled out at the roots. You and I, Nox…we had far grander fish to fry. From the looks of it, I made the right call."

She caught the flash of feathers out of the corner of her eye as Zaccai found his feet, standing behind Nox to flank her. Whether she was leading them on a suicide mission remained to be seen, but he'd made it clear he'd stand with her while she went down.

"Look at you, dear. You've found a pet," Millicent crooned. "So have I."

Millicent no longer wore the long, black gloves that had been a staple of hers for years. Her gray, fatal arm was now a proud, threatening fixture. She raised her deathly hand and gave it a flick to gesture for the Hammer to advance. If he was the brawn, she was the brain with an unforgiving bite.

Nox had neither the time nor the energy to waste on the Hammer.

She took a step to the side as if the mountain of a man hadn't existed, mind filled with Emily's red hair and kind smile as the woman had put herself in danger to help Nox escape from the Selkie. The news of Emily's death was the final sharpening blow she'd needed.

The world vignetted as she focused entirely on the woman whose hand had earned her infamy. Nox had no care for the colossal monster at her side whose very steps shook the stones of the throne room. She didn't look to Zaccai as his wings flared and his sword drew across his body in a stance of readiness. She saw only Millicent and the woman's venomous smile as she thrust her hands to her side, flexing her fingers into claws as she eyed the young queen.

✦

"Elil!" Ash's cry was strangled and hushed as he called to his father.

He and Tanith had practically fallen into the dungeon, given how they'd flown once they'd slipped into the circular stairwell undetected. They used the small gift of time to their advantage, darting across the castle's prison to the last cell on the end. The fae man looked off into the wall of the cell as if his son didn't exist. "Elil, the castle's under siege."

"From Sulgrave?" the man finally asked. He looked not at them but beyond them.

"No, you narrow-minded bastard," Ash barked, battling to keep his emotions under control. "Aubade is upon us. You can either die in your cell or you can fight with us. The south is here no matter how you stand."

Whether he'd gone mad with his own obsession or if he was truly bored with any topic that didn't involve the isolated mountain kingdom of fae, the reever remained impassive. Elil slowly turned to them with a look of boredom until his eyes landed on Tanith, hunched unmistakably in red beside his son. He offered a small, humorless smirk and looked away once more.

Footsteps pounded above them. The men would close in shortly. They hadn't yet found the stairs, but once they did, they'd have no time.

"Elil, will you fight with us?"

His face remained fixed on the wall, lost to his thoughts.

"Father!" Ash's tone hitched in desperation as he begged, but the man did not return his pleading stare.

The denial told Ash one thing: Elil knew no son. He knew no loyalty. He believed in a world divided into two: his dispatch, and those who stood against it. Ash had made his stance clear when he'd chosen Tanith.

There would be no alliance here.

Tanith set a small hand on Ash's forearm. He wasn't sure why it surprised him, but in the face of their assured end, his breath hitched against the small comfort. Tanith was still far from declaring herself friend to Gwydir. She had never said a word to denounce her faith nor to distance herself from her beliefs and her calling. Perhaps if they'd had more time together, if he could have spent another year with her, she might have come around. Even still, her comforting touch against the half-blood fae who disgraced magic was remarkable.

It was wonderful. And kind. And didn't matter in the slightest if they didn't survive.

The sounds of boots distracted him from where he'd lost himself to the gentle graze of her fingertips. He clenched his jaw. "Elil, I can't ask again. If you won't fight with us, I have to leave. I don't want you to die."

Elil laughed, eyes unfocused as they stared into some thought behind the chilled stone of his cell. "Your unwillingness to do what needs to be done is why you'll never be great."

Ash closed eyes in one hardened, tensed rejection of whatever treacherous emotions might have wanted him to fight with his father. His human heart wanted him to beg the man to see compassion and reason. It wanted to grab the iron bars and clang against them until Elil saw him. This was the part of him he needed to banish so he could find the strength it took to leave his only living parent behind.

"Let's go," Tanith urged quietly.

She got to her feet and tugged at Ash.

He sent one last glance to his father, feeling hollow, bitter contempt. He didn't bother with a parting goodbye as they turned toward the passage that was meant to lead them to the woods beyond the river. They'd scarcely shifted toward the tunnel before the encroaching shouts of men came not only from the stairwell but from the exit beyond.

Ash grabbed Tanith's hand as his hope evaporated.

They exchanged bewildered looks, knowing with petrifying certainty that their last resort had been foiled. Troops were invading from above and below. In moments, the dungeon would be flooded by the cleansing force of Aubade as they lay claim to the castle and everyone in it. From somewhere behind them, Elil began to laugh.

Chapter Forty

"FLY ME!"

Yazlyn couldn't meet Amaris's eyes. Her answering scream was disjointed and terrified, pulling on some deep, long-held fear she'd never revealed to Amaris. Yazlyn struggled to stay on her feet. Tears poured freely from her as terror consumed her. Frantically, Yazlyn choked out, "The crows! I can't!"

Amaris cried out again. "There are no crows! Fly me!"

Yazlyn winced against the threat from above, thrashing at the unseen enemy. Her shoulders hunched and her hair shielded her as she lifted her hands to protect her neck, her entire body trembling. Amaris had never seen the young woman so much as exhibit fear, but this wasn't just fear— this was something wholly petrifying. The sergeant's sword clanged uselessly to the ground as she used both hands to protect her face and ears, utterly lost to her terror.

Amaris ran for the sergeant and grabbed her shoulders. "There are no crows!"

Yazlyn trembled, spit dripping down her mouth as she thrashed against Amaris in utter, lurid panic. Amaris only shook her harder. She had no idea what the fae saw, nor did she have any idea of what she spoke, but whatever gripped Yazlyn was going to destroy them.

"Yazlyn! The crows are not real! Look at me! The crows are not real!"

Yazlyn forced her squeezed eyes open, but flinch after flinch tore through her body the moment she did. She couldn't hear, couldn't function as she gagged on all-consuming fear.

"Listen to me!" Amaris shook harder.

The ghouls grew closer every second while Moirai ran farther and farther away. They were losing precious seconds. Amaris raised a palm, smacking Yazlyn across the face to try to get her attention. The slap rang out with a sharp, high-pitched sting. Yazlyn blinked through her tears, dragging at her breath. She fought to look at Amaris.

"The queen has the power of illusion. She doesn't want you to fly. Do you know what's real?" Amaris had to stop her speech as she flung her sword and heard the metal crunch against the exposed spine of a ghoul. It fell sideways but was already picking itself back up. She kicked at it and shoved Yazlyn forward. "I'm real! The ghouls are real, Yaz! And they're going to tear us limb from limb if you let Moirai get in your head! There are no crows!"

Amaris swung toward an approaching skeleton, the impact of her short sword blowing it backward. The reanimated dead grew nearer with every passing heartbeat, but unless she could pull Yazlyn out of her hysteria, they were done. Her wings flared to protect herself against the razor-sharp talons and pecking beaks Amaris could only imagine. Her hands kept flying to her ears, so Amaris knew the perception attack had to extend to whatever banshee shrieks invaded the sergeant's every thought.

"Look," Amaris begged.

"I can't see anything," Yazlyn cried back, choking on each word, face contorting with her tears. "It's black with crows. They're as thick as smoke."

This time, when she slapped her, she used every ounce of force she possessed. This was no quick smack. This was the angered, aggressive urgency to knock sense into the fae. A bright red welt immediately lifted on the wide-eyed face of the fae woman as she gaped at Amaris.

Amaris waited on bated breath. If she left Yazlyn panicking on the passage floor, she'd be condemning her to a certain, shredding death. Within the next ten to twenty seconds, the skeletal remains of the undead would close the gap between them. Either they took to the air right now, or they would fall at the hands of the undead army.

"Please, Yaz: the queen is using illusion against you. I need you to trust me. Close your eyes if you must, but we have to fly! The ghouls *are* real. We need to go!"

Yazlyn raised her arms against a final crow before releasing an angry, primal cry as she grabbed for Amaris. Her sobs had stilled as she did her best to nod, tears still pouring over her cheeks. Her eyes remained tightly clenched as she took to the air, lofting the pair barely out of the swinging swords of the living dead who had reached gaps beneath them as she shot blindly upward.

They nearly crashed into the ceiling of the subterranean passage. As one of Yazlyn's wings touched the rough stone, she jolted in alarm, convinced it was the scraping attack of a bird.

Amaris screamed, "Open your eyes! Open your eyes!"

Yazlyn opened her eyes only to bolt toward the floor, veering wildly to the side to dodge invisible enemies as another blade-sharp crow made a threatening screech and grab for her. They spun toward the ground, Amaris's stomach in her throat as gravity dragged them downward.

They would be overrun by the undead army the next time their ankles were within grasp. "Please, by the All Mother, good goddess Yazlyn, trust me!"

Yazlyn hovered over them where they treaded in the air, motionless as she beat her wings just out of the grip of the bones and flesh and putrid smell beneath them. Her eyes were still closed so tightly that not even the barest hints of light could get in.

"See? Your eyes are closed. Nothing has touched you! Nothing is in the air, no matter what you hear! We've been in the same spot, and nothing bad has happened. Please listen to me, Yazlyn. Ignore anything you see in the sky. I promise you: I will not let us die!" Amaris was still screaming, throat raw as each sound shredded her vocal cords, desperate to be heard over the groan of the undead and the shriek of whatever invisible enemy tormented her friend.

Yazlyn twisted her face in a hardened anger. When she opened her eyes, it was with the mask of a warrior. While her eyes, nose, and chin remained scrunched in something between fear, disgust, and the need to be sick, she nodded at Amaris.

Amaris pointed her short sword down the passage after the queen. Yazlyn attempted to close her eyes again as she jerked to the side, but every time she did, they took a dangerous zag and dip against their forward trajectory. Still, she powered forward.

Amaris was desperate. "There is nothing in the air! Listen to me! All you see is passage, ceiling, wall, ghouls! Passage, ceiling, wall, ghouls! Say it back to me."

Yazlyn was nearly hysterical as she yelled the mantra back with an unholy, unhinged volume. Her wings continued pumping as they tore through the air like an arrow after the queen. Her voice echoed against the curved stones of the tunnel. She again cried the mantra back to Amaris as she clutched at her. "Passage! Ceiling! Wall! Ghouls!"

Amaris yelled back. "There are no crows! The crows are invisible! Passage! Ceiling! Wall! Ghouls!" All she needed was for Yazlyn not to hit the obstacles above or the corpses below.

"Passage!" Yazlyn screamed again as her entire body reverberated against a shudder. "Ceiling!" she yelled, forcing them to stay high enough that no ghoul could grab them without running into the roof of the passage. "Wall!" she cried, staying in the center of the tunnel. "Ghouls!" Her wings tore through the air, keeping them free of the threat on the ground.

Yazlyn took another dip in altitude, and the chipped, rusted blade of a corpse nearly clipped Amaris's foot. The animated carcass loosed a disgusting, moist cry as they passed, barely missing its weapon. Amaris realized the fae was holding her breath.

Amaris had never felt so devoid of hope as she pleaded with her friend, words tearing through her throat as she begged, "Goddess, Yaz, breathe! Keep going! Stay high!"

The passage had been straight until it emptied into another room full of crates and storage. There was a fork in the path, both routes seeming to be intermittently littered with ghouls. Their numbers had decreased as the primary congregation seemed to have found them in the last circular room, but Yazlyn and Amaris were not out of the woods.

"Where?" Yazlyn barked.

Amaris fought against panic as the threat of imminent failure pressed in on her. She stared between the two passages. "I have no idea."

They wouldn't be able to discern anything over the thundering beat of the fae's wings. She closed them, and they rocked the earth below them as they touched down. Yazlyn landed and Amaris nearly clawed at her to stay airborne, but Yazlyn was apparently taking a warrior's gamble knowing they had at least fifteen seconds before the ghouls reached them. Without the beating sound of her wings, she could buy them a moment of silence.

"Listen!" she hissed, her voice fast and demanding.

Amaris strained her ears beyond the groaning noises of joints, bones, dirt, and metal. The smell of carrion pressed in from all directions. Carcasses in various states of decomposition sought out any moving, breathing thing as they scraped against the caramel-colored stones of the underground tunnels.

Then she caught it. A distant noise seemed to differentiate itself off and to the side.

"Left!" Amaris yelled, but the word barely left Amaris's lips before Yazlyn scooped her up and shot into the leftmost passage. Amaris's internal compass told her they were going to the outermost perimeters of the castle. The tunnel to the right may have veered back beneath the primary residences, but the one to the left seemed to have a damper, saltier scent of the distant sea. If Moirai was going to escape, she clearly intended to find a rowboat waiting.

"My bow!" Yazlyn growled, doing her best to carve a straight, airborne path. If they found the queen, they needed to be able to take her down at any cost.

"I can't get it over your wings until you land!"

"Just get ready!"

The smell of the sea grew stronger, brine, fish, and kelp mixing with the dust and mortar of the tunnel and the rancid odor of the dead. They had not yet escaped the castle's underground labyrinth, but they had to be getting close. As they plunged into the next passage, Amaris was shocked to find Moirai just before she shot out of the tunnels. "Drop me!" Amaris screamed.

Yazlyn understood the command. She dropped Amaris, sending her to tuck and roll to the ground as she continued with an arrow's precision toward the exit, landing squarely in front of Moirai.

In the flash of the single drop and crouched landing, they had the queen surrounded. The fleshy sound of ghouls continued to shuffle through the passages, the foul sewage of their once-human bodies leaving greasy, slick trails of rot in every step. It would be only a matter of time before the skeletal army of the undead had ascended the cliffs and blocked off their exit.

"Drop!" Yazlyn screamed.

Amaris fell into a crouch as Yazlyn loosed an arrow directly for her; the queen was pinned between them. It glanced off Moirai, skidding uselessly to the ground beyond her. Without missing a beat, Yazlyn nocked another arrow. It would have embedded itself in the heart of its mark if something hadn't been shielding the queen.

"Save your arrows," Amaris growled from her end of the passage. "It's her ward. It's acting as armor."

A slow, wicked grin spread over the queen's face in response.

Amaris doubted the ghouls could harm her while she wore her protective ward. This was how she was able to continue to run so confidently down passage after passage as she made her escape, no matter how many guards or centurions fell to defend her. Moirai merely intended to wait out the undead until she could wander back into her vacant castle.

"You can't hurt me!" the queen taunted, fingers wiggling at her sides. Her emotion was nearly one of delight. She would outlast the reever who desired magical balance. She would burn Raascot off the map, along with the winged fae she blamed for her daughter's fate. She would escape, unharmed, and Yazlyn and Amaris would be left to rot in the tunnels.

Moirai had all the time in the world.

Amaris and Yazlyn had no time at all.

Ghouls encroached from three points of entry as their stiff, disjointed, grasping hands and feet crawled up from the sea, entered from the new rightward passage, and followed from the tunnel from which they'd come. Yazlyn wouldn't be able to hold her containing position of the queen for long.

Amaris heard the scraping, dragging sounds of exposed bone and the squish of rotten skin and muscle tissue as it dragged over the yellowed stones of Aubade. Soon, she'd need to either turn and fend off the ghouls and allow Moirai to escape, or she'd have to ignore the corpses in an attempt to contain the queen. Moirai played the waiting game, knowing that both women would have to choose sooner rather than later.

Then she flicked her hands beside her as if the motion was meant to do something. For Amaris, nothing happened. In a heartbeat, the reever could see Yazlyn's flinching increase until her face changed from bravery to horror.

"Amaris!" Yazlyn shrieked. "Real or fake!"

Amaris followed the sergeant's gaze to a passage and saw nothing but empty space, save for the bodies of two deceased soldiers making their slow advances. She bellowed from her diaphragm, begging her friend to believe her lavender eyes and their true sight. "Passage! Ceiling! Walls! Ghouls! Queen!"

Amaris couldn't regard Yazlyn to see if the fae trusted her as the warrior shuddered with every step between her and the added unseen enemy. She struggled to differentiate threats as she finally turned to focus her attention on the corpses, every sense deceiving her.

Amaris didn't know what to do with the moments afforded to her each time the fae raised her sword to meet the carcasses of the ghouls. Amaris had thrown a knife. She had slashed at the queen, attempting to grip and grab as she'd jumped skyward. Yazlyn had wasted two arrows from across the room. The queen was impenetrable. Moirai was merely waiting. Why was she waiting?

If the ghouls couldn't kill her because of her ward, then there was something else she needed that either she or Yazlyn could have the power to affect. There was something other than the threat of weapons or pain or death that could disrupt Moirai's escape. There was a reason she paused.

Amaris understood their only course of action.

"Yazlyn! Listen to me!"

The sergeant looked up from where she'd been swinging, choosing to trust Amaris regardless of what she heard or saw.

Amaris bellowed with all the force of her lungs. "Dive down to the cliffs! Destroy any boats you see! Moirai is waiting for a chance to escape by sea! Go!"

Moirai's screech confirmed everything as the woman's features flashed between anger and fear. "You don't know what you're talking about!" the queen gasped, but her tone betrayed her.

"What about you?" Yazlyn shouted back.

"I've got her," Amaris said, wholly focused on Moirai.

"Stop!" Moirai cried, fury and disgust thick in her useless command as Yazlyn turned to move.

With a twist of wings, Yazlyn took to the sky.

She made one beat forward and then paused, hovering as she felt an unseen hand stop her.

"Yazlyn—"

"Wait!" Yazlyn jolted, narrowly avoiding the exposed bones and ligaments of fingers that grabbed at her ankle. Amaris watched her with frenzied confusion as the sergeant supplied a single, vital piece of information, "The ribbon!"

Amaris met her intensity with baffled urgency.

"The ward is her crown!" Yazlyn shouted.

Moirai paled at the word. "No," Moirai said again, hands flying to the circlet that rested on her curls, "no." She had nothing else to say. She began to take steps away from Amaris, fingers securing the golden ward atop her head.

Amaris struggled to find her voice as she looked helplessly after the queen who clutched at her crown. "I can't grab her. How do I—"

"Your power," Yazlyn cried out over her shoulder, off like the very birds she feared, darting through the passage to find the boat that undoubtedly awaited Moirai and her escape.

The goddess had given Amaris the gift of shock wave. It had been a peculiar power, and what use it would serve hadn't been entirely comprehensible. Her wave had never been able to collapse walls or destroy cities, though furniture, windows, and people had all been jolted and rocked every time she'd used it. Her eye for enchantment and true sight had made sense: if she was to break the curse, the goddess needed her to see through it. Persuasion had been the icing, gifted by the All Mother to smooth over the bumps and obstacles she might come up against. The final gift had remained: What purpose did the shock wave serve?

Moirai remained poised in a defensive position as if to fight her off, certainly knowing she was untouchable as long as she retained her crown. Amaris could not stab her, could not kick or punch or thrust or fight. She wouldn't even be able to touch the crown to remove it from atop the sovereign's head as Amaris intended harm on the royal. No one could snatch the crown from atop Moirai's unbound, gold-brown curls. Moirai's grin returned as she saw Amaris exhausting her options and coming up short. Only a few more moments and the ghouls would be upon them, and Moirai would go free.

Chapter
Forty-one

"THEY'RE COMING," TANITH SPOKE ONLY TWO WORDS, BUT IN them was a prayer, an anguish, a desperation. Ash heard it all, and he knew he'd die defending her.

The impulse came from something so deep and true inside of himself that it couldn't be logically explained or reasoned with. All he knew was that he could not let her die.

Footsteps sounded in the hall that Zaccai had planned to be their exit as Aubade forces thundered in from the frozen forest and rivers beyond the dungeon. The arctic blast of the winter wind whooshed in front of the infiltrators as a warning, for whatever door they'd come in through remained propped open to the elements as it ushered in Aubade's men. If the harbinger of freezing air was any indicator, the men would be here any second. The stairwell filled with the echoing of clamor and men as the opposing army descended on every remaining inch of the castle.

When Aubade was finished with them, nothing would be left.

Ash looked at Tanith and truly saw her.

He had spent months knowing her and several of those overseeing her as his charge. He'd hated her. He'd thrown things at her and dodged the things thrown at him in return. He'd tolerated her. He'd grown fond of her. He was angry at her. He was happy to know her. He'd known her to be insane, yes, but also to be controlled, intelligent, calm, and strong in a way that was so distinct and profound from any reever or soldier or person he'd met on the continent. And when he'd fallen for her, their barbed, arduous road smoothed over, and nothing else mattered.

They had created a narrative about who Tanith was and what she was. They'd seen her power as a threat, as a danger, as a menace. They'd contained her, and she hadn't fought. She hadn't struggled, bitter or angry.

But there was something Tanith had that Elil did not.

As Elil had grown and studied and traveled, his hate had consumed him, dark ink of a singular narrative swelling until it blotted out anything good that had once existed.

Tanith's exposure to this life and those in it had popped a hole in her worldview, draining the thoughts, the notions, the anger she'd felt until the hate that had been forced upon her had dissipated and she was able to write her own story.

She was not evil.

She was not his father.

The soldiers' uproar mingled with cold as it spilled into the room and they closed in on them from both exits, above and beyond. They had twenty seconds. Then ten. Then five.

Aubade would be fully upon them. Ash had been looking into her eyes and she into his for what may have been seconds and what may have been lifetimes. Nothing more was spoken. Nothing was nodded or implied or agreed upon.

He raised the flat key filled with Gadriel's gift that had been meant for Elil's cell and brought it to her silver cuffs.

Her eyes didn't even widen as it happened. She made no move to change, to react, to alter in any way. Somewhere in the white noise of the distance, intermingled with weapons and armor and shouts and soldiers, Ash discerned the outcry of Elil's horrified screams as the hateful reever, possessed with

476

one singular fixation, watched the seamless cuffs clatter to the dungeon floor. The cuffs clanged in a high-pitched ring that made so much noise and no noise at all. The elder reever yelled, crying and yanking against his chains from where he'd been secured to the floor of his cell.

The bodies of Aubade's men closed in. The pale, wind-pinked faces of the southern invaders banged and knocked and pounded and smacked against every stone between the stairs, the exit, the prison. The sounds were a deranged symphony, harmonies and counter-harmonies mingling with the crazed minor key of destruction. While their music swelled, Ash looked at her, and she at him.

He didn't wince. He didn't flinch. He didn't command, ask, or beg. Ash only watched Tanith's dark eyes as they bore into his.

"Close your eyes," she said. And then, she raised her hands.

With a deep, prolonged inhalation, Tanith summoned the groundwater of power that flowed through the universe.

✦

Beside an oak, the Hammer was a redwood. Next to a hill, he was a peak. If the Hammer had raised his outstretched palm and captured the second in command, Zaccai's entire skull would have fit easily within one colossal palm. Each step he took caused the tremors throughout the throne room, miniature earthquakes rippling from each motion.

And Zaccai was facing him alone.

Nox steeled herself against the fear that vibrated with each step, shaking her body but not her mind. She kept the Hammer cautiously in her peripherals while she focused on the object of her hate.

She had no doubt that the mammoth of a human had been an easy selection for Queen Moirai after losing the murderous, bloodthirsty Eramus. But it was no wonder that someone selected for their enormity was a man of skill rather than wit.

How pleasant must it have been for Moirai to discover

that in her very dungeons was a malevolent, brilliant, industrious killer. Between the Hammer's sheer force of power and Millicent's reliable cunning, coupled with her singular touch of unforgiving death, Moirai had crafted an unstoppable pair.

"What did she promise you?" Nox asked, making slow steps to the side.

"What more could I want? I'm the Hand of the queen." Millicent's teeth reflected the fae light of the throne room. Elongated shadows gave Millicent the horrid, sunken appearance of the dead.

"Did she tell you that you might rule here in the north by proxy?"

Millicent laughed. "Why would she need to tell me that? Darling, did you learn nothing?"

Nox flexed her hand to keep from jumping as the Hammer swung at Zaccai. She fought the urge to cry out and warn him, relief washing through her as he dodged the first blow easily. The brute was formidable, yes, but between his weapon, his armor, and his muscled appendages, he was sluggish. His strength would land a killing blow every time, but only if his crushing strikes landed.

Nox forced herself to remain fixed on Millicent, though her heart thundered for Zaccai. Millicent studied her face from across the room, delighted at the fear her counterpart brought, waiting for Nox to react.

Every time the titan struck, Zaccai hesitated for the moment it took the Hammer to raise his weapon before he leapt to the side. Once the heavy mace was already on its downward arch, the man was unable to course correct.

Their battle was one of timing. Nox had to believe that Zaccai would master the steps to the dance. Each time the Hammer brought his weapon down, he was left exposed for Zaccai to strike.

"What was I meant to learn?" Nox asked, narrowing her eyes. She held Chandra loosely in her fingers, glaring at the woman with cold calm. Each step she took belonged to a different dance than the commander's sharp, militant movements. This one was graceful, intentional, and elegant.

Millicent practically sparkled. "The power of suggestion is so much greater than force or promise. I suggested to you that the one you loved was held north, and what did you do for me?"

Nox fought her internal battle, soothing the fire that raged within her with cold determination.

Millicent played with her, pressing. "Do you know how many you've murdered? The forces you collected? The men you consumed to save her? A subtle prompt: that's all it takes. Even the most powerful can be manipulated with the proper nudge, whether it's a succubus under my roof or a queen on a throne."

With a single, chilled laugh, Nox said, "I don't deny that you're clever, Millicent. I knew you craved power. I was under no illusion that every man I consumed served you as much as it served me. My error in judgment occurred long before that."

Millicent feigned a curious frown as she continued her steady, circling steps.

The battle raged over Millicent's shoulder. The Hammer raised his weapon again, this time swinging it backward from where it had landed, the weighted spikes coming upward in a deathly cut. Zaccai avoided it with two backward beats of his wings, pausing again in a crouch to lure the monstrosity into another downward blow. Each time the Hammer swung, Zaccai lunged.

The tide within Nox turned as she watched the commander's expert strike. No longer did fear or fire threaten her. A smile tugged at the corner of her mouth. Nox became so unbothered by the whale of a man that it was as if he weren't there at all.

If there was one thing she had learned in the upheaval of a life in Priory to the road with the reevers and her days in Castle Gwydir, it was who and what to trust. And Nox believed in Zaccai.

The women shook involuntarily, their steps jolting as the Hammer's weapon embedded itself in the throne room floor. It required a mighty yank to free it from where it had made an indentation in the blue cobblestones. While the Hammer focused his efforts on freeing his mace, Zaccai slashed at the small, exposed space on the back of the man's neck between his helmet and the upper edge of his armor.

The Hammer reacted with an uncoordinated flail, swiping at the commander as if he were a mosquito as Zaccai shot skyward into the lofted space of the throne room again before the giant had time to recover. Blood dripped down the back of his neck. The red nearly drew Nox's focus, hoping for a killing blow, but the wounding cut had not been fatal. Still, she caught Zaccai's grin from where he hovered above and behind Millicent with the wicked delight of the undaunted.

Feeling more emboldened with every moment that passed, she said, "My error wasn't in trusting you, Millicent, if that's what you were wondering. You were always wicked. You showed your cards so early, it's truly embarrassing. I'm ashamed on Moirai's behalf for putting someone so transparent in any position of power."

Millicent winced almost imperceptibly, her gray hand flexing as she resumed the slow, wide circle of the throne room. Nox didn't want to put the Hammer at her back. She stopped matching Millicent's steps, advancing instead, forcing Millicent to be the one to move back. Agitation flashed through her as she reacted.

With a contented sound, Nox said, "I see where I failed so clearly now. My error had nothing to do with you. My mistake, Millicent, was in underestimating Amaris. Listening to you was my own fault, only because I hadn't believed in the strength of the ones I love. That's why Zaccai will beat your Hammer. That's why Gwydir will not fall today. That's why no matter what you or Moirai throw at us, you have no hope of victory. I won't make my mistake again. I believe in us, and we've already won."

480

Zaccai shot into the air, and instead of arcing, he dropped in an immediate downward plunge.

Millicent's gaze flicked to him for only a fraction of a moment, but it was all Nox needed. It was not with anger, fury, or violence that Nox moved. She felt nothing but trust. She believed at her core that Chandra would find her target. As she stepped and released, the deadly weapon circled through the air with such precision that she almost wished it had lasted a second longer for her to admire the silvery, singular power of the axe before the crunching sound of muscle and bone as Chandra chewed through the Madame's arm and severed the limb. The blow sent Millicent to the ground, skidding backward as her head smacked against the stones.

The sound was sweeter than music, the blood more beautiful than sunrise. Nox grinned with true, succulent joy as a banshee's wail tore from Millicent's throat. Crimson waves flowed freely from the Madame's once-mighty arm.

Her scream snagged the Hammer's attention like a dog attending to its owner. And that was all Zaccai needed.

The commander came down with his sword, plunging it into the gory slash that marked his target. His weapon was perfectly straight as it punctured the exposed space between the helm and the armor on the back of the giant's neck, finding the soft, fragile spaces where the spine weakened. His sword pierced skin and tendon, drilling between vertebrae, making a sick, popping sound as esophagus and muscle gasped and gurgled.

The titan's eyes widened with realization. He'd been beaten.

The Hammer sank to his knees, the entire throne room shaking in the avalanche of his fall. The mace clanged to the ground. He collapsed, his body emptying itself of its blood.

Nox stepped up and put one foot on Millicent's chest.

The witch's gray hand twitched like a spider's dismembered limb, phantom spasms still encouraging it to flex and jump in unnatural ways as the death magic that had possessed her, given her strength, and fueled her wickedness for so many years ebbed out uselessly beside her. Nox could almost see the motion in Millicent's face as if she were still trying to force the phantom limb to do her bidding. The woman's eyes darted in all directions like a mouse in a trap, settling on nothing.

She pressed her foot harder into the Madame's chest to gain her attention. "It's done, Millicent."

"Choke on your superiority," Millicent spat.

Nox leaned her weight into her foot.

The Madame's lips pulled back in a snarl. "How can you think you're better than me in any way, whore? After all you've done? After what you've become? Do you know what *I've* suffered? Do you know how my mother died? How my father abandoned me? How I was sent off, unloved, shown down and discarded—"

Nox rolled her eyes. She took her foot from Millicent's chest, sighing as she plucked Chandra from its place on the ground. "Hey, shh, shh... Listen very carefully to what I'm about to say to you, because I won't allow you to die with any misconceptions between us. We've all had horrible child-hoods, Millicent. Who among us couldn't blame the world for how it made us grow cold? You've had all the time in the goddess's lighted kingdom to heal. You are no victim. And yes, I'm a whore. But I'm also a fucking queen. Maybe if you're lucky, the All Mother will pity you more than I do."

With her final words, she raised her axe overhead and brought it down in a liquid, grinding motion as Chandra's razor-sharp blade ate through Millicent's frantic pleas, slicing her wicked face perfectly in half. One eye bobbed sickeningly upward, rolling into the back of her head as the axe pierced not only bone but all the connective membranes and tissues that had once given this witch the audacity to purchase and sell bodies as if they belonged to her. Millicent had bought her, used her, had subjected her to unspeakable abuse. Nox was not stronger because of what she went through. She was strong in spite of it.

She pushed her foot harder against Millicent's chest as a counterweight to yank her bloodied axe free as she rejoined Zaccai.

There was admiration in his eyes unlike anything she'd ever seen.

"Didn't think I had it in me?" Nox winked.

"I—" He swallowed, surveying the carnage. "You have been more of a queen to Raascot in one winter than your father was in decades. There is no one I would rather have on this throne."

✦

Ash and Tanith hadn't discussed her powers.

Weeks had become months as the fall turned into the dead of winter, and their time together made one thing known: whether or not it was wise or permanent or describable, Ash trusted her, and he believed she would not let him die.

Now they were out of time.

Aubade poured in from both sides as men swarmed the dungeon. Tanith tilted her head forward. He understood her nonverbal signals and threw his arms around her, closing his eyes tightly as he clutched her, touching his head to hers.

He felt her hands raise over them as she pulled from the magic that coursed through the world itself. Electricity had been her freshwater spring, but Tanith had access to the groundwater. She could do anything.

Crackling, sizzling intensity exploded through the dungeon. The hair stood up on the back of his neck, his entire body, as the atmosphere buzzed with tangible power. The air filled with a metallic-scented flame, both hot and acrid as everything electrified. The men did not scream. They said nothing as they crumbled, skin, bones, and clothes evaporating in the silver-blue light of Tanith's all-consuming power.

Ash clutched her more tightly, his fingers digging into the red clothes on her back while he held on to her. He didn't open his eyes. He didn't question her power, nor did he presume to understand its functionality well enough to dare burn his eyes on her white-hot gift.

The silver sounds of death and horror and power filled the room, and then it was gone.

When the enemy vanished, it was with the ringing violin's string of a final note, poignant and complete. Cold, dark air rushed in once more. And he knew it was done.

Ash's grip became an embrace, pulling her even more tightly toward him before he opened his eyes. She held him close, hugging him in return. They clutched each other with a strength and ferocity they'd never shown. Ash opened his eyes to turn to the cell to see if his father had survived, but Tanith stopped the turn of his chin with a soft, small hand.

"Don't look for something you don't wish to see."

His throat bobbed. Ash leaned forward again, resting his forehead briefly against hers. They shared the moment for the longest of heartbeats before the shuffle of men overhead told the pair that the castle had not yet eliminated its threat.

Tanith was on her feet in an instant. She grabbed his hand and tugged him upward.

"Come on," she said. "The battle isn't over."

Chapter
Forty-two

S HE NEEDED GADRIEL.
Amaris panicked as Yazlyn winked out of sight. She was alone with the queen, an army of the undead, and a single, impossible task. She'd never been able to summon her shock wave of her own volition without Gadriel present, no matter how many times they practiced.

The groan of cadavers overwhelmed all, drowning out her frantic dread as Amaris stared at the queen with no idea what to do. Moirai remained flexed in some prepared state of attack, perhaps unaware that, no matter what she did, her illusion would have no effect on Amaris.

The scraping and dragging of cartilage and remains scratched and chafed against the stone floors, making it impossible for Amaris to focus. She couldn't hear her own thoughts over the putrid, soggy skin-sacks as they dragged their dripping carcasses through the passages. Even Moirai couldn't remain stoic and unaffected. The queen gagged miserably, though she did not appear to be afraid.

That made one of them.

If the ward was to be believed, the only harm the army of the dead could do to Moirai would be to inconvenience her while she waited for Amaris to die. Then she could scramble over the corpses to the shore.

And if Amaris failed…

Perhaps Yazlyn had made it to the sea by now. If the sergeant overcame her fear of the illusions, she could find whatever it was that Moirai had waiting on the other side. Then even if Moirai escaped the tunnels, perhaps Yazlyn could contain her. But she could not harm her. Not with the crown.

It would be useless.

Yazlyn had known it before Amaris had. Her crown could not be grabbed or ripped from her head. Yazlyn would be helpless to take Moirai down. The curse would remain intact. This was the culmination of her training, of her gift, of her very life. This was why she'd been born: to take down Moirai without ever having to touch her.

Amaris closed her eyes and relaxed, calling on the power within her.

Nothing happened.

She flexed her hands, her muscles, her tendons. Her abdominals tensed along with her quadriceps, biceps, and forearms. She balled her hands into fists, fingernails biting into the tender flesh of her palms. A cord in her neck spasmed as she strained to summon her power.

"Come on. Come on!" Amaris fought against the threat of helpless tears.

Moirai eyed her with the confused, bewildered specula-tion of a cornered animal. She blinked repeatedly, frustrated and agitated that Amaris remained planted between her and the exit. She decided she could wait no longer. She had to try her luck with blowing past Amaris before her boat was damaged.

Moirai rushed for the passage. Amaris blocked her with her body weight, throwing her shoulder into Moirai. The queen bounced backward, grunting in frustration. Amaris could play the defensive game as long as she needed. At least, she could have played such a game if dripping bodies weren't crawling their way toward them from the ocean, over the cliff, and through the passage.

In minutes, they would surround her on all sides. The ghouls pouring down from the castle would catch up. Others would close in from the passage at her back.

Think, think!

Moirai rushed her again, and Amaris did her best to grab at the queen in order to drag her, but the slippery surface of her ward was like well-oiled glass encompassing her.

"You can't touch me, witch!" The queen wriggled free with her slick, invisible gloss. "You have no power here, reever!"

Just buy time, a quiet voice begged.

Once, that had been all Nox had begged of her. Buy time.

She had been waiting for Nox to save her. She'd waited for Nox to save her at Farleigh each market day, or during the visit of the bishop. She'd waited for Nox to save her in the form of Eramus as the captain of the guard had sprinted into the ring. She'd counted on Gadriel to rescue her as she plummeted into the pit in the Tower of Magics at the university, and for Zaccai to protect her as she'd been Ceres's prisoner. Amaris had allowed her story to be written by other authors. She had merely been a plot tool for their actions and heroisms. Her life had been a string of efforts to stave off danger long enough for someone better, someone stronger, someone more worthy to come along.

But no one was coming.

Gadriel had no idea where she was. He would not find her in the underground passages in time for her to summon her shock wave. Nox was in Raascot. She had no clever plan. No one Amaris had ever loved or trusted would seal her fate tonight. One truth remained: she was ready, or she wasn't.

Maybe she wasn't.

Maybe she would never be.

But she had no choice.

Moirai got to her feet. The smallest corner of the queen's

lips tugged upward in a cruel grin as if she saw the clock run out over Amaris's head.

"Moirai." Amaris swallowed, buying time, knowing it was all she could do. "There's something you should know before you die."

Amaris took an authoritative step forward and offered the ghost of a smile as Moirai responded in a reciprocal backward step.

"How dare you threaten me," the queen of Farehold hissed, voice low.

Through gritted teeth, Amaris said, "The prince you've tried for so long to cast and preserve with your illusion? He was a fiction from the beginning. The boy was never your grandson. There wasn't a drop of royal blood in his veins. Daphne bore no son."

Moirai had been ready to barrel toward the sea. She had been tensed to push past Amaris and take her chances with the cliffs and its corpses. But Amaris had succeeded in catching her attention.

"Don't lie to me, demon-lover," she snarled.

Amaris shut out the sounds of the undead. She remained focused on Moirai. "Daphne had a daughter. She knew exactly how evil and horrible her mother was. Your daughter? Princess Daphne? She never wanted someone so wicked to know about her child. Daphne wanted you to die without knowing that your granddaughter existed."

"Keep that venom on your tongue!" Moirai yelled. "Keep your poison to yourself and the snakes you serve!" The queen attempted ferocity, but her tone was wrong as she tilted her head in a quick way meant to deflect and reject the words as they hit her. She took a second step backward. Amaris took another step toward the center of the room, buying both time and space.

"Daphne bore King Ceres a daughter. Did you know that? Their love child came into the world."

Moirai balked, the skin on her face growing taut. Her

wrinkles looked almost like scars in the gloom of the underground tunnels, refusing to disappear no matter how hard and tight her anger became. She squinted against the information as if dust were hitting her in the eye, each word more horrible than the last. "I cradled my grandson, you childish bitch. When he was snatched from me, I kept his memory alive and well for his people. The king of demons played no role in Farehold's future."

Strength swelled through Amaris as she advanced, one move at a time. "The curse you intended to keep them apart came too late. Daphne was already pregnant. You failed, Moirai."

The queen bared her teeth in feral hate. "Lies. I've held this kingdom together after what was done to my family. You have no idea what I've sacrificed to maintain Farehold's stability. I've given everything—"

Amaris spoke with her whole chest as she said, "Daphne brought her daughter to an orphanage along the northern border hoping that her father would find her. She picked an orphan child that matched her human husband's hair so that you wouldn't know the difference. The crowned prince that you've been casting for all of these years? The boy you've tried so hard to preserve so that the people wouldn't know that his father beat him to death? He was a peasant, exchanged from an orphanage, so that the true heir would never be harmed by her festering scab of a mother."

Moirai shook with vitriolic denial. "You're wrong."

Amaris's fists remained flexed at her sides as she advanced. Every step she bought in driving Moirai backward was more space, more confidence, more time between her and the undead. "Do you know the best part?"

She was met with an angry growl.

Moirai raised her hands in front of her face, blocking the horrors from reaching her ears. She didn't want to hear it. She didn't want to see it.

"The daughter now sits on the throne in Castle Gwydir.

489

Ceres gave the northern kingdom over to its new queen. And as soon as your evil fucking crown topples from your worthless head, Daphne's true heir will ascend in Farehold as well."

Amaris had done everything she could. She'd wrung every second clean, and it hadn't been enough.

A soggy hand clamped around her ankle. Its bony, protruding fingers dug sharply into her tender flesh, unencumbered by any barrier of fingertips. Sheer bone sliced into her tendon.

A second corpse pulled her in close as the rancid, bloated body of a drowned sailor dragged her into its clutches.

Amaris cried out. White-hot pain overtook her.

Moirai saw her chance for exit and began to run, her arms stretched in front of her to block and defend anything that intended her harm.

"Die with the unholy alliances you've forged, reever!" she screamed, crawling through the ghouls as if swimming in a nightmarish river of bodies.

Agony, helplessness, and terror cut Amaris down the middle. She cried out, and as she did, she threw her hands to the side in a thrust of unadulterated power.

Her fists balled in all the anger of years. She flung her helplessness, her pathetic, empty life. She flung the times she'd been hidden, her years stowed away. She threw every time she felt she was weak, every worthless moment that she hadn't been enough into her fists as her power found her.

She threw her loaded punch, hands stretched before her in a push as her shock wave thrust the world into chaos, everything rippling beyond her in a circle as the universe crumpled against her ability. Her mouth opened in a scream louder than had ever torn from her throat. Her call was louder than that of any babe ripped from the breast of its mother, any dying maiden, any mourning soldier. Every injustice and violation or wrongdoing burned through her. In a singular, sweeping moment, her boom shook the dead that had clutched her and tossed them backward into the passage as magic uncoiled from her.

Moirai flew from where she'd been rushing, blown back by the wave, sailing toward the center of the passage on her back. She shuddered with a horrified convulsion, skull smacking against the ground. The explosion of energy echoed through the chamber, dust and bits of mortar raining from the sky as the tunnel groaned. The queen's golden dress blew nearly above her head, her hair to the side, crown jostling far out of reach with a high-pitched clang.

"No!" Moirai shrieked with primal panic. She clawed against the stones like a rabid animal, which told Amaris everything she needed to know. "No!" Moirai screamed again as she wriggled for her crown.

The blast settled, and the world in its wake seemed to move in slow motion.

Moirai twisted in response to the thunder, her upper body moved as if with a snail's pace as her fingers reached for the crown that bounced and reverberated beyond her grasp. The gold and jewels moved in one-half time, each ringing and clatter taking an eternity as Moirai clawed, knees hitching on her crawl toward her crown.

The ghouls recovered from the blow, advancing from every passageway, closing in on the queen.

If Amaris waited, she could have seen the army of the undead tear Moirai to shreds. The queen's death was a victory no matter who achieved it, but Amaris would have no peace of mind unless she was the one who made the killing blow.

She limped toward the queen, each laboring step taking everything she had.

"You bitch," Moirai growled, voice rising with hysterics. She had no coherent thoughts, only shock and agony as the unholy terrors closed in on her vulnerable, fallen form. "You bitch!"

Amaris reached her along with every unholy creature from beyond the grave.

"I owe Daphne thanks," Amaris shouted over the groan of the dead, voice stretched thin with pain. Her eyes narrowed with intensity. "She's the reason I exist. I was born to kill you."

491

The skeletons tore and scratched and writhed, closing into a pile of corpses as the reever mounted the fallen body of Queen Moirai and pinned the screaming monarch beneath her weight. Amaris's short sword came up in the brief amount of time it took for her to plunge it through the throat of the queen of Farehold as the backward tension of the undead tore against her bicep and shredded her pale skin. Her weapon found its mark.

Moirai's obscene, animal cries were cut short as Amaris pulled her blade upward, red with the queen's blood. Ghouls overtook them then. They bit and scratched and tore and swung whatever rusted weapons they clutched.

Amaris had done it. She'd killed the queen. And the monsters were there to ensure that, though Moirai had died, Amaris would be fast on her heels as they plunged to meet the goddess. She swung her bloodied short sword as she hacked at the ghouls, but they were ten thousand and she was one.

Fingernails and bones tore against her face, her neck, her back as she tried to raise herself to her feet. Dead bodies scrambled for her, sensing the last remaining living thing in the passageway.

As they wrestled her to the ground, Amaris let out a rasping, husky growl. She hadn't thought it would be enough, but the magic was undaunted by the crescent of her waning life. Her blast shot the creatures back with an intensity she'd never summoned. They weren't just knocked to their backs; they were hurled so thoroughly against the opposing walls that joint separated from bone, scattering them on impact.

She'd created space, but their clawing and scratching had already caused too much damage. Her vision swirled, the light of the moon over the sea fading as all colors leached into a single, dark shade.

Amaris grabbed for her throat. A tangy copper filled her mouth, its accompanying gurgle forcing her to choke on her own blood. One hand pulled away, as red as the paint she had used to decorate her lips before the banquet. Her free hand braced the ground, hovering above Moirai's lifeless body as the world began to dim.

She couldn't even begin to assess her wounds. She had no tonics. She had no more weapons. She had only the shredded remains of her gauzy gown and its star-flecked jewels as they slowly dyed themselves crimson with the remnants of her life. The ghouls around her were getting to the sticky, bony remnants of their feet. Her vision grew darker, the vignette of blackness closing in on her peripherals. Amaris's fingers slipped against her wet throat, trying and failing to stop the fresh flow of blood.

She looked at Moirai with the last of her dying light, a chuckle as her final feeling.

I did it, Nox.

Time slowed as she collapsed on top of Moirai's soft, still-warm corpse, knowing that her death had meant something. She'd broken the curse. She'd killed the queen.

Chapter
Forty-three

I N THE MOMENTS FOLLOWING THE CASTLE'S SIEGE, ASH KNEW
he would follow Tanith anywhere.

They'd found Nox and Zaccai in the throne room,
still amidst the carnage of whatever formidable opponents
they'd faced.

"Ash?" Nox breathed as they burst into the room.

"Cover your eyes!" Ash had shouted, and they hadn't
resisted. Zaccai had covered Nox with his wings the moment
Aubade's soldiers had poured in, blackening the room like
flies. Tanith had knelt with one hand outstretched to greet
them, total destruction coursing through the hall and eliminating the wave of soldiers.

When Tanith's magic blinked out, there were no corpses,
no clothes, no remnants that anything had existed.

"What the hell happened?" Nox demanded in the quiet
shock following her flex of power.

"Tanith happened," Ash answered.

Securing the castle in the aftermath of invasion was a surreal
experience. They drifted from room to room, finding broken
windows, splintered doors, and splatters of blood where injury
had stained the walls, even though no bodies remained.

The storm had not relented.

The blizzard outside was in white-out force, wind whipping and snow blinding beyond the castle before Aubade's troops were depleted. The blizzard pushed on the windows, discarding any remnants of the men or their footprints. Any soldier who hadn't already made it into the castle had been consumed by the arctic as the All Mother finished their job. If it weren't for the lakes of blood in the throne room and the enormous corpses left by Nox and Zaccai, there would be no evidence that anyone had infiltrated Gwydir.

They were safe.

Zaccai led them to a hiding place where castle attendants had been uncovered in the kitchen. Those who served Gwydir and its residents had found refuge in a crawl space meant for root vegetables and other such storage, carefully pulling a trap door and rug over to hide them. Nox extended her hand to every one of them, helping the people to their feet. A servant Ash heard Nox call Leona wrapped the young queen in a hug meant only for those who had narrowly escaped death. The invasion had been intended to level, claim, and destroy. After the blizzard dissipated, they'd have to venture into the city to see what damage was done to Gwydir and its residents. For the time being, the breathless silence of survival gagged the castle. No one could quite process the trauma that had been intended for annihilation.

It was incredible to watch Nox in her queenly role as she helped her people. She ensured everyone was safe and cared for as if she'd been born for this.

Tanith slipped her hand wordlessly into Ash's and led him away, leaving Nox and Zaccai to their tasks.

Ash frowned after her uncertainly as they bypassed the rooms, the training center, the throne. The shock that followed battle kept him mute as she led him through the castle's corridors, twisting and moving on an unspoken mission.

His frown deepened as they descended into the dungeon. Ash had gone through too much, been through too much, to fully comprehend what she was doing. Tanith knelt in front of Elil's empty cell. Numbly, Ash joined her on the ground. He didn't turn his face. He didn't want to see the space where Elil was meant to be. He didn't want to see the scorched black charcoal marks against stone. He didn't want to see the empty chains.

Instead, Tanith lowered her hands to the silver cuffs that had been wrapped around her wrists. She lifted them gingerly and, with the slowness of time, offered them to Ash.

He was still too dazed to fully comprehend why he now held two silver cuffs in his hands. He blinked at the manacles in his hand that had once covered the length from Tanith's wrists to her elbows.

Ash closed his eyes tightly, shaking himself awake. He reopened them to focus on Tanith. She was still on her knees before him, but her forearms were now extended, held together, and outstretched for him.

Ash's lips parted in silent shock.

She was offering her wrists.

Ash drew in air through his nose, forcing a sense of clarity into his muddled senses. He couldn't allow the anesthetized numbness to consume him now. The column of his throat worked hard to swallow the knot in his throat. He lowered the silver cuffs to the ground beside him and, instead, took her hands in his own.

He wanted to laugh but thought he might cry instead. He set the cuffs on the ground between them.

She looked at him with the same almost-vacant serenity she'd maintained through so much of her stay at Gwydir. Her eyes were speculative as she calculated him.

He smiled and brought her hands to his mouth, brushing a kiss to her knuckles.

"I trust you."

Epilogue

I T WAS LIKE THE FIRST GLITTERING FROST ON A GRASSY LAWN. Like iced sweets. Like long sleeps on chilly nights beneath warm covers.

A distant nostalgia tugged pleasantly at Amaris. She remembered looking up at the stars while she drifted through the woods toward the university on the back of a cart. She remembered holding Gadriel as his head wound rendered him unconscious, singing to him in the forest. She remembered the cold.

She didn't like the noise. It was unpleasant, and she wished it would stop.

This called for lullabies, not for the sound of teeth, of gnashing, of clawing. She heard the ripping of fabric. Amaris was conscious of each scraping sound as dirt and rocks and pain bit into her from somewhere in the distance. At least, she knew it was supposed to hurt.

There was a rawness to her skin, as if the same piece were forced against sandpaper time and time again. It didn't belong in this late-morning nap, in the winter comfort, in the distant forest where young, hesitant love bloomed.

The smell should have been pine or moss or maybe warm

soup after coming in from a day of chores on a chilly evening. Yes, that would have been nice. The odor of carrion and the choked, gurgling noises didn't quite fit in her strange, bobbing dream.

This was not a nice dream.

This was not a nightmare.

What was this?

At least the pain had stopped. It made it easier to settle into the beckoning call beneath the duvet, lulling her deeper and deeper into blissful calm.

The voice was so familiar, so friendly. Another joined it, then another. So many voices. Perhaps too many. Yet what lovely music it was to hear speaking sounds that didn't belong to cadavers. Any voice that wasn't Moirai's was decidedly pleasant. As nice as their voices were, she wished they'd let her sleep.

There was so much rust in her mouth. Hopefully it would go away soon. She felt a discomfort and tried to swallow, but her throat told her that no, swallowing was no longer for her. She didn't argue. Her throat knew best.

Amaris wasn't sure if her eyes were opened or closed, but they saw nothing. Perhaps this was what death was like. She supposed she didn't know, as it would be her first time dying.

She had hoped death would be less uncomfortable, but there was little she could do about it now. Death was very, very cold. The arms of the All Mother didn't smell as lovely as she had imagined. She'd hoped for plums and cinnamon to be the last things on her mind. But one couldn't always have their wishes.

Death was also noisy. Once the scraping and dragging stopped, she kept hearing a sentence. She didn't care for it. She didn't listen to it.

"Stay awake!"

What an unpleasant command. No, she didn't think that was something she wanted. If death had to smell like bones and flesh and raw, angry wounds, at least she could sleep.

Something wanted her eyes to burn less, but she couldn't blink them. She still didn't know if they were opened or closed.

The displeasing sentences of the voices above and beyond grew fuzzier and fuzzier. It was a garbled sound against the waves of unconsciousness. Yes, sleep was much nicer. She preferred this. She would ignore the voices.

"Amaris?"

Amaris could finally close her eyes. She hadn't known if she still possessed such an ability, but she found herself blinking. She looked around uncertainly but couldn't quite identify her surroundings. So much of the misery had fallen away. The worst parts of the nightmare had passed.

The stars burned overhead. And, if she wasn't mistaken, it felt quite like summer.

She lifted an arm to see that it was bare. There were no scratches or wounds. Her fingers floated dreamily to her throat to find with quite a bit of joy that it came back free from any trauma.

She was perfectly whole.

In fact, as she looked down at herself, she was quite sure that her gorgeous, silver-speckled dress was still intact. She was so glad. She had truly loved this dress.

She looked up to see who had spoken her name and was pleasantly surprised.

"Nox?"

If she wasn't mistaken, she was dangling her legs off the cliff outside of Aubade. It was a delightful night with a large, silver moon. The sea had never looked so lovely. The crashing waves specked with flotsam were so soothing. She was glad that Nox could witness her in a dress so beautiful. Nox had only ever seen her in linen dresses at the orphanage, followed by fighting clothes. How wonderful it was to be dressed up for once with gauze and silver and white, red lips painted for the occasion.

Nox crossed to her and knelt.

"I don't think you're well," Nox said, eyes searching her

as if reading a book. They darted to and fro with too much intensity. She should sit down and appreciate the stars.

Amaris frowned. "I feel perfectly fine."

Nox shook her head so hard that Amaris could hardly mark the motion, dark hair a blur as it whipped around her. Her voice shifted into an alarming pitch as she said, "You're rippling. Something is wrong, Amaris."

Amaris smiled at the silliness.

"Isn't the summer lovely?" Amaris asked.

Nox grabbed at her again, her voice too loud for the gentle night. "What happened? What happened in Aubade?"

Amaris felt like she should frown, but she didn't want to. Her dress was too pretty. The night was too nice. Nox was here. Why would anyone want to frown?

"I killed the queen."

"After that!" Nox demanded, shaking her.

"Don't yell," Amaris chastised in a friendly, dreamy tone. She made a dismissive motion, stopping to examine the way her hand shimmered as if losing its fullness. It was a curious visual. She had never seen her hand make such a motion, as though she were made of the same water as the ocean beyond. She twisted it in the moonlight and was pleased to see her pepper diamond.

"Did you know this ring was a siphon?"

Nox's breaths came in strained, uneven pulls. She tightened her hold on Amaris's arms, grabbing her dress, her hair. Her eyes grew larger in unfettered panic. Nox's hands kept moving as Amaris was disappearing like sand between her fingers.

"Nox, you're so beautiful. I'm glad you're the last thing I see," Amaris said serenely.

Nox's voice broke in a sob, her voice piercing and terrible as she cried for Amaris to wake up. Amaris was distinctly unhappy at this. Nox yelled. She hit. She slapped. She pulled. She hurt. Nox's anguished expression grew deeper and deeper. Amaris wanted to sleep. She enjoyed the ripple.

She wanted to listen to the waves and soak in the silver bath of the summer moon. She wished Nox would leave her alone and just lie next to her. She had worked so hard, she deserved to sleep.

"Wake up!" Nox's cries were the banshee wails written of in bestiary tomes, her hand making contact time and time again with acute focus. The ringing sounded in Amaris's ears, becoming stronger and stronger with each blow. She began to feel a sensation cut through the numb as Nox raised and lowered her open palm over and over again. Amaris blinked at her, reaching a hand toward Nox's face as if to cup her the way she had on their last night together.

Nox remained, though her frantic screams went silent, muted by an invisible wall.

"She's here! She's with us!" a deep, male voice called out as rough hands shook her. The voice shouted things, demanded things, begged for things. His familiar voice was so near her ear, growling through the summer night, talking over Nox.

"I'm not the only one who's hard to kill, witchling."

Amaris looked for the sea and the cliffs but couldn't quite understand what she was seeing. She couldn't focus on anything. A dark-haired girl bent over her, and she tried to reach her hand upward for Nox, but it fell limply at her side as Yazlyn's chestnut curls filled her vision. That wasn't who she wanted to see. She tried to ask for Nox but had no voice. She wanted to go back to the cliffs. She closed her eyes and searched for the sweet release of a star-soaked night.

About the Author

Piper CJ, author of the bisexual fantasy series *The Night and Its Moon*, is a photographer, hobby linguist, and french fry enthusiast. She has an M.A. in folklore and a B.A. in broadcasting, which she used in her former life as a morning-show weather girl and hockey podcaster and in audio documentary work. Now when she isn't playing with her dogs, Arrow and Applesauce, she's making TikToks, studying fairy tales, or writing fantasy very, very quickly. Connect with Piper online at pipercj.com, on Instagram @piper_cj, on Twitter @pipercjbooks, and on TikTok @pipercj.